London Bridge

Nana Malone

COPYRIGHT

This is a work of fiction. Names, characters, places, and incidents either are the product of the author's imagination or are used fictitiously, and any resemblance to actual persons living or dead, business establishments, events, or locales, is entirely coincidental.

London Bridge

Cover Art by Najla Qambar

Photography by Wander Aguilar

Edited by Angie Ramey, and ReGina Kaye

Published in the United States of America

Chapter One

Emma

It had taken me six weeks to get back to bloody London.

I was in New York with my mother when I got the note. The reminder that my work wasn't done.

Francis Middleton is the worst of them. You cannot let him walk.

A year ago, this journey had started with a note just like this. Printed on heavy ivory card stock. That message had pointed me to the Elite, the secret society my brother would have been part of. The same secret society that had been responsible for his death. I'd gone to the only people I could for help. Ben Covington, East Hale, Drew Wilcox, and Bridge Edgerton. My brother's closest friends.

They'd promised me retribution.

But now at the finish line, things had stalled. And instead of telling me something, *anything,* they'd gone silent and shuffled me away from London... presumably for my own safety.

But one, I didn't need saving. And two, this note had found me in New York, so how safe had I been really?

East, Ben, and Bridge hadn't been kidding when they said they'd take care of everything. Bridge and the boys had bought my mother's house, regardless of what it was actually worth, just like that and put it wholly in her name. As if it was nothing. And then they forced me back to the States with my mother. Which, God, I loved my mother, and it was good to see her. But it wasn't for them to decide who I was or what I wanted to do. I wasn't a child anymore.

Hell, they'd even gotten me a dream job. But the whole time I was there, not a single word came about my brother, his killers, or what they were doing about the final one.

Which meant I had to take matters into my own hands. Which meant returning under cover of night so to speak...if I didn't want the four assholes of the apocalypse to send me right back to my mother like a recalcitrant child.

I'd need to fly under the radar. And not tip them off that I was back. While I was still doing marketing work for my old company remotely, I'd also need a job here in London. I'd been careful though. My passport had been stamped in France, and then I'd taken the train. Immigration would mark that they'd seen me come through, but Bridge wouldn't have access to that. East's fiancé, Nyla Kincade might with her Interpol connections, but I didn't think she'd rat me out like that.

The point was, they didn't own me. I was the one who'd gotten them started on this vengeance thing to begin with, and now they wanted to kick me out of it?

Toby was my brother. I deserved vengeance just as much as they did. I deserved to be part of the takedown, but they'd tried to keep me out of it.

Well, not anymore.

I'd been watching Bridge for the last two weeks, and what I'd heard was true. He and Mina had broken up, so he'd been rambling around that house by himself. Sometimes, when he'd work late, he'd stay at his suite at the hotel. I'd been watching the house all day, and he still hadn't returned, so it meant he was very likely going to stay at his suite.

I parked my car and walked the block up to the house in

Belgravia. I smiled to the security guard, who I recognized from the last couple of times I'd been there, and he said, "Oh, Miss Varma."

I flashed him a winning smile that said I belonged there. "Yes, I'm here to see Mr. Edgerton. Is he here?"

He shook his head. "No. Not according to the logs. He won't be returning this evening."

Even better. I would grab his laptop, have a quick look, and I'd be in and out before he even knew anything. Sure, he'd see me on the security cameras eventually, and the guard would tell him I'd been there, but I'd be long gone by then. And I'd stay hidden.

"Would I be able to go in? The last time I was here I left something behind, and I sort of need it now. I have the code."

The furrows of his brow eased before they even started to form. "Oh, you know the code. Please type it in here, and you may enter."

That was the thing about being forgotten. While we'd been meeting, we all had our own personal codes so as not to deal with security every single time we came. Even though Mina's had been changed, there was no reason to change any of ours. Bridge had simply forgotten that I had access to his house. *Amateur.*

I typed in my code and then said a little prayer to every god I could think of. I'd been raised Catholic, but I hadn't darkened the door of the church in at least fifteen years. But now, it seemed like as good a time as any to find my faith. When the screen lit green, he nodded and pressed his own code to open the gate. "Just use the same code for the front door and you're good to go."

"Oh, excellent. I won't be but a minute."

I went in swiftly, as if I owned the joint. Bridge thought he was so slick in keeping me away from all of this, but what he didn't understand was that I would not sit back like a little woman. Toby would have expected me to be a hundred percent myself. And this was me being myself. Bridge Edgerton could kiss my ass. He'd been telling me what to do for years, but I was done with being controlled.

Emma

When I let myself in the house, a giddy sense of excitement tripped over my skin as his scent hit me. No longer was there a hint of femininity in the house. No bowls of potpourri, but the scent of sandalwood lingered in the expanse. It made a part of me deep inside clench. I loved that smell. Why did he have to smell so good? Honestly, he was a pure asshole, but he smelled like a fucking delight.

I thought back to that one kiss we'd shared when we were kids. Possibly the hottest kiss I'd ever had in my life. But he'd walked away, vowing to never touch me again, which was fine, because I had zero interest in being controlled for the rest of my life.

Liar.

A quick search of the house told me his laptop wasn't there. And that's what I fucking needed. There was a prick at the back of my eyes as I resisted the urge to cry. No. All this meant was that I was going to have to go to his suite in the hotel. And that would take a little more ingenuity, but I wasn't giving up. Bridge Edgerton had another think coming if he thought I was just going to sit back and do as I was told.

* * *

Bridge

I hadn't been staying at the house lately. Suddenly, it seemed I had turned into Ben before Livy came along. I had a big fancy house and refused to stay in it. I'd only opted to stay in the house tonight because I had a meeting on this side of town in the morning. But I'd avoided my own staff by slipping in through the back during a shift change.

I wasn't going to subject any of them to my mood.

What the fuck was wrong with me?

What's wrong is that the woman you thought you loved was hired by your fucking father.

It was like the old man would never cease to be a thorn in my side.

He wanted nothing to do with me publicly, but he still wanted to control me.

I grabbed the pillow and rolled over in the bed again. I was hot. Tight. Itchy. I just wanted out of my own fucking skin. Sleep was so far off in the horizon, I felt like giving up. I was in the process of rolling over again when I heard something in the other room.

What the fuck was that? It sounded like a light scraping noise.

I sat still, calmed my breathing, and waited. That was definitely a muttered curse coming from the living room of the suite.

Fucking Christ, that was the last thing I needed. There had been a time when I'd been a different person, rough around the edges, the one that was likely to end up in jail. Angry all of the time, and I was angry for reasons I couldn't control. I'd smoothed those rough edges and made something of my life, but now, it seemed like the old me needed to come to the forefront or something very bad was going to happen.

Under my bedside table, I reached for the one thing vested in my former life that I kept handy. The switch blade was just as I remembered it. Cold. Delicate. Deadly.

Just like Mina.

I shoved the thoughts of my ex out of my head. I didn't want to think about her and all her lies.

I sprung up out of bed. As usual, I slept commando, so I padded over to the closet and eased the bottom drawer open on the far left. I took a pair of boxers from it and tugged them on. If I was about to have a fight, there was no need to have the lads flying about uncovered.

Luckily, I slept with my door slightly ajar, so easing into the living room didn't cause any unwanted sound. Then I saw it. The shadow in the study, going through my things.

What the fuck? How had anyone gotten in here?

My feet moved of their own volition. My rational brain was

chirping up with things like, 'Call security. You are closer to the door than to the study, so just leave.' Or the oh so helpful, 'At least put a fucking shirt on.'

No, I wasn't going to do any of those things. I was going to find out who the fuck was in my suite.

The study door was open, and I saw someone dressed in all black. One of my fucking employees? I could play this scenario one of two ways. I could approach, turn on the lights, and ask them what the fuck they thought they were doing, or I could jump them. I was irritated enough that option two seemed excellent to me.

With a step-over-step motion, I slid against the window to the living room. And then, it was easy.

One arm in a choke hold, the other pressing the knife against the jugular, leaning close. The person was small, delicate. A light floral scent hit my nostrils and I inhaled deep. A woman? The slight stature, the curves, definitely a woman. Not Mina though. She was shorter and not as strong. The woman in my arms delivered a half decent elbow to my ribs. Enough to make me grind my teeth.

And why did she smell so fucking familiar?

My fucking dick didn't seem to know any better. This wasn't some game with a girl who liked it rough. This was deadly serious. But God, why did she smell... and then I knew why. I whipped my intruder around so fast that she squeaked, and with my hand on her throat, I backed her up against the wall and placed the knife to her jugular again.

"What the fuck are you doing here, Emma?"

Chapter Two

Emma

Maybe this was not exactly how I wanted things to turn out. After all, it looked bad. Me caught, first of all. Second, Bridge with his hand around my throat was not ideal. Unless you were into that sort of thing. And third, a knife at my jugular. Again, none of this was a good look. I licked my lips. "Bridge, I didn't know you were home."

"Clearly. What the fuck do you want, Miss Varma?"

Just the way he said *Miss Varma* sent a shiver into my spine. But then again, Bridge Edgerton was always doing that. Making me want things. Making me need things that he had zero intention of ever delivering on.

We'd kissed once when we were kids. Okay fine. *I* was a kid. My brother had sent him to look after me because I was fifteen and unruly. God, I really was a terror. My poor brother, Toby, hadn't been able to come home for break, and he'd promised me a concert so he'd sent Bridge in his stead. But God, Bridge acted more like a father than a cool mate of my brother's. He wasn't as much fun as he was now. If this could be classified as fun. He'd been barely eighteen, but he acted like he knew more than I did. Like he was better, smarter. He wasn't.

And as much as my little crush on him had developed, it hadn't changed over the years. He was still *that* person. From a distance of thirty paces, he could still make me tingle with just a look or an arched brow. But he also made me want to hit things. Which, let's face it, was a volatile combination. "This looks bad, but I can explain."

"Start talking, Emma."

"Well, first of all, let's do away with the knife, shall we? We both know that your leanings are toward protecting me, not actually killing me. So, put it down."

His furious gaze bored into mine, and we stood there locked in our little dance as if we had all the time in the world to make our decisions. And I could see it, the constant war inside him. The war between what he *should* do and what he *wanted* to do.

Somehow, what he wanted to do always seemed like he was on the verge of kissing me. But he never gave in, not voluntarily anyway. The last time he kissed me had been under duress. Well, fine. He could pretend he didn't want me all he wanted if he thought he could keep it up. I knew he did, but he would never take that step. All because of the promise he'd made to my brother. Which was such bullshit.

Toby was gone. Long gone. And aside from vengeance, I didn't owe him anything. He would have wanted me to be happy. And he had loved the lads. If I had ended up with any one of them, he might have been a bit miffed in the beginning. Mugged off, actually. But if one of his mates had shown he had the stones to date his sister, he would have been happy. Because what's better than to have your mates *actually* be in your family.

Toby had been closest to Bridge if I had to guess. Because Mr. Edgerton took the whole *look out for my sister* thing a little too literally. Because of that, he wouldn't touch me. "Now, now, Bridge, let's not be hasty." I shifted my hips ever so slightly and watched as his eyes flared. "Is that whiskey on your breath?"

"I had one fucking drink."

"'Course you did." I rolled my eyes. He was so predictable. "Never out of control, are you? I'm just shocked you even had one drink. Imagine what that would do for your personality. It might loosen you up."

"I'm still waiting for you to tell me what you're doing here. You know me. I'm patient."

Yes, he was, wasn't he? He would wait until I gave him a goddamn nod. The problem was, I was stubborn too. And so God only knew how long we could stay locked in this little dance of ours just to see who would crack first. But neither one would. There was no give and take with me and Bridge.

It was either find our corners or go all out rumble status. Though that was rare. Because hell, in a rumble, there stood the chance of him putting his hands on me. Anywhere would do. Just something to alleviate the ever-present pull low in my belly when he was around.

Three years or so ago, I'd resolved to stop overthinking this whole pull to him, and I had almost shagged Logan Mann instead. It was an exercise in futility when it came down to it. I hadn't wanted Logan as much as I'd wanted Bridge.

Bridge had been my first kiss. That kind of crush I couldn't forget, despite his complete ambivalence toward me.

As I stared at him and licked my bottom lip, his gaze narrowed and focused on it. And my inner diva stood up and cheered. He tucked the knife away and backed off, then he tossed it on to the table nearby. He didn't remove his hand on my throat though. "Emma, I'd hate to leave a mark. Talk."

The way he was staring at my lips with his body so close to mine, his scent wrapping around me, all musky and intoxicating like spices, I took a chance that he was as distracted as I was. There was no way I was telling him what I was really doing there because I knew he'd send me away.

"Okay, fine. I have been following you."

That surprised him. "What? How?"

"You should know by now not to ask how I know things. You haven't been home in a while."

"Not really your business."

His grip loosened, but he didn't entirely remove his hand.

I shifted my hips, and he frowned at me. "Stop it, Emma."

"Stop what?" I asked innocently.

"I know what you're doing."

I lowered my lashes, bit my bottom lip, and rolled my hips again.

He released my throat then. "Stop."

"Touchy-touchy, Bridge. Don't you just want to give in? Do what you've always wanted to do?"

There were mere inches between us. If I wanted to, I could reach up and press my lips to his. Would he respond? Would he act like he didn't care? Would he give in?

Fuck if I knew. I was desperate to find out, but how many times did you have to be rejected by someone before you got the message? I tried to play nice. "I wanted to talk to you." More like make him read me into the plans the lads had for their payback on Francis Middleton.

"Bullshit. What are you fucking doing here?"

Okay fine, so he could read me well. "There's no need for that kind of language, sir. We had a deal. The five of us. I gave you the information necessary to stop the men who were responsible for Toby's death. You got two of them. Congratulations. But the third and final one? What the fuck are you doing? You lot are sitting on your bloody hands."

The muscle in his jaw flexed. "We have a plan in play."

"Well, then you just have to let it right out." I crossed my arms, putting a little space between us. Because when he was this close, I couldn't pay attention.

"I'm not telling you what the plan is. It's for your own safety."

He took a step back. Immediately, I missed his heat, his scent... even the smell of whiskey. Why was he drinking whiskey? Every now and again, Bridge would have a scotch, but he was so tightly controlled it was very rare. I didn't think I'd ever seen him drunk. Hell, I'd never seen him truly let loose and have some fun. Never. Not once. "We had an agreement, remember? And you boys tried to cut me out of it. You sent me away."

"I made it so that you could spend some time with your mother."

"Yeah, see, I love Mum, and she is enjoying New York immensely. But that wasn't the deal. I'm back now, and I want in."

"You have a job."

"One I'm working remotely for. And I intend to find out what the fuck is going on."

"Like I said, there's a plan in motion. Don't get involved."

He turned from me, and I grabbed his arm, leaning into him and pressing my body into his. And just for the briefest moment, I could feel the shiver run through him. "Are you backing out? You know, I intended to be part of this. If you don't talk to me, if you don't share, if you leave me out of it, I'll go around you."

I watched him visibly swallow even as his gaze narrowed. "Time's up. It's late. You have two options. I'll put you in a car with my security and they'll take you home, or you can stay here and I'll take you home in the morning. Where are you staying?"

I pressed my lips together. "I'm not telling you that."

"Right, so your mum's house it is."

Yes, I *was* staying at my mum's house, but that wasn't the point. The point was that I wanted to get the lay of the land before picking a new flat. I'd already asked Telly to see if there was a unit at her building. She lived right above Vauxhall Station. Good location. Central with quick access to the tube and a gorgeous view. "It doesn't matter where I'm going. About my second option?" I purred as I leaned in to him. "Should I help you keep your bed warm now that it's been cold for a while?"

He hissed. But I could see the way that his gaze flickered to my lips. I licked them for good measure, trying to see if I could tempt the devil to come out and play. He'd never taken me up on the offer. It didn't matter what I looked like or how I acted, I just wasn't one of those women that he would ever touch. But tonight, the way he was looking at me like I was finally on the menu, it was my turn to shiver. "You've been trying to tempt me for years. What happens when one day I take you up on it?"

The question hung between us.

Heat bloomed in my chest, spread out, and concentrated itself at the apex of my thighs. Bridge took a step, closing the gap between us. I held my stance and lifted my chin so I could meet his gaze. "I'm tired of the dance, Bridge."

His low chuckle as he leaned close sent another shiver of piercing need through me. "If I finally give you what you've been asking for, are you going to run?"

I held his gaze. "I don't run. I'm pretty sure it's going to be you who can't handle this."

If there were awards for bravado, I would win. Little did he know that he was capable of shattering my soul.

Best not to tell him that then.

Never.

I would never tell anyone. Because all my concentration was on getting revenge, making Francis Middleton pay for my brother's death. After that, I'd go off and live my full life.

One Bridge kept insisting I needed to have. The one my mother worried about constantly. But not before then.

"Emma," his voice was a rasp.

"Go on, Bridge. I dare you."

Bridge

Why was it always like this with us?

Emma Varma, the one woman I couldn't touch. I'd made a

promise to her brother once, a promise to look out for her. At the time, it had been some silly little incidental *watch out for my sister at some concert* sort of thing. He hadn't known that Emma was exactly my kind of kryptonite. I loathed her. I really did.

Lies.

She had this energy about her. It was almost frenetic. She was always bouncing. Jumping here and there. And she had this way of laughing. It was so bright and sunny and hopeful. And every time I looked at her, I wanted to strip off that hope until she was bare and she could see the realities about the world.

Well, aren't you a dark fucker?

That laugh. It was like she was mocking me with her sunshine. She had this enthusiasm about her. She never did anything measured. And she always added a dose of radiance, which, dear God, it was a wonder she was still alive. I should know. I'd pulled her out of enough scrapes.

And why did she always have to smell so good? She was like that tempting flame that you knew you shouldn't touch. But still, there it was, dancing in front of you, laughing at you, mocking you. And sure enough, you just had to reach forward like a moth to the flame.

That was Emma Varma in living form. Her dark locks were pulled back into what appeared to be a low, tight ponytail, and she was dressed head to toe in black. The top and the black leather pants hugged her body closely enough to make her appear almost naked. The way she would look in a silhouette. Fucking hell.

What was it about me that wanted to steal some of her light for myself and hold on to it?

She was close. So close. The scent of jasmine wrapped around me, testing me, tempting me, teasing me. Ever since the first time I'd met her, she had been trying to destroy me. It was the only explanation for her behavior. She was always there, demanding a smile, trying to make me laugh. And when I didn't, she would pout. I remembered the first time I saw her. I'd been struck dumb.

Completely frozen in place when Toby's little sister had bounded out of the car. It had been a parent's weekend. Mum hadn't been able to come because she'd had to work, and obviously, my father wasn't coming, so I planned to just hang out with my mates. Toby's mum had come, along with Emma. The first time I'd seen her, Toby and I were thirteen, she was ten. She'd straight up asked me where my parents were. And that had stung. It was like she could see straight to the loneliness that was eating me alive.

When I told her to mind her business, it was like I could see her digging in her heels, determined to spread sunshine my way. By the end of the twenty-four-hour visit, she'd made all of us friendship bracelets with these intricate, woven designs that I didn't even know were possible. The ones that kids at school did were always some simple concoctions. But no, not Emma Varma, because God forbid, she wasn't going to do anything halfway. Her mum said she'd stayed up half the night making them. Mine was the biggest of them all. She said it was because I needed more friendship than the rest.

God, I hated her. I hated that she saw me so clearly. I hated that she knew what I needed. At the same time, that little girl had chewed me up on the inside. I'd kept that damn bracelet.

My little sliver of sunshine. But that girl was now this woman, teasing me, tempting me, grinding her hips against me, trying to make me break. Why was she *always* trying to break me? I'd never done anything to her. I'd only ever been minding my own bloody business. And yet there she was, finding ways to demand that I give her some of my time, my attention, my soul. Well, I had no interest in giving my soul.

And also, you told Toby you'd protect her.

And in that moment, the things that I wanted to do with her had nothing to do with protection. She was in my house. Up to no good. Demanding that we read her in on the Middleton situation.

Eleven years ago, our mate, Toby, her brother, had died in our secret society initiation. For ten years we'd thought it had been an accident. Something unavoidable. And then we'd found out that it *wasn't* an accident. That it had been preventable. The brothers on duty had deliberately not helped him. They'd let him die. We'd taken down two of them, and there was just one left to deal with. And we were hell-bent on bringing down the final one. The Elite had made a lot of mistakes over the years. We had the opportunity to change it, or we could burn it down. We were leaning toward changing it, but burning it down was still an option too.

But Emma... Emma couldn't be part of it. We'd all agreed to keep her away. We'd learned the hard way just how dangerous our so-called brothers were. What they'd been up to, what they were willing to do in order to hold onto their power. *We* could handle the fallout, but I'd be damned if we'd let Emma get caught in the crosshairs. Try as I might though, I couldn't get her to listen. I couldn't get her to agree to walk away.

Six weeks ago, I'd sent her away. I'd gotten her a dream job with an advertising firm working in their crisis management department. I called in a few favors. Her mum was originally from New York and had family there. And Pamma Auntie had been looking for a change. I think the anniversary of Toby's death really did her in. So I'd arranged for her to be taken care of. She had a sister in in New York and one in Toronto So we set her up in New York, and she could build a life there while going to Toronto as often as she wanted. The last I'd heard, she'd gone back to school and was even dating again. The idea of Pamma Auntie dating made me want to laugh. Although, she had that same sunshiny aura about her that her daughter did.

Her sunshine doesn't bother you though. Only Emma's.

"You look like you want to eat me alive, Bridge. Do you?"

Fuck me. "Why do you do this?"

"Do what?" She angled her chin at me defiantly.

"You're trying to push me to my breaking point."

"And you're close. I can tell. Just let go. You'll feel better."

She rocked her hips in a small figure eight again, and I had to clamp my teeth down hard. I slid my hands up her back and then to her hair, then wound her ponytail around my wrist. "Do you understand that you are *not* ready for this?"

"Oh, on the contrary, Bridge. I think you're the one who's not ready. Go on, have a taste. I know you want to."

I swallowed hard. I was always right on the edge of control with her. Always just desperate enough to give in. This was her fault. I didn't do things like this. Sure, I liked women. And since Mina had proven herself to be such a conniving bitch, I was availing myself of all the available, and not so available, women in London. And there were many. I could do mindless and easy. It was like a workout. And fuck, I liked sex. I liked it raw and dirty. Fun and playful. Any way I could get it. I didn't realize that Mina had kept me on this tether for years, doing my father's bidding. Jesus Christ. I blinked rapidly and shoved Emma away from me. "Enough. You can have the room down the hall to the right."

She glowered at me. "Why do you do that? Pretend you don't want me."

"I'm not pretending Emma. I don't want you."

Liar.

I could feel my inner self doing a double-take so hard I almost spun myself around.

"You don't want me? Fine. It's bullshit, but fine. You know I could fuck anyone, right?"

The fuck she would. It was better not to tell her that though. It would just make her run out and fuck the first guy she saw. Not that she'd actually get that far because I would stop her and lock her in this house until she saw reason.

Oh yeah, that sounds completely rational.

She rolled her eyes. "God, you're so fucking uptight. Would you relax? I didn't come here to steal your ever-present virtue. I want Middleton's head on a spike. And I'm pretty sure Nyla would have shot me if she had caught me at East's. And well, you know Olivia and Ben. I would have gotten an eyeful of something I didn't want to see. So that left you. And Drew... Well, Drew is sort of a prick."

"Drew is *not* a prick." Okay, sometimes Drew was a prick, and something was up with his wife, so she was smart to avoid that ticking bomb. "I love hearing that I'm the last resort."

"Yeah, pretty much. You think I would voluntarily come and talk to you? I don't know what the hell I ever did to you that makes you always act like such a twat. You made a deal with me. You made me a promise."

"I did no such thing. Ben made you a promise. I told him to keep you out of it. He has reconsidered now."

"Not my problem. If you're upset about it, that's too bad. Jesus, are you really not going to help me?"

"No, I'm not. You're going to get yourself killed. I want no part of that."

"Then help me."

"God, you're so fucking obstinate. You won't listen to anyone. You think you're the only one who misses Toby?"

"I'm his goddamn sister, aren't I?"

I ground my teeth and tugged her back. "Get in the fucking bedroom."

"Oh yes, you do know how to talk to a woman." She shook off my hold. "Make me."

"Emma..."

"Bridge," she mocked.

"You're staying here. It's too late for you to go back to your mum's."

"Like I said, you can't make me. You're not going to hold me like a fucking prisoner. You're not my father. Need I remind you that he is the worst kind of arsehole? I don't need another one in my life. I'm going home."

I stepped in her path. "You're staying the night, Emma. It's fucking 2 a.m."

"Yes, and? You know, there are a million bars that I could go to all over London that are still open right now. Find me a nice bloke. Shag in a nice dirty alleyway."

She'd pressed herself against me again, and I steeled myself. I couldn't stop the blood reeling in my veins though. "Fuck off, Emma."

"Don't you wish I would?" She giggled then, twirling away and heading toward the hallway that would lead to the foyer and right out my door. She really didn't think I would do it. Well, as it turned out, Emma Varma didn't know me that well at all. I marched out after her, and she cast a look back at me as if to ask what the fuck I was doing. But before the words could tumble out of her mouth, I picked her up easily, flipped her over my shoulder, and carried her down the hallway to the bedroom.

She screamed, battering me with somewhat ineffectual hits on my back. She tried kicking, but I wrapped my arm around her legs and then swatted her ass with my free hand. "Behave. It's just for the night. And trust me, the last thing I would want to do is join you. I'm just keeping you safe."

"If you don't let me go right this instant, I swear to God, I will fillet your skin off your stupid muscles."

"Oh, you noticed those muscles then?"

That only made her kick harder, which earned her another swat on the ass.

Her shocked gasp had my blood heating.

Oh no, you don't. We're not doing that. Not with Emma. She deserves better than you.

Once at the bedroom, I marched to the bed and dropped her down unceremoniously. She landed so hard she bounced. I worked hard to keep my lips from twitching at the sight of her with her dark ponytail bouncing along and cascading down her shoulders and her furious scowl as she glowered at me. "This is kidnapping."

"Sue me." And then I marched out, using the keypad outside the door to lock her in.

The room was designed as a panic room. I had converted it into a guest room, but the panels were still there. The only difference was that there were *two* panels. One on the outside and one on the inside. And I locked her in. If I had a heart, I'd have been slightly concerned that I was keeping her against her will.

But this was Emma. I knew just how much trouble she could get herself into, so I got over that fast.

Chapter Three

Bridge

I wasn't a complete monster. It wasn't exactly like I'd *kidnapped* Emma.

No, just unlawfully detained her.

For her own good.

I'd eventually let her out. I unlocked the door that morning before I left at five-thirty. I'd also left her a note, letting her know that security would take her anywhere she needed to go and or would have her car driven to her.

I knew she wouldn't appreciate it, and she would be well mugged off. But when I looked in on her, she was passed out in the most hilarious fashion. Emma slept like a starfish. A sloppy starfish to boot. The covers were kicked off the bed and she laid right across the center of it, hair in a tangle around her face. I had to resist the urge not to go and smooth her dark locks away so that the moonlight could hit that beautiful cinnamon skin. But of course, I didn't touch her because that would be creepy and also one hell of a temptation I did not need.

So I'd walked away and stuck to my program. A quick early morning text to Mum to remind her to take her medication. I'd also set several alarms at her house. But I knew how she was when she was working on something new. She ignored lots of alerts and warnings. Then I headed for a workout. My trainer and I hit the mats for forty-five minutes. The jiu-jitsu got my blood flowing, and I could already think more clearly.

Ever since my first time on the mats, when I'd had my arse thoroughly handed to me, I'd clicked with the sport. It hadn't felt good to fail so spectacularly the first time out, but the moves had felt good to my body, like something I could learn. It calmed down some of my wild, angry energy. And that was exactly what I had needed this morning, especially after a fitful night of sleep while thinking about Emma.

A nice Zen hum.

Was it the jiu-jitsu or the blow job from the yoga instructor right after that brought on the Zen?

Sigh.

Honestly, I was *almost* disgusted with myself. What was her name again? Lizbeth? Lilibeth? Something. Lily? I honestly didn't know. But she was always there setting up for her class that was thirty minutes after my training session at the gym. Sure, I could have had my instructor come to the house. It would have been more convenient. But I liked the routine of leaving home, going somewhere. Being responsible to someone else. It forced me out of some of my more selfish habits. Almost made me seem human.

In retrospect, I was well aware that in the past I had been eager to leave Mina's bed just to avoid early morning complaints. The blonde instructor had made it apparent from day one that she was more than happy to jump on my particular ride.

I'd never taken her up on it until this morning. I'd still had all that edgy energy from the round with Emma. I just needed something to take the edge off. She had wanted to kiss, and I'd told her I didn't do that.

Which was a lie. I actually loved to kiss. It was the seduction of it. Learning about someone, feeling them out, finding out just the right tempo and slide. Kissing was amazing. Even with the women that I had zero intention of ever seeing again. It was part of the fun.

But the blonde gave a very clear *I might be a clinger* vibe. When she looked disappointed about the kiss, she'd offered to blow me instead. She likely thought that a blow job would change my mind. She had a certain level of skill I appreciated. Clearly, she'd done that before. Many times. But there was something too cold, too calculating about her. Practice makes perfect and all.

Too much like Mina. When she'd left me in the shower gasping from release and told me she'd see me again, I knew I had been right. That possessive glance in her eye told me our little interaction was a one and done. I didn't need that harassment.

And still, you think a blow job isn't going to earn you a stalker?

It should be easy enough to avoid if I had to.

What the hell happened to you? The bloke who once hated the way other men used women and discarded them.

What the fuck had happened to me was Mina. And my father. I deserved to let loose just a little. Finding out your fiancée was a mole planted by your own father had a way of souring you on love.

When I walked into the office, it was 6:59 a.m., and I stopped short. Ben sat on my chair, feet up on my desk, shoes and all. *Twat.* East was over among the couches, laptop on his lap. Drew was on one of the club chairs, sipping back coffee like it was a job. His eyes were bloodshot, and despite the crispness of his suit, he looked like he'd maybe slept in it.

What the hell was going on with him? East would have to ask. East was the sensitive one. The one with the heart. People liked him. They told him shit, right?

There was also an unexpected visitor on one of the couches opposite of East. Brenda Fornace. She was our publicity person. "Was there a meeting on the calendar?" I asked.

Ben shook his head and pinned me with a glare. I wondered what the fuck had crawled up his arse.

Brenda stood. "Bridge, it's good to see you."

"Likewise. What's the matter?"

East just shook his head at me. "Mate, did you have to get caught? By paps no less?"

I frowned. "Caught doing what?"

Drew laughed. "Well, we could draw you a diagram, but from the looks of the photo, you already know who we're talking about."

I glanced around at my mates. "What the fuck are you on about?"

Brenda brought the paper over. "This ran this morning."

It was a photo of me looking disheveled, unkempt, and freshly fucked at the Bornan Benefit last week. Oh yes, Anisa Bucker? She and her husband were always on the verge of divorce according to him. "Yes, it was a little cliché, but what's the problem? I didn't notice anyone with a camera afterward."

"Well, it's a problem now," Brenda muttered as she planted her hands on her hips.

Bullshit. After all the shite Ben and East had pulled over the last several years, I'd be damned if she was going to crawl up my arse because I'd shagged a model. "Why? First of all, the photo doesn't show me actually shagging the woman, so what's the problem?"

Ben stood up. "The Zicks Hotel, remember them?"

I really had slept like shit. My normally sharp mind was sluggish. I tried to piece together why the hell everyone was pissed off. We were working on their merger. The Zicks hotel chain was one of the largest privately owned hotel conglomerates in the world. While Emma had been asking what the fuck we were doing about Middleton, this merger was part of that.

Francis Middleton had had a hard-on for the Zicks account for their private management and branding for years. Rumor was that he'd dated the one and only Zicks heiress and the family had deemed him inappropriate and run him off. Which was ridiculous. His father was a lord. But ever since, he'd wanted in with the company.

"You were caught, mate. The grand dame, Fredericka Zicks, has already emailed about it. She wants to discuss our future partnership."

I cursed under my breath. "Are you fucking kidding me? That was nearly a done deal."

Drew winked at me. "Well, until you undid another deal. Was it a socialite this time? A model? Who was it?"

I scowled at him. "Shut it. We'll just do a charity benefit or something. Take the attention off."

Brenda laughed. "No PR campaign is going to make her *unsee* this. You literally look like you were just shagging someone in the cupboard. Were you?"

Yep, sure was. I winced. "Fine, I'll meet with the old lady. Smooth her feathers. Not a big deal."

Brenda's phone buzzed and she excused herself for a moment.

When she was gone, Ben leaned forward. "It's a big deal. This was how we were going to go after Middleton," Ben said. His eyes were direct and clear. No joking. No laid-on charm. He was serious.

I slid my gaze to East for help. There was no way I had fucked us so badly with one transgression. I refused to accept this.

East only shrugged. "Mate, I have tried to find every other avenue around Middleton. He is squeaky clean. The only way we get in is this way. And let me break it down for you; he knows his mates have already gone down. He already suspects it was us, but I have a feeling he's going to be slippery. We can't afford to lose this opportunity."

Brenda strolled back then with a glower pinned on me.

"What do you want me to do about it? Like I said, I'll talk to the old lady."

Brenda sniffed. "That's not going to be enough this time, pretty boy. But I could come up with a plan for you."

"Oh, yeah? Fine, whatever it takes. I'll do it."

"I'm so glad to hear you say that, because this plan involves you getting married."

I turned my head to glare at my mates and laughed. "You have got to be kidding me."

She shook her head, her red bob bouncing along her stout shoulders. "No, I'm not. You need a reputation change. You've gone a little off the rails since Mina. This will fix it."

The fuck? Like I needed some kind of public lobotomy. It wasn't happening. "Then I guess we're not fixing it because getting married is the last thing on earth I'm doing."

* * *

Emma

That motherfucker.

He had locked me in a room like an intractable child. I was going to murder him.

I'd woken up to find the door open, so at least last night wasn't a staged kidnapping to make me his sex slave.

He'd have to want you first.

Fine, my ego could take the hit. What did I care?

I'd headed home that morning, and then I'd put out the 999 to the women. I probably should have gone to them first anyway. I just had thought that Bridge was my direct line. Because my brother, like the lads, had been part of that world. And I knew that they loved him nearly as much as I did. They'd gone to all this trouble to make things right. Except, it seemed they wouldn't make the final step.

They will. They're just not letting you take it with them.

God, I hated them.

No. You don't. They're your family.

With my mum splitting her time between Toronto and New York with her sisters, and my father just as absent as he'd ever been, the lads *were* my family. Which was why it hurt so much that they were shutting me out. After a shower and a strong coffee, I'd sent out the SOS to the girls text group. The group consisted of Livy Ashong, Ben's fiancée; Nyla Kincade, East's fiancée; Telly Brinx, Livy's bestie; Amelia, Nyla's partner at INTERPOL and the women from the Winston Isles. Penny was the queen, and Jessa, Ariel and Bryna, were all princesses. It had been Telly, our resident tech genius, who had replied first. And then all the girls in the group chat had chimed in. Penny and Ariel had been all about the have-to-make-them-pay attitude. Okay, who was I kidding? That was mostly Ariel. She was terrifying when she got going. There was almost no line that was too far to cross short of murder. And I loved every ounce of her.

But Penny, Ariel, Bryna, and Jessa weren't here. So it was going to have to be Telly, Livy, and Nyla. Telly suggested meeting up at her place so that the boys couldn't spy on us. Which was smart. Because as down for the cause as Livy and Nyla were, the boys made it impossible to keep anything a secret. And once one of them knew, they all knew. They gossiped worse than teenagers.

So that night as I skipped up the walk toward Telly's place, I glanced around. I loved this complex of flats. They had that whole work-living feel to them, and if you were lucky, you could get one that overlooked the Thames. Those were more money of course. I had some money saved from my last job, but I had to ask Telly and see if I could even afford a small studio there.

And that was why the next line item was to get a job. Luckily, the job that Bridge secured for me in New York to keep me out of his hair completely overpaid me, and they'd made me an offer to let me keep working while I was back in London. I just had to write marketing plans, which were easy, and I could do it in my sleep. And that would tag me over until I had something more permanent.

Telly buzzed me in, and I strolled in to find all the girls already there. With hugs all around and a large wine glass placed in my hand, Telly plopped back on her massive sectional, which took up nearly the whole room. "Tell Mama Telly everything. Who are we killing?"

I laughed even as I glanced around for her wife, Carmen. "Is Carmen here?"

She shook her head. "Carmen and I are having a disagreement. So she is off in Bristol, checking on the clinic there."

Olivia slid Telly a look. "Mm-hmm," was all she said.

Telly threw up her hands. "Don't look at me like that. I didn't start this argument."

Livy rolled her eyes. "This is classic you, Tell. The moment things are going well, you need to sabotage them. I'm surprised you even got married."

Telly scoffed. "Ugh, harsh."

Livy just shrugged and took a large gulp of wine. "Mm, true."

My gaze darted back and forth. "What's happening?"

Olivia pointed at Telly. "This one is mad at her wife because her wife wants a baby."

Telly jumped in then. "I'm not *mad* at her. I'm just confused because we agreed we weren't having children."

Olivia shrugged. "Well, it looks like she wants to revisit the idea."

Telly shook her head. "No, we've only been married for six months. Plus, I was very clear that I do not *like* children. They are sticky and snotty and loud. So loud."

I frowned. "Wait, didn't I see you happily munching on the cheeks of Penny and Sebastian's daughter?"

Her eyes went wide. "That is different. She's a cherub. A little brown cherub. And her cheeks... My God, she has cheeks for days. She has extra, so I alleviated her of some. Look, babies are adorable. They're cute, especially fat babies. Fat babies are the best. I don't trust a skinny baby. But look, I don't want to have my own baby. They smell bad ninety-nine percent of the time. Whether it's that sour milk smell, or the poop smell, or the vomit smell, they just always smell. And they demand attention. Plus, I love our flat. We can't have a baby in a flat. You need a home with a garden and all that stuff. And I am not the pram mommy running around, you know, at brunch and things. Clearly, as much trouble as we get into with heists and the danger... I mean, come on."

Olivia shrugged. "I'm just saying, maybe if you heard her concerns..."

"I don't *want* a baby. In fact, I said I don't want a baby before we married, and she agreed that she did not need children. But now she says, 'Oh, but wouldn't it be great?' I know what that means, so I told her to take some time and think about what she really wanted out of our relationship. So she went to Bristol."

I winced. "Telly, don't throw this away. You have to talk."

She waved a hand. "She'll be back. She will see that I am being sane and rational."

Livy sighed. "For starters, no one would ever call you sane and rational. Secondly, I'm not suggesting that you have a baby, especially since you're so adamantly against it. What I'm suggesting is that you communicate and hear what she's got going on, because sometimes the baby isn't really about the baby."

"No, you haven't seen her. She's got that look. The one where she seems to squish every chubby cherub around. We can't walk ten feet on Sundays for brunch without her just going, 'Ohh, look at the baby.'"

We all sighed. Nyla came in from the kitchen. "Did someone say babies?" She looked terrified.

I laughed. "You're not a fan either?"

She shrugged. "You know, I'm actually not opposed. But God, I love sleep. And sex whenever I want."

"Uh-huh. God, you do have layers. What about you, Liv?"

Livy smiled. "Oh, I love babies. And I think left to his own devices, Ben would have me knocked up and pregnant all the time. I just also happen to love my job. So it's about timing. I'll have to decide when I'm ready. And Telly, when that happens, you can squeeze all the cheeks you want."

Telly clapped. "See? This, I love. I am Auntie Telly. I'm not Mummy. God." She said it really slowly. "And you have great tits, Livy. Your tits would withstand a baby. Mine would not. Or Carmen's. Carmen's already sagging a little bit. I like them though because they're so big. But look, they're not going to withstand stretchmarks and a baby tugging on them all the time. My God, those are *my* boobies."

Livy snorted so hard she nearly spilled her wine. "Oh my God, I love you, Tell. Jesus."

Telly shrugged. "What? Priorities."

I rolled my eyes. "Guys, can we get back to the problem at hand? Mine?"

"Yeah, sorry." Telly frowned. "Okay, so you're saying Bridge locked you in the bedroom?"

"Yes, but that's not the point. The point is, I asked him to let me help with Middleton, and he refused. He won't tell me anything. He won't give me any information. He's completely gone back on his word to let me be involved."

Livy pursed her lips. "Yeah, Ben's become reticent as well."

Nyla crossed her arms and paced. "Yeah, you know, East is the same way because, sure, I mean, I came in late. But after we dealt with Garreth Jameson, you'd think they'd be happy to take care of this final asshole, but it's like they've got some plan and they're not sharing."

Telly nodded. "I mean, not that you want to spy on your fiancés, because that would be awful. But... If you *did* want to spy on your fiancés, you know, there are easy ways to do that."

Nyla frowned. "You've met my fiancé, right?"

Telly laughed. "Yes, and I'm a better hacker than he is. I'll have his passwords in no time. If you, you know, if you were to give me permission." The truth was, they were both great hackers, but East was a hair better. No one ever dreamed of telling him that though.

Nyla shook her head. "No, I can't do that. I don't *want* to do that. But there must be other ways that we can look into what they're doing."

I shook my head. "What if we just let them do their thing and we did our own?"

Telly nodded, leaning forward. "Go on. I'm here for this."

Livy shook her head. "Honestly, let me just ask Ben."

I shook my head. "No, I don't want to know that there *is* a plan. I want to be part of it. Toby was my brother."

Everyone glanced around. It was Nyla whose voice was surprisingly soft. She didn't usually take the empathetic route, but she surprised me when she said, "Ems, have you ever thought that they're just trying to protect you? Toby was your brother, but they loved him too. And the fact that you were the one who pointed out their failings means they feel responsible to fix it. And the fact that this has been so remarkably dangerous means they want to keep you out of it and keep you safe. They think it's the least they can do for him."

I shook my head. "There has to be a better way. He was my *brother*. I wish I could explain. I feel unsettled, and it's like there's a hole in my chest. I can't move forward. I am stuck. And until that last asshole gets what's coming to him, I will stay stuck. I have no closure for myself. Mum has been able to move on past it, but every time I turn around, or I have a question, or some bloke fucks with me, I miss him. I need my brother."

Telly took my hand, and her smaller one was warm as she squeezed hard. "Well, we're here for you. If you want us to go on our own lady heist, I'm here for it. We're Ocean's Eight."

I rolled my eyes. "Well, fun, but not really the best premise for a movie."

She laughed. "Right. Because honestly, what was Anne Hathaway even doing in that movie?"

"Right?"

We high-fived.

Livy just chuckled. "Look, you know we are the bad idea crew. Or rather, the boys are. How about we be smarter? Think this through. Maybe there's another way to get to Middleton. One we haven't really considered. One the lads haven't considered either."

Maybe she had a point. No reason to fly in blind as we often did. But then a colossally bad idea. I knew it was bad the moment it dawned on me. "Hey guys, I'm back now and I'm looking for a job. Something a little bit more permanent. Why don't I get one?"

Nyla's sharp gaze narrowed on mine. "Please tell me you're not thinking what I think you're thinking?"

I grinned. "Why don't I apply for a job with Middleton Communications?"

I should have known by their faces that this was the worst idea I'd ever had. Livy and Nyla's brows furrowed, but Telly clapped. Her enthusiasm alone should have told me this was a very, very bad idea.

Chapter Four

Bridge

My bloody head had been pounding all goddamn day. How the fuck had this happened? When I strolled into my flat at the London Lords hotel, I tossed my keys haphazardly onto the counter. I wasn't sure which part of my day was worse, Brenda slapping down that image of me or suggesting I get married to fix everything. It was an image I hated. I looked wrecked. Out of control. Like the person I'd been once.

If I saw that picture of me, I wouldn't bloody do business with me either. I'd seen a million blokes like that. Where I had grown up in East London wasn't exactly the gritty working-class area it had once been. But there were still many neighborhoods that weren't exactly desirable. And that's where I'd grown up. Mum doing her best. Dad pretending I didn't exist. So many of my friends who looked like they were whacked out and out of control.

And that's what you look like now. Full circle.

I worked my ass off to shake every ounce of my upbringing and become something that challenged my father. I normally stood by a moral compass that he didn't have. I took care of business that he didn't. And now, I'd thrown that all away for a round of stupid decisions.

You can make different ones.

I knew that. I was wishing I had made different ones. The problem was that with the fury and the loathing came rash decision-making, wanting to fulfill my own prophecies. And so yeah, Anisa Bucker had happened.

Wife to Darian Bucker. Wealthy financier, rich kid set for life. His wife had been eyeing me. Bought me a drink. So yeah, I'd dragged her into the wardrobe and shagged her. I didn't care about her, hadn't thought about her, really. All she'd said to me was, 'So, I hear you no longer have a fiancée.' And that had been it. I didn't know that there was someone around to capture a photo.

Because you were careless. You lost focus. You were finally everything that your father ever said you were.

And now it was going to fuck with our plans.

But still, Brenda's idea was no kind of solution. I wasn't fucking getting *married*. I'd just finally dropped Mina. All the tabs knew about Mina was what we'd fed them. Under no circumstances was I going to let her come up looking like roses. All they'd been fed was that I'd broken up with her. Which was important. And we'd cited irreconcilable differences. People could read between the fucking lines. And ever since the split, the women had come out of the bloody woodwork.

Not that I was complaining. After all, I was a bloke. I liked women. But when I'd been with Mina, I hadn't stepped out once. I wasn't my father. He was more of a pompous ass who didn't give a fuck who he hurt. Mina hadn't been an exactly right fit. On paper she was, but there was always something a little aloof about her. But once I'd made my decision, she was it. Only to find out I'd been wrong about her.

It happened to the best of us. But it was never going to happen to me again. I was not getting married for the sake of the London Lords. I was not getting married for the sake of Toby Varma.

Toby had been one of my best mates. When he died, it had rattled me. Toby had been like me. Someone who didn't belong.

The product of our fathers' extracurricular indulgences. Someone unwanted, shuffled around, discarded, and forgotten. My mates were like brothers to me. Ben, Drew, East. We were thicker than mates; we were family. But Toby, Toby had been the one who got to me. And then one day he was gone. Just gone. A lot of what I did now was to make up for him too. But this... I would not get married. Not to fix this. We'd have to find another way. We just would.

There was a knock at the door, and I checked my phone to see if security had texted me. Nothing. I frowned as I approached the door and checked the security panel. The woman on the other side was more than familiar with her dark hair pinned artfully in smooth coils and a sophisticated up-do. She wore a mid-length cocktail dress that looked like it had been painted on but was somehow still sophisticated. Diamonds on her ears. I debated not opening it, but I needed to find out how the fuck she got up here.

So I opened the door. "What do you want, Mina?" As exes went, I sure could pick them.

Her lips were glossed in *Pink Perfection*. Her signature color. I should know because I had taken her to Brew's Cosmetics when she'd been under the delusion that she wanted her own cosmetics line. We had gone as far as testing out some samples, and then she'd gotten bored. I'd spent a lot of money on endeavors for her, and she'd always gotten bored. There was nothing she seemed to like doing at all. That lipstick was the only one she'd done. Pink Perfection.

"Is that how you talk to your fiancée?"

I choked a laugh. "We broke up. Don't you remember?"

"Yes, I remember that you were a bit miffed with me. Do you mind us not doing this in the hallway? It's conspicuous."

I crossed my arms and leaned on the doorjamb, not allowing her in. "No, we can do it here just fine. You're not coming in. There are security cameras left and right. I want to make sure the time-stamps are clear."

She lifted an arched brow. "What do you think is going to happen?"

"With a woman like you, I don't know. You'd do just about anything for money, wouldn't you? You really think I haven't seen it all? I have. I won't have you accusing me of hurting you or anything. You're staying right out there."

She blinked rapidly. "You think I would do that?"

She seemed to have forgotten she'd promised to tell everyone about my supposed cruelty. I didn't want to know what that entailed, so better to have her on camera. "That's the point, Mina. I don't know what you would do. So every conversation we have is going to be public. I don't have anything to hide, so I don't give a fuck who hears. But there will be security footage. *Always.*"

She sniffed. "What I wanted to talk to you about, we can't talk about out here. It's private."

"You want to talk about all the times we shagged and I wondered if you were thinking about someone else?"

I watched as her skin went pink from her breast up to her neck, to her pale cheeks. "We never had a problem in the bedroom."

"Well, I made sure you didn't." My personal philosophy was no one went to sleep until my partner came. That morning's yoga situation was an anomaly. It still didn't sit right.

She blinked rapidly. "That is uncouth, Edgerton."

I shrugged. "It's also the truth. What do you want, Mina?"

"Look, I saw the papers. The photos of you. I know what they're saying. Playboy Bridge Edgerton, really living up to the moniker. Bridge Edgerton has gone off the rails. Heartbroken. Spinning out. I know that can't be good for you. I am willing to help you."

I laughed genuinely for the first time in weeks. "What? How do you plan on helping me?"

"I know they're making it seem like you're spinning out, but we can spin this. We'll just say we got back together and we've been working things out. We'll make up some bullshit about couple's therapy, and everything will go back to normal. Let's be real; you've missed me."

I tipped the corner of my lip up into a sneer. "Oh yeah? What makes you think I've missed you?"

Her smile was pure evil. "You forgot what happened in your office not too long ago?"

My fucking office, right.

She'd walked in, begging me to take her back, stripped naked, and then straddled my lap. Refused to let me lock the door, hoping someone would interrupt us. And okay, I'd given in. I fucked her the way I'd always wanted to. The way she would never allow.

Completely unrestrained. Mina had been very strict. She only ever had sex in the bed or the shower. Nowhere else. She had zero interest in it. Even in the house, she rarely would let me eat her out, and most of the time she didn't want me touching her breasts.

I wasn't allowed to leave bite marks, beard rash, or other marks on her skin. Everything expertly restrained. For years I thought someone had hurt her, so I'd done my best to be gentle. But that day, I hadn't felt like being gentle, and she'd said and done all the right things. And hatred or not, if I was going to fuck a woman, she was having an orgasm.

She had come—twice. But there had been something in her eyes. They were empty, calculating. And I could see that the whole scene had been about control. And I made a vow that I was never touching her again. I knew from that moment, everything had been a lie.

"Look, this is dangerous for you. I know how you worry about appearances. All you have to say is that it was me you were with. Hell, I'll say it. That we were making up. Everyone will like the love story, and we can go back to our lives."

"Your life? You mean the life *I* gave you?"

She pressed her lips firmly together. "The life I've gotten accustomed to. I wanted to become Mrs. Bridge Edgerton. But you've been distant for the last several months. I know your friends have poisoned you against me."

"Oh, really? You think it's them? The only one that hated you was Ben. Now I know that the others knew about you. And they thought I loved you enough, so they didn't tell me. Ben though, God, he has always hated you. And he could see it. I don't know why I missed it."

She pursed her lips again. "He just didn't like that I had your time. He's very controlling, you know."

"Right, *he's* the controlling one. Got it. Get on with it, Mina."

"Fine. I will help you. We'll get married. Something quick, not big and lavish. Just a hundred people or so. Tasteful. At Hyde Park or something. We'll invite the paparazzi."

"Uh-huh, this sounds amazing. What do you get out of it?"

"You mean besides the honor of being your wife? A ten-million-pound payout. A million pounds a year for ten years. After that, we can go our separate ways. Tell everyone we gave it a good try."

I laughed. "Oh, is that all? Ten million. It's a drop in the bucket."

But she wasn't done yet. "And well, you're going to give me Belgravia. After all, I decorated it. And the equivalent of one of your hotels, so I can continue to earn money."

I laughed then. "Oh, wow. So all that, and what do I get?"

She tilted her chin and met my gaze. "And then I won't tell anyone about that dirty little secret you have at the Austrian boarding school."

I studied her. I had always thought Mina a magnificent beauty. Her pale alabaster skin. Her dark, sleek hair. There had been something vulnerable about her once. Like she needed taking care of. But I could see now that had been part of the act for me. This Mina was cool and calculating.

I had thought I loved her. I thought she needed me. All those things were appealing to me at the time. But I don't actually think I ever really loved her. Not the way I should have. "Wow, you're just going straight for the blackmail."

"It's not blackmail. I'm just saying, you're already in trouble. For you everything carries on, I don't tell anyone about Austria, and I get my life back."

I pushed myself to my full height then. And that was the only time she took a step back. What? She thought I was going to hurt her? I'd never put my hands on a woman.

You did spank Emma last night.

I ground my teeth just thinking about her. I swallowed hard against the flash of need. The immediate tingling.

Fucking Emma. Intruding on my thoughts right now. It was always inconvenient.

What about all those times you fucked Mina and thought about her?

Nope, I was not doing that. Not right now. I shoved those thoughts back into their locked dungeon in the recesses of my mind where they belonged.

"Well, Mina, you've given me quite a thing to think about."

She sighed. "The clock is ticking. The offer only stands—"

I held up a finger to her, interrupting. "Well, my first answer is not if you were the last fucking woman on earth. Not if your pussy was lined with gold. That's my initial answer. I will come up with one that is more thorough with a little time."

Her eyes went wide. "What did you say to me?"

I slowed down my speech so she could hear me properly. "I said..." I inhaled deeply, wrinkling my nose at that rose water scent she always used. It was always far too much, trying to smell sweet when honestly she was decaying on the inside. "That I wouldn't marry you even if your pussy was lined with gold."

She raised a hand to slap me, and I grinned and tsked. "Uh-uh-uh. Cameras, remember? Cameras."

As it turned out, Mina gave not one fuck about the cameras as her palm connected with my cheek, quick and sharp. The thing was, I think it hurt her hand more than it hurt my face.

I glowered at her. "Now, if you darken my doorstep again, I will have you removed. How did you get up here anyway?"

"Everybody knows me. They know I'm your fiancée. They assume we're still fucking."

"Then I'll fire them. Every single person you talked to from the moment you walked in this place, I will fire them. Don't come here again."

"Why, you—"

I simply stepped back into my loft and closed the door while she was still speaking.

Chapter Five

Emma

I tugged nervously on the sleeves of my Chanel blazer. I'd gone casual with jeans but paired it with a silk blouse. I knew Francis Middleton. I'd known him for years.

I still remember his father as he'd come inquiring how my mother and I were getting on after Toby died. I remembered his father's calm demeanor, affable smile, warm hand. He'd brought his son as a shadow. Francis didn't say much, but I remembered his eyes on me.

Curious.

As if he was looking for something in me. I didn't understand at that time what it was. I was too numb honestly. They'd come not a month after Toby had died. They offered their help and, assistance. A job for Mum. A new school for me. A fresh start. At the time, I thought it was because our father was one of them. One of those special men in fancy cars with tinted windows. Men who exuded power.

I didn't know anything about my father really, or the Elite then. But Francis and his father were just like him. Slick. Powerful. Rich. Those qualities exuded off of them in waves. It was unavoidable. You could tell.

Over the years, Francis had checked in. A call here. A visit there. Running into each other at an event. He was polite, but his gaze was always searching. He was handsome in that beautiful, pale, and very British sort of way. *Bland.* Even though he had centuries of wealth behind him and a name nearly as old as the queen's herself. But he'd always watched me with keen awareness. It wasn't until later that I'd learned that he had been one of the ones responsible for Toby's death. So what had he been looking for?

Maybe he was looking for some kind of awareness that I knew deep down his family had covered up Toby's death. Hushed up my brother's death when they could have prevented it. They could have saved him, protected him.

But as I waited in the sitting area of Middleton Communications, I tried to force a placid smile on my face. If I wanted access and answers, I was going to have to play the part. Act my ass off, actually.

I heard the padding of feet before I felt the tingle of awareness. As always, it carried a hint of... Danger might not be the right word, but it carried a certain feeling that made me uneasy.

"My God, Emma Varma." He skirted around the massive oak table in the center of the room to come over to me and take both my hands in his . The crisp scent of his Tom Ford cologne enveloped me as well.

"Francis, it's good to see you."

"You can imagine my surprise. I didn't realize that you were on the schedule today."

"Well, I called earlier. I told your secretary I wanted to surprise you."

He lifted his brows. "I welcome the surprise and lucky for you, I have some time. Do you want to grab lunch?"

"Well, maybe in a bit, but I mostly wanted to talk to you about something."

"Ask anything. I have always said, as has my father, that if you or your mother ever needed anything, we're here to help you. Toby was a friend."

I ground my back molars but forced my face to stay neutral. Francis had been no friend to Toby. I knew that. But the lie tripped off of his tongue so easily and with such skill that my sense of unease prickled again.

"Of course. Actually, I'm just back from New York, and I'm looking for a job."

His brows lifted and he dropped his hands, slipping them into his pockets. "Oh, really?"

"Yes. Of course, I wanted to just see what you might have open. I wouldn't want to use our connection. I assure you, I'm more than qualified."

He nodded. "Of course, of course." He waved his hands dismissively as if that was even a question but he'd go ahead and find me some job that I may or may not be qualified for, simply because I knew him and he owed me. "Well, I can talk to our Director of Marketing. I'm sure she could help find room for you on her team."

I gave him a wan smile. "Actually, I've been in crisis management for the last several years. I worked for Turnings and Forster." The crisis management division was where I'd find anything pertaining to my brother if it existed.

He blinked rapidly. "Oh, wow. All right. I know they're mostly United States-based, but they have some foreign clients, and for those that they can't handle, we do some work with them."

I smiled. "Yes, I'm aware. Which is why I'm here."

"Oh, I just assumed that because we knew each other, you wanted to catch up."

"Of course. It's always lovely to see you." I lied through my clenched teeth. "My job at Turnings and Forster was great. I had some amazing clients. And while I enjoyed New York, I figured it was time I return to London. I missed being here. So, here I am."

He cleared his throat. "Right. Of course. I mean, when was the last time I saw you? Two years ago? Or maybe it was a year?"

"About a year and a half, I think. Somewhere around there."

"Yes, yes. I remember you said you were thinking about going back. I hadn't seen you around, so I just assumed that you hadn't returned."

"Yeah well, I had to get Mum settled. She's had a foot here and a foot there for some time. She has moved permanently to New York now."

"Well, that's good to know. I'm so glad things are working out for her. She has family there, doesn't she?"

The small talk was killing me. *Get to the bloody point so you can give me a goddamn job and I can get out of here.* But I didn't say that out loud. "Yeah, you know, she's happier there." I shifted on my feet. "I, however, missed London and my people. So while looking for a job, I figured I'd come to the best."

He smiled wolfishly at that one as he eyed me suddenly, assessingly. I was aware of the way men looked at me usually. I knew some would always try and please me, and some would try to determine ethnically what I was. Though I was quite brown, I screamed Indian or Middle-Eastern or something, at least. But they were never quite sure.

"Turnings and Forster, that's impressive, Emma."

"I'm aware." I left it there. I felt like women were socially programmed to make men comfortable. I had zero intention of doing the usual bullshit, talking a lot, trying to explain why I was as good as my male counterparts. He clearly knew the firm I worked for and what I was capable of. So I knew he would make some calls and find out that I was good at my job and that I wasn't playing. "I'm not sure I have anything available for you, Em. But, like I said, I can ask a few questions."

"You do that. But might I just point out a couple of things?"

He chuckled and then crossed his arms. "All right, point away."

"Well, first of all, I recognize that Middleton Communications has an image problem. You don't have enough women on your executive board. You don't have enough women on your team. And the last two women that you had on your team of crisis managers, specifically senior executive level, both quit for undisclosed reasons. Now, while that in itself doesn't say much, it does scream to a lot of old-boy cronyism."

"Says the woman who's in my building asking for a personal favor from a friend."

I forced a smile on my face as he said *friend*. He was no friend of mine. "Actually, I just asked for time from a friend. My resumé speaks for itself."

His brows popped. "Does it now?"

"In fact, it does. So you can call Turnings and Forster, find out if I'm any good at my job, which then will tell you that I, in fact, am. You can examine your own company policies to see why there aren't women in executive positions and really recognize that I am here to solve a problem for you. Now, I don't expect to be part of the executive team immediately. I need to prove myself first, of course, and I'm willing to do that. I just want an opportunity to do what I am good at. Before you walked in, I took the liberty of sending you both my CV and my client list. You'll see politicians, actors, athletes, all of whom would be more than thrilled to give me a glowing recommendation. And you will see the proposal I made for you to fix your lack-of-women problem. Because as things are shifting worldwide, you and Middleton Communications haven't really changed with the times. If it is a cultural problem that will need to be solved, I'd meet with you and your father so we can talk about the problem and resolve it. But if there's a toxic environment at your company, at the higher levels especially, I know that you would want to solve that to make it an equitable work environment. Am I correct?"

The corner of his lips twitched, and his keen gaze took on an icier glint. Had I miscalculated? This was the wrong way to go, wasn't it?

"You, Miss Varma, are different than I remember."

"Well, I have grown up just a little."

"All right, you have me intrigued."

I gave him a small smile and tried not to look too smug.

"Why don't I take you to lunch, and you can tell me more about how I can fix my woman problem?"

"Well, I mean, don't you want time to review my proposal first?"

"No. You managed to walk in here and disrupt my day and make me a pitch that's interesting enough for me to take notice. I think you'll pitch better in person than it will on email."

Fuck. He was going to make me have lunch with him. Fine. I would just have to watch what I ate. Because there was no way I was going to stomach several hours with him. What I wanted to do was force him to tell me what had happened to my brother, what he'd done, his part in the whole tragedy, and see if he could look me in the face. But I knew that I had to be patient. Because he was not going to tell me what I wanted right away. This was going to take time. And during that time, it looked like I might be working for the enemy.

* * *

Bridge

I accepted that I had cocked up the plan.

That crow didn't get any better tasting when it was decided that I needed to go plead my case to the old lady. Apologize for being a philandering cunt.

Except I wasn't a philandering cunt. I was just a single bloke, working some shit out with his dick.

Great. Go ahead and say that. See if the old lady likes it.

I stood at attention when her assistant called me forward. "Mrs. Zicks will see you now."

When I strolled in, Fredericka Zicks scooted from around her desk. Her face looked like what a grandmother should look like.

Softly round and heavily lined with wrinkles with a wide smile at the ready.

But I knew better than to let the immediate warmth fool me. Fredericka Zicks was a shark. And she'd been swimming in shark-infested waters for decades. She knew how to run a business, how to run a successful hotel conglomerate that her husband left her over twenty years ago when he died. She was a force to be reckoned with. And while she might look like the kind of granny who made biscuits and always had a toffee for you, she wasn't. But still, she gave me a warm smile and reached her arms out to me, warmly gripping mine. "Ah, Bridge Edgerton. I always did say you were a handsome devil. If only you and my daughter had ever hit it off."

I forced a tight smile. Her daughter, while actually genuinely kind, was not my type. She was timid. I was sure that it wouldn't work because I knew that I was gruff and well, if I was being honest, at times, I would terrify her. I terrified most people. That fact normally didn't bother me. But she was actually nice. No need to corrupt the youth.

"I think that ship has sailed."

She tsked then got right to the point. "Well, it seems that you've gotten yourself into a spark of trouble, doesn't it?"

Oh, so we were jumping right in, were we? "Fredericka, I appreciate you taking the time to see me, but honestly, we don't need to talk about that. That's gossip. You know what the tabloids are like."

She nodded and gestured for me to take a seat in one of the fine-leather couches she had in her office. "Yes, they are rags. And I'm only relieved that my husband, Timothy, passed before he saw how bad they could really get. Although, you know, when the princess died, things were already pretty brutal. You witnessed that, of course. But nowadays, anyone is fair game."

"That's true. Anyone is fair game. Even when you're not looking for trouble."

She smiled at me. "Darling, I know why you're here. I'm sure it reached your ears that I had some concerns when I saw the photos of you."

Well, I did always like her directness. It made my life easier. "Yes, but there wasn't any merit or truth in what they were saying."

"My boy, I'll have you know I wasn't born yesterday. I know what young people are like."

I winced at that. "Yes, but I promise you what they're saying isn't true."

She pressed her lips together, and I could see the fine lines around the edge of her mouth. "I understand that you broke up with that fiancée of yours."

I nodded. I'd taken Mina to some charity benefit two years ago and I thought Fredericka had met her then. I couldn't remember for sure.

"Honestly, I was never particularly fond of her."

My brows lifted in surprise. Well then, this was certainly easier than I thought. I thought she'd read me the riot act. But she already disliked Mina. And truly, she would understand. "We had our difficulties. It was just time to separate. However, I wish her well because she's not a bad person, per se. It's just that we were incompatible."

She waved a hand. "Sure. I don't need to read between the lines, boy. I understand she's probably hurt you deeply with her actions."

I frowned. "Come again?"

She lifted a brow. "My darling, you can't possibly not know."

My stomach churned. "Know what?"

She sighed. "Well, I mean, it's all water under the bridge now, as you two have been separated."

She was right. It was all water under the bridge. But at the same time, I did want to know. "Right. It doesn't matter anymore, does it?"

She frowned and nodded. "Unless you are thinking about rekindling things. Perhaps the two of you will wed?"

I definitely avoided the question. "Mina and I are not rekindling. It wouldn't work."

She frowned again. "Right. It's just that this hotel is my family's legacy. My husband and I built it from the ground up. Our core values are based on family, elegance, and beauty too. But mostly *family*. We have great family values here. It's about tradition."

"I understand. And I promise you the things you read in the press about me, they're not true. The London Lords remain an excellent partner for Zicks. We've been working on this merger for so long. Please don't let rumor and innuendo sour what would be a fantastic partnership."

She sat back. "Do you think me born yesterday, boy?"

I winced. I hated that form of address. As if I was nothing better than a child. I was a grown man who knew his job well.

"No, ma'am. Of course not."

"I know sometimes men need to serve their bravados. I just would prefer you to do it at the right time."

"And that's not the case?"

She held up a hand. "I've heard the rumors. Granted it was not while you were with Mina, but after. You and your mates, as you say, were a wild bunch once, weren't you?"

I opened my mouth to argue, but it was true to some extent. Mostly Ben. But I wasn't going to throw him under the bus either. "The things we did when we were young are not what we do as adults."

"Of course not. But your teammates are settled. They have moved on. And the moment you were no longer engaged, all I saw were stories of you in the papers. You can understand why I would be concerned."

I could see it then. This was really a problem. There would be no easy smoothing things over. I could say all the right words, do all the right things, and she would still see that image of me strolling out of the wardrobe, hair mussed, clothes askew. Fuck me. The lads were right. I really, really had fucked this up. This was on me. This couldn't be blamed on anyone else. If this deal went south, we'd have no one to blame but me. All the work, the plan of vengeance for Toby, all depended on me getting this right. I cleared my throat. "I didn't want to say anything. but the photo, the woman I was with, she's not some illicit affair. She's someone who has been a friend for years. Obviously, I was with Mina for a long time, and things didn't work out. And my friend was comforting, and we realized that we've had some very strong feelings for years, but we never acted on them. That night, what you saw in that photo was us giving in to them."

I was lying through my bloody fucking teeth. And as long as Anisa went along with this and didn't say anything, nobody would know it was her and not some hidden woman that I was in love with. Whatever the hell that meant.

Fredericka's eyes went wide. "Oh, a love affair."

"Oh, it's hardly an affair. We're just not ready to go public. You know, the timeframe with Mina and all. It's for the best if we remain quiet for a while." My brain was offering scenario after scenario on the fly. There had been a time when I could lie with the best of them. Where I'd scammed and played and worked the system in my favor, because back then, it had been about survival. But I didn't live like that anymore. Except... When the chips were down, I apparently went right back to that. Disgusted with myself, I sat back. "You know, privacy and all that. And if we're going to be together, I don't want her shunned. You know how society can be. People taking sides. I wanted to give a bit more space between Mina and I before we go public."

And to my shock and surprise, Fredericka was grinning at me. Jesus Christ, she was buying this? The old lady was shrewd. I'd been certain she smelled deception, but oh no, she was giving me a soft gaze that women gained babies from. What the hell was wrong with her?

"This could not be better news. You're in love?"

I cleared my throat. "Um, yes. I'm in love. But you know, it's still new."

She waved me away with a hand. "Uh, you men, always so cautious when it comes to love. You've been in love with her a long time?"

I nodded. "Oh yes, since we were kids. Before I even knew what love was."

The more I blabbed, the more she believed me, and her expression grew softer and softer. "Oh, I see now. Ugh, these tabloids. If only you hadn't been seen."

"Yes, that was careless, to say the least. But we were trying to just get a few moments together while at a public function and not be seen, but you know how these things go."

She chuckled. "Yes, of course. I was in love once. I was young once. Don't let the withered skin and the white hair fool you. I know what it's like to sneak off with someone you care about."

Was this actually working? She was believing this pile of shit. I wasn't sure if I was relieved she was buying it or disappointed. Either way, I was going with it. This was so much better than producing some fake fiancée. Now I didn't have to say anything or do anything about it.

"I insist on meeting her."

I frowned. "Excuse me?"

"Your new love. I want to meet her."

"I— But, it's still so new."

"Oh, come on. When you know, you know. You just said you've been in love since you were kids. You are going to marry her, right?" And I could see it now. I was in a corner, backed against the wall, and Brenda had known it would happen. The old lady, shrewd or not, a modern businesswoman or not, she was feeling grandma fairy tale vibes, and she was going to get them one way or the other.

"Now, let's not jump ahead of ourselves."

"Young women these days, they're so used to time wasters. You're not young anymore. And I promise you, if you were on your way to getting wed, not that I'm pushing you because I know what that's like too, but if you were on your way to getting wed, that would certainly curb the speculation on Mina because I'm sure she's quite sore she has lost a catch like you."

Oh yeah, that was me, some catch. "Yes, well. Mina is not worried about me."

The old lady pursed her lips again. "Now, I'm not one who tells tales, but that woman has every intention of keeping her claws in you. If you love the woman that you're involved with, I would lock it up. Mina is not done. And I promise you, she will make trouble. You're lucky you never had a child with her."

I thought of the threat Mina made last night, and my stomach roiled. "Right. I'm lucky."

"So, before you go, let's get Charles out there to put something in the books. I want to meet your girlfriend."

I smiled wanly. I'd done it now. I had put my own foot in it. I had told this lie. The same lie I'd gotten all over Brenda and the lads for. So now I was going to have to fix it. The question was, with who? I didn't have the time to hire someone.

Or, you can ask someone you already know.

I frowned. Livy was obviously engaged to Ben. Nyla was also engaged to East and the others were all taken as well. "I'll try and convince her to meet you then. I'm sure we can make time."

She clapped with glee. I was so fucked. "I love, love. Surely, you're going to get married soon?"

I tried to play it off. "Yeah, we're taking things slowly, but pretty soon."

Just as soon as I found someone to pretend to be my girlfriend. I'd fucked up. And either the old lady believed everything I was telling her, or she was calling my bluff. The problem was I didn't know which. So I had to act as if every word I'd said was true.

Chapter Six

Emma

The thing about great ideas was that sometimes the execution didn't go quite how you planned. As I sat across our lunch table from Francis who was wearing a crisp white shirt, no tie, with his suit jacket impeccably cut to fit his frame, I was losing some of my earlier nerves. "So, *Miss Varma*—I have to call you that now that you work for me probationally—how have you been? You certainly look well. No longer the skinny knobby-kneed girl I first met." His gaze swept over me slowly, settling at my breasts and then moving back to my face. I didn't budge. I was not going to show my discomfort.

The thing about Francis was, he was handsome. Perfectly cut jaw, good physique, a wide smile that screamed charm and elegance, and well, money. He exuded the cockiness of someone who was born rich and white. Smooth hair, expensive cut. Everything about him screamed money, wealth, access, and privilege. But there was definitely something off about him. And I was afraid that my face showed exactly what I thought of him.

I had nothing but disdain for him, his family, his apathy toward what had happened to my brother. The way his family had covered it up said that *we*, the Varmas, didn't matter. A part of me knew he was just a kid at the time, doing as he was told. But I knew him. I knew his family. They'd been running spin for so long, I was sure that they had no idea what the real truth was.

"Well, Toby's death was a very long time ago. I certainly am no longer knobby kneed. I'm a grown woman now."

His grin twisted with just a hint of a leer. "Well, I would certainly agree you are, in fact, a grown woman. So tell me the truth, now that your unorthodox pitch is over, what makes you really want to join Middleton Communications? In the car on the way over, I did a brief background check. You certainly do have an impressive resumé. Internships and all. Plus, I know your father well."

Way to get punched. "Probably better than I do." He cocked his head as if he didn't understand what I was saying. But he did. I knew he did. Everyone knew who my father was and that he'd had as little to do with us as possible. "I've had great work experiences. A chance to really dig into what I want to do. And while I love marketing, I think crisis management is really my angle. Which is basically marketing of a person or a corporation to be exactly what the public expects it to be. To deliver on the promise of a premise, as they say."

He smiled broadly. "I love that. To deliver the promise of a premise. Excellent. Look, you're practically in the family. You just have to tell me what division you want to start in and where you want to go. We could talk about it now, or maybe later over drinks as well. You can ask me anything. I want to make sure that you are aware that I am completely open and available to you for anything you might need."

I had to work hard not to roll my eyes. He was disgusting. Vile.

The whole time I was sitting there, all I wanted to do was scream, *You killed my brother. It's your fault he's dead.* But I didn't. Instead, I walked him through the positions I had done research on and found most interesting and appealing. Also, they paid the most. Because I was going to take him for as much as I could before I found a way to take him down.

Suddenly, I could feel it... a tingle of awareness at the back of my spine, the hairs on the back of my neck standing at attention, and I glanced around. I couldn't find the source. Usually, that was the way I felt when Bridge was around. I couldn't explain it, but suddenly I was a little too tense, a little too aware. But maybe that was just because I was talking to slime and some primordial part of my brain was trying to tell me, *Danger, danger! Get out, get to safety.*

As Francis droned on and on about company culture, their core mission, and what was really important, I wondered how the hell he would know. After all, he was the Vice President. He had no idea what company culture was, or how the people, the 'proletariat' as he put it, responded to things. And that was the problem with getting this pitch from him.

I wanted the job because I wanted access to him. And he was giving me access in any way that I wanted it. But to do what I was going to need to do, I'd have to swallow that throw up at the back of my throat. Stomach it. Shove it down and be this close to one of the men responsible for my brother's death. Could I do it?

I'm not sure you have to.

And just then, in my peripheral vision to the left, I saw Bridge coming through the crowd. Women watched him with interest. He stood above most of the men, and even they gave way to him as he prowled my direction.

My brows furrowed. What the fuck was he doing here? If he saw me with Francis, that was it. He would know what I was up to. I wondered if one of the girls had spilled. Livy couldn't be blamed, honestly. Word was, Ben often used sex to get her to tell him things. How good *was* he in bed? Because the two of them were like the same person. If you told one, the other automatically knew. I should have known. It could have been Nyla too. Because she was law and order, after all. She would probably be concerned about my safety. But it certainly wasn't Telly, that was for damn sure. Telly was all, *Burn them down and hack them while you're at it.*

I stiffened and tried to use my hair to cover my face slightly as I answered the questions about how I liked to work. Plastering that fake smile on my face, even as one part of my brain tried to analyze how quickly we could leave the restaurant without Bridge seeing us. But it was too late because he'd already seen us. I saw when he spoke to one of the hostesses and she pointed him directly at our table. Oh fuck. I didn't even have time to make it to the loo before he came for me.

It might be likely that he'd lock me in the loo, wouldn't he?

God, I hated him.

Uh-huh, sure you do.

And then he was at our table. I was almost startled as he approached because he moved with such force, like a man on a mission. And then something happened to his face. His lips curved up in an alluring smile and a dimple appeared. Except, it didn't reach his eyes. That smile was a fake one. One perhaps used to lull the unsuspecting into complacency. He did not come in peace. I knew it in the core of my bones when he opened his mouth and started to speak, grinning at me and Francis widely.

Francis stood and the two of them shook hands then clapped each other on the back. When Bridge turned to me, the smile reached his eyes a little bit more. But then he was leaning over me and saying something to Francis. My brain finally clicked into gear just at the tail end of what he was saying. "Thanks for looking out for my girl for me."

Francis stuttered. "W-what? Your girl?"

And then the impossible happened.

Bridge Edgerton leaned down and dusted his lips over mine. Too shocked to move, I sat stock-still, staring up at him. Okay, fine. I was too surprised to slap his arse into the middle of next week.

It was pure shock that kept me from releasing my coiled hand straight across his face. That was the reason behind the gasp and the parting of the lips. It wasn't my fault that his tongue delved in ever so slightly and his lips whispered over mine again before he pulled back and sat down far too close to me. "You don't mind if I crash your lunch, do you? When security said you were here and I was already on the other side of the courtyard for a meeting, I couldn't resist coming to say hello."

I blinked at him. Security. Security? The fuck was going on here?

Francis's gaze slid between Bridge and me, and confusion etched his brow. "I don't understand. I didn't know you two were in touch."

Bridge turned that surprisingly knicker-melting smile to me and winked. "Well, Em and I have known each other for eons. Even before *you* knew Emma." I could see it then, the animosity just under the surface with Francis. Bridge brought it out of him. They loathed each other. But they could pretend for the masses.

"You're together?" The hint of malice wove around each word.

Bridge grinned. "It's new. Well, not new because..." He turned to face me. "We've been in love forever, but I was with Mina, and she was in school in the States and then working in New York. But now, the stars are aligned. Now that she's back, I'm not letting her out of my sight."

I was dumbfounded. It was the only explanation for me just sitting there like a mule cow, just staring at him. And then I realized... Wait a minute. What the fuck was he on about? What was he doing?

Slowly, the pieces started to sink in. He'd said, girlfriend. Long time. Together. What the fuck was going on? I knew something was happening. Something had to be going on. Bridge Edgerton always had a rhyme and reason. He didn't just do things to fuck with me. Was this their plan? Had they really had Middleton in their sights all along, but I hadn't believed it and now I was messing it up?

I decided I'd better play along, so I leaned into him then. "Darling, I thought we weren't telling anyone."

He grinned. "Sorry, I know you're trying to keep it private for a minute. He leaned in and kissed me again. This time, his hand cradled my cheek and his thumb slid over my cheekbone. "But Francis is a friend. He won't tell."

Francis sat back and lifted a brow. "I'm confused, obviously. If Miss Varma here is your girlfriend, why aren't you giving her a job?"

Before Bridge could interject and ruin this, I chimed up. "Because I don't want to work for the man that I love. It would make for a contentious relationship at home."

Bridge's arm clapped on my shoulder more tightly, even as he was gazing at me with love. "Well, you know her, she's stubborn. She wants to do everything on her own. I begged and pleaded, tried to make her change her mind, but she'll do what she wants. She's damn good at it. I could use her, but apparently, she prefers you. And she wants to be all on her own."

Francis nodded slowly. "Well, I guess I respect that."

Bullshit. Like he knew anything about striking out on his own. But I forced my face to stay in its complacent smile. "Darling, I'm in the middle of an interview. If you don't mind..."

Bridge laughed. "Oh, I didn't mean to ruin your day. Okay, love, I only wanted to say hello. I'm sorry." He leaned in for another kiss. "I'll be back at the office. Have Hans drive you, yeah?"

Fucking Hans. I *knew* I was being tailed earlier. I'd felt it. Of course he'd put security on me, because he was a controlling dick. "Oh, you know I hate that. I'll just take the Tube."

"Darling, you will not take the Tube. Have Hans drive you. I'll see you after you're done with your lunch. Francis, be good to her."

And then he was gone, striding out the door like he owned the place.

"I'm so sorry about that. I didn't know he was here."

Francis studied me closely. "You didn't mention you were Bridge Edgerton's girlfriend."

"Well, like I said, it's new and private. Is that a problem?"

He frowned. "No, not a problem. Are you serious about this job? Are you sure you don't want to work with him? I'm sure he could scrounge you up a position." The way he said the word *scrounge* had my hackles up. Mostly because I was still on edge from what the fuck had just happened, but also because of the subtle implication that I wanted to take the easy way out and play office lovers.

"Like I said, I'm my own woman. I want to stand on my own two feet. I want a career that's mine that no one else gave to me. I want to know that I earned it. I can't do that at the London Lords."

He nodded. "Well, in that case, Miss Varma, I am truly looking forward to getting to know you better. After all, like I said before, you're already a member of the family, aren't you?"

I nodded. "Indeed, I am. I can't wait to get to know you better."

* * *

Bridge

There was something about the hum of adrenaline when you knew a storm was coming. When I was younger and I would get into trouble, it wasn't that I liked doing dumb shit; I liked the feeling of being alive when I flirted with danger.

And I was under no delusions. That stunt I'd just pulled was the equivalent of taking a surfboard out into a tsunami because I'd always wanted to ride a big wave. It was reckless. And Emma could have eviscerated me.

Hell, I'd almost been felled when my lips had met with hers. Just the whisper of her lips was enough to send a bolt of electricity down to my cock. I was shocked that Emma gave me a reprieve. She didn't say anything when she walked into my office a little later, but when I stood and then angled my head, letting her know that we'd be heading down to Ben's office, she still said nothing. Just eyed me skeptically. She smiled at my assistant, Tracy, waved at one or two people that she knew, and then I realized that she knew most of the people who worked here.

What the hell had she been doing with Middleton? But even as my attention was firmly on her, she looked straight ahead and walked with purpose. Marched, really. I knew that I had a lot to answer for. First of all, locking her in a room. I hadn't seen her since the other night. She was probably still pissed off. And then there was putting a security detail on her. Very likely, she was still irritated about that. And then, well, the whole kissing her and pretending we were together thing. Even I didn't have an answer for that except that I was desperate.

Desperation was the only thing that would have made me kiss Emma Varma voluntarily. I knew danger lay that way. She was, for all intents and purposes, a praying mantis.

Is it voluntary if it's under duress?

When we marched into Ben's office, he looked up from his laptop and raised a brow. "Emma, Livy's not here. Did you try her office?"

"I'm not here for Livy. I'm here about him."

Ben nodded at me and directed us both to take a seat. As Emma spread out her skirt prettily around her, she grinned at him. "Oh, that's cute, Bennet. You have absolutely no idea what's about to happen to you, do you?"

Ben's brows lifted as his gaze turned toward me. "What the fuck did you do, Bridge?"

I shook my head. "Let's wait for the others. It'll be better if everyone hears about this ongoing drama at once."

She just shrugged. "Oh, I didn't start the drama. It's all you."

When East finally joined us, I looked behind him to see if Drew would follow. "Drew coming?"

East shook his head. "No, he already left a couple of hours ago.

Didn't know we would have an impromptu meeting. Who did you shag this time?"

I sighed and grumbled, "Fuck off."

East grinned at Emma. "Hey, Little Tobes, what are you doing here?"

"Oh, you don't know either?" She slid me a wide grin. "This is going to be entertaining."

I scowled at her. Why the fuck was she having so much fun with this? I was clearly not having fun. I was uncomfortable. She had me by the balls, and she wasn't even playing with them. It was really disappointing to say the least.

When everyone was settled, Ben slid his gaze to me. "Are we going to need to drink for this?"

"You two won't, but I probably will."

Emma smiled. "I'll have to take a sparkling water if you have it." She turned her gaze to me then. "Sweetheart, will you get it for me?"

I ground my teeth. She was having fun. My life was in shambles, and she was having a goddamn good time.

East chuckled. "Sweetheart? If that didn't sound like she was plotting your demise, I don't know what would."

Emma laughed. "Oh what, Bridge didn't tell you? We're in love now. He loves me. He looooves me," she said with an exaggerated flutter of her lashes.

She drew out the word love. She was teasing me. I didn't feel like being teased. I wished she would just fucking get on with it. And when she didn't continue, I said it. "I went to see Fredericka today."

Ben pushed to his feet. "You did what?"

I waved him back down. "Relax. I wanted to apologize and let her know that what was being said in the news wasn't at all who I was or what I was about. The problem is, either I got played by her, or she really just isn't budging. So I improvised."

East crossed his arms, chuckling. "Oh, God. You? Improvising?

I remember who you used to be. What game did you play this time?"

Fuck him.

I cleared my throat. "No game. I just followed through on what Brenda said."

Ben laughed. "Wait. You said you were getting married?"

When I didn't respond, there was a deafening pause that hung in the air, and then East howled with laughter. "Oh my God. Oh my God. You told her you're getting married to *Emma?*"

"Well, I didn't name her specifically. But the old lady wasn't interested in the mea culpa at all until I said that the person I'd been with was someone I'd known for a long time, and that it wasn't what she thought. I told her that we were just two people who were trying to work our way to being together."

Ben chuckled. "Oh my God, and she bought that?"

"Either she bought it, and I was too good of a liar because she wants to meet my new girlfriend, or she didn't believe a word of it and she's running a game on me because she said, 'Oh my God, what a relief it must be to get to be with the woman you love, and when is the wedding?' She wants to be part of our love story."

East whistled low under his breath. "Holy shit, she ran a game on you."

"That's the impression I get. Yeah, so here we are. And since there's no one else I have known for that long, Emma it is."

Emma grinned. "Oh, you should have seen how he approached me in the restaurant when I was meeting with Middleton."

East and Ben sat still for a moment, obviously surprised and displeased. East stood up, frowning. "You did what?"

"He hired me. I work for him."

All three of us gaped at her.

"What? You weren't bringing me in, so I made it happen."

I glared at her. "You are a dead woman, *my love.*"

"Well, considering you need me and I need you, it looks like we're going to have to learn how to work together, aren't we?"

Chapter Seven

Bridge

There are a few things worse than having to explain to your mother that you are getting married to someone she knew quite well, but clearly not someone you were dating. And the real question was, how much should I tell her? I didn't want her to worry because she knew just how powerful my father was. Knew what he could do. My father and I had a detente regarding my mother. He stayed the fuck away from her, and I didn't kill him. When I was younger, before I was properly entrenched in the Elite, he had lorded his money to gain access to her. And I had been powerless to do much.

But now that I had power, I sheltered her from any of his mercurial whims. Once he'd brought a woman to her restaurant, just to taunt her. All because I had refused to meet with him regarding an Elite matter. He could hurt me through her, because for some reason, he was under her skin.

A part of her still loved him, and I would never understand it. But as I stood outside of Lush Souls, my heart squeezed just a little. I had made her a promise once when I left for Eton, the lying, the bullshit, it was stopping. I was never going to be that boy again. Because I wanted to be someone better for her.

Except, here I was, about to embroil us both in lies and bullshit again.

She saw me before I even walked in. I was coming in from the back of the restaurant. She was speaking to someone who was cashing out in the front of the house. Was that the new manager? Her gaze flickered up, and she gave me a broad grin.

Mum had a wonderful smile. It was the kind of smile that was broad and open and completely guileless. I'd always loved her smile. It had a way of warming you up even when you didn't have money for heat or food. She had a way of making you think that everything was okay just because you had her love.

I opened the backdoor and walked in. A busboy I'd never seen before came over to tell me that the restaurant was closed. But I inclined my head toward my mum. "Ah, you haven't been paying attention to her locket. That's me on the inside of it."

He stammered then. "Oh, sorry."

I shook my head. "No, you're just doing your job."

Mum came over then and wrapped her arms around me, and I leaned over her miniature frame. At five-one, she was small. Always had been. I had towered over her by the time I was ten. "So you don't call, you don't write, you just turn up when I've just shut off the ovens."

"You don't have to feed me, Mum."

She tsked and started tugging me toward the kitchen. "I'm cleaning up anyway. You can help me. We'll make you some quick bangers. How you can find them comforting after all the good food I've introduced you to is beyond me but—"

"No, Mum, I ate already."

"But there is always room for dessert."

I knew how this was going to go. The moment I stepped into the kitchen, I would be handed an apron and put to work. It was how she kept me out of trouble when I was a kid. She figured if I was cooking and eating, my hands wouldn't be so idle. And for the most part, she was right. Sure enough, when I stepped into the kitchen, nodding my hellos at the hostess and the dishwasher, someone put an apron in my hands. I put it on easily. I moved to one of the cabinets to pull out flour and spices. I still had no idea what I was going to make, but the way Mum was busying herself, following after everyone to make sure they'd done their jobs, I knew this could take a minute because she was going to be rocked when I told her what I had to tell her.

As we made the sauce for what would end up being a single-serving tart, she slid her gaze to me. "All right, tell me what the problem is."

I frowned. "What do you mean, problem?"

"I know you. When you just want me for a visit, you do the usual things. You call me. You set up a date, and then you made sure the kitchen is stocked. And I get to be as messy as I can be and you follow after me and you clean. I cook you things. Things that your housekeeper doesn't know to do."

"I will have you know, I cook for myself."

"Oh, I know. You should be able to. I taught you myself. When your mum is a chef, she has high expectations."

"Yes, but when your mum is a chef, she's a control freak."

"Yes, that too." She said it with a shrug and a smile.

"Why can't I show up at the restaurant?"

"You only come here when there's something on your mind. Otherwise, I see you once a month. When you want to treat me, or if it's my birthday, you'll have me come over. You'll send a car, the whole thing. But you're turning up here, knowing I'm busy and knowing you're busy. So, what's wrong?"

I shifted on my feet, slicing strawberries nimbly with the sharp Nesmuk knife with the rosewood handle. "I needed to tell you something, and it wouldn't keep. So here I am."

I watched her make quick work of the dough for the tart. Her hands, though thin and delicate, were strong. After all, those hands had raised me, hadn't they?

"Spit it out, boy."

I stiffened. "Mum, you realize I'm a man? I'm nearly six-foot-three."

She whipped around and pointed a finger at me. "And I'm still your mother. I can tell when something is wrong. Neither one of us has time for this, so what's the matter? Is it Darcy? Do we need to switch schools again?"

I frowned thinking about my sister. "No. This one seems to be holding. I haven't gotten a call this month, so she's fine."

She nodded. "Then what is it?"

"I—" Why was I nervous? My mother wouldn't understand. "I'm getting married."

She whipped around so fast that she was a blur and jabbed a finger at my chest. "You don't listen. That Mina girl, she's no good for you. Never has been. Earlier, before, I kept quiet, and I've always hated myself for it. I should have said something straight from the start. Not that you would have listened, mind you. And now here you go, even after everything you found out her being in cahoots with your father, and you still insist on marrying her? What is wrong with you? I didn't raise a fool."

I blinked at her. "Damn. Tell me how you really feel, Mum."

"God, Bridge you would think I didn't raise you to be cunning and aware. You have a brain. Just use it. Must you insist on thinking with your dick? I mean, she's beautiful, but there are a million beautiful women out there."

I blinked at her. First, the use of 'dick'. Second, the suggestion that I should whore around London. Thirdly, ewww. "Mum, no, I'm not marrying Mina."

She was in the middle of jabbing her finger on my chest and starting on another tirade, and then she stopped short, mouth agape, finger poised a mere inch from my chest. "Oh." She dropped her hand. "Tell me what the hell are you talking about."

"I, um, I have been seeing someone."

She lifted a brow. "Yes, I've seen the someones you've been seeing all over the newspapers."

I winced. "M-most of those are made up, Mum. The paps can't be trusted."

"And there was one in the Sun. You looked disheveled. I know that look. I saw it once with Gemma Repiori. Remember her? You were what, fourteen? Fifteen? When I caught the two of you attempting to go at it like bunnies. Did you even know where to put your hands, boy?"

I hot flush crept up my neck. "Mum."

She chuckled. "What? You do know how you got here, don't you? No point in being embarrassed."

"Oh, Jesus, I should have done this on the phone."

She shrugged. "But you didn't, so you get what you get. So who's the lucky lady, or do I have to guess?"

"Why does that sound like a question? Like an incredulous one at that."

"Well, who is she?"

I swallowed hard. "Actually, you know her already."

She lifted a brow as she neatly cut out the excess of the pie crust. "Know her? Oh God, Bridge, not one of my employees. Please, tell me no."

I coughed a laugh. "No, Mum. No, it's Emma... Varma. Toby's sister."

She blinked. Blinked again. And then a smile started to curve over her lips until she was showing teeth and her cheeks creased to make one of her dimples appear. "Oh my God, Emma. I knew it. The two of you have been bickering and circling each other for years. Emma. Well, I'm well chuffed on that one." And then she frowned at me. "Wait, how the hell did you convince her to marry you?"

It was my turn to stare at Mum. "Are you serious right now?"

She shrugged. "Oh, I suppose you're right. You are a billionaire, and you're not terrible to look at."

I coughed a laugh. "Jesus, Mum, why are you like this?"

"Well, I had to learn to be a smartass once you started being able to talk. It was either that, or you were going to destroy me."

I laughed. "Why do you seem so at ease with this?"

I stirred the strawberries, blueberries, and blackberries gently, cooking them down just a little.

"Because even when you were a teenager, I saw the way you watched Emma. When she would leave the room, when she would come back, if she was in the car, or when Pamma came to pick up Toby. You would act like you weren't watching, but I'd see you from the window. You've had a thing for her for years."

There was no way she could know. "No, I haven't."

"Well, clearly you have because you're marrying her, aren't you?"

"It's complicated. It's not like that." I winced thinking about how I was going to maintain this lie. "It's just that it's very complex and... I don't know. But yes, we are getting married."

My mother laughed. "She's British. You don't have to give her a UK passport."

"I know. It's just... our relationship is complicated. The whole thing is *complicated*. But we're doing this."

She chuckled again. "Why do you look like you're doing it under duress?"

Then she gasped and clasped a hand to her chest. "Oh my God, you're giving me grandchildren. Thank fuck. I was worried you might die alone. Okay, when is she due? I will bake the best gender reveal cake ever."

I shook my head. "Mum! Why do you always do this? You get carried away and you go off on a tangent. She's not pregnant. We're not having a baby."

Her body sagged. "Oh, way to deflate me."

"You're insane."

"I'm your Mum. Now, are you going to tell me the real reason you're marrying Emma Varma, or am I going to have to beat it out of you?"

I blinked. "I care about her. It's complicated and stuff, but I *do* care about her." At least that much was true.

She rolled her eyes. "I'll wait."

And before I knew it, I was telling her the whole story. My mother sat there silent, saying nothing until I was done.

"Wow. Your pickle sure has gotten you in a pickle, hasn't it?"

"Mum."

She laughed and then took the spoon from me and filled the tiny tart tin. "God, you're so easy. So, the little tantrum you've been having over the last several weeks, this finally ended it?"

Tantrum? "Yeah, it appears that way."

She nodded. "Okay, look, this whole thing is unorthodox, right? But I think what I said still stands. Emma Varma has been under your skin for years. You can deny it all you want, but honey, I've seen it. Call it whatever you want, but that girl has got your number. I, for one, think this is fantastic. And I'm baking the wedding cake."

I sighed. "Mum, don't go overboard."

She lifted a brow. "My son is finally getting married. That in itself is cause for celebration."

"It's not real, Mum."

"I know. I know."

She might insist that she knew, but it bothered me just how comfortable she was with the idea of Emma and I being all too real.

* * *

Bridge

The next day my conversation with Mum still rang in my head. Why the hell did she think Emma and I were inevitable?

It was more likely that one of us would kill the other. But one point was true; we were in this mess together. Emma didn't trust me. I didn't trust her. And now we were stuck. Locked in this little war. But despite what she thought, there was no way in hell I was going to give her what she wanted in the end. We would take down Middleton. That I could promise her. A promise made down deep in my soul somewhere. But making her part of it, involving her, was not going to happen. I hadn't been able to protect Toby. But his *sister* I could protect. Just like he'd asked me to do all those years ago.

Oh yeah, like you're protecting her now?

After Brenda left the two of us alone in the office, Ems wanted to go over details on how it was all going to work. I told her I already had a plan for that, but my only plan at that point was to go to Ben's. From there we'd have a better plan.

But as we headed back to Belgravia, she was trying to nail me down. "Okay, so I don't have the final word from Middleton yet, but I think I'm in for a hire. So you lot just have to tell me exactly what I'm looking for. I'll find it. In and out. This won't take long."

"Why don't we curb that enthusiasm until we have a little more information?"

"Oh no, you don't. Don't talk like I'm being impulsive. I'm not. I do have a skillset to offer here."

"No one's saying you don't have a skillset, Ems. I'm just saying we don't need your skillset yet. Take a breather. Take a moment. Take a pause. We're trying to keep everyone alive and out of the nick if you don't mind."

She smirked. "Aww, worried that you're too cute for prison?"

She had no idea that there were things worse than prison. Despite being Elite, if we didn't do this just right, Middleton would find a way to burn us.

A burn was a complete annihilation of someone's life. Financially, socially. Utter desolation. You only got one burn and The Five, the advisors to the Director Prime, had to approve it. And you were never allowed to burn another member of the Elite. But there were ways around every rule.

"I'm not going to prison. It's not what happens when you're rich. But I'd rather live out my last days somewhere with lovely amenities instead of stuck in some no-name island hell. It's not my idea of a good time."

She chuckled then. "My God, you *really* think we're going to pull this off?"

"We'd better. Otherwise, your plan or mine, none of us gets what we want."

At Ben and Livy's, we let ourselves in. I could immediately smell Livy's cooking. I could tell the difference because Ben's, while it tasted okay, never smelled this good. When it was Livy's turn, she was always adding some exotic spice. Ben called it her secret sauce that she wasn't going to share because she was afraid he'd leave if he knew the special concoction. Livy just always rolled her eyes and said he was just more impatient when he cooked, which I believed.

Livy came bounding over and gave us both a tight squeeze. "Well, glad to see the happy couple is here."

Emma groaned. "Is now the time for jokes?"

Telly poked her head from around the pillar of one of the makeshift desk stands while she peered at security monitors. "Hi, you two. Needed a shag on the way in, did you?"

I glowered at her.

Telly only chuckled. "What? You're both entirely fuckable. I would." She snorted then. "Okay, honestly, not you, Bridge, but Ems for sure."

Emma, who was used to Telly by now, just rolled her eyes. "I know. Have you seen this ass? It's a sight to behold."

And like a fool, my gaze dipped for just a breath of a second, but still, they dipped. Because I was a glutton for punishment and didn't know better.

Fucking hell.

"Are you two done? We have real problems here, and we need your help."

When we were all gathered in the living room, even Drew, with his glass of scotch, gave me a slap on the back and a head nod for Emma. "Well, we thought we would be up a creek. But look at this, shotgun wedding and all. When did you knock up our boy Bridge here?"

I rolled my eyes. "Hardy-har, you twat. Can you lot be serious for fucking once?"

Nyla came in with drinks, handing one to Livy. "Oh, right. As if you lot are a serious crew. Come on, you stole a massive diamond and managed to throw me off the scent, all the while cracking jokes."

East stood and wrapped his arms around his fiancée, kissing her neck. "Oh, come on, you know you were never going to arrest us."

To take down Bram Van Linsted, we'd stolen a diamond from him for one of The Five. Bram had been one of the three responsible for Toby's death. His family had stolen the diamond from the Elite member's ancestor decades ago. We merely returned it in exchange for his assistance. Nyla had been onto us at the time from the Interpol perspective, and it had taken a lot to throw her off our scent.

Ben chose that time to come in from the kitchen bearing a platter of cooked meat. "My eyeballs. I can't wash them out. If you two don't mind."

Nyla snorted. "This coming from the man whose bare ass I have *actually* seen."

Ben flashed her a grin. "I know. You've never seen anything so nice, have you?"

Nyla just rolled her eyes. "How are you people my family? Emma are you sure you want to be tied to us forever?"

There was no undoing this. We were going to have to make this look real. When Drew turned his back, I took his scotch. Then he turned back and scowled. "Oi, mate."

I shrugged. "Keep an eye on your drink, man."

With a shake of his head, he pushed to his feet and headed back to the bar.

"All right, Ben, you called this little tête-à-tête. What do you need?" I asked.

"Well, for starters, I know Brenda talked to you two. She called me after she left."

"Excellent. Are you here to scold us? Am I not making this shit look real?"

He shook his head. "No, you're here because Livy insisted that you guys might need a little lovey-dovey coaching."

Emma laughed. "You think I need coaching on how to be affectionate?"

Livy rolled her eyes. "I swear to God, Ben, you don't know how to explain anything properly."

He chuckled as he blew a kiss to his fiancée. "I'm sorry. What I mean is, I know Brenda gave you the rundown on all the things you have to do. But I thought maybe this would be a good opportunity for you guys to, you know, act like you're together while you're here."

Emma snorted. "Oh, come on, you can't be for real."

East sat forward, placing his elbows on his knees. "Unfortunately, we are. Old lady Zicks wants to meet you. She's no fool. She mentioned earlier today after our meeting that she wants to have dinner with you two."

My stomach flipped. She wanted to ascertain just how real and how tight our connection was. Fucking hell. "When?"

The question had East giving me a tight grimace. "Ahh, tomorrow."

I cursed under my breath. "No fucking way. We don't have time for that."

"Well, that's why we're here. For starters, Bridge, you didn't even offer your girlfriend a drink. You should probably do that."

I stared over at Emma, who was perched on the edge of the

couch. I never noticed before, but that was her usual spot. Anticipating a fast exit, I assumed.

Emma declined. "Ah, no, I'm not thirsty."

I frowned at that. "Come on, this is practice."

Nyla nodded. "It helps if you actually know the drink she likes."

I had no idea. I'd known Emma since we were kids, but that was the whole point, she'd always been a *kid* to me.

Well, she's hardly a kid now. Have you seen the tits on this one?

I frowned. I was hardly taking directions from my dick right now. The bastard twisted in my trousers as if trying to get my attention, and I forced myself to give Emma a tight smile. "Well, what would you like to drink?"

"I don't actually like to drink. I have a few options that I use when I'm out and about so that I don't look unusual. I'll take a Tanqueray and tonic. And honestly, I'm a little partial to rum. But generally, I don't really like drinking that much."

I studied her. How hadn't I known she didn't drink? Because I distinctly remembered one weekend on holiday when she'd been with her mates. They'd been suggestive and flirty and I'd discovered a bottle of vodka amongst their bags. I remembered her being blitzed. *Are you sure about that?* "When did this start?"

"Since always. You just always assumed I was a party girl. You never bothered to ask any questions."

"Fine. Whatever. I'll fix you a non-alcoholic drink."

She shook her head, but Nyla stepped in. "I know you don't want one right now, but it helps to look the part. It would help to know if Bridge can prepare you a drink too."

She shrugged. "Then give me one."

"Are you sure this is absolutely necessary?"

Livy smiled. "Well, it'll help. Don't worry, we'll all be at dinner. Right there with you. Together."

Emma laughed. "Hardly together."

And then Drew spoke up, like the knob that he is. "You know Bridge, you need to look like you like touching her."

I handed her a drink. She gave me a cheer, and then I hovered slightly. "What do you mean look like I like touching her?"

"Maybe don't match her outfit, like you do when you're on stage. But sit close. Look at her like she hangs the moon and the stars."

I rolled my eyes. "Oh, come on."

Emma sat forward. "Fine. Fine. You lot think that this is really necessary to make the old lady believe you?"

They all nodded. East especially. "Fredericka hates liars. It's the fastest way to get your arse fired."

When Emma approached, sashaying over to me, I held my breath. Then she took my hand, sliding her fingers between mine, and fucking hell. Off like a rocket, my dick was circulating some ideas of his own, so I sat and brought her down to my lap then wrapped an arm around her. "Is this better?" This was more difficult than I thought. Having her lush arse on my lap made my mental synapses take a holiday.

She held my hand then smiled. "The two of us, we're together in this. Together forever." She was good at putting on a show. Good with people. Good at making them believe. And then I knew we were going to be fine. We could play the part. The problem with that was, my dick wanted in on the game.

* * *

Emma

After several hours of being coached in having to hold Bridge's hand and smile up at him like a loved-up simpleton, my brain was melting. "Oh my God, are we done yet?"

Liv smiled. "Well, the two of you are semi-believable."

I glanced up at Bridge, my gaze drifting over the sharp line of his jaw, and I knew it wouldn't be hard to pretend. A part of me had cared about him since we were kids. It wouldn't be hard to pretend that I wanted him or that I could fall for him. The difficulty was remembering that this wasn't real. This wasn't something that I could look at in the future and go, 'Yes, I have his heart.' So I needed to pretend and make it look real but feel nothing.

Easy.

Fucking hell.

I could do this. I was tough. Every time I started to waver I just needed to remember I was temporary to him. That painful twinge would keep me level.

"The other thing we need to do is move you into my house here in Belgravia." He said it nonchalantly like he was casually mentioning his workout schedule.

"I beg your pardon? I can't move in with you." With him? And his shirtlessness? I was weak. No way, no how.

"It has to look real Ems, considering the position we're all in."

I swallowed hard and glanced around. Everyone was looking at me expectantly.

And then Telly, traitor that she was, said, "Weren't you just looking for a new place? This takes care of that."

Oh God. My stomach pitched. This was real. I was going to have to live with him.

Bridge lifted a brow and I could see it for the challenge that it was. "Is there a problem? A reason you can't stay with me?"

Fuck. Fuck him and his fucking smug face. "Nope. Not at all. I'll consider it." I lied through my teeth.

I turned the attention to something even more pressing and let go of his hand. "Okay, now that I have sufficiently mooned over him, can we get to the real brass tacks here? What are you planning to do about Middleton? You need to tell me what's happening. I'm in a position to help now."

Bridge shook his head. "No, you don't. Because you're not going to be part of it."

"If I do this to help you, you have to let me take an active participatory role."

Ben stared at me.

"Too risky Ems." That came from East.

I shrugged. "Look, you people won't tell me anything, so I took matters into my own hands. I walked into his office, had lunch with him, and then applied for a job."

Bridge threw his hands up. "You see what I'm dealing with?"

East shook his head. "This is a bad idea."

Telly grabbed a handful of nuts off the center tray. "Why? She's smart. Emma isn't going to get caught up in anything. She could poke around. You just have to trust her."

"It's Middleton that we don't trust. Especially after the way I essentially peed all over him at that restaurant. He's seen that she's mine. It was like waving a red flag in front of a bull."

I scowled at him. "Yeah, we never did talk about that. But besides that point, we're not a thing. And I don't think he's that weak of a caveman."

All the men nodded. Even Drew, agreed. "Ah, sorry, love. He one hundred percent is a caveman. We know him. If he saw that you were Bridge's, he would want to disrupt that."

I shook my head. "That's not what we're talking about here. What is *your* plan exactly? We had a plan for Van Linsted. Jameson presented his own plan. Middleton is slick. We can't half-arse this."

East sighed. "The first step is getting this Zicks account. Middleton has had a hard-on for it since we can remember. At least five years. But Fredericka Zicks turned him down. Rumor is that he was trying to get in the pants of the old lady's daughter. He has, of course, never had anyone turn him down before. So he's taking it personally."

"All right, so you get the company, and then what?"

The lads exchanged glances. "Well, then we hire him."

I grinned. "That is excellent. What the fuck is the hen house without a wolf?"

Bridge rolled his eyes. "We hire him, to make sure it's exclusive. He gets the kind of access he thinks he wants, and we get access to him. And then we do the usual. Find our leverage. Apply pressure. Take away everything he actually really wants in this world. Eviscerate it and make him watch."

I blinked at Bridge. What was interesting about Toby's best mate was that as affable as he was, and as much as he liked to fool around and have a good time, as much as he enjoyed being outrageous, there was a steely core to him. One where he didn't take anything for granted.

"All right, then let me help. I can get better access to him than you can."

"And if he doesn't trust you?" That was from East.

"He will."

Bridge shook his head. "He won't. You're Toby's sister. Plus, as far as he knows, we are together. Obviously, he knows that we've been instrumental in taking out the others. So he's going to have his guard up."

"Not with me though, because I will play dumb and naive."

Bridge laughed. "Nobody smart would ever think you're dumb or naive."

"He underestimates me already. What is your problem? And while he's looking around, I'll have access. Besides, this is our deal Bridge. I do this whole getting married thing, and you let me take an active role."

"I said I'd let you take an active role, but I didn't say what that role would be."

"Semantics. If you go back on this, no deal. You and I are not getting married."

He shrugged. "Trust me, the last thing on earth I want to do, is marry you. There is not enough payback on the planet to make this at all palatable to me."

Pain bloomed in my chest. Fucking hell.

"Bridge, we had a deal."

"No, *you* want a deal."

"It doesn't have to be this hard. Just let me help. Let me do this for Toby."

Bridge tucked me back into his side then, but I resisted.

"I can get closer than any of you can. You're going to have to realize at some point that I can do this. You're going to have to trust me and let me help."

Bridge was already shaking his head. "You are going to be helpful, but not the way you want it to be. You'll be watching him as a surveillance."

I turned to face him. "Watch me. I can do a hell of a lot more than surveillance."

He sputtered and stared at me. "Just what do you think you're going to do?"

"You lot have been trying to get dirt on him for how long now? You haven't found anything. East, you and Telly have tried hacking, and you can't get past his firewalls. I can get what we need from the inside."

"Over my dead body."

My slow grin was designed to grab him by the balls. "Hope you enjoy being cold and still, Bridge, because I'm doing this."

And there was nothing he could do to stop me.

Chapter Eight

Emma

I really needed to rethink my decision-making processes. How the hell had I ended up at this dinner wearing a dress that left me not much room to breathe, sipping on wine that I wanted to guzzle, and pretending to be with the one man I couldn't have?

Because you want revenge for your brother and this is how to get it.

Except, I'd told myself a version of this story over and over again since Bridge had kissed me in the restaurant, and every time I examined it, there was a small voice inside that called me a liar. That called out that I would have done anything to feel Bridge's lips on mine.

Which made me pathetic.

It was too easy a role to slide into. I should be more alarmed. I should be better at hiding my feelings. Because if I wasn't careful, then he would see right through me. As it was, his hand was on my thigh in full view of anyone who happened by, and I was sure everyone could see how flushed I was.

But nobody seemed to notice as I sipped wine and made small

talk. They were all acting completely normal as if I wasn't having a little earthquake everywhere near my vagina.

Bridge flashed a grin at me, and I was so dickmatized by it, I stumbled through words trying to get back on topic. Which was again... Fuck. What the bloody hell had we been discussing?

He gave my knee a tight squeeze and just answered for me. The squeeze was a reminder to get my shit together. "Ems has a job offer from Middleton Communications. Though I wish she'd change her mind and work for me."

Oh, was that the question? "Well, darling..." The word nearly caught in my throat. "I do need some freedom. We need to keep things interesting."

Overall, though, dinner turned out not to be so bad. Fredericka was funny and engaging, and she had stories about the hotel industry up the ying-yang.

She even had Bridge relaxing and laughing a little bit. That was until she asked about the wedding date. When he tensely mumbled the date we'd agreed on two weeks from now, he looked like he wanted to bolt.

But he'd eventually relaxed and sometime during the night, the touches had gotten more casual. Not as deliberate and calculated. Bridge had his own set of touches. One where he would smooth a finger over my cheek and tuck my hair behind my ear, another where he'd wrap his hand around my shoulder and then rub my shoulder with his palm. That was his favorite. I'd gotten accustomed to those touches. So when he started telling some animated story about Ben and East at one point in their early days when they were trying to get their first hotel up and running, he reached over and laughed, bringing me into the story, talking about how my mother had come to visit and Ben had been up to no good. Then he put his hand on my knee. At first, it was a casual touch. I didn't really think about it, but then it stayed there. Stayed put as he held on to me. His thumb gently stroked the inside of my thigh, and he looked relaxed. Happy.

This was the Bridge I'd seen glimpses of when we were kids, the Bridge I'd secretly watched. The guy who would laugh when he was with his mates because he was the most comfortable he was ever going to get. This was the Bridge that was hard to ignore, the man that I couldn't help but watch and be enthralled by. It was almost as if he had no idea of the catastrophic nature of his looks or his charm when he was on. Of what he could do to my soul. He had no idea he was capable of that. It was too easy to fall for this man. When he gave me a gentle squeeze, the look he gave me was so adoring, I cleared my throat.

"If you'll just excuse me, I must powder my nose."

Livy made a move to stand, but I shook her off. "No, I'm all right. Enjoy your dessert."

Bridge frowned at me then, his face scanning mine, looking for deception or a reason for it. But when he couldn't find it, I skipped off to the bathroom. I just needed a moment. A moment where he wasn't believable. A moment where I didn't one hundred percent think and believe it was real. A moment where I wasn't caught up in the lie. I needed a reset. Because I was susceptible to him. I was, and I couldn't help it.

Because you've been in love with him half of your life.

Yes, fine. I had a little crush. Everyone had crushes. It was totally normal. And like everybody else, I'd get over it. It wasn't hard.

Oh, sure it's not. Just stop caring about him. Stop thinking about him. Stop obsessing over him. Stop wanting to believe that this is real.

I groaned. I had to do something, or this was going to be bad.

Luckily there was no one inside the powder rooms, which was helpful. When I let myself in, the attendant smiled at me and pointed at all the open stalls. I smiled at her politely and then locked myself in the stall for a moment. I didn't have to pee so I just sat down and did deep breathing exercises.

All the therapists I'd seen were always trying to tell me about it. The thing to manage my raging anxiety was to take deep, calming breaths. One therapist told me that it was okay to be still. That was a load of crap. I didn't want to be still. Being still meant that I was going to have to deal with everything around me. Being still meant that I would have to look at myself, my family, all of us, coping in our different ways.

Nevertheless, I took a deep breath. It was all I could do, really. And then I stood and opened the stall again. The attendant smiled at me again, and I noticed there was someone else at the sink washing her hands. From the back, she looked vaguely familiar, but I couldn't quite place her.

It wasn't until I was standing next to her, washing my hands, that I knew exactly who she was. "I see that you are very cozy with Bridge. I knew from the moment I saw you with him that you were up to no good."

I turned the faucet off and took the towel offered by the attendant. "Mina, I wish I could say it was good to see you, but I'd rather not see a bitch. However, you know, when life hands you bitches, smack them down." I said with a shrug.

She scowled. "You're uncouth."

I snorted a laugh. Honestly, I couldn't help it. "If you say so. You were the one who slapped me, remember?"

She scowled. "I knew that you were a gold-digging home-wrecker. I could feel it."

"Mina, I didn't ruin your relationship with Bridge. You did that all by your lonesome. I had nothing to do with it. All I know is that as much as you hate me, I didn't interfere with your relationship."

"I'm sure you really believe that, but I can see that you're with him because you wanted my life. Just watch out. He has more secrets than you could ever know."

I frowned. "There's always something pathetic about the woman who *thinks* she's been wronged. You're desperate to have someone to believe your rendition of the past. You don't know anything about me and Bridge."

"And you don't know anything about *him*. You should ask him about the boarding school. He never really even intended for me to find out that secret. And then when I did, he lied to my face. If he was willing to marry me and he was still going to lie, imagine you. He's not ever going to marry you."

I swallowed hard because, on the contrary, he was very much planning to marry me. But what secret was she talking about?

You know Bridge. You've known him since you were ten. If there were secrets, there were probably reasons for them.

"Look, I don't know what kind of fucked-up dynamic you two had. All I know is that he's with me now. So it looks like you're out of luck."

"You think you're so smart? Just realize that if he did it to me, he'll do it to you. He'll find someone younger who he thinks is more malleable."

I had to laugh at that. "Look at me. What part of me do you think is malleable?"

Her gaze swept over me. "I see the personal stylist has been with you."

I pressed my lips together at that. "These are just clothes. It doesn't change who you are. I'm not being controlled."

"Sure, you aren't. You think you're exhibiting control by picking those god-awful colors? Soon you'll be in beige and black and gray like the rest of us. A basic clone of every woman he's ever been with. As far away from where he grew up as possible. Only when he has you there will you even be close to having him. And even then, you won't really. You'll always come second to the lads, his mum, the company. You will always, always be second. He doesn't even love you. He was with me for three years."

"Just because he was with you doesn't mean he was actually going to marry you, Mina. You never knew him."

She stepped forward, trying to crowd me. She was taller than I was in her heels. But I didn't back down, and I knew how to plant my weight into my heels. So even when she tried to intimidate me by towering over me in her sky-high stilettos, I didn't budge.

"You think he's going to stay with you? He belongs to me. He's just bored. We just had a little disagreement, so he's exerting his independence. You don't matter."

"The fact that you've cornered me in the bathroom after following him to dinner tells me that I do matter. At least to you. And right now that's all that's important. And when he sees that, you're done for, Mina."

"Why you little—"

But I didn't give her the satisfaction. I turned on my heel and strode out, determined not to believe anything she'd said about secrets and lies because that wasn't the relationship Bridge and I had. I didn't deserve to know any of his secrets because none of it was real. And so all this burning pain in my chest about being left out in the cold again, I had to displace that, because none of that was real either.

* * *

Bridge

Something was wrong.

When Emma returned from the loo, she was decidedly quieter. She had been polite and a sweetheart at dinner, but then the mood suddenly shifted. It was like something in her had been switched off. For the first time, I actually believed we might pull this off. But I could tell, something had irritated her, and I couldn't figure out what it was.

"Are you all right, Ems?" I frowned at her.

"Yup, never been better."

"All right, what did I do wrong now?"

She shook her head. "Nothing, Bridge. I'm just tired. Did you get what you needed at dinner?"

I searched her gaze, trying to identify what was wrong. "Yeah. You were brilliant, actually."

"Well, I aim to please."

Something was off about her tone. Had I fucked up? It was always hard to tell. I was always being told by corporate strategists that I had low empathy.

"You've got to tell me what's wrong Emma."

"Nothing is wrong. Let's just get home."

As we arrived at the security gate, I could see her tension. It was in her shoulders and the set of her mouth.

We pulled in and security gave me a nod. Someone was here.

Before I even engaged the car into park, I knew who it was. And now I was tense. I glanced over at Emma. "What are the chances that you'll stay in the car for a moment?"

She laughed. "You're kidding, right? What's going on?"

"Nothing. Just stay in the car, would you?"

"Well, the fact that you want me to stay means I'm not going to. Tell me what's going on. I can help, or is this—"

Something caught both of our gazes, and it was Mina coming out of the front of the house. "Well, twice in one night. She is determined," Emma muttered.

What the fuck was that supposed to mean? "What do you mean, twice in one night?"

"She cornered me in the bathroom at the restaurant."

I cursed under my breath. "Fucking hell. You should have told me."

"Yeah well, here we are."

Emma shoved the door open and I cursed under my breath as I followed her out of the car. "Ems, wait."

But she wasn't listening. Instead, she was strutting up to the front door. "I mean, if you had this much of a hard-on for me, Mina, maybe we could have arranged something. Honestly, I have never kissed a girl, but... I mean you're beautiful, but I'm just not into you. But if you're this insistent, we could get a room. Hell, you're more persistent than my past boyfriends."

Mina gave her a wan smile. "Wow, Bridge, I see you're aiming down."

"Mina shut it. No one wants to hear your bullshit. What are you doing here?"

"Well, you gave me a month to pick up all my things. I've come to collect some of them."

"Right now?"

She shrugged. "Well, I was at a dinner and saw you, then I figured you wouldn't be out with your new whore for much longer. I didn't know it was a short engagement."

Before Emma could unleash, I wrapped an arm around her middle and pulled her back.

"Are you going to just let her talk to me like that?"

I gazed upon Emma, hopefully communicating my need for her to be quiet and hold herself together. This was what Mina wanted. Ignition. And then I turned to Mina.

"No, Ems, Mina knows you're no whore. Which is why she called you that. She's furious because she fucked up and she no longer has a place here. So she's lashing out at everyone. She's the one who's a whore."

The words coming out of my mouth felt like I was a stranger. The same words that had been hurled at my mother for her choices and how she took care of me. From boyfriends, from my father. They couldn't understand our relationship or how the hell I'd gotten here. I felt ill for going the same route, but it would get her attention.

"Bridge, there are some matters I need to discuss with you privately that we should deal with before I go."

"Mina, we've already covered this. You had the same matters to discuss when you came into my office and again when you found me at the hotel. Anything you have to say can be said in front of my lawyer."

She slid her gaze to Emma. "After everything we've been through?"

And just like that, she knew the angle to play. She knew exactly how to press that button and that I would cave because she knew the truth about the little sister that my father had abandoned. He'd essentially left her on my doorstep so I would look after her, and being the ass that he was, had somehow named me as her goddamn father. I loved Darcy, but she wasn't mine. However, I did what I could to look after her, and goddamn it, this was the last kind of scandal we needed right now. Even the lads didn't know about Darcy.

At that moment, I regretted so many of my past decisions. As I took in Mina's oak brown ensemble, I wondered if I'd ever seen her wear color. She was a beautiful woman I'd thought I loved once. Had I been the one to choose that? A life devoid of color?

"Mina, now is not the time."

"Well, you know, it needs to be the time. Because I did come to your office already, and well, we were sidetracked."

She leaned forward and winked at Emma, who wanted to dive for her throat. Once again, I stopped her. "Ems, she's trying to get your goat."

"Well, it's bloody working."

My lips twitched. That was the thing about Emma. If there was a fuck to be found, she hadn't found it yet. She really would knock the hell out of Mina. I suspected it the first time Mina had slapped her. Emma had *let* it happen so that I would no longer be able to unsee who Mina really was. And once those glasses were off, it was impossible to put them back on.

"And then I came to your hotel, but you seemed to be under the misguided impression that I wanted to shag you, which I didn't. But we do need to have a bloody conversation."

"Mina, now isn't—"

"All right. We can talk, or you'll love the news report about it."

Ice formed in my belly, and I knew she would do it. Expose

Darcy. Expose me. I had to figure out a different solution because Darcy was not getting dragged into all of this. Not for any reason.

I cleared my throat and then cocked my head at Ems. "Go on inside, Ems. I'll be right there."

Emma's eyes went wide. "You're kidding."

"No, this is just something I have to take care of."

I hated the smug look on Mina's face. She was getting what she wanted, stitching me up and twisting Emma's emotions. She always was a master at this.

"You can't be serious, Bridge. We've just come from a fantastic night out. Your ex is here, in *our* house demanding to speak to you, and you are just going to entertain that?"

"Emma, I'll explain everything later, okay? Just get—"

Emma shook her head. "Nope. The good news is, this time when I leave, you can't really stop me. Enjoy your night, Bridge. Mina, I wish I could say it was a pleasure, but two sightings of the devil incarnate in the same night? I should take that as a hint."

And before I could stop her, she was already sauntering to the security gate. I shouted for Lars and Max to stop her, but they'd already gone back into the garage and Emma had already gone out to the main gate. With a couple of quick taps of her fingers, she was on the street.

Fuck me.

I turned to Mina. "What the fuck do you want?"

"My God, your fiancée is so *scary*."

"What the fuck did you say to her?"

"I just pointed out that there are secrets that she doesn't know about you. Things she doesn't understand the way I understand you. You're not in love with her. You were never going to marry her. Just re-instate me, and if you like we will draw up a new agreement about how I'm supposed to stay exactly a hundred feet away from your father, and then we'll go back to normal."

"The fuck we will. You really are delusional."

"You need to stop saying that. Look, in case you've forgotten, I was supposed to go up to pick up Darcy from school. End of term is approaching in a few weeks, remember?"

Fuck. I'd forgotten. "We're not doing this."

I'd forgotten to remove Mina from Darcy's contact list. I would do it first thing in the morning.

"I don't need you doing me any favors."

"Well, I care about Darcy a great deal. We've gotten close."

The hell they had. Darcy always looked uncomfortable around Mina. Probably because Mina didn't care for children. She hadn't wanted any children of her own. Oh, and she said she knew and understood what was expected of her because I did want children. I didn't know, maybe it was a way to reset the sense of a father. Who the fuck knew if that shit worked?

"I'll take care of it."

"What, and this responsibility goes to your new fiancée?"

"You need to understand something. She's going to be my wife. Not you. And while you're at it, give my father my regards."

"You don't understand, Bridge. He forced my hand. What was I supposed to do? Go back to my old life? Scraping to make ends meet? I love you." She reached for me and I easily stepped out of her hold. "I know you're angry, but everything I did was for you. Sure, yeah, you were a job at first. But I actually fell for you."

"Oh, so much so that you just lied to me continuously for three years?"

"You must know he threatened me. I was actually protecting you, Bridge."

I laughed. "You know what?" I turned from her and lifted my face toward the moon. "A part of me almost believes you."

"You should believe me. I never wanted to hurt you. Maybe if we could just go away somewhere and be honest with each other, really talk things through, I think—"

"Leave, Mina. Don't come back. I'll have all your things that are still here packed and sent to you. Every stitch of artwork and antique furniture is going in the vault and will be sold at auction.

You will not receive a dime of those proceeds. I'm being kind and generous and letting you take your favorite pieces out of here. If I see you again, I'll burn it all. Do you understand me?"

She stuttered then. "N-n-nothing changes. You know you'll never be happy."

"*You know, I'm getting that impression.*" I mimicked her.

"You're miserable, cold, and terrifying. God, so fucking terrifying. Imagine what would happen if I told people that I've been scared for my life?"

I lifted my brow. "See if that works out for you because I have Emma. She'll be doing nothing but shouting from the rooftops how in love she is with me and how sad she is for you. We can keep playing this game, or you can finally slither back under the rock from whence you came."

She passed me then, making sure to brush me with her breasts. "You loved me once."

"You know what, I'm not actually sure I ever did. I'm revoking your security pass."

"Well, you can certainly try, can't you?"

Chapter Nine

Emma

"My love, where the hell are we?"

I looked up to see Telly pushing through the door of the roof. I spread my arms and said, "Welcome to my thinking space."

She glanced around. "Beautiful plants, but whose place is this?"

I pointed to the other roof across from us. "Do you see that place across the way?"

Telly plopped on the seat next to me in one of the fold-out chairs I'd hauled up there and then grabbed a beer. "Yes, but why are we stalking people like you're Joe from *You*?"

"We're not *stalking* anyone." I pointed at my father's flat. "That flat across the way is the flat my father bought for my mother. Neither one of them uses it anymore. It sits empty. He doesn't even lease it. It's a ghost property. There is no record of it in his name, nor any connection of it to him or his family, nothing. My mother doesn't use it either, but he still holds on to it. And I should know because I come here to see if he's put anybody else in it. But like he promised her, it was a place for her, for the *two of them*. Crazy, right?"

I took another long pull of my beer. P.S., I hated beer. It just felt like the thing to do, and I felt like rum would get me sloppy real fast.

"All right, darling, so we're watching a flat that your parents used to shag in?"

"You know, that's what I thought it was when I first found it, but honestly, when I followed my mother there once, they didn't even shag. They only like talked and shit. They watched the telly like a boring married couple. Talking when they could have been shagging."

Telly frowned. "How long have you been coming here, luv?"

"I was fourteen when I found it. You see, my father couldn't be bothered to turn up for a birthday or Christmas or anything like that. Because, God forbid, if his new family found out about us, they'd disown him. But star that he was, he always managed to meet her here once a month."

Telly's voice was soft when she asked, "Did she tell you about it?"

I shook my head. "No. I tried to catch her several times, but I always missed her."

"Then how did you know they met?"

"It was how she was after. The first time I caught them, I think she knew they'd been found out. After they'd meet, her mood was always melancholy. I always thought, oh, you know, Mum was just depressed because she had her period or something. Nope. She was dickmatized."

Her brow lifted. "Hypnotized by a dick?"

"No, *traumatized* by a dick. It's a little different, you see?"

Telly snorted and then choked back a cough. "Jesus. I thought my parents were fucked up."

"Nah. I think I take the cake on that one."

"So why do you come here and watch their flat?"

"I don't know. I think sometimes I'm looking for my father, hoping he'll turn up because he misses her."

"Has he?"

I shook my head. "No. But a cleaning crew comes in once a week."

"How do you know that?"

I took another pull of the disgusting beer. "Well, I broke in once or twice. Do you know that in that flat, there are photos of me and my brother? School photos. Like, ones where we looked weird. There were also goofy candid photos that were clearly taken by Mum. She decorated it as if we lived there like a family."

"I mean, it sure is pretty complicated. Families often are."

I shrugged. "Yeah, complicated. I'm sure that was it. There were even like these photos of Toby playing football with his kit on, the kind of things that were taken from a distance. I noticed one in particular. A game Mum wasn't there for since she had to work, so she negotiated with me and insisted that I go and sit through his game."

"Well, that's the way of these things, isn't it?"

I could tell she thought I had lost it. That I was having a full mental breakdown. "There was this one time though, I saw a man taking photos, and he was dressed smartly. But not too smart. Like most rich weekend dads, you know?"

She nodded. "Yeah."

"And I walked up to him because he was taking photos of the game, and I asked him which kid was his. He vaguely pointed in the direction toward my brother's team and said, 'Oh, that one,' and then called out one of the other numbers in the team. He said that was his nephew. I was a kid, so I wasn't really paying attention, you know. But I remember thinking he looked really familiar. It had been that long since I'd seen my own bloody father that I couldn't remember what he looked like." I swallowed the fresh stab of pain.

Telly was silent for a beat. "Fuck, I'm sorry."

"Oh, it's not your fault. My father was a complete twat. But anyway, there's a photo in there. Toby's just full-on mid-air kick, straight into the goal. His dark hair was sweaty and matted into his brow. I mean, it was an awful photo of him in the face, but God, the glory it captured. He would've loved a photo like that. Anyway, that's in there. And I remember the game too because it was coming down in buckets.. And I was certain Mum never took pictures really. She'd make signs though. *Go, Tobias!* And we'd paint our cheeks in obscene colors and such, you know?"

Telly nodded. "Yeah."

"My dad took that picture of my brother. There are other photos of me at school things. Debate and such. Can't tell if it was mum or him who took them. But there are photos in that flat, littered all over the place, of our childhood, of us growing up, of momentous occasions. All of which he wasn't there for."

Fuck, I was getting maudlin. Which was not the purpose of having Telly come up here. "Sorry. I just... I come up here when I need to think, or I need to rage, or when something seems unfair. I come up here a lot."

Telly nodded. "How in the world did you get a key to come up here?"

"The handyman. I was quite flirty in my youth. I used to sneak up here and he caught me a few times. He's older. Thought it was a shame I didn't have a dad."

Telly groaned. "Oh, please tell me you didn't."

Then I realized what she thought. "No. No. Not like that. He was nice. Didn't want anything in return. I think one day he caught me and I was so upset and I told him about my dad. And then he just gave me a key. I've had one ever since."

"Is he still the handyman here?"

I shook my head. "Nah, he moved on a few years ago. But now it's his son. No one bothers me."

"Jesus, Ems, what's got you in a twist? What's going on that's forcing you up here, waiting to see if your Dad's around?"

I thought of the look Fredericka had given her daughter over dinner. The magnitude of the lie I was tasked with pulling off. I thought of how alone I felt. "I don't know. I just... With that dinner tonight, I had my mind on family."

"Makes sense. You were probably missing your brother."

I was missing them all to be honest. I forced myself to blink back my lonely tears. "Thanks for coming. Did you bring it?"

Telly sat back and pulled a device out of her bag. It was about the size of a phone and not much heavier. Black and smooth.

"This will do what we need?" I asked.

She licked her lips. "I know that I was on board with this idea, but I feel like I need to warn you how dangerous this is. I won't stop you, but maybe you should have one of us visit you at work and in the midst of an introduction, we copy it."

"That will be too suspicious."

She chewed on her bottom lip. "If he's as dangerous as you say, then maybe—"

"Telly, are you with me or not?"

"Of course I am. It's just dangerous, so a little caution wouldn't hurt."

"I hear you. I promise I'll be careful." Well as careful as I could be and still get what we needed. Access was the first step. Then proof.

"Fine. If you promise. How'd it go tonight?"

I furrowed my brow as I thought about how easily Bridge touched me. It was all so simple. So casual. Hell, I knew the score, and even I believed him. "Better than expected. As it turns out, Bridge Edgerton is a hell of an actor."

"Well that's good, isn't it? That it went well."

"Too well," I snorted. "She believed us. We are a couple in love. Even when we told her our impending nuptials were going to be a small ceremony with close friends only, she insisted on attending. So in a month, we are *all* going to be lying."

Telly shrugged. "Uh, you know, with all the shit that we've gotten up to over the last several years, there's been a lot less fuss about lying than there used to be."

It wasn't the lying that bothered me so much. "I've always had a dodgy relationship with the truth as long as it served me. But this feels... I don't know. It doesn't *feel* like a lie." It felt like I could get caught up in it.

Telly nodded and sat back. "Ahh, so this is the route. I thought something was up the last time we were all together. You two looked distinctly... uncomfortable with each other. I'm sorry I didn't see it sooner."

"Yeah well, it's just that tonight felt real somehow."

She smirked and lifted her brow. "Did it now?"

I laughed and shook my head. "You mean Bridge actually having an inkling that something else is going on in the world other than his own selfish agenda?" I shook my head. "Nope, not one bit. To him, I'm just annoying Emma. A means to an end."

She gave me a gentle shove. "Ems, come on, you know he doesn't think of you like that."

"Oh, but he does. I mean, imagine forever having to look after your best mate's sister."

"I don't know. I've seen the way he looks at you sometimes. I mean, he's exasperated, yes. But he's curious. And you know Bridge, he keeps himself so buttoned up. I always have the urge to muss him just a bit to see what he'd do."

"Yeah well, I *have* mussed him, and all he does is sit there in flat, not-so-silent condemnation. And tonight, I thought... I don't know what I thought. But it turns out, I'm still just annoying Emma, because when Mina showed up, he went off with her."

Telly straightened in her seat. "The fuck?"

"Oh yes, it was quite entertaining. She cornered me at the restaurant, which meant she was following him. She basically told me to lay off her man."

"Oh, Jesus Christ."

Precisely. "Yeah, it was a bloody delight. Very exciting."

"Fuck, Ems, I'm sorry."

I shrugged. "Not your fault. And then, well, she turned up at the house. She tried to tell me that he was keeping secrets and hiding things from me. Which, as it turns out, he was."

"What are you going to do about it?"

"Well, the only thing I can do. I agreed to marry him, not because of any teenage feelings I have for him, but because he and the lads can help me get justice for Toby. So, I'm going to do my part. If I was going to break into a secure laptop, and I only had a few minutes to do so, how would I do it?"

Telly sat up then. "Are you thinking of doing what I think you're thinking of doing?"

"Yes, I certainly am. I'm going to break into Middleton's computer, get the dirt we need, and so then maybe I don't have to marry Bridge at all."

She sighed. "Then we're going to need a plan. C'mon, let's stop stalking your parents' ghosts and get to work."

* * *

Bridge

Emma hadn't come home last night or the night before. There had been a small part of me that had thought maybe she would. We'd been working together as a team. I thought she would understand. Come home. And God knew she was temperamental at times. That was half of our problem. I was always too controlled, and she lacked any control. She hadn't come home, and the security team hadn't been following her, so I had no fucking clue where she was or where she'd spent the night.

Conventional wisdom told me she was at her mum's. I checked there first, but I didn't see hide nor hair of her there. There were some hints that maybe she'd been there over the last couple of weeks. Open drapes, that sort of thing. But yeah. If she'd been there in the last day or two, I certainly would've known.

Fuck. Why the fuck did you agree to speak with Mina?

Over the last thirty-six hours, I'd convinced myself that talking to Mina had been necessary. But had it? It always went the same.

Her trying to convince me to let her come back. The first time, admittedly, I'd been ambushed in my office. So that one wasn't really my fault. The second time, at the hotel, I'd sent her packing. But this time, I'd fucked up, thinking that this was part of her getting her things and then she'd swept me by the balls with the one chip she had left. My one and only secret. Even East didn't know about Darcy. At least I didn't think he did because we had a rule; no peeking around in each other's lives. Anything we did publicly was fair game. But it was the only way the four of us could work together. Trust. And most of the time, we told each other everything anyway. The way Ben and East loved gossip, it was like living with teenagers.

But fucking Mina, she knew the one thing, *the one thing* I should have kept to myself. But I'd honestly thought I was going to marry her and we were going to start our lives together, so I'd shared. Because Darcy was going to need someone. Not just someone to look after her, but someone who understood her. When Mina and I got together, Darcy was eleven and needed a woman to talk to. I already wasn't very good at talking.

Every three months or so, I made time to go see her. Take a couple of days. Actually take the bloody weekend off. And if there was time, I'd take her skiing or do something that she wanted to do. I figured sooner or later she'd get tired of her big brother, but she never did. And Lord, did she love to talk. About anything.

The last time I'd seen her, she had asked me about the hotels. Taking a full-on interest, like she was an up-and-coming investor. I wasn't really sure why until I realized that she'd been trying to take an interest in my world so we'd have more to talk about. Which was quite smart of her, and really what I should be doing. But who the hell knew what a tween was interested in? She really likes to read. So every time I went to see her, I'd find some rare edition of some fun book and get it for her. There was an author called Darcy Morgan, and she wrote these fantasy stories. At first, Darcy loved her just because she had the same name. But she wrote about dragons and princes and things that really kept Darcy firmly entrenched in her books.

One time, when the newest book was coming out and hadn't been yet released, I'd managed to get her a copy. I'd never seen that little girl squeal so hard. Honestly, I was worried she'd been stuck with something and was bleeding everywhere. But no, all she was bleeding was enthusiasm. I couldn't help the tug of a smile on my lips when I thought about the way she'd marched herself at me, wrapping her arms around my neck. That really was the best feeling.

And so, when Mina had pressed that button, the reminder that Darcy was going to need more than I could give her, I had to give in. She knew how to get to me, and she worked it. Pushed on my weakness, and I'd fallen for it. I hadn't seen that pressure point being applied until it was too late. So now it had been two days and I hadn't fucking seen Emma.

Ben shoved his way into my office with Drew on his heels. "Mate, what did you do at dinner?"

I frowned at him as I looked up from my laptop. I had the Dubai project file open, and I was fully focused on them. The build was going fine. There were some problems with one component that we had to solve. The engineer still hadn't gotten back to me. "What are you doing here?"

Drew grinned, heading straight to the bar. Had anyone else noticed he was drinking a lot? It was only bloody two in the afternoon.

"I don't know what either one of you are on about."

Ben laughed. "You should. Fredericka bloody *loves* you. Even more, she bloody loved Emma. Now she is insisting on throwing your reception."

I groaned. "Oh, for fuck's sake, are you serious?"

In the back of my mind, I had hoped we might never even have to get married. That we could have one of those long engagements that just never seem to pan out. But it looked like we were moving forward, and there was no pulling this train back. "Well, I'm glad we performed."

Drew tossed his drink back. "So why don't you look happy? You should be over the moon. It's starting to look like someone kicked your puppy."

"Since neither one of you seems to know what this is like, I actually have bloody work to do. We have to break ground in Hong Kong in a couple of months and you two are worried about my love life?"

Drew chuckled. "Well, it's not your *real* love life."

Ben lifted a brow. "Drew is right. I can't believe I'm actually saying that, but what's wrong with you? You seem out of sorts. You've got that laser focus turned off. So what if the old lady wants to throw your reception? The idea was a very private ceremony. We all go to a party, you smile at Emma adoringly, and then we get on with this. Zicks gets signed over. The deal is a month away. What is your problem?"

I rubbed the back of my neck. "Nothing. It's fine. Everything went as planned. No surprises."

Ben lifted a brow. "What aren't you saying?"

I could lie, but I was already quite done with that. "As it turns out, we did so goddamned well that we got people like Mina nervous."

Drew whistled low. Ben's brows just popped. "What does Mina have to do with this? You're not still seeing that cunt, are you?"

I scowled. Not so much at Ben, but more about the fact that he'd been right. All along he had been right, and I had ignored his blatant hatred of her. He'd had known more about her than I had. But at the end of it, even before I decided to marry her, he'd never really wanted Mina for me. I hated the constant reminder that he had seen something I hadn't. Like it had a lot to say about my abilities.

"No, she's... we're done."

He visibly relaxed. Drew just nodded his head as he poured himself another scotch. "So if you are done with Mina, what's the problem?"

"She came by the house making another plea for reconciliation. Emma was with me, and I just had to focus on the problem at hand."

This time, Drew's brows went up and Ben leaned forward. When Ben spoke, his voice was slow and coaxing, as if talking to a scared, wounded animal. "Please, God, please, tell me you did not shove aside Emma to talk to Mina."

I frowned at that. "Mina was the problem at hand. I had to deal with it before it blew up in my face."

Drew whistled again. "How is he the calm and rational one?"

My gaze jumped between the both of them. "I maintain that it was the right call. Mina is a grenade that can go off at any moment."

Ben shook his head. "Mate, for someone so fucking brilliant, you are an eejit. How can you not know that was going to set Emma off, first of all? That all Mina wanted to do was start trouble, second of all. And that no matter what, there is nothing you can give Mina to make her just quietly go away. You need to make severing your relationship painful. Definitive and final."

"I thought we weren't trying to make noise and make waves. With the induction of the new initiates, with their training, and with everything else we have going on, the last thing we need is another crisis. Didn't you just give me that speech the other goddamn day? About how I am shit with a fucking distraction? So I dealt with the problem."

Ben shook his head. "Let me guess, you haven't seen Emma since?"

I frowned at that. "No. I went by her mother's, but she wasn't there. I called Livy, and Nyla, and Telly. No one has seen her. Or if they have, they're not telling."

Ben muttered under his breath. "Now it all makes sense."

I frowned. "What makes sense?"

"Last night, Olivia was on the phone talking with someone. Calling someone a fucking idiot. With her, it could have been about an episode of *The Bachelor*, who the fuck knew? When I asked her about it, she just rolled her eyes. She was in no mood to tell me. But it was her you're-a-fuckup face. Turns out, I'm the fuckup by proxy. You messed up, which means you have to fix this."

"How am I going to fix something with someone I can't find? Who, if I could find, wouldn't talk to me, and whom I don't understand at all. Not to mention, she's working at Middleton's office, so she's also not safe. It's like she's deliberately trying to fuck with me."

Ben shook his head. "I have a solution for that, actually. I've put Alex in play there."

Alex was one of the new Elite recruits. Ollie, Alex, and Liam were part of our attempt to do things differently. The three of them were still in training. "Is he ready for that?"

"It's strictly observational. When the three of them indicated for specialties, he requested media. So this is a good fit. Anything out of sorts, and he'll alert us."

I still didn't love it. But at least she wasn't entirely alone. Drew chose that moment right then to size me up entirely. "You mean, someone you have the hots for is running away from you? Ben, mate, tell your friend."

Ben shook his head. "I'm not claiming him. Not with these kinds of fuckups. We'll give him to East."

"But East isn't here."

I scowled. "You know what. I've about had it with you lot."

Ben shook his head. "I'm sure that's what Emma is feeling right now too."

"It's not that bad. How mad can she get?"

Ben laughed. "Mate, I can't believe I was ever even mildly

relieved about you having a fiancée and seeing you settled. You haven't got a clue. Emma Varma is about to make you pay."

Something about the way he said that made me realize he was telling the absolute, unvarnished truth. I'd fucked up. And Emma would get her pound of flesh.

Chapter Ten

Emma

I would be a liar if I said I hadn't been watching my phone all day. For two days. two goddamn days, not a word from Bridge. I half expected him to have someone watching me and come find me on the roof on Saturday night, but he hadn't. Nor had he called yesterday.

So, I started my new job at Middleton Communications wondering just what the hell I was going to do with him. I was already in this hornet's nest. I had made my bed, and I had to live in it. The good news was, I actually was good at crisis management. I hadn't lied my way in there; I did have the skillset. And that was going to come in handy because when I rolled in on Monday morning, it had been a hoard of client files. So many.

Most of them were fairly simple. Basic image checks. Nothing major. But when Francis poked his head into my office at 5:30, I was starting to wonder if I'd ever get the stink off of me. So many of his clients were utter sleazeballs. There were so many sex scandals to deal with that I couldn't even count them.

I knew the rules. Our client was our client, and our only job was to keep their name out of the press or put it in the press, depending on the situation. So that was beg, borrow, steal, and brand as much as you had to. I couldn't help but be swept up in half of what I was reading. There was one guy, a lord, who'd carried on a sexual relationship with a sixteen-year-old. He was married too. And while the age of consent in the UK was sixteen, it was still gross. Really gross. Not to mention, his wife was the reason he had any fortune at all. His family, while they had the title, had lost their money nearly a century ago. So they'd been marrying rich heiresses for decades. And to make matters worse, he was using his wife's family money to pay for his mistress.

Really, mistress? She was a teenager. How could she be a bloody mistress? She didn't even know anything. Anyway, he was using his wife's money to pay for her flat, and an overly zealous pap had gotten a photo of the two of them making out on the balcony. Good God. No wonder he was looking for a crisis management company if he was going to do shit like publicly make out with his teenage girlfriend where cameras could see them. It wasn't like they had high privacy fences or anything.

That was the file I was looking at when Francis knocked on my desk. Two sharp raps. It worried me that I hadn't even heard him come in. My head snapped up and I startled and pushed back automatically. "Jesus Christ, you scared me."

"Sorry." He held his hands up. "You were so engrossed I don't think you heard me knock."

I'd let him get away with the lie, even though I had the transparency function turned on in my bloody earbuds. They weren't noise-canceling. I found that wearing them and piping in low levels of classical music helped me concentrate better, but I never, ever put the noise-canceling on. It was like asking to get murdered.

"Right. Sorry." I tugged them out of my ears. "What can I do for you?"

"Ah, I see you have the Webster file."

I pursed my lips. "Yup, sure do."

He frowned at that. "Remember, we don't pass judgment on our clients."

The way he said that made me highly uncomfortable, but I covered it well. "No, it's not that." I forced a smile of neutrality on my face. "My concern is that he's a moron."

Francis choked a laugh. "Oh. Yes, I generally don't like stupid people either."

"Why would he do something so reckless as to make out with his girlfriend on an open balcony? Dumb."

He laughed. "Yes well, never let it be said that our clients are always playing with a full deck."

"It's frustrating. I could do a much better job if people would just follow the rules. Don't do anything in public you wouldn't be comfortable plastering as a front-page headline on a newspaper."

He guffawed. "Do you mind coming with me? There's something I want to show you."

I forced a smile on my face. God, he was sleazy. He was the kind of person who gave the profession a bad name. Everyone always looked at crisis managers like we were devils hiding things.

We were not hiding things. Some people just really had no idea how to weather a situation. A good crisis manager could get you through that. But Middleton, Jesus. The kind of clients he had, I wasn't sure I'd ever be able to get this stink off.

I got up and grabbed my phone and the little black device that was directly under it. Wherever he was taking me, I might actually have a chance to use this thing. If I could just show the lads that I could copy his phone and do something helpful, something useful so that I wouldn't have to stay in this job for too long, that would be ideal. I followed him into his office and in there was a stack of paperwork. "Sorry, HR brought this to me. I figured you and I could have a drink and find out more about each other as you sign."

"Right, more paperwork. I thought I signed everything already."

"Yeah, it's more NDA clauses."

"Well, you know I'm not going to sign anything else without my lawyer actually reviewing this, right?"

His brow furrowed. "What's the problem?"

"Nothing. It's just not smart. And I know you wouldn't accuse me of not being smart, would you?"

"It's HR paperwork," he pressed.

"Yes. And the last time I signed HR paperwork, I had my lawyer present. So, I won't be signing anything else. This isn't an exemption."

I hoped I wasn't being foolhardy. Middleton stared at me, and I got the distinct impression I was being examined as if I was on a petri dish.

"But I'm more than happy to get to know my new boss better." I grinned at him in that coy manner that seemed to convey that I was good-natured even though I was saying hell-fucking-no. I sat down on the low leather couch and grinned up at him as I ignored the stack of papers in front of me.

"I can't say I love this turn of events."

I smiled at him, determined to put him at ease and not choke on it. "Oh come on, considering that I didn't get this paperwork until just now, it can't be that urgent. Either you got too busy and just realized that it had to be signed, which is fine, or it's a power play in which you expected me to comply and just sign them. See, I'm too smart for that. I'm not sure what kind of game you're trying to play, but it's really unnecessary."

His brow furrowed even deeper. "I assure you, Miss Varma, I'm not playing a game."

"Okay then, if you say so. In which case, I will still ask that you allow me ample time to call my lawyer to come and review the documentation. In the meantime..." I leaned forward, grabbing a glass and pouring some of the scotch that he already had on the table then holding it up to him as if I meant to offer cheers.

He frowned but raised his glass with mine. And while I raised my glass to my lips, pretending to take a dainty sip and then deliberately wincing, I did not swallow an ounce. I was somewhat bolstered to see that he swallowed easily and quickly. But I never trusted a sleazeball. He could have put something inside of my glass that I didn't notice, so I certainly wasn't going to touch it.

"So I was looking at some of the other clients that you have, and there are some with redacted files."

He nodded slowly. "Yes, you don't have a clearance for those clients yet."

"Don't I?"

He sat back and laughed. "You don't. You just got here. I want to see what you're capable of first."

"Well then, you have to actually give me something needy. So far, the clients you sent me are how to make someone look good after a divorce, boring things. There are a couple of corporate clients in there that would be more interesting, but I can do better."

He chuckled as he nodded, reached into his pocket, and then, bingo, placed his phone on the coffee table. I leaned forward to pour him another glass and he shook his head. "Oh, I'm not drinking alone. I learned that scotch is like a woman... to be savored."

He laughed out loud, throwing his head back. And I inched my phone even closer to his. He was so preoccupied with his musings as he poured his own scotch that he'd missed the telltale flicker on my phone that told me the cloning program was working.

What I was doing was dangerous because if he caught me, or had an inkling actually, not only was I going to lose the element of surprise, but if he was as dangerous as Bridge kept saying, then I would potentially be in real danger.

All right, so keep having drinks with the crazy.

If this was going to get me closer to who hurt my brother, then I could do it.

But still, that little voice inside my head kept talking to me, kept trying to warn me that maybe my impulsive nature, just this once, could get me into trouble. That maybe my normal level of impulse was not a good move.

Middleton sat forward then, and I smiled up at him as once

again I lifted my glass, let the liquid touch my lips, and winced, swallowing my own saliva to appear as if I'd taken a sip and swallowed. He noticed that my scotch level was not diminishing like his was.

"Is scotch not your drink?"

"Earlier, when you said something about needing to savor it, I'm trying to apply that advice."

His gaze narrowed even further as he watched me. "I can't put a finger on you, Varma."

"I didn't know you were trying to, *Middleton*."

He chuckled. "There's something shrewd about you. You're smart, and you know it."

"Ugh, what a shame it would be if women didn't know their own worth."

He inclined his head, nodding slowly. "What a shame indeed. So tell me, how was your first day?"

"Oh, you know, as first days go, you spend half of it trying to look busy, the other half of it wondering if you've acted too impulsively and taken the wrong job."

"And did you?"

I smiled then. A somewhat genuine smile. "Too early to tell. But I am already learning so much." When telling a lie, you should just stay as close to the truth as possible. In this case, I wasn't lying. I had already learned a lot. I had learned that Middleton didn't have a line. He and his company would take any kind of client. So far, what I had seen told me I needed to watch my back, because he had the kind of clients that you read about in the papers. The kind of clients who were slick enough to get away with whatever charges were levied against them. The kind of clients where the word unscrupulous still made them look like angels. A word to the wise, be cautious.

When he finished up his scotch, he leaned forward. "Can I ask you a real question?"

"Sure. I might not answer, but you can ask."

"Fair enough. What's the deal with Edgerton?"

"What do you mean, what's the deal?"

"I mean, the deal. Are you really seeing him?"

"Why? Didn't it look like we were seeing each other?"

"You just seem smart. Ambitious. Edgerton doesn't seem like your type."

"Oh, you know my type now, do you?"

I leaned forward to pick up my phone and the black device that was hiding underneath it. But he leaned forward and wrapped his hand around my wrist. "You're brilliant, but you know that. You don't seem like someone who would put up with bullshit. You need someone who can keep up with you mentally and wine you at La Costa Reina in Barcelona, the best paella in the city, mind you. And you clearly need someone who can handle you."

I lifted a brow as I glanced down at his hand on my wrist. "Handle me, you say? You mean someone who sees me as an equal and doesn't try and tamp down my fabulousness just to make himself comfortable? Someone who doesn't think that I needed to be *handled*?"

He frowned. "I'm not saying you need to be handled. I'm just saying a woman as strong as yourself requires a certain finesse."

I laughed at that. "Let me guess. You know someone who's better with that kind of finesse than Bridge?"

His gaze met mine. "I might."

"Well, if I'm ever in the market, you can introduce me to them."

He chuckled. "So you're serious? Edgerton?"

"And what's wrong with Edgerton?"

"Nothing. He is, after all, a friend."

The way he said friend told me that he and Bridge were anything but, but I made no comment about that. "Well, Mr. Middleton, it's late and your friend is waiting on me. So, if there's nothing else, I'll have my lawyer join us tomorrow for the final signing of the paperwork, or you can just go ahead and send it to their office. If there are any problems, they'll make me aware of them."

He frowned. "It's still early. I thought we'd spend some more time getting to know each other. After all, you haven't finished your scotch."

I left it where it was. "Yeah, as it turns out, I really am more of a rum girl. Thank you for the drink though. And I will tell Bridge you sent him your regards."

He lifted a brow. "You'd do that?"

"I'm sure he returns them."

He chuckled. "You're probably correct."

I lifted the phone and the disc in one full sweep as I pushed them to the edge of the table before placing them against my side. "Thank you for the drink, Mr. Middleton."

"I've already told you, since we're old friends, you can just call me Francis."

I thought of Bridge's tendency to call him anything but Francis. "Did you have a nickname growing up?"

He frowned at me. "No, why would I have a nickname?"

"I don't know. Don't the lot of you all have nicknames?"

His brow furrowed. "Nicknames are juvenile."

Well, that went well. Excellent. "Well, good night then, Mr. Middleton."

"Oh, Miss Varma..."

I cursed under my breath as I turned around slowly. "Yes?"

"Just so you're aware, you could do better than Edgerton."

I swallowed hard. "Thank you for making me aware. I will take that under advisement."

He nodded at me. "Yes, you do that."

I tried to hold my visible shudder until I was well down the hallway. I could see why the other women on his team quit. The difference was, I couldn't quit. Not yet. There was still work to do.

* * *

Bridge

Whoever said making soufflés was stressful just had no idea how to make them. The reason I was stress-baking still hadn't walked through the front door. I'd expected her yesterday, but today she hadn't come by the office, or called, or texted, and I was starting to get antsy. And since she hadn't come back to the house, I decided before I did anything stupid, like calling her, going to fetch her and bring her back, or essentially kidnapping her off the street, I should resort to baking.

When I was a kid, we didn't have much, but Mum always seem to have the ingredients to make something. Or she'd barter for it. Everyone knew that she could bake. So sometimes, they would barter for ingredients, or she'd have leftovers from someone's birthday cake or something. And so I'd learned to make all kinds of things. And even though I wasn't fancy then, just a kid from the East End, after all, I could actually *do* fancy shit in the kitchen.

Granted, my father had fixed all of that, hadn't he? The more I thought about it, the more I wondered if I'd have been happier going up to a culinary school or something like that. A part of me often thought I would have been much happier. But that wasn't exactly how things turned out, was it?

The front door opened, and I quickly checked the security camera. My heart lunged in my chest, ready to do battle. But for no good reason, because it wasn't Emma. Instead, it was my mother. She strolled casually into the kitchen. "Explain to me why you're baking."

"Because I like to bake."

One quick sniff and she muttered. "Soufflé. Nice. Chocolate and raspberries?"

I nodded. "Your nose never fails you."

"No, it doesn't." She pulled wine out of the bag she was carrying. "I may have a famous restaurant now, but I still like cheap wine."

I laughed. "Oh, Mum."

I grabbed glasses for both of us and then uncorked it for her.

"Aw, that's a good boy. So you're home baking, instead of with this fiancée of yours?"

"It's complicated."

She rolled her eyes. "I know. At what point are you going to call her and tell her that your mum wants to see her? Or even better that you have a sausage you want to share with her?"

I blinked rapidly. No, she really hadn't? Had she? "Mum."

"Please, Bridge. I'm a chef. You think I didn't hear worse with you and your friends when you were a lad?"

I frowned thinking about that. I really didn't want to think about what she'd heard or seen.

"Well, have you talked to the woman?"

"I... I messed up, I think."

Her brow lifted. "You think, or you know?"

I sighed. "I know."

"All right, if you know you made a mistake, how are you fixing it?"

"I'm not fixing it because it wasn't really a mistake."

My mother took a long sip of the wine. "Ugh, I didn't raise a fool, did I? I tried to raise you right. Did I make a mistake somewhere?"

I frowned at her. "Mum, I'm fine. She's the one who's stubborn."

She shook her head. "The number one thing I taught you was to be the first to apologize when there's anything in question. Are you doing that?"

"No, because there was nothing in question. *She's* wrong."

My mother raised a brow. "Bridge."

I sighed. "Look, we had dinner. Mina turned up. When we didn't engage with Mina at dinner, she turned up here to pick up a few of her things."

"And let me guess, Mina manipulated you into talking to her in some way?"

I frowned. Was I that transparent?

My mother shook her head. "Jesus, Lord. I did raise a fool. I tried so hard. A single mum, all by herself. I tried not to raise a moron."

"Hey."

"You're a good lad, Bridge. Smart, self-contained, but God, you're so emotionally unaware."

"Yeah, I know Mina manipulated me."

"Yes, and let me guess, Mina manipulated you into having a conversation with her. Did you invite Emma to take part in that conversation?"

I frowned. "No, because it had to do with Darcy."

My mother frowned. "Yeah, and?"

"You know how sensitive that situation is."

"I do. Your father dumped his daughter on our doorstep, telling us he was going to tell the world she was yours if we didn't raise her. Now, I could have dealt with that consequence, and you did right by her. We both did."

"She's my sister."

"Yeah, she is. But you hiding her away isn't doing either of you any good. People are using her against you. And at some point, it has to stop."

"I need to keep her protected."

"I understand the compulsion," she said. "You always want to do the right thing because you're a good lad. But at some point, you won't be able to protect her if you haven't protected yourself. Mina knowing your 'secret' will only make things worse for you. It's not a secret. Your father has manipulated the situation to his advantage, mind you. This has nothing to do with you. So she knows about Darcy. But Darcy is getting older. She's a teenager now. Soon it won't matter. She's a good girl, strong, smart. A little manipulative, but that's just a girl figuring out her power. That's all."

"Yeah, I wish she didn't do it at my expense."

Mum laughed. "Ah, she's figuring herself out. But you have to stop beating yourself up for letting Mina get too close. You don't have time for that. The sooner you can let that go, the sooner Darcy won't feel like an Albatross. But let me guess... You decided to talk to Mina so she wouldn't spill the secret, and then what? Emma wanted some explanations?"

I shrugged, mindful of the timer on the soufflé. But I didn't pay attention to timers. More often than not, I paid closer attention to the smell, and it wasn't quite there yet. "Yeah, Mum. I may or may not have messed that up."

She rolled her eyes. "Oh, lad. Fine, you made a mistake, but explain to me why my son, who knows better, has not apologized yet?"

"Because Emma is stubborn and she—"

My mother shook her head. "She didn't fuck up here. You did. And maybe she's making some demands on you, but if you need her, you want to sort this out instead of stewing in here and making soufflés that will no doubt be delicious. Matter of fact, I'll help myself to one. But maybe you should go find your bride-to-be, not just because you need her, but also because you were taught the right thing to do."

"Mum."

She shrugged. "What? You're going to start policing me now? That's not a good idea."

I rolled my eyes. "Why are you so difficult?"

"I had to learn to be to deal with you. Now, get."

"But the soufflé..."

"Boy, do you think I can't get a delicious soufflé out of the oven?"

"But it won't be warm when I get back."

"It doesn't matter. Something tells me this is more important."

I sighed. She was right. Just one problem; I had no idea where to find her. She had given my security boys the slip. The good news was, I at least knew where she worked, so it was easy enough getting her last known location and trying to track her from there.

This would all be a lot easier if she'd just moved into the house like I told her to.

Key words there being *told her to*.

I frowned at that. My mother had a point. This was not the way to get compliance, not with Ems anyway. I couldn't bulldoze her. If I wanted her cooperation, she was going to need a softer hand. And if not that, at the very least, an apology. I knew Emma, she was going to make me pay for my poor choices. She was such a fucking ballbuster.

The real problem was that every time I thought about her and that spark of fire behind her eyes as she narrowed them at me, asking if I really was going to let Mina stay and have a conversation, it made my dick hard. It was just a slight motion. You would have missed it if you weren't paying attention or looking for it. But goddamn, when I thought about it, my dick hardened. What did that say about me that I got a hard dick at the thought of Emma Varma ending my life? I was going to find out because, one way or another, I was going to track her down. And then I was going to eat some crow.

Chapter Eleven

Emma

I'd made a deal, and I was going to honor that. It wasn't exactly like I was playing games. I wasn't being deliberate or callous. I showed up exactly where I was required at the time. The Green Initiative luncheon, talking about sustainable efforts of the London Lords Dubai build, and I'd been very cooperative. I smiled, wore the appropriate outfit, and said the appropriate things.

I slipped my hand into Bridge's and let him stand forward. I was the perfect billionaire's plastic wife. If I could have taken a picture of the expression on his face, I would have. He'd been surprised to see me when I walked in at the appointed time.

I wasn't sure why he was surprised. I'd given him my word, after all. Maybe that was what was unusual. Someone giving him their word and keeping it. He'd been so surprised his mouth had nearly hung open. But then I'd smiled with him just in time for the press to capture a picture. A pretty picture it was, too. Our lips grazing and me smiling up at him.

Calculated. Pristine. Anybody watching would think, *My, aren't these two in love?* Except, I wasn't in love. Was I?

You're not fooling anyone. You caught a case of feelings. And now you're regretting these feelings.

It was bound to happen. What had made me think that I could slide in undetected? That nobody would know. Hell, that none of those feelings from long ago would surface again. I should have known. But like a fool, I ignored the warnings. Like a fool, I thought I could control this. But I couldn't, and now it was coming to bite me in the ass. Because here I was, pretending for the cameras. Pretending for him. Pretending to be in love.

Except you're not pretending, are you? So what is it? Pretending to pretend?

I was in so deep now, there would be no extricating myself. And when I landed, there would be pain.

The whole luncheon, he'd held on to my hand tightly as if he was afraid I was going to vanish again. And he was right. As soon as this was over, I was going to go back to my hidey- hole. I could have stayed at Mum's. Instead, I'd chosen a cozy hotel in Victoria. After I'd hatched my little plan with Telly, I took the last couple of days trying to outline my plan. Middleton was excited about me and what I could bring to the table, which was a boon. He already had clients for me and a project that required travel. It was just a one-day thing, but we'd be together. Alone.

I was glad Telly had come through for me with the cloning device. It would certainly cut down on the amount of time I had to spend in his presence. I wasn't sure who was the better hacker, Telly or East. My guess was it depended on what kind of hacking you needed. But watching the two of them battle it out non-stop to see who was better was very entertaining. And it benefited me. In this case, since I didn't want Bridge knowing what I was doing, Telly had been the better choice.

Would East be faster? Sure. Could East actually protect me if some shit went down? Again, probably. But would East tell Bridge what was going on? One hundred percent, undoubtedly. Which I couldn't have. So, I had a plan. All I had to do was execute it. Oh, and not get killed or exposed in the process.

At one point during lunch Bridge leaned over. "We need to talk."

I nodded mutely through my forced smile. He narrowed his gaze at me as if he didn't believe me. The thing was, I had Nyla's help making my escape. As soon as his back was turned, she directed me out the side door.

As I scooted past her, she grinned. "You know, normally I don't agree with playing games. But if he's going to be a dick, then he deserves what he gets."

"I appreciate it. And it's not a game. I just need time. This is all moving quite quickly. And if Mina is still in the picture, maybe I'm not needed at all."

She frowned. "Please God, not Mina, okay? She's a right stropping cow. Just the worst. The absolute worst. If you want him, go get him. Don't give in to Mina."

"Well, currently we are very much on the *he should come and get me* angle. I'm not chasing anyone."

"And that I agree with. You, my darling, are excellent. And he would be lucky to have you."

"Thank you. But let me get out of here before he notices I'm gone."

I marched across the road, my heels making a *clop-clop* sound on the cobblestones. More than once I wobbled slightly, nearly turning an ankle. I finally flagged down a taxi and hopped in.

The car was pulling away just as the side door opened and out came Bridge, gaze trained on me. My phone buzzed in my hand. When I looked down, there he was.

Bridge: *Where the fuck are you going?*

I considered answering, but I didn't bother, and as the taxi approached West London, I had the driver take a detour. I don't know what led me back to the rooftop across from my parents' secret flat, but I just needed a moment to clear my head. I had plans. Crazy dangerous things I was planning on doing. All in the name of my brother.

The best part was, it didn't even occur to me that it might not be the wisest course of action, but at least my goal was singularly focused. Make the men who hurt Toby pay. There was that little voice at the back of my head that said, *And what happens after? What happens when you make them all pay? Then what will you do with yourself?*

It was a question I didn't have an answer to. And one I probably wouldn't have for some time. I was this close already. There was no turning back. No second guesses. This was it. One guilty party to go, and then maybe I could see about getting my own life. Finding love if that was even a thing. I saw it happen for Livy and Nyla. And Telly too. But even Telly was having a moment where love might not be enough. And I didn't even know if someone like me could have love. I was perpetually unlovable even to my own father. Oh yeah, because that made a perfect fact for a dating profile.

You just stay focused. Focus on the important thing. Catch Middleton. Make him pay. And then you'll be free.

Whatever the hell that meant.

It was the creaking sound of the roof door that had me whipping around to find the one person I never thought would find me. "Jesus Christ, Bridge, what the fuck are you doing here?"

His voice was a low growl as he approached me like a jungle cat. "Don't run from me. Do you understand? It took me a few days, but I found you. You run from me again, and I'll find you again. You don't run from me, do you understand?"

I scowled at him. "Oh really? You're going to stop me?"

"Yes, you damn well better believe I am." With every stride toward me, I could see the intent on his face, the fury. He wasn't used to anyone telling him no. He wasn't used to anyone defying him. But as he approached, all I did was lift my chin up, ready to do battle. He would not control me. And he certainly would not control my heart. At least that's what I thought before he fisted a hand into my hair, tugged my head back, and slammed his lips on top of mine.

* * *

Bridge

She stole the breath from my lungs. I couldn't breathe. Jesus fucking Christ, *I could not breathe.* I didn't even know what had possessed me to kiss her. I didn't know what I needed or why. Just seeing her ratcheted up the tension in my body to a roaring hum. All I knew was she tasted incredible. Like everything I needed but everything I shouldn't want. She was sweet and soft.

I could feel her surprised gasp straight to my dick. When I clasped my hands into her hair, fisting gently, tightening just a little, she gasped, and then it happened. That moan, that low moan at the back of her throat that told me I wasn't the only one suffering. That I wasn't the only one feeling this. That I wasn't the only one dying.

I knew all of the reasons I *shouldn't* want Emma. I knew all of the reasons I should stay away from her, all of the reasons why she was trouble. But I couldn't stop. As her tongue glided over mine and our teeth clashed, I pulled her to me, our bodies melting together.

Her mewls ratcheted up the electricity coursing through my veins. All I wanted to do was take more, fist her hair, hold her there as I ravaged her. As it was, I was probably fisting too tight, but somehow I couldn't make myself let go, couldn't make myself stop. I was drowning in the sea of her scent wrapping around me. The need for her building and building, layer upon layer, until all I was going to see every single time I closed my eyes was her. She was already more than a distraction and so much more than I could take, and at the same time, she was everything I needed, everything

I wanted. For three years I had thought I wanted something else. Something cold and distant. Something that was the opposite of this, because I had known that dancing this close to a flame, I was going to get burned.

But still, with my other hand, I cupped her cheek, pulling her in and daring myself to dance even closer, needing more from her. Demanding that she respond. And did she. When I finally released my hold on her hair, I slid my hands over her back down to her ass, bringing her soft curves in closer contact with my muscles. My dick practically jumped with joy. "God, this fucking arse has tortured me."

I didn't realize I'd said it out loud until she whimpered. And that moan sounded a lot like my name, but who the hell could tell because I had my tongue in her mouth, and I was taking out my frustration and worry on her. The fear over the last few days of not knowing where she was, what she was doing, if Middleton had hurt her or she'd done something reckless. I would have lost it.

But when she turned up today in that god-awful gray, I wanted to shoot whoever had dressed her. Because that wasn't Emma. Emma was full of color. She was adventurous and always loud and unpredictable. Emma was alive. And as I kissed her, stroking my tongue over hers, fucking her mouth like I wanted to fuck her body, like I wanted to use my fingers and my dick, tilting her ass just so she could feel the full length of my rigid erection, I knew that now that I'd broken the seal, there would be no reprieve. Now that I'd tasted her, there would be no getting the sugar and spice off my tongue. There would be no forgetting this, no putting Emma back in her box, because now I was lost.

I wanted more. But instead of taking more, I tried to let go. But Emma wrapped her arms around my neck, holding on close. When I released her, shifting my hands across her hipbones and trying to make her back up, she held tighter and rotated her hips just the way I wanted her to. That simple, small action had me tightening my hands on her hips so hard, I might have left bruises. Against her mouth, I muttered a low, "Fuuuuccck."

And I could almost feel the tip of my dick weeping. Begging me to just give in. Please God, for once in my life, just take the thing that I needed more than air, to take this dangerous thing without the consequences.

But I was fooling myself because deep down inside, I knew that with Emma, there would be more than one time. There would be no *just this once*. If I went there, I would have to go there again, and again, and again, because I was already an addict. And all I had done so far was kiss her. So even as she held on, I very deliberately reached behind my neck, unclasped her hands, and stepped away.

"Fuck, Emma."

We stood there for a long moment and she blinked slowly, trying to get her brain synapses back online. "H-h-h-h-how did you find me?"

"It doesn't matter. This can't happen."

I watched as her eyes narrowed. "Are you fucking serious right now?"

"Yeah. Let's not muddy any lines, okay? It's too complicated."

Pain sliced through my heart as I watched her shutter her eyes. The softness I'd just seen in them, the vulnerability, vanished and sassy Emma came out.

She always had this flicker in her eye, pure mischief and trouble. "Oh, gosh. Wouldn't want you getting the wrong idea with you kissing me and all that. I guess you end all your arguments that way, huh? By kissing people? My God, that must be hot as shit to watch you and Ben, opposite ends of the spectrum, him so fair, you so dark, making out every single time you have a fight. God, it must be some hot action. Do you grope his ass the same way? You know, inquiring minds. I want to get visuals properly."

I blinked at her. "Shut it, Emma."

"What? I'm asking for a friend. Me, I'm the friend." She raised a hand. "If you're telling me that's how you end all arguments with your friends, I am here for it. I approve this message."

I was not going to do this with her. "Come home."

"No. That's not my home."

Bloody hell. Maybe force wasn't the way to do this. "I'm sorry, okay? I'm sorry. I shouldn't have stopped to talk to Mina. We are a team. You and me. I should have respected that. I didn't mean to discount what you were feeling. I just... There's nothing to say except I fucked up."

"What's to keep you from fucking up again? After all, it's Mina. She knows all your secrets."

"I don't know." That was the truth. I didn't know. Hell, I had no idea. I might fuck up again. "I might screw up. But I'm aware of it. I have a blind spot there. She doesn't need me. But we have a job to do, okay?"

She blinked up at me slowly. "Oh, we have a job to do. But just for future note, never kiss someone like that to apologize again. It's not a good look."

And then she turned around toward the door of the roof and yanked it open.

* * *

Emma

I had no idea what to think about that kiss. And the way he'd run off afterward as if I'd burned him... What the fuck? This was the most fucked up scenario. And I kept falling for it.

My plan had been to go back to the house in Belgravia. My little sojourn could only last for so long because somebody would notice that Bridge and I were living separate lives. As I was headed down the stairs of the roof, I got a text from Francis.

It was just an address. I could try to ignore the summons, but something told me that would be a bad idea. I forwarded the address to Telly, Nyla, and Liv, letting them know the madness I was partaking in just in case. Then downstairs, I grabbed a taxi to Westminster, not Belgravia.

I needed to do this assignment. Needed Middleton to trust me enough to take me with him to Barcelona. So far, I was the only one close enough to find out what the hell he was up to. I double-checked the address where I'd been summoned and there was a hustle and bustle of a couple of people from the office as I strolled in.

"What's going on?"

Francis met me at the door. If he noticed my glammed up look, he said nothing about it. He looked freshly showered and shaved. Where had he been tonight? Was he at the same benefit I'd been at with Bridge? "This is Weston Price. His wife and daughter are missing."

I blinked rapidly. "Where are the police?"

He frowned at me like I'd asked something ridiculous. "We were called first. There is an off chance that his wife took his daughter and left."

This picture was wrong. Maybe you don't call the police if your wife is missing. But your daughter? "What? Are they missing, or did she leave him?"

"Unclear. So we need to handle this. We need to treat this like they are missing persons. Unless..."

My stomach dropped. "Fuck, did he kill her?"

Middleton's eyes went wide. "No. This isn't anything like that."

"Well, it's going to look like that to the police. So, what are we doing? When did you get here?"

"Five minutes ago. He called me ten minutes before that. It's only been fifteen minutes."

I shook my head. "Assume he freaked out for fifteen minutes. So it's already been a half hour. If they're missing, we need to call the police right now."

"Manage the crisis, Varma. Take care of your client."

I stared at him. "You have to be kidding me."

"You wanted to prove yourself, right? Well, here's your chance. Fix this. Crisis manage."

"All right, first and foremost, call DI David Strickland." I handed one of the assistants my phone. "He's in there. He's a friend. He'll come. His district isn't exactly Westminster, but he'll come and make the appropriate calls on the way."

I brushed past Kara, one of the assistants, and walked up to our client. "Mr. Price, I'm Emma Varma. I work with Francis. When was the last time you saw your wife?"

His gaze slithered over me to Francis, and I stepped in his path to block his view. "Don't look at him. Look at me. I'm the one here to help you. This is my case. If you lie to me, I will throw you to the wolves and I will destroy you. I will make sure the police arrest you on suspicion of murder. Now tell me, where are your wife and daughter?"

His mouth hung open, again trying to glance at Francis, and again, I stepped in his path. "Was I not clear when I said, I'm the one in charge? Tell me what I need to know."

He swallowed hard. "Her car is gone. I-I wasn't home the last couple of days."

"Were you traveling for work? Where were you?"

He cleared his throat. "I, um..."

"Before you think about that lie that's trying to formulate itself, think again. I already warned you what would happen if you lied. I have a police Detective Inspector on his way right now. He's a close personal friend. If you lie to me, I will tell him that you're suspicious, and I could give two fucks about my job." I turned around to glower at Francis. "So do not lie to me."

"I take two days out of a month to go away. I-I have a dominatrix."

Inside, I howled and bent over with laughter. On the exterior though, my face was the picture of composure. "We need his or her name and address."

He hesitated. "I need discretion."

"You will have no such thing if your wife and daughter are missing via foul play. So, you need to have less discretion with me right now. Name, address, alibi, right the hell now. When did you get home?"

He'd stopped looking at Francis now. "Thirty minutes ago. I wasn't worried. But Asha, my daughter, she had piano lessons at seven. They should have been home by eight-thirty at the latest. My wife is a stickler by the schedule, and they weren't here."

"Did you try her phone? Call friends?"

He nodded. "Then I called Francis."

"Okay, you're going to need to remember exactly what you told me, make sure your story doesn't waver because it's the truth. Is it the truth, Mr. Price?"

He blinked at me and nodded. "Yes."

I watched him carefully. His hands were jittery. It could be anxiety because his wife and child were not where he expected them to be. But it could be something else too. "Were you leaving out something?"

His head snapped up. "What do you mean?"

"What are you leaving out? A lie by omission is still a lie. And that would make me very annoyed indeed."

The assistant came by and handed me back my phone. "He's on his way."

"Yeah. It's the DI. He's coming. Now is your chance. Truth or dare. The dare part is you take your chances with the Detective Inspector on your own."

I watched him visibly swallow. "My wife, we were having troubles. She wanted to leave. My, uh, proclivities were not to her liking."

I sighed. "So she might have just left. Did you check the bank account?"

He frowned. "Uh, no."

"Check the accounts." Another assistant ran by. "Get Mr. Price some water and also get him a washcloth and a comb. He should look slightly rumpled, but not completely disheveled. And is that whiskey on your breath, sir?"

He nodded. "I-I poured a drink."

"Where's your glass?"

He frowned at me. "My glass?"

"Yes, your bloody glass."

"I-I drank from the bottle, I guess."

I stopped another assistant. "Grab me a glass."

When he brought it over, I slapped it on the table next to what looked to be a very expensive bottle of scotch. "Someone get Mr. Price a toothbrush. And someone grab me a shirt. Make sure that you rumple it on your way down. We're going to change your shirt because you have spilled some whiskey on you, and you smell like a distillery."

Price just stared at me.

"Move."

In the hustle and bustle, my brain was whirring. Had he done something to his wife? Because I had not signed up for that nonsense. There was justice for Toby and then there was actively supporting a murderer. That I could not do.

When the shirt was brought over, it wasn't rumpled enough, so I grabbed it, balled it up, rolled it around, and twisted it. When I unfolded it, it was a disheveled mess. "Put this on. Somebody take that one, bag it, and give it to the DI."

The other assistants were off with it. "Mr. Price, grab the glass."

He wrapped his fingers around it. "Okay, no one has touched your wife's or your daughter's rooms?"

He shook his head.

"Is your blood up there? Anything that suggests that, you know, in a fit of rage when she'd tried to leave, you *Dextered* her?"

He frowned. "What's dextered?"

"Never mind. Okay." I turned to my boss. "Have I handled the crisis well enough for you?"

He nodded. "Um, yeah." He watched me with his hands stuck in the pockets of his trousers. "You are certainly better than I anticipated."

"Like I said, I'm good at my job."

Over the course of the next thirty minutes, Inspector Strickland showed up. He'd been the one who'd handled the inquiry into my brother's death. For a moment I thought Francis would recognize him, but he didn't seem to. Not that it mattered. Strickland interviewed Price and asked some questions.

When the other DIs from Westminster District turned up, they all had a conversation. Strickland pulled me aside. "Right now, my money is on her leaving. Texts have all gone unanswered. Most clothes and toys are still there, but there doesn't seem to be a whole lot. With this much money, you'd probably overindulge the kid and the mum. I'd say she probably left."

I said the thing that we were both thinking. "Or someone made it look like they left."

His gaze narrowed on mine. "Is there a reason you called me?"

"Um, well, he's a client, so I'm being careful with him. I figured a friendly face never hurt, but I also know that if he's up to something, you are like a dog with a bone and won't let it go until you find it."

He smiled. "It's good to see you, Ems. All grown up now, eh?"

I shrugged. "We all have to grow up sometime, don't we?"

"Well, it looks good on you. Your mum must be proud."

"Mum wants me in New York. You know, living a quiet life, on the dating apps, trying to find a nice husband."

"Not for you?"

I shrugged. "Well, I wouldn't mind a nice husband. But did I mention these were Indian matchmaking apps?"

He grinned. "Oh boy."

"Oh boy is right. She is determined that I don't make the same mistakes she did."

"Send her my regards. I'll have my lads talk to the Westminster boys. I'm sure the wife will turn up, but we'll double-check. Check the accounts and everything."

"I appreciate it."

When he left me standing in the massive marble foyer, Middleton made a comment behind me. "You handled that well. How's that for a test?"

"Well, not bad," I said.

"What would you have done differently?"

"Well, I would've called the police as soon as he called me."

He raised a brow. "Ah, so you're saying I made a mistake?"

I nodded. "Yes, because if in fact he did harm his wife or do away with her, the clock is ticking."

"He's my client. Isn't it my job to protect him?"

"Yes. Protect him legally, as much as possible. Get him the best deal possible if, in fact, he did do away with them. But helping him bury evidence or running down the clock on possibly finding them alive, no. Because that makes you liable and an accessory."

He nodded. "I'm pretty sure, Helena just left."

"Is that her name? Helena?"

He nodded. "He was a shitty husband. The dominatrix is the least of his predilections. I promise you, she's probably in St. Tropez or somewhere similar. If you check the accounts, I am certain they've been cleaned out."

"Did you check the accounts?" I asked him.

He shook his head. "No. I wanted to see if you were going to or let the police do it."

"I could do it. But it's better if the police find it. That way he looks cooperative that he's given them access, and he gets to look surprised."

He smiled at me. "You, Miss Varma are certainly better than I expected."

"Which is a shame. You should have expected me to be excellent."

"And I did. Don't go fishing for compliments."

I shrugged. "I don't need them. I know how good I am." And then I left him there. There was something off with this situation. I'd handle it, but something was eating at me. And before the night was out, I knew I'd be texting DI Strickland about Helena Price.

I didn't know the woman. Her husband was a client. I'd handled the situation the best I could at the moment. But something was gnawing at me, and I knew I wasn't going to be able to sleep until I had some answers.

Chapter Twelve

Bridge

As a general rule, my father didn't speak to me. Not in public anyway.

Not once after a single Elite meeting had he ever approached me. How many of these monthly meetings had we had where, post business, he had not acknowledged me in any manner, pretending I didn't exist?

There was a time in my life when I used to think about my father and pretend that he wanted me. I'd pretend he was that kind of father that we hear about in books. The kind that would kick the soccer ball around with you. The kind you would speak to.

My father only ever spoke to me when he was laying down a mandate. Something he expected to be done. Granted, he'd learned early on that it didn't go well for him. It didn't stop him from trying though.

Wednesday's meeting started no different. With the exception that I kept hoping for a text from Emma. Why the fuck wouldn't she just listen?

Maybe because you dry shagged her on the roof then took off like your left bollock was on fire.

To be fair, molten lava had been flowing through my veins.

But it didn't matter how many times I looked at my phone, there was still nothing. I shoved my phone into my cubby before I got dressed.

Tonight's meeting had required robes but no masks. We merely reviewed the initiation rites with the new recruits, and then we went about Elite business, deals, and partnerships. There was one burn request, which was wild.

For an Elite member to burn someone meant complete, utter desolation. If a burn was requested, it meant every member in the Elite would completely sever ties with the burned member. Whoever got burned would have no recourse, nowhere to go short of changing their name and living off the radar. There was no way to come back from burn. You didn't get bank loans. You couldn't even get a license to get married or hell, a license to drive. You were going to be alone and truly burn, and that was it. Disavowed from humanity. Requests were not taken lightly.

The member had to show cause, provide evidence, get it past The Five and the Director Prime, in this case, Ben, before it went before the general membership. And each member only had one. So the burn request had better be for some serious shit. The members of the Elite didn't vote on the merits of the burn, whether it was petty or not, the group voted on impact to the Elite.

When you put in a request to burn someone, chances were they were powerful. And if they were powerful, it meant someone in the Elite was going to get touched by whatever the fuck they touched.

Sometimes there were lengthy conversations, discussions, and arguments, and it rarely ever came to this. A burn request was rare, and the approval of one was even rarer.

In the eleven years I'd been in the Elite, I'd only seen three. Most people were mere nuisances and not even powerful enough to know someone in the Elite. And we couldn't burn our own brothers. Although, sometimes I wished for the capability. So when you wanted to annihilate someone in the organization, you had to get more creative like we had.

Otherwise, I would have long ago burned my father. Just done it. Pulled a trigger to rid myself of him.

If you wanted to rid yourself of him, you could have just left.

I could have. But leaving the Elite was difficult. Even non-voting members still got called back for initiations. It was like a life-long cult. And no matter what you did or how weak you became, you still could never quite escape at the side door. Unless, of course, our little plan worked. Removing Middleton from the equation would be taking down one of the most powerful families in London. After all, they'd had the juice with the authorities.

Even Toby's father had been hushed about his death. Merri-weather was an enigma. He never saw his children. It was one of those things that Toby and I had bonded over. We both had pricks for fathers. He'd kept up with their lives and paid attention with a sense of pride. Watched over them. But no contact.

Was that the agreement he had with his wife? Was she so horrid that she forbade contact with any of his children? I had no idea. All I knew was that, unlike my father, Merriweather paid attention. But even he hadn't been able to get any answers about Toby's death. He'd been dealt the same lies we all had.

After the meeting, I headed straight for the doors to wait for Ben, East, and Drew. Drew, unlike the rest of us, didn't hate his father. They got along well. They had a rapport. As the two of them were chatting about something, I gave him a nod when I walked by. As usual, East was dodging his father. The old geezer didn't get it that neither one of his children wanted anything to do with him. After what he'd done to East's sister, I didn't blame them. And Ben... Well, Ben loathed his father, but the old man had, in his own way, come through. Although he had the nerve to insult Olivia, so he stayed on the shit list.

Once I was out, I inhaled the cool fresh air that greeted me. I stood on the glass walkway over the koi pond, no longer needing to nod and smile at appropriate times and no bodies to clash and brush with. All standing too close, talking too much. The peace was refreshing.

"I see you never learned the social niceties."

I stiffened at that voice. It was one I knew well. One I'd learned to loathe. "Ah, old man. You had to ruin someone else's night. Do yourself a favor and go back inside. I'm not feeling particularly charitable at the moment."

My father laughed as he joined me and stood by my side. "If only you could learn to be more grateful for your opportunities and show that gratitude. Without me, you wouldn't be where you are now."

"Without you, I would probably have a much happier life. But here we are,"

The old man shook his head. "Is it true what I hear? You and the Varma girl?"

"Where did you hear that?"

He spread his hands. "Mina. Where the fuck else?"

"I love that, you know, you just bring out in the open the fact that you planted a prostitute to someday become your daughter-in-law."

My father waved his hand in the air. "Please, she was never going to actually become my daughter-in-law. She was just meant to keep you happy enough. She did her job for three years, and the ruse could have continued a few more too."

"And you're not worried about the blowback on you?"

"Of course not. It was part of my contract with her to never actually marry you."

"Well, I love that you don't see anything wrong with this conversation."

"You need guidance. If you won't let me do it directly, I have to do it subversively. I'm not sorry about that."

"Why do you think I need guidance? You've never given a shit before when I was running roughshod all over East London, learning to pick locks and boost cars. Did you give a shit then? I mean, I was ten. Imagine the life of crime I could have led."

He scowled at me. "I plucked you out of there, didn't I? Put you in a good school. Let you have my name. Why, aren't you happy now?"

"Because the whole time, you were choking me. Which is what you really want, Lord Edgerton. But your plan didn't work. I'm not going to marry Mina. I'm not going to hold her in my arms anymore and have her stay by my side. She's no longer going to feed you information. That's over."

"You can't marry Merriweather's daughter."

"Is there a reason for that? Or is this just one of your edicts?"

"You can't. Merriweather is not a good ally."

I lifted a brow. "For me or for you?"

"I'm trying to do you a favor, son."

"Since when do you call me son? Look, old man, you've been trying to control me for too long. It's done. Tell your whore not to darken my door anymore because I'm not going to be responsible for what happens to her next time. Stay the fuck out of my life. You can take the guttersnipe out of the gutter, but he will never lose those sharp edges."

"You go this path, and I can't undo it for you."

"You know what's interesting? After all these years, you think you still have any say on who I am and what I do, the decisions I make. You walked away from Mum. Maybe you never intended to get caught up in her. Maybe gramps and gran wouldn't have approved. But after meeting gramps the one time, I'm pretty sure they could have cared less. So all of what has happened was all you. You are the antagonist in our lives."

"You're going about this the wrong way. But you're not going to listen to me, are you?"

"Absolutely not, you've already proved yourself untrustworthy. So, if we are done here, I'll be on my way. I'll get to avoid you for another good solid month."

"Stay away from the Varma girl."

"Thanks, Dad. I don't intend to," I called out as I left him behind with the koi and the massive white pillars of the gazebo. What was his game? What did he want from me now? The sooner I found out, the sooner I'd be able to sidestep it. We had a plan we needed to execute, and I wasn't going to let my past stand in the way.

Not this time.

* * *

Emma

I returned to Bridge's late Wednesday night. My roller bag was making that consistent rolling sound on the marble floor along with a light squeak. The marble was pretty and light, but the house felt like a museum, complete with the expensive art hanging on the walls. But the art even felt like it was meant to show sophistication and wealth, not actual joy or fun. I could change this place out so fast and add color. So much color. Rugs, and art, and photographs that I loved.

Except, this isn't your house.

No, it was not. Not at all.

The silence was deafening, and the house was dark. I knew that Bridge was in the house somewhere because all the security team were outside. Jack, Mark, Liam, Andrew, a four-man team for the night shift.

See, I *had* been paying attention to my briefing. But where was he? The house was dark. Was there a chance he'd already gone to bed?

I turned the lights on as I went, like a little Tinkerbell leaving fairy dust in my wake. I left my bag at the bottom of the staircase because I remembered the rules. If I was in the house sleeping, I needed to be in his room. Which, to be fair, was over a thousand square feet, so there was plenty of room for the two of us. The nights I'd stayed, he had been on the couch and I'd taken the bed. He had his own personal people from the hotel cleaning the main bedroom. But still, I roamed around downstairs. The massive foyer, the library to the left. I hadn't even gotten the chance to really explore. I knew from what Nyla said that it was expansive.

It had only been three days, and I'd been throwing myself into work, looking for angles and an opening to be away. I'd also been avoiding getting settled. But if this was going to work, Bridge and I were going to have to start acting like a team.

I was amazed when I reached the gorgeous chef's kitchen at the back of the house. I knew the layout was in some ways similar to Ben's, but Ben's house was far more open. And it was almost twice the size of this place, but he'd taken two houses together and knocked them out and built one big place. This house had one additional floor than his did. Both had subterranean levels for the gym, and the sauna, and the squash court, which was ridiculous. In the middle of London? Why not go outside?

I could poo-poo all the wealth and opulence in front of me, but at the same time, I was too afraid to touch it, to explore it, to make it mine, because I would get comfortable. All those things I had wished for and dreamed of when I was a child were right there at my fingertips. I could get far too comfortable here, and I wasn't staying.

So much for teamwork.

Oh, we were a team all right. We were joined together at the hip now whether I liked it or not. And as much as I hated to admit it, Bridge was right. Something about Middleton the night before had sent a shiver down my spine. I couldn't put my finger on it, but I'd seen it. He was just as dangerous as I'd been told.

Bridge had tried to warn me, but I hadn't listened. Unfortunately, I had this awful suspicion that I was in his sights, and not in the kind of way that made me interesting. If I thought maybe he just found me attractive, that, I knew how to handle. But the way he looked at me like I was interesting in some other kind of way was just wrong. Like I would be fun to play with, and not in a sexual manner at all. It worried me. And that was why I'd turned tail and run back to this place. Because while Bridge was a hundred percent a predator, I trusted him a hell of a lot more than I trusted Middleton.

The smash of something falling turned my body around, and I frowned at Bridge's study. Was that where he was? I marched over and didn't even knock because my heels made that *clip-clop* sound on the marble, and I assumed he would have heard me. Besides, I wasn't going to give him the opportunity to reject me now, was I?

Inside the room, I stepped on glass shards and instantly stopped. The brown liquid on the ground told me what had happened. When I lifted my gaze, I found Bridge's shocked one snapped to mine. Eyes wide, brows lifted, mouth slightly open. "What the fuck are you doing here?"

"Well, as I was informed, I live here now. Is that not the case?"

"You left me, so no, not really the case."

My heart squeezed at the sound of that. And something about his voice shattered me into finer pieces than his broken glass. Because while the glass might be able to be reassembled, after that phrasing, my heart couldn't be.

"I didn't leave you. I just... I needed to think."

"You fucking *left*. Turn around and go back."

"No, Bridge. I'm not turning around and going back. You're right. I shouldn't have left. I should have stayed so we could talk. I was hasty, and I'm sorry."

He scowled at me. "I don't need you. I'll figure something else out."

"This isn't about you needing me or not." I deftly avoided the glass and closed the door behind me. And then I leaned up against it, well aware that his hand was gripped around a glass bottle of amber liquid. And were those... scones on his desk? There were crumbs on the dark wood and a few around his mouth. Who ate scones in the middle of the night? "I-I need you."

He pushed away from his desk, standing straight as he put the bottle down. "What's the matter?"

"I—" What the hell did I say?

Apologies work well.

The idea of an apology made my mouth dry out. I wasn't usually one for them because the way I figured it, if I was being my authentic self, I had nothing to apologize for. But now was not the time to be stubborn.

"I'm sorry, I shouldn't have left. And you were right. Middleton is dangerous. I think I've bitten off more than I can chew."

His eyes went wide. "Did he hurt you?" Before I knew what was happening, he was striding toward me, but his body had lost some of the grace that I was used to. Instead, his charge was force-ful. Determined. I had nowhere to back up to. When Bridge reached me, his big hands roamed all over my body, but not in a sexual way. This wasn't about wanting me. This wasn't about the kiss on the roof. He was checking me for harm.

"I'm okay. He didn't hurt me. He just scared me, I guess."

"I'll fucking kill him." His voice was barely more than a guttural growl.

The scent of scotch wrapped around me and also a faint vanilla scent. "While that would make me ever so happy, I don't think that's going to work. Something tells me he's hard to kill."

Bridge frowned then, releasing me and taking a deliberate step back. "What happened?"

"It was a job." I inhaled deeply, and then let the air whoosh out of my lungs, emptying them. My body sagged, the tension rolling away with his nearness. "He was testing me, I think. I handled it like I would handle anything. This guy, Weston Price, his wife vanished, right? And it was like Middleton wanted to see what I would do with the details. The first thing I always tell my clients is that I will not to be lied to. I can't help them if they lie. We want to avoid judgment even if we have done terrible things. We don't want to be ostracized from the community. Little lies can be dealt with, but big lies, like, 'Hey, I killed my wife, now you help me cover it up,' I'm not okay with that. So I ran down my spiel to him and said that he shouldn't lie to me. If you killed your wife, let's call the police. Let's get you a lawyer. We'll find a technicality to get you off. Those kinds of things, that's what I say to my clients. And then—"

Bridge frowned and interjected before I could go on. "You think he killed his wife?"

I shook my head. "I don't know. I don't think so. There were some clothes missing. A few kid clothes and toys too. I think she left. Middleton claims that Price had told him they'd been having problems. But there was something about the way he said it. Like he knew a lot about their family. A lot about the wife. I don't know. I wish I could explain, but it just... It sent a shiver down my spine. He asked me what I would do if Price *had* killed his wife. I told him I'd call a lawyer and get the police there. And while my answer was right and he said he was very impressed with it... I don't know. I felt assessed in this kind of way that frightened me. I can't explain it. Can I say I came back because I was scared and I got a bad feeling about all that?"

Bridge nodded slowly. "Of course you can, Ems. Middleton and his friends, they did that to Toby. By all regards, it was negligence, but it might have been deliberate. They left him to die. These people are deadly and dangerous. And of course you should be scared. Knowing what I know now about the inner workings of the Elite, do I think more than one of them is capable of actual murder? Absolutely. Do I think Middleton is one of them? A hundred percent. So you're right to be scared. That's why we wanted to handle this together as a team."

I nodded. " I see that now. And I should probably listen. I just don't like to be left out. I thought that's what you were doing. I still think you're doing it, but I am pretty sure you are also trying to keep me safe."

Bridge nodded as he shoved his big hands in his pockets. "Exactly."

I lifted my gaze to him. "Are we going to talk about that kiss?"

He swallowed hard. "Ems..."

"We have to talk about it. I don't want to be in this house with you at war. You kissed me. And yeah, okay, cool. I get the impression you're pretty pissed off about it. I get it; you never wanted me. But if we're going to live here together, you can't do that hot and cold thing. You can't kiss me like you want me and then go all cold and distant again. It's confusing the hell out of me. And because we have to pretend kiss in front of people all the time, it will make it worse. I like to know where I'm at."

His gaze blazed on mine. "You think I don't want you?"

I laughed. "Fine. Since we're doing the honesty thing right now and I come with my tail between my legs, I'll have you know, I've had a thing for you since I was little. Since I was ten years old. Through the years, you've made it very obvious you don't feel the same. Which I get, because God, I was a pill. A really hard one to swallow, I know. I'm a lot to handle. I get it. And that's fine. Although, there's clearly something wrong with you if you don't want me. But since we have to fake it in public, I'd rather you didn't fake it when no one's around to see it."

"You know I'm still going to kiss you. I have to."

Why was he acting obtuse? "I know, but what I'm saying is that I don't want you to kiss me when there's no one to see it. It confuses me. It's not fair. After all, you know how I feel about you, and it feels like you're toying with me, which isn't fair, and it's cruel. You're a lot of things, Bridge, but you're not callously cruel. I know that as a fact."

"You think I was being cruel when I kissed you?"

"Weren't you?" My voice was husky and soft, and I forced

myself to tilt my chin to meet his gaze. He was searching mine. But he nodded.

"I won't kiss you again."

"Right. Awesome." My heart squeezed again. "Now that that's taken care of, you want to tell me what the fuck happened with the glass shards?"

"Ems..."

I shook my head. No more displays of emotion in front of him. "Why are you having lots of scotch lately? Last time I checked, you barely even drink. You only have one glass when you are with the lads. But I noticed it's become a regular occurrence lately. What is happening?"

He looked like he wanted to say something but then stopped himself. Then he opened his mouth. "My father, that's what's wrong. Tonight he approached me after the meeting. As a matter of fact, he told me to stay the fuck away from you. And he admitted that he paid Mina to pretend to be in love with me for three bloody years. I've known that for months now, but hearing him say it so casually sort of set me off. That first glass of scotch wasn't even doing the trick. I didn't know where to direct my anger, thus the scones. And when I was still mad, the glass."

"Is that going to be a habit now?"

He shrugged. "It's no secret that I like my control."

"What? You need to be in charge of things? I'm shocked. I never would have guessed it, honestly. I always thought you were a little fast and loose."

The corner of his lips twitched then, and that warmed the center of my chest just a little. I liked that I could at least start to pull him out of his dark mood.

Because you're a glutton for punishment.

"I really tried with Mina. I had to be that guy. I tried to be open and tried to be what she wanted. She was the perfect kind of woman. At least what I thought was perfect then. Now I realize that all she represented was all the things I'd been denied as a kid.

The kind of woman my father was with instead of my mother. Sophisticated and poised. I didn't even realize that through the years I'd been conditioned to want a woman like that because that's what had been denied me. I was Lord Edmond Edgerton's son, but I had none of the things that came with the name. And as a kid, I thought I wanted it. But almost from the moment I had Mina, I knew something was off. I *felt* it. And still, I thought it was me. So I tried to make her happy, tried to atone for not knowing all the things I should, not having all the things I should, even though as an adult, I have more than enough. And hearing my father try to control me and keep me from you just... I don't know. It set me off. He insisted I give up our charade. He doesn't want me marrying you for some reason."

I frowned. "I don't even know your father."

"That's just the point. It's not about knowing him. It is a matter of him trying to control me. Again."

"Ah, so let me guess, you're more determined to marry me now?"

To my surprise, he shook his head. "I was going to marry you before he even said anything."

I told myself this was no different from what I already knew. I'd just said that I was done with the whole let's-not-play thing. But then there I was, wishing that he'd come forth with feelings for me.

Idiot.

"I promised you I would see this through. I promised you that I would get justice for Toby. I gave you my word. And currently, this is the only way. The safest way, because your way was dangerous. And so I give you my word. Unfortunately, that requires you marrying me. Now, if you don't want to, I will find some other way. But you've waited eleven years, and you deserve closure. I promised I would give it to you. So here we are."

I watched him. There was something about him that reminded me of the boy I once knew. "Bridge, you don't have to do this."

"It's not about having to do anything, Emma. It's about wanting to. You should go to bed. I'm going to get this mess cleaned up."

I frowned at him. "You're not going to call someone?"

He hung his head and shook it. "No. My mess, I clean."

I watched him for a long moment, and then I turned and walked out of the study. That was the most information Bridge Edgerton had ever given me in my entire life. The most he'd spoken about his feelings. He was trying to help me find closure for Toby. And I'd been fighting him.

The problem was, even though I had resolved to not let my feelings get in the way of what had to be done, his quiet declaration of how he was doing this for me only made me fall harder.

So much for determination.

I went to the kitchen and grabbed the dust bin, a wipe cloth, and some brushes. I immediately returned to the study to help him clean up. I found him in the exact same position, but with his shoulders sagged. I stood in front of him, and he lifted his misty gaze to mine.

It crushed me to see him like that, but I tried to ignore it and handed him the rag. "I'll get all of the big pieces, you wipe up the rest."

His gaze searched mine and then dipped to my lips before lifting back up to meet my eyes again. "What?"

"We're a team, Bridge. And when we're a team, your mess is my mess. And my mess is your mess. Come on, let's get this cleaned up and get to bed. I have the impression that we're going to have to revamp our plans tomorrow."

And for the first time since I'd agreed to this arrangement, Bridge and I worked together.

Chapter Thirteen

Emma

I knew it was a dream. I always did. But cognitively knowing it was a dream and actually experiencing it as a dream, were two different things. Because in the moment when the fear wrapped around me, and I wanted to cry, it was no dream.

"Daddy, Daddy, please don't go. Please don't go. Don't leave me." And the man whose face I could never see clearly would peel me off of his legs and walk out the door. Like he was making a narrow escape for his life. It didn't matter how many times I chased after him. I could feel it in my bones, the fear, the sadness, the worry. All of those were real as I lay there in my bed, wishing, hoping, and praying that Daddy, whoever that was, would come back. But he never did.

I could feel the warmth of my mother's arms around me, holding me, her voice crooning and shushing me, telling me that it would be okay. But I knew better. I knew that it would not be okay. Nothing would ever be okay again.

And then there was Toby, chasing after the car on his bike, his little legs going as fast as they could. He was throwing things at the car and shouting until his bike crashed into a telephone pole. And he laid there, his little body on the street, my mother running after him, screaming, "Tobias, Tobias, get up. Get up." And there I was sitting on the pavement, watching other cars right on the road. Some pausing to make sure that the little boy at the side of the road was okay, others driving on. My mother screaming after Tobias, running after the man in the red car. I was sobbing and wailing because the man had left us. Walked away never to be seen again.

I knew it was a dream. But still, every single time it happened, it felt so real, so palpable, and crushing my very soul. I woke up in tears, sobbing and gasping, the pain all too real and vivid. The pain was like fresh wounds torn asunder, bleeding and weeping over everything.

"Ems, are you okay?" Bridge's strong arms were on my shoulders, shaking me alert as I sobbed and blubbered.

Slowly I dragged my eyes open through the sorrow. "Uh, ah, what?"

"Ems, you're crying."

I scooted back against the headboard and wiped my tears. "I'm sorry. It was just a dream."

Bridge eased back on his haunches. He was shirtless, wearing nothing but boxers. I got the impression that the boxers were for my benefit and that maybe he slept nude. But just the idea of it made my whole body warm, and soft, and pliant. "I was... I have it all the time."

"That's some dream, love. What's it about?"

I shook my head. "Don't worry about it. Go back to bed. I'm sorry I woke you."

He watched me for a moment. "You don't have to be sorry. We're partners, remember? You can talk to me."

It was at the tip of my tongue to tell him that I didn't need him and that I didn't need anyone. I was fine. The same lie I'd been telling myself for years and years. The same lie that wasn't accurate or true. Or useful, honestly. Instead, I whispered, "I think it's a memory of the day my father left."

Bridge rolled forward on his knees and braced his arms on the edge of the bed as he listened.

"I think I was three, so Toby must have been six. He looked about that size. The man, who was presumably our father, climbed into his red BMW. No, it was maroon, I think. That's a more accurate description. I wrapped myself around his legs as I begged him to stay. I knew if I could just hold on tight enough, he would feel so guilty and he wouldn't want to go. Instead, he just picked me up and hugged me, gave me a bit of a squeeze, and told me to be strong for my mama because she was going to need my help. And then he left me there on the bottom stair. In the dream, I break down crying. My mother wrapped her arms around me and held me tight, telling me it would be okay and that she loved me. Toby chased after the car on his bike, but then he crashed against some kind of pole, and then my mother chased after him and I was left there, crying. My whole family was devastated by the man in the maroon car who drove away. And that's when I woke up crying. So sorry about that."

Bridge's voice was soft. Full of gravel, but soothing. "I'm sorry. That's terrible."

"Yeah well, like I said, it could be a memory. It could be made up to fill in the gaps of what happened with my parents, you know?"

"That's why you still go to their flat, isn't it?"

I nodded. "How did you know?"

He shrugged. "You're not going to like the answer."

I tucked the duvet around me, under my armpits. "Tell me."

He sighed and gave me a sheepish smile. "Ever since, you know, what happened to Tobes, Ben, East, and I, we've been looking out for you. Your mum didn't like it, so we stayed out of sight. Whenever you were having trouble at school, or she seemed stressed out, we'd put a private investigator on it. Someone just to look out for you. Security from afar, I suppose."

I frowned. "What?"

He shrugged. "Yeah, sorry. Except, I'm not, because one of the guys followed you to the rooftop of a flat across from another building of flats. A little investigation, and we found out that the place had been rented by a corporation. East, of course, being East, unraveled it. It's your mum's flat. Your father bought it for her. And every now and again, you would go when you were feeling sad. Or even when something good happened, you would go and sit up there and drink. I can only imagine how much it hurts."

"Well, you don't have to imagine. You have access to your father, and you hate him."

"Yes, but your mum and dad were different. They loved each other. My mum was just a fling who got knocked up. He stuck it out for the first year, all right. He'd send her money and things, but then it all dried up. He didn't turn back up again until I was ten and off to boarding school. He insisted. So to really piss him off when I got there, I changed my name to his."

My eyes went wide. "You changed your name on purpose?"

He nodded. "I mean, I could do whatever I wanted, right? After all, he gave his consent by putting his name on my birth certificate. And like it or not, he is actually listed on my birth certificate as my father."

That surprised me. "He allowed it?"

"I think in the early days, a part of him wanted to claim me, but as my mother's demands increased, he wanted none of it anymore. But it was too late for him to change his mind like that. Although I had my mother's last name, he was listed as my father. So at boarding school, I took his name on purpose to piss him off. You should have seen it. Ugh, he was well ticked off. He came to school once screaming at me about why I did it. But there was nothing that could be done about it unless he wanted a scandal, which, of course, he didn't."

"So he has never claimed you?"

Bridge shrugged. "Only when I was tapped for the Elite. I think he hoped I would fail the tests."

I frowned. "What are these tests?"

Bridge chuckled. "Nice try. You know I can't talk about that."

"Oh come on, these tests killed my brother."

Bridge's gaze snapped to mine. "The tests didn't kill your brother. Toby passed the tests with flying colors. Initiation night killed your brother. Three men killed him. Two of whom, we've made to pay. We're working on the third."

I watched him. "There's something about the way that you say you're going to make them pay. Is it bad that it gives me a little bit of a thrill?"

He laughed. "Not bad, exactly. It just makes you an odd duck."

"Oh, I'm odd." He didn't know the half of it.

He smiled. "It's okay. I like odd." He pushed to his feet.

"Bridge?"

He smiled down at me. "Yeah, Ems?"

"Would you, um, just stay with me for a minute? Just until I fall asleep. This dream, it just lingers." I was embarrassed. Humiliated, because hadn't I just given a big speech about how I wasn't going to chase him anymore? But this wasn't about that, and I needed something, otherwise, the melancholy would drag me down and take days to shake. I just needed comfort.

He nodded. "Of course. Slide over. It's a big enough bed for the both of us."

Except, when he got into the king-size bed, sliding between the cool Egyptian cotton sheets, the bed no longer felt nearly as big. It felt crowded. He was enormous. Over six feet, with a wingspan like an eagle. Jesus. And I wasn't exactly petite either.

He reached over and took my hand. His big one wrapping around mine. "It's okay, Ems. I have you. You can sleep now."

I didn't know how the hell I was supposed to sleep. This was a poor, poor idea because now he was holding my hand and electric shocks were running up my arm. Even though I'd said I was going to stop, let him go, and not do this to myself anymore. But here I was in bed with the man whose attention I'd been trying to garner since I was ten years old. He was holding my hand in bed with me. Shirtless. Not like this was a recipe for disaster at all. I was likely to be up the rest of the night, but at least the warmth that he shared with me chased out some of the darkness. So even if I was going to be awake all night, I wasn't alone.

* * *

Bridge

It was warm in the bed. Warm and sweet, and it smelled like vanilla and jasmine, and God... I wanted to stay there forever.

I reached out and pulled the scent closer. It smelled like soft, warm woman. I knew this was a dream, but I was not letting it go. As my hands sneaked up a shirt, wrapped around, and cupped her breasts, I smiled. "God, you're so fucking soft."

The dream woman turned, and her face was Emma's. I was slightly alarmed, but Emma felt fucking incredible. Jesus Christ, she was smiling at me. For once, her guard was down and she wanted me. I couldn't for the life of me remember why we couldn't do this, why we couldn't be together. I couldn't think about a single reason why I had stayed away from her. I held her closer until her backside met the length of my straining dick, and she wiggled against me. "Bridge."

"Yes, Ems. God, you smell incredible, and your ass... I have been dreaming about this for so long." I mumbled that into the back of her neck as I kissed along her spine. Then I moved the kisses over to her shoulder, between her ear and the joint, then nuzzled in where her scent was strongest. Under her shirt, the soft cotton pulled the back of my knuckles, and my thumb found her nipple. I brushed it back and forth, rolling it around until it pebbled.

"God, you're responsive too. I've been an idiot."

"Bridge, please."

"What do you want?" I asked her, my voice full of gravel.

"Bridge."

I pulled her closer and angled the kisses better, open-mouthed. This time, I tested the weight of her breasts fully. She filled my hand, and I squeezed gently. Her ass started to move against me. More insistently now. I tucked my free hand down the front of her shorts. When her legs squeezed it, I mumbled against her, "Open. I'm just going to make you feel good."

She groaned. "I can't."

"Yes, you can. I would never hurt you." She hesitated for a moment, but I whispered, "Open, Ems. You'll like it."

She shifted slightly so her hips were opened wide to me. My fingers found her slick folds. Who knew Emma Varma was smooth and slick? She'd waxed. Fucking hell. Her warm slickness coated my fingers, and I hitched my breath. My other thumb and fore-finger plucked at her nipple. She burrowed in my arms, and I bit into her neck. "God, I have dreamed about this moment since I was eighteen and you kissed me outside of that club. I knew you'd be soft. I knew you'd be so fucking soft. I knew when I touched you that you'd be hot and slick. Fuck, I want you so bad, Ems."

She whimpered. "Bridge, please... Just don't tease me."

"I wouldn't tease you."

And as my fingers found her tight button and slid over it, an electrical hum ran over my skin as she groaned low. I repeated the motion. I needed to turn this around. This was an awkward arrangement.

If I could just climb over her, I could suck on her tits. I'd spend my morning feasting on them. I could kiss on her belly, slide her shorts down, and then I could set my mouth on top of her sex and not come up for hours. She burrowed again in my arms, thrashing now.

"Bridge, God. Oh my God."

Something was wrong. She kept thrashing. "Ems, hold still."

She wasn't trying to get away. She was trying to twist around and get closer. "Easy does it. Here, come here, climb on top, and I'll..."

Suddenly there was a hand pressing against my chest and I groaned. I tried to lift my eyes to look at her face, but my eyes wouldn't open. What the hell? Why wouldn't they open? I tried harder, and finally, I cracked one open and Emma's wide gaze filled my field of vision. "Bridge."

Her voice was sharp, and I blinked as the ethereal wisps of the dream vanished. All except for one. My hand was very much still up her tank top. And my thumb... Fucking hell. My gaze was hooked right where my thumb brushed over her nipple. "Oh fuck, Emma."

I released her and backed up. "I'm sorry. Fucking sorry. I didn't—"

She was panting. Her pupils were wide and dilated. And she was biting her bottom lip. "Yeah, I figured that was a dream. And just my luck, my dream won't let go."

"Oh God, did I hurt you?"

She frowned. "Hurt me?"

"I... Fuck, I was dreaming Ems, and I, um, we have... this was... Oh God."

"Relax. You fumbled around my shorts for a second, but you couldn't find the clasps."

I was a prick. "Jesus. I'm sorry. You needed comfort and I... Well, I guess you know who you're dealing with now."

She stared at me for a long beat. "When we're awake, you act like you don't want me. But when you're asleep, you want me? What is this?"

"Ems, I'm sorry."

"No," she said crisply. "You have made that perfectly clear."

Fuck. I ran my hands through my hair and sat up. "Emma, yesterday you said a lot of bullshit, and I let you say it because it was easier and I could separate myself from you more."

She inched away from me. "What? What are you talking about?"

"You're busy sitting here thinking I don't want you, when you are all I have ever wanted since the moment we first kissed. Hell, even way before that. Before I even understood. You are infuriating and stubborn, and fuck, so alive. I wish I was like that. I wish I could be like that, but I can't. And I have responsibilities. I made your brother a fucking promise. I made him a *promise*, Ems. Someone like me touching someone like you is not living up to my end of that promise."

Her bottom lip trembled. "You made Toby a promise, and that's why you won't touch me?"

"Yeah, that's why I won't fucking touch you. I promised to look after you, and I always will. I know it seems dumb to you, but he was someone I really cared about. I don't care about many people. Toby and Drew and Ben and East, they are my family other than my mum. So I have to keep that promise. It's like an oath to me. But just so we're both really fucking clear, I do want you. Very much. I'm not trying to push you away. I'm not trying to hurt you. I'm trying to keep you as safe as possible and untouched by me. It's been an impossibility for fifteen fucking years. Now you're here, and it's even harder."

I thought she was going to punch me. She looked like she *wanted* to punch me. But then the weirdest thing happened. Emma's lips twitched, and then she snorted and fell over, howling with laughter. "Oh my God, I can't believe you just said that."

I frowned, not understanding. Was she mocking me? "What?"

I didn't like how it felt. I liked her laughter, but not when it was directed at me. It felt like all those years ago when the fancy boys from Eton had mocked my accent.

"Oh my God, you said it's hard." And she erupted in another fit of giggles. I sat back, replaying the conversation. And then I heard it. And despite myself, I started to laugh. A real, genuine upfront laugh. And just like that, the tension flowing and ebbing between us, ever so taught and ready to snap, eased just a little.

She sat up again, trying to contain herself, but then she just kept howling. "I could feel it was hard."

And then she erupted in another fit of giggles. And before I knew it, the two of us were laughing like kids.

I'd never had this. And I realized that this was what was missing. All that time with Mina, the easy laughter, the ability to relax, the knowledge that everything was okay. I'd never had that.

Finally, Emma turned to me. "Your first mistake was telling me that you want me. Because now it's my mission in life to make you give in. You made a promise to my brother. And you're keeping it because he made me promise him that no matter what, I would do what makes me happy. I think when Toby said to look out for me, he meant to look out for me from other people, not from you. That's what I think. You want me? All right. One day, very, very soon, you're going to give in. Mark my words. Meanwhile, you stay hard. I'm going to grab a shower."

And then she slid out of bed and sauntered away. Her ass jiggling in those tight boy-shorts over her brown skin made me want to bite it.

She's right. One day very soon, you're going to give in and give Emma Varma exactly what she wants.

Just one problem with that. I was certain I wouldn't have any control.

And I was going to terrify her.

Chapter Fourteen

Bridge

That light feeling from waking up with Emma didn't last. No sooner did I hear her turn on the faucet to brush her teeth, than my phone buzzed on the nightstand. Blearily I glanced at the bedside clock. It was barely six-thirty.

I snatched it up quickly. "This is Edgerton."

"Mr. Edgerton, this is Sister Mary Luce from St. Catherine's Academy. This is about your sister."

People always acted as if panic was hot. For me, it was icy and cold.

Brain already in speed mode, I growled, "What's happened?"

"I'm sorry to have to say this, but Darcy broke curfew last night. We discovered she was missing this morning."

My fucking sister. "Right. I'll be there in a few hours."

"Thank you Mr. Edgerton." She sniffed the sniff of the indignant. I knew that sound of exasperation well. It was the sound you heard anywhere near Darcy.

I wished I could explain the feeling, the worry, the swirling panic, the way it gripped my gut and twisted it, and those little minions with pointy pitchforks that would stab at intermittent times. Off campus. For the love of Christ. Anything could have happened to her. Of all the reckless behavior. She knew better. Fury coursed through my veins. I couldn't show that though. I needed to stay calm. I couldn't let Emma see me like this.

"Is something wrong?"

Her soft question from the door brought me out of my reverie. I swallowed hard. "I, uh—" I cleared my throat. I was already jumping out of bed. "There's an emergency."

Emma strode over quickly, which dislodged her tank top, exposing a full breast with cinnamon-tipped nipples. I swallowed hard and turned around immediately.

"There's something I have to take care of. Family thing."

"Let me come. I can help."

I shook my head as I shoved on my boxers. "No, I don't need your help." I could hear her stomping around to stand in front of me before I could grab the rest of my clothes and jump to the shower.

I glowered down at her. It was my full-on glower face. It usually worked wonders to get people out of my way, but it didn't work with her.

"We just had a whole moment, you know, where I had a bad dream, I talked to you about it. You were supportive. And while we're not in a real relationship, we are family, aren't we?"

My mouth was dry. And there was stinging somewhere in the region of the upper part of my nose. What the fuck was that? I nodded slowly. "Yes, but *I* have to do this."

"Yes, I understand that. I'm not saying that you don't. If something's wrong with your mum, you have to go. So, let me help you. In case you haven't realized, you have a crisis manager here. So you go and take a shower, and while you're doing that, I'll go turn the coffee maker on and fix something to eat, because you need to eat before you go deal with whatever it is. Then I'll have a shower, and I will come with you. Do you understand me?"

I wasn't sure if it was the steel in her gaze, or the set of her lush lips, or just the steadiness of her. I've never pictured Emma as steady. In my head, Emma was lively, peppy and always bouncing. As if she couldn't settle. But there was something so solid about her now. Grounded. She knew I needed someone, and she was stepping up. No questions, no hesitations. Just 'let's go.' I could feel myself nodding. "Okay."

"Right. You have five minutes." And then she turned and was already running out of the bedroom and heading for the stairs.

She didn't give a shit that she was in her tank top and panties. She didn't give a shit that there was staff crawling around the house. She gave no fucks. And fuck, I wanted her.

And not in the same way that I'd wanted her my whole life. Not in that constant sexual hum kind of way, but one that was solid and everlasting. I wanted to hold on to her because even though I was worried, the tension in my gut somehow eased when she was around. Knowing that I didn't have to carry anything alone anymore, that was all Emma.

Within thirty minutes, we were out the door. Emma's hair was still wet, and she was grappling with something in her purse, but we moved without stopping toward the car. Steven, one of the replacement guards I'd found, drove us to Heathrow.

When she realized where we were headed, she frowned and asked, "Where are we going? I thought your mum was in London."

"Just a quick flight to Austria."

She seemed satisfied, and after that she didn't ask me any questions. It wasn't until we were on the flight on the private London Lord's jet that she sat back, folded her hands over her middle, and leveled her gaze on me. Her dark eyes saw straight through me, to the soul. "Is this the secret? The one Mina was telling me about? When she alluded that I didn't know you?"

I glanced up from my laptop and cursed under my breath. "Yes, this is the secret. I..." What would I say? How did I explain this?

She shook her head. "I can see you're doing the thing where you're looking to apply a filter, wondering how little you can tell me. Don't do that. I'm on a plane with you to Austria. Unless you plan on killing me, you need to tell me what's going on. I didn't ask any questions, but I could tell you needed me, so I came. And now, since we're here, I know you have some things to do, but just tell me what they are. Tell me what's happening so I know what to expect when we land."

She was right. I needed to be more open somehow. We were in this together. Like it or not , we were a team.

I closed the laptop and turned to face her. "All right, that phone call was from a school in Austria. St. Catherine's. It's a boarding school."

There was nothing on her face, no expression. She was completely stoic. "Okay, so boarding school, right. What's the problem?"

"Darcy, she's been missing for eight hours. No one knows where she is."

Emma just blinked at me. "Okay, and who's Darcy?"

I sighed. "She's my sister."

That was when Emma frowned. "But you don't have a sister."

"Yeah, we've managed to keep that pretty much under wraps."

Her brows lifted. "We? Ben and East?"

I shook my head. "No. Even they don't know about Darcy. Mum knows. And well, I guess my father."

"I need you to start at the beginning."

I didn't want to get into this. I didn't want to have to go into the lies that summed up my family because then she would have all the tools she needed to permanently damage me.

Or maybe she won't. Maybe, for once, you can trust someone.

Considering she was on her way to meet Darcy, there was no way of avoiding it anymore. "All right then. When I was almost eighteen, my father had long since fucked-up my mother. He turned up one day with a child. A baby, really. She wasn't even one. You know how kids have those like, two middle teeth on the bottom, that's about how old she was. She had these big dark eyes. They kind of remind me of yours. Curly dark hair. Full on baby rolls. She was so fat. If there ever was a picture of what a baby should look like, healthy, happy, giggling, that was her. Darcy. My mother almost had a heart attack when she opened the door to find my father on the doorstep. Then he just handed Darcy to her and said, "I need you to look after her."

Emma frowned then. "Wait, after he'd walked out on your mother and barely acknowledged you, he turned up and left a baby with her?"

I nodded. "Yeah. He'd had some French mistress who he got knocked up. I guess she was trying to give up the baby for adoption. When he found out about it, he was furious that his child would have ended up in someone else's hands, or maybe just that he didn't have control over the situation, who the fuck knows? Anyway, he took the baby and brought her to my mother for her to raise, because God forbid that he should claim the child."

"That is so fucked up."

"Yeah, it is." I sucked in a sharp breath. "What's more fucked up was that her birth certificate named her mother one Claire d' Mall and her father one Bridge Edgerton."

That was it, the moment where her eyes went wide and she sputtered. Had we not been talking about me in this situation, it would have been funny. "What the fuck?"

Once I joined The Elite, I'd looked up Darcy's mother. She was living with some Italian count, wanted nothing to do with her daughter, and said if I ever brought Darcy to her that she'd tell the world a story that matched my father's version. "Yeah. Isn't that great?"

"You are on the birth certificate?"

I nodded slowly. "Either he had it forged, or that's what he told Claire his name was, or fuck if I know. I was just shy of my eighteenth birthday and he dropped off this kid and made it seem as if I'd fathered her."

Emma leaned forward then, elbows planted on her knees,

hands clasped together, her forehead on top of her intertwined fingers. "I can't even fathom this bullshit."

"Yeah, welcome to my world. Anyway, he left her and started sending mum a stipend. Admittedly, it did cover most things for Darcy, like school and such. Then he walked out and that was it. And when my mum threatened to tell the world that I wasn't the baby's father because all it would take was a simple paternity test to prove it, he threatened to release that I was the baby's father. He threatened that he would remove me from Eton, and all the hard work I'd put in would all be in vain, and that my life would be over before it even began. So mum didn't really have much choice. We took in Darcy and raised her like my little sister. Lucky for her, she had access to the best schools for a while, but the money ran out when she was going to secondary school. Dad couldn't be reached, so I paid for her school and all that stuff. She knows I'm her big brother, but she doesn't know who her dad is. At some point, it's going to come out that I'm on her birth certificate and she's going to hate me, even though I haven't done anything wrong."

Emma sighed and sat back. "Forgive me for saying this, but your family is fucked up. Also, I would very much like to kill your father."

"Join the queue. I get first dibs."

"What happened to ladies first?"

I smirked. "Not in this case. For once, let me be the big strong bloke and deal with the arsehole."

She was insistent. "I promise you, I'm deadly."

"Are we really arguing which one of us is going to kill my father?"

She nodded. "Hell, yes. That's despicable, Bridge. That's so awful."

I nodded, feeling completely numb. "Yeah, it is, isn't it? And Darcy had been a handful ever since she went to secondary. She's a pain in the ass. It's like she's looking for something that's missing or trying to figure something out about her place in the world, and I can't help her. Sometimes I wonder if she's just desperate to find out where she fits in, who she really is. Maybe she's sensed it. Maybe she knows. But she doesn't know she was adopted. She thinks my mum is her mum."

Emma sighed. "Oh, Bridge. I don't know when the right time is to tell someone something like that, but you do have to tell her at some point."

"I know, but she's just a kid. And she's my sister. So I'm hesitant to tell her about it because I know she'll be mad, and I'm afraid we'll lose her."

"And you love her."

I couldn't help the smile that spread over my face. "Oh, undoubtedly. She's the only thing I've ever done right, you know?

That confession was difficult for me to make. There were a million times I'd done all the wrong things. A million times I had regrets or wished I'd done things differently. I'd managed to make enough right decisions to end up exactly in this position right now, but there were a million other little things that I wished I had taken a chance on and been willing to accept the risks.

Like Emma.

No, not like Emma. She was off-limits.

Then she lifted her gaze and met mine. "Thank you for telling me."

I could see it in her gaze. It wasn't so much what I'd told her but that I had trusted her when I trusted nobody. And as much as I loved my mates, even they didn't know about Darcy.

She and Mina were the only ones. Mina only found out because she'd seen paperwork from the school. But she'd believed that I was Darcy's father. Full-on believed it. She still believed it even though I told her the truth.

"There's just something about you that makes me trust you. I know you won't use this against me."

"How could I? You actually care about people. I mean, you have that fuck-everyone demeanor. But deep down, under that hard cement shell, you're an all right bloke. You're even kind and considerate."

"Oh, easy now. I have a reputation to protect."

She just stared at me for a long moment. And then nodded slowly. "I'm sure she's okay."

"I bloody hope so."

* * *

Emma

The whole flight I'd watch Bridge try to control his emotions, but when we took the helicopter from the airport to a helipad on the school premises, I watched some of that control slip and prayed he wasn't going to be too hard on his sister when we found her.

Maybe I felt a natural affinity for Darcy because I'd *been* her. Angry with the world and not sure why. Desperate for someone to love her. Wondering what was wrong with her that she didn't have a normal family like everybody else. Sometimes all that rage expressed itself in unhealthy ways. Like stalking your parents and watching their flat from a rooftop across the street.

From the moment we'd landed, he'd been on the call with an investigator that was following up with parents of the girls she was friends with and barking orders that sounded a lot like, *Roar, roar. Bloody roar. Sister roar.* Not that I could blame him. He was terrified.

And I could offer little more than platitudes.

But when we walked into the headmistress's, office, I saw a myriad of emotions play over Bridge's face. We found the headmistress in a massive leather chair behind a dark oak desk surrounded by shelves of books. We *also* found Darcy sitting in what looked like a minimalist wooden chair , covered in mud with streaked tears on her face.

A devastating wave of relief washed over Bridge's face. He

almost collapsed into my arms when he saw her. The squeeze of my hand must have given him the strength he needed because just behind the relief, fury, incredulity, and exasperation were hot on its heels. "Jesus fucking Christ, Darcy, what were you thinking?"

The nun in the corner muttered something like, "Tell me about it," then crossed herself. Though it was unclear if the sign of the cross was for all wayward girls like Darcy, for Bridge's cursing, or for herself because she agreed with him.

Darcy, like every wannabe bad girl on her own, plastered on a no-fucks-here face and shrugged. "They shouldn't have called you. I know you're busy."

Bridge's face started turning an alarming shade of lobster red. "Busy? You're my sister. When I hear that you've gone missing, of course, I'm going to come."

Darcy rolled her eyes. "Is that what they told you? I wasn't missing. There was a concert."

Bridge blinked slowly as if trying to parse out her words into an order that made sense. "A concert?"

"More like a festival. I was with friends. I was fine. I even left a note."

Bridge's glower turned to the headmistress. "She left a note?"

The headmistress nodded. "Yes, but she was still missing from campus, so we had to call her parents."

Darcy stepped up. "He's not my father; he's my brother."

The headmistress sighed. "Since you are the one responsible for her, we called you."

Bridge just shook his head. "I wish you had notified me that she'd left a note this morning when you called. I would have still come, but perhaps I wouldn't have lost three years off my life." To Darcy, he said, "You couldn't shoot me a text and say, 'I know they're going to tell you I'm missing, but I'm just off to a concert'?"

Darcy tilted her chin up. "You're telling me you wouldn't have come?"

He scowled. "Of course, I would have come."

She smirked then. And I could see the confidence she felt that she had his love. It was making her bold. I stepped forward then because this was going in circles. I knew how this was going to go. Lectures from both sides. Her sitting there and taking them in and then internally vowing to never listen to them because they didn't know anything.

I had been there. "Hi, Darcy. I'm Emma. I'm your brother's fiancée."

Darcy's gaze went wide as she assessed me, trying to figure out if I was like Mina or not. But then Darcy jumped up, ran to me, and gave me a tight hug. "Oh my God, thank God, because I loathed Mina skanky pants. She was the worst."

I hadn't expected the hug, to be frank. Or the skanky pants nickname for Mina.

Bridge scowled at me as if he hadn't wanted Darcy to know.

"Yeah, well, I'm not too fond of skanky pants myself."

She grinned at me as if she had a co-conspirator already. "So when's the big day? Are you going to spring me from this place for the wedding?"

"Oh, we're likely to elope. More than likely."

Darcy frowned. "Oh my God, you let him talk you into that? Bridge, I know you hate people, but God, you're not even going to give the poor girl a wedding before she's settled to you for the rest of her life?"

Bridge looked like he wanted to throw something. "Sister, can you give us a moment?"

"Gladly." She stood with a huff then sighed. "Please when I get home, can we have a wedding? I love weddings. Love, love, love." She was effervescent and sweet. Gone was the scowling adolescent.

"Ah, something tells me you just love to party."

She grinned. "But isn't it the best part?"

I nodded. "Yes, weddings are about the celebrations."

"So," she sat back on her seat. "Tell me who you are."

"Um, well, I've known your brother for a long time. He and my brother were best friends."

Darcy's gaze cleared all of a sudden. "Oh my God, *that* Emma. At last, Bridge."

I turned my gaze to Bridge then. I noticed his wide eyes, and then he cleared his throat. "I'm not here to listen to anything you have to say about that. I'm very disappointed in you, Darcy."

I put my hand up. "Bridge, give the poor girl a break. Darcy, what were you saying?"

She gave me an impish grin. "I remember your brother. Uncle Toby. He came to the house before."

"How did you know Toby was my brother?"

"You look like the softer version of him. The girl version. Mostly, it's the eyes. You have the exact same eyes."

I'd never heard that before. "Yeah, I suppose we do."

"Bridge has been obsessed with you forever. One time, I found letters that you'd written him in his room. He was holding them and stuffed them in a drawer."

The hot wash of embarrassment hit my face.

Oh. God.

The letters. I did not want to think about those letters and the things I wrote in those. Fucking hell.

I cleared my throat. "Letters?"

"Yeah. Hot stuff, really. Well, I mean, to a nine-year-old which is when I found them. They were well worn too. As if he'd handled them a lot, mind you. Did you know he held on to them?"

The heat crept up my neck, to my face, to the tops of my ears. Oh, God. I couldn't look at him. I could not look at him.

I'd sent those letters after the concert. The one where this bloke had tried to manhandle me. Bridge had taken care of him. But then after, before he put me in the taxi home, we kissed. It had been single-handedly the hottest experience I'd ever had. Granted, I was only a teenager and hadn't had any life experience at all. So I'd written those letters to try and get my thoughts together about my feelings for him. Big mistake. He'd never written back. I had assumed he'd tossed them or possibly never even gotten them. I'd sent them to Eton, after all. Or worse, maybe he and his friends had laughed at me.

Although, I couldn't see Toby putting up with that. So I knew he at least hadn't told the others. Ben and East had never said anything. And Drew would have teased me mercilessly. But I'd forgotten about those damn letters.

"Oh, the letters. Funny you should mention those."

Darcy grinned mischievously. "Oh yeah, really. I mean, you were my introduction into like all these feelings things."

I swallowed hard. "Oh boy."

"Yeah, and of course, Bridge was livid when he saw I'd gotten into the safe and that I was reading them. He told me they were 'well inappropriate.'"

I couldn't help but mutter, "Wow, you are a handful."

She frowned then. "Everyone always says that."

I laughed. "Well, I would have said that about me too."

"You know what? My brother didn't say that. He just said, 'Emma,' and then made a stern face."

I laughed. "Yes, I know the stern face well."

Darcy laughed. "I like you a lot more than the other one."

"Thank you. But maybe you could cut your brother some slack, yeah? Because he was worried. And having been you, I don't think I ever gave any thought to the consequences of my actions or about who might be worried and looking for me."

She frowned. "But I did leave a note. I'm not selfish."

I stepped back, watching her curiously. "I know, but did you think your brother wouldn't come?"

She pursed her lips then. "I didn't ask him to come."

"He's your brother. Don't you think he loves you?"

Another purse. "Yes, but I didn't ask him to come. It's not my fault. He made a choice."

I nodded. "That's fair. He did make the choice. But the choice was you. It's always you. But you know that, don't you?"

She crossed her arms then, staring at a spot just over Bridge's shoulder. "I'm not sure I like you anymore."

"Well, I mean, one former bad girl to another, you don't have to like me. But I'm speaking the truth, and you should pay heed. There are easier ways to get your brother's attention. Much easier ways. You don't have to self-destruct to do it."

"I lied, Bridge. I don't like this one very much at all. Can we get Mina back? She at least thought of only herself."

Bridge chuckled. "Mina's not coming back. And I'm pretty sure you're the one who wanted her to go."

Darcy scowled. "This one thinks she knows too much."

Bridge shrugged. "You know she's right though. You don't have to try so hard to get my attention. If you want to see me, see me. Just call me. I'll come any weekend."

She frowned. "You're busy. You're *always* busy."

"I am busy. But for my sister, I can make some adjustments or have you come home."

She lifted a brow. "Mina is not there, is she?"

"You think Emma and Mina could ever stay in the same place?"

She laughed and then her gaze focused on me. "No, Emma would eat her alive."

"You're right. Mina's not my favorite person at all."

I was surprised to find Darcy sitting back as she assessed me again. "Fine. You're not so bad."

"Hmm, I have the approval of a teenager. Be still my heart."

Darcy just rolled her eyes. "Okay, can we go get ice cream since you're here?"

Bridge rolled his eyes. "You're not getting a reward for sneaking out and going to a concert and making everyone worried. Now, we'll go get something to eat and we'll spend some time together because I recognize I haven't seen you in a month, and that's got you feeling insecure. But we're not going for ice-cream. You're not six anymore."

Darcy pouted about that. And I watched Bridge. He might not be her father, but he certainly had that daddy energy going. Which was extremely sexy. "Yeah, I think dinner is a fantastic idea."

He searched my gaze and I nodded. I recognized that he was looking for some kind of indication that he'd said or done the right thing. But I knew that eventually I was going to have to answer some questions about the letters. Questions I wasn't necessarily ready to answer.

Chapter Fifteen

Bridge

At the London Lords hotel in Vienna, the heels of Emma's boots made a sharp clopping sound on the marble entryway as she looked around and said, "I've got to say, you boys have taste."

I smirked. "Ben has his specific flare on things. He's very particular about warmth and elegance. East, on the other hand, is more modern. I like more of a collective flare. Still modern, but home to African and Indian pieces and paintings. That's where we show our personality."

She turned and smiled at me. It was wide and broad. "And how does Drew fit in to all of this? I always feel like poor Drew is the ginger stepchild, you know, the ugly stepsister."

I coughed a laugh. "I wouldn't say that to Drew if I were you. He might be the wealthiest of us all. After all, he controls most of our money. Or Wilcox Financial does. They have forty percent of our asset portfolio, so he's very much an integral part of things. He's just the only one of us who chose to actually work for his father. The only one of us who doesn't hate his father. So, there's that."

She turned slowly. "I knew when you guys first talked about doing something together, Toby was so excited. He had it all figured out. Then everything changed. You all left Eton and went to Oxford and Cambridge and the university in America, and then you came back and had these grand plans. He would have been so proud. He just wanted to be with his mates, you know?"

I could feel a fissure forming along the middle of my heart somewhere. Every time I thought of Toby, I couldn't help but think how I'd failed him. Something had been off with him. Some secret he was keeping, and I hadn't been paying attention.

"His legacy is in our mission statement. We did it for Tobes. When things were hard, we'd talk about it and then we became these ruthless businessmen. We built this fucking empire from shit to really stick it to our fathers. Aren't we a predictable lot?"

She gave me a soft smile then. "The prodigal sons." As she stepped down into the living room of our suite and took in the view of the Alps, she whistled low. "Oh my God, Bridge, this is stunning."

I smiled. "Yeah, it is, isn't it? This is where I always stay whenever I come to see Darcy. She loves it here. I let her have a birthday party here once. God, that was such a mistake. A dozen tween girls running amok in the hotel. God, it was worse than the lads, I swear."

She rolled her eyes. "A few pre-teens and you wanted to shoot yourself?"

"You don't know what they did. There were three broken lamps and a chandelier that had some kind of feather boa stuck in between the light facets. We had to take it down and have it cleaned. And then there was the makeup. Jesus. It was everywhere."

Emma just laughed. "You sound like a doting father."

I shivered at that. "God, I don't want to stifle her."

"You mean like you did with me?"

I scowled then. "You needed stifling. God, you were such a pain in the ass. Your only goal in life was to be rebellious for no reason. Your mother adored you. You were brilliant and smart, top of your class, vibrant and vivacious. Already a force of absolute nature. You just wanted to be you. But being rebellious, what was the point?"

Emma turned back to the view. "You know what's funny? I wasn't really difficult on purpose. To my mum, never, and to Toby only when I really wanted to stand up for something. Usually some bit of freedom that he wasn't giving me. And for anyone else who got in my way, I just wanted to make my mark. Be seen. It's all I ever wanted. But you know, with Mum, I didn't want to give her any trouble. She'd had it bad enough. And I was smart enough to realize that no amount of rebellion was going to bring my father back. No amount of begging, pleading, or acting out could do it. He didn't even see me."

"His loss, Ems. His loss."

She turned to me then. "You saw me though. Unfortunately, at my worst."

I grinned. "No, not at your worst. Just at your most handful-like."

"I hated that you were there for those things. I hated that you were there to see me stumble and fall and flail. And God, you were so smug about it all."

I grinned. "I'm not smug."

"You're always smug, Bridge."

Just staring at her with the early evening sun lighting her features, kissing her cheekbones and the straight edge of her nose, literally made the day for me. My gaze dropped to her lips, and the words came out before I could even stop them. "I never meant to stifle you. Wanting you was like trying to catch a firefly. Ethereal and impossible to pin down. And every time I thought you were in my grasp, you weren't. But then I learned that you don't capture something so beautiful. You just build it a big wide net and let it think it's free."

"Oh, so you were merely letting me think I was free?" She turned to face me.

I nodded slowly. "Yeah, because you were always mine. You have always been mine, Ems. And with everything that happened, I could let you go that far away."

I expected her brash laugh. Her rejection of that notion that I'd built this web around her to keep her close. Always in my orbit, but never in my hands. Instead, she stepped forward. "Bridge Edgerton, when will you realize, if you would have only held out your hand, I wouldn't have tried to run."

She stepped into my space, and I inhaled deeply, my brain suddenly going fuzzy with the intoxicating scent whirling around me and making me dizzy. Making it impossible to think or focus. And then she raised herself up on tiptoes and kissed me on the cheek. I held my breath, willing the moment to still and freeze. But just as quickly as she'd been there with her lips dusting my skin and teasing me, she stepped away. And in that breath, with the sun setting over Vienna, my control snapped. I reached a hand out, gently placing my hand over her bicep. "Where are you going?"

"I'll probably grab a shower. And then we should eat something, right? Before we head back tomorrow morning?"

"No."

Emma lifted a brow and then looked at my hand. She tilted her head, offering a challenge. "No? We've been over this Bridge. I'm not putting up with your teasing anymore. It's cruel."

She tried to shake me off, but I gripped tighter. "And I keep telling you, you're mine. I'm just fucking tired of fighting it."

Her brows lifted and she blinked at me wildly. I pulled her to me, willing her to stop the madness and put an end to it, because if she said no, that she didn't want this, I would let her go. I would have to. When I slid my hands into the hair at the nape of her neck, I gripped gently and heard the sharp intake of her breath.

"If you do this, Bridge, you'd better mean it."

My gaze searched hers. "Tell me no."

"Not on your life."

And then I crushed my lips to hers, and the dam broke. The

one I kept such a tight hold on, all the feelings, the frustration, the pain, the hurt, the joy, I poured every last emotion I had into that kiss. And Emma absorbed it all. When my tongue slid inside her mouth, sliding over hers, licking inside, exploring, tasting, taking, demanding a response, she rose to the occasion, sliding her tongue against mine as she whimpered and moaned. Her breasts pressed into my chest. I could feel them through the soft silk of the blouse she wore. All day, the sheer softness of the damn thing had been teasing me. Her bra underneath was this cinnamon brown color that sort of matched her skin, but every now and again, she would shift and I would see a bit of lace peeking through. So while I couldn't see through her blouse, and that was maddening enough knowing that there was lace underneath covering those perfect tits that I had spent far too long fantasizing about, I was a goner.

Emma's hands dug into the lapels of my suit and pulled me forward.

"I'm leading princess." I mumbled the words against her lips, and I could feel her smiling. I could also feel her laugh. A surge of warmth started spreading out from the center of my chest out to my extremities, and I could feel myself buzzing, humming. That constant *bzzzz* running through me, that low electrical current that if I let get out of hand would eviscerate me. But it was too late because it was already building in my blood, and I could feel it coming for me.

Emma was no demure kisser. Swipe for swipe. Tongue for tongue. My hand was in her hair, hers sliding through mine, her nails scouring my scalp, and I backed her up against the window. Needing more. Begging for more. When I slid my lips to her jawline, kissing along her delicate bone structure from her ear to her chin and then dipping down to her neck, I was like an animal. Slow open-mouthed kisses, my tongue sliding along her skin, finishing with a teeth chaser.

Emma hissed. "Bridge, Jesus."

And then, I sank my teeth into her, giving her a love bite. That was going to leave a mark even on her darker skin.

She started to slide one leg up my leg and over my hip, and I helped her, holding her in position. "Wider."

She widened her stance, and I picked her up so that her legs wrapped around me. I slapped a hand on the tempered glass behind her. It was cold to the touch. And I knew it would be cold on her skin when I bared her to it.

I kissed along her neck and her collarbone, leaving more bites, more kisses, more evidence that she was mine and that I had claimed her. And then I kissed lower. I was stopped by a button, which I growled at. And then I snatched my hand from her hair and used both hands, easily tearing the fabric down the middle.

"Fuck, Bridge."

"I'll buy you twenty more just like it."

I couldn't even meet her gaze because my eyes were glued to the swell of flesh pressing above the lace demi-cup. My hands went to her ass, lifting her even higher, bringing her tits right up into my mouth.

"Yeah, that's more like it."

I buried my face between her cleavage and suddenly, it was like I was a teenager again. So enamored with seeing tits for the first time that the current of electricity stirred up of my spine, and I moaned trying to think of something else that was less sexy. That was less... Emma.

But as I inhaled her spicy scent, I couldn't think of anything else. The buzzing grew more insistent, and so did my dick. I could practically feel the precum leaking out of me. Fucking hell, she was gorgeous. My hands dug in tighter into her ass, and I grazed my teeth over the soft flesh. "Do you know how many times I have dreamed about popping your nipples into my mouth?"

She was already shaking in my arms. Her head thrashing back and forth across on the glass. "Oh my God, Bridge, if you could just... I need it."

"You need a lot. But I'm going to start with your tits. Bring your straps down."

Her head kept lolling on the glass. With my right hand, I swatted her on the ass. That brought her head up, and her eyes flashed with fire as she glowered at me.

"You like spanking me too much."

"I'll stop when you tell me to."

She opened her mouth, more than likely to eviscerate me, but then she snapped it shut. "Don't be a dick."

I grinned at her. "I am the one with the dick, if that's what you mean."

She rolled her eyes. "Why is it you have to be such a... ahhh—"

My teeth grazed over the swells of her flesh again, and she groaned, unable to finish what she was about to say. "Dick."

I grinned. "Is that you telling me to stop?"

She snapped her mouth closed and glowered. And then I swatted her again. This time, I noticed the hitch of her breath and the way her hips canted for it. "Ah yes, my Emma liked it."

By nature of who I was, I was domineering. I wasn't super into kink or anything. But with Emma, I just felt the urge to swat her behind for all the times she had done stupid shite. For all the times she'd scared me shitless. For all the times she'd made me want her. I wanted to teach her those lessons that teasing me was a recipe for disaster for her. That teasing me was going to get her spankings and kisses and finger-fucks and titty-fucks , and ass-fucks.

Easy does it. We're not scaring her off yet. Not when we're finally here.

It's like my brain and my dick were finally working in tandem, and they had decided that I had fucked up for far too long. They were going to finally have Emma Varma, and I had better not screw this up for them. It was like an out-of-body experience because I could see what was happening and could feel it in my body, but I was not in control anymore. The wheels were off now, because I was touching her. And now I was going to have everything I'd ever wanted.

"I said, take your straps down now."

Still glowering, she hooked her thumbs on her straps, and then dared me with her eyes. I could see them sparkling. And when she didn't immediately comply, I licked over one nipple through the lace. Emma's gasp was shaky. "Oh, fuck you."

"Yeah, that's the plan. Bring down the straps now."

She did as she was told, baring her full C-cups. I almost wept for joy because, God, she was fucking perfect. High and proud, her dark nipples peaked and called my name.

I sucked her into my mouth, tugging sharply with my tongue, and she gasped, hands in my hair, holding me close. I licked and laved and sucked. I nipped with my teeth, scraping ever so gently and causing her to shake.

I applied the same attention and feral lack of control to the other breast, sucking it as she held me even tighter and started to shake against me. "Oh my God, Bridge. I just... oh my God."

And then I could feel it, her body tightening, her back bowing, the sharp, rugged pants coming from her lips. I dragged my lips off her nipple and stared at her. Her eyes were screwed shut, her mouth parted, her teeth grazing over her bottom lip. "Look at me."

Her eyes snapped open and met my gaze.

"Are you coming?"

She tried to close her eyes again, and then I slapped her ass with my palm, and she moaned. "Oh my God, Bridge. Bridge, Jesus."

I ever so gently slid my fingers over the seam of the jeans she wore. And the trail of expletives that escaped her lips was like a siren's call. Holy fuck. She'd just come, and all I'd done was lick her tits. I was keeping her. Never, ever, ever letting her go.

Better not tell her that, or she will run. You're going to have to let her think she came to this conclusion all on her own.

I grinned at her as I placed a sweet kiss between her cleavage. "You recognize I could do that all day?"

Her hands were still fisting my hair, tugging it tight, trying to bring my head back to her nipple, and I grinned at her before placing soft, sweet kisses there. "Oh, that's my girl. Fuck, that was so hot."

In my arms, she still bucked and jerked and I just held her tightly in place, watching her come apart again with the aftershocks quaking through her. If that could happen with just me sucking on her nipples, what would happen if I put my mouth on her sex? What would happen if I sucked on her tits as I was fucking her? What would happen if I pinched them as I took her from behind?

Fuck. My dick was a rod of steel in my trousers, begging for release. Begging to be inside her slick, wet heat. And so far, I was just happy to suck on her tits. Jesus. If I wasn't careful, Emma Varma was going to own me.

Then my dick chimed in. *Are you saying she doesn't already? Because I am about to detach and go and live with her. She gets me in the impending divorce.*

Just the thought of divorce caused rage to flare in my blood, and I squeezed her ass as if I could remind her with sheer possession who she belonged to.

I eased her down and she slid against the window. Her knees buckled slightly. "Are you all right?"

"Um..." She shook her head and swallowed hard. "I-I don't... Oh God."

She locked her arms around my neck and held me tight. Her hips seeking mine as she rubbed herself against me suggestively. "I don't know. I've never... wow."

Laughing, I dipped down and placed a soft kiss on her lips. "Oh sweetie, we're just getting started."

I stripped her of her shirt and then reached behind her and with two fingers, deftly unsnapped the bra.

Emma's eyes went wide. "Well, I see you've done that before."

I grinned. "A gentleman never tells."

"Except, I thought you were no gentleman."

I chuckled then, but I couldn't take my eyes off her tits on full display. When I reached for them, weighing them, I eased her back against the cool glass, my thumbs rubbing on her nipples, and her nails dug into the skin of my shoulders. "Oh my God. Oh my God."

"God, you're so responsive. I could fucking do this all goddamn day. I love your tits."

"Ah, a boob man, I see."

"Actually, I'm generally an ass man. You'll see."

Her eyes blinked open and her brows raised in surprise. I had to chuckle at that. Just the ultimate shock in her gaze had that light feeling zipping through me, and I laughed. "Oh my God, you are... Wow. Those expressions. Everything is on your face."

"Um, I've never..."

"Relax, that's something I take my time with. Right now, I'm going to fuck you. I'm going to take what I've been wanting from you my whole life. And then I'm going to hold you. And later, much later, we'll talk about how much of an ass man I am."

"Bridge, I—"

"Turn around, Emma."

She did as she was told, hands planted on the glass, bare tits against its coolness. "You know what's interesting? You didn't ask if anyone would be able to see you. You just turned, plastering those perfect tits on the glass. Do you know how hot that is?"

She swallowed hard. "I think you're possessive enough not to let anyone watch me like this."

Of all the things she could have said in that moment, the fact that she'd seen me so clearly worried me. This was the first moment of hesitation I'd had since we started kissing. "You said that with confidence."

"You know me well, but I know you too, Bridge Edgerton. You don't share."

"I don't. But if it would turn you on, just once, I might do it."

The breath came out of her in a soft puff. I wrapped my arms around her waist, my big hands easily spanning it. And when I went to the top of her jeans and hooked my thumbs inside, unzipping and peeling them off her skin, I was met with gorgeous bronze skin and a lacy pair of thong panties that matched the bra.

Jesus fucking Christ.

She started to turn around, but I planted a hand in the middle of her back. "You just need to stay here."

She nodded. "Okay."

She dropped her forehead to the glass, and I could hear her breathing. I could see her shaking. One leg at a time, I released them from her jeans and then slowly dragged the panties down.

With her bare and naked in front of me, I sank to my knees. With a sight like this, what you should do as a man was get on your knees and fucking worship. From the front, Emma Varma was the most captivating creature I'd ever laid eyes on. And from the back, she was pure elegance and sophistication. Carved by a master to tempt, taunt, and tease. "Emma, legs wider."

She hesitated then.

"I said, wider. Now."

"Don't get bossy with me," she snapped.

I glanced up at her, ready to swat her ass, but her gaze met mine. "You tap that arse again, and you better be ready to knuckle up."

The rich laugh that filled the room was a sound that swallowed me. It took me a moment to realize that it was me laughing. Proper laughing. I smoothed my hands over the smooth skin of her hips and ass. "Oh yeah? What's going to happen?" I gently tapped her flesh with my fingers. "What are you going to do to me, Emma? And do I have enough condoms for that?"

It was her turn to choke a laugh. "I'm just warning you now."

"Okay, if you say so." I didn't want to be predictable, after all.

It was quick work undoing my trousers and letting them fall.

Stepping out of my boxers and pants and then kicking them aside. When I pressed my body against hers, Emma's voice shook. "Jesus Christ, you're huge."

"Yes, thank you for noticing."

My whole body covered hers, and my dick pulsed insistently against her ass. Precum had pooled at the tip and was already sliding down the thick shaft. I groaned and rocked my hips against her ass, my dick sliding over the seam, back and forth. "Oh my God."

I palmed her ass, humming a little as my dick slid between her globes, sliding back and forth, with me providing the lube. Emma's body started to shake again. "Jesus. Bridge, I... wow." she choked out.

A couple of times, the tip of my dick brushed against her pucker, and I could feel her tense. I smoothed my hands up over her back, down, around and cupped her breasts gently. "Relax. We have all night. For now, I'm just feeling you. Can I feel you?"

She whimpered and then nodded. "Yes. Oh fuck, yes."

The tremor in her body only ratcheted up the tension in mine. Fuck. What was I doing? This was not the kind of sex you had with Emma Varma. Emma Varma should be in a bed surrounded by rose petals and candlelight.

My brain took over. *No, we're going to fuck her. And then we're going to fuck her again. And probably again. But the fourth time we'll go slow. Right now though, we're going to tease her. Get her worked up again. And then just like this, we're going to take her against the fucking glass. So shut it.*

Well, nice to know my body had its own set of expectations.

I notched my hips again, the tip pausing at her pucker and grazing it, making me hiss. Emma whimpered as I slid past once again. "How are you feeling?"

"I-I don't know. I've never... I don't know. Was it supposed to feel good?"

I stilled. "Emma, it's supposed to make you feel good, but if you do not like the sensation, then we are going to stop this right now." I didn't want her to do anything she wasn't comfortable with. "Now tell me, how does it feel for you?"

"I... When you move, um, I don't know."

I leaned in close, rocking my hips against her ass. "There's nothing you can tell me that is embarrassing or that I shouldn't know. You have to talk to me, Ems."

"I like it. Am I supposed to?"

I chuckled against her ear before kissing it gently.

"Ems, if this gives you pleasure then it's something you are supposed to feel, a hundred percent."

"Oh, okay. It feels good." So I did it again. And again. And then she whimpered. "Oh God, Bridge."

I was releasing more precum at this stage, and if I kept going like this, sliding the thick length of my erection between her cheeks, I was going to explode outside of her, not in her snug velvet folds. I eased back, pushing myself away from the glass. I snatched up my trousers and found my wallet. I had a pack of three condoms that I kept in there. Ever since Mina, I'd had to make it a habit. I only kept three in there because it was safer. I could at least have some self-control if there were only three. Except now I was horrified that there were only three. So for all these extra-curriculars with Emma, where the fuck was I going to get more condoms?

It didn't matter though. I grabbed one, tore the foil and rolled it down my full length and then I was back.

"Push your ass up for me."

"Wait, I thought—"

I laughed. "No, we're not. But I still need you to stick your ass up. You're smaller than I am. The angle won't be—"

"Oh, right." She did as she was told, and I glanced at her ass, my hands palming her curves. Jesus fucking Christ. She was so soft. So beautiful. And then I slid my thumb between the seam, all the way down until I found her slick wet center, and then up until I found her clit. Gently, I rubbed the soft button and her legs started to shake. "Oh my God, Bridge. Bridge, oh my God."

And then I slid my thumb away, back to the folds, sliding into her velvet richness and then back up over her pucker, pausing for a moment and swiping in smooth circles over her hidden place. Emma moaned low, and I knew one day I was going to take her there. But today, today the fact that her sex was right here waiting for me meant I couldn't wait. With a hand around my base, I notched my dick against her sweet center, and then I hitched my hips and slid up until the tip of my cock hit her clit.

She whimpered, "Oh God. Oh God. Oh God."

"Sweetheart, I need you to slide your fingers down. Find your clit."

I could feel her hands trembling as she met mine. "That's it. Right there. Use your fingers. Part your folds for me."

When she complied, I slid my dick over her clit again and again and again.

And then I waited for the telltale hitch of her breath. "Oh God, Bridge. Bridge, please, please, please."

Then I slipped away for just one second, notched myself against her entrance, and then slid home, teeth grinding. In front of me she stiffened and whimpered. The whimpering, begging woman in front of me changed to one who was tense and unyielding. "Ems, what's wrong?"

"Oh, wow. You're big," she panted. "So big."

I kissed her shoulder. "Yeah. I know. You'll be okay. Your body just has to remember how to open for me." I slid back and inched myself forward again. Again, I was met with stiffness. "Ems, relax. It's just me. Let your body relax."

When I slid back again and inched forward, she was more relaxed. I took it easy, inch after inch. Slowly sliding back home like I belonged there. And eventually her hips started to push back against me. "Yeah, that's it. Remember the sensation. I'm big, but I belong here. And it's me. You just tell me if anything doesn't feel good."

"Wow. I'm so full. Of you. Oh, Jesus."

I picked up my pace slightly. My fingers sliding with hers over her clit. "Yeah that's it, keep touching yourself. Tell me what you like. Do you want it faster? Slower? Or is this just right? Like Goldilocks?"

She coughed. "Oh my God. Why can't I... oh..."

I could feel her body easing around me, going fluid as she rolled her hips back to me. I picked up my speed. "Is this what you wanted Emma?"

"Bridge, oh my God."

"You've been teasing me for years. Is this what you wanted?"

"I-I didn't know what I wanted."

"Well, you've got my attention You have got my dick inside you now. And this is the last dick you're going to have for a long time, do you understand me?"

She nodded vehemently against the window. "Yes. Oh God, I didn't... I didn't know."

"Well, now you do."

My fingers found hers, guiding them back into circles over her clit, and then she started to shake again. "Bridge please," she whimpered.

I reached up, palming one of her breasts, pinching her nipples just as I started to feel her body quake around my dick.

When she tossed her head back on my shoulder and her body started quivering and shaking and gripping my dick, milking me from tip to root, I gritted my teeth and held on. "Yeah, that's it. Good girl."

I wanted to come so bad, more than anything in my life. I wanted to come, but I held on to that because when I finally came, I was going to be looking her in the eyes.

The rise was sharper on this one, and the fall was debilitating because Emma couldn't stand anymore.

I could still feel the aftershock on my dick, and I groaned into her ear. "Jesus Christ, you are killing me."

"I... Oh my God."

I eased back, and she hissed. "Aww wow. How are you still..."

I turned her around gently and planted a kiss on her lips. "God, I have been waiting for you my whole goddamn life."

She blinked up at me with a lazy smile. "Same. Same."

I leaned down and picked her up, and she gave me a squeal. "Um, Bridge, how can you... Why are you still hard?"

I laughed. "Oh, we're not done."

Her eyes went wide. "Um, we're not?"

"No, we're not."

"Oh, wow. You—do you do drugs or something?"

I laughed. "I haven't come yet, love. I've been waiting on you."

She blinked and blinked again. "Oh." And then I could see the pink chasing up her chest, hitting her face, giving her a red tint to those gorgeous cheekbones. "Um, right."

I carried her into the bedroom. "Ems, what's wrong?"

"I just... I thought you were having..."

I frowned but laid her on the bed and crawled up between her legs. With my dick notched between her legs, I put my weight on my elbows so I didn't crush her. "What's wrong? Just talk to me."

"I-I've never done this before, so I didn't know. And now I'm embarrassed."

I frowned. "What do you mean you haven't done this before, Ems? You've never had an orgasm? Just who the fuck have you been sleeping with? I'm going to kill all of them for never giving you one. Also I want to beat my chest because clearly I've given you two, or did I miss one in there?"

She ducked her head. "K-kind of two and a half. The first one took me by surprise."

"I can't believe no one's ever made you come before. Well, we're going to make up for lost time because that's ridiculous."

I smiled down at her and leaned down and kissed her. On her

face, her expression was wrong. She didn't look happy or relaxed. She wasn't reaching for me. "Talk to me." I watched her swallow hard, and I couldn't figure out what I'd done wrong. "Did I hurt you?" The shame slapped me quick, cracking my heart into a dozen pieces.

You were never worthy of her and then you fucked it up.

"Fuck. Are you hurt? Was I too rough?"

She shook her head. "No. I'm not hurt, obviously."

"Ems, help me out because I don't understand what's happening."

She cleared her throat. "I've never had sex before until now."

I blinked down at her. "What?"

She licked her lips nervously. The pink tip of her tongue peeked out to lubricate her bottom lip, and I groaned because my dick was notched against her very wet cleft, and fuck...

"Wait. Repeat. What the fuck do you mean you haven't had sex before?"

"You don't have to be a dick about it. This was just my first time."

I started to push up and away from her. Unable to process the words. But she wrapped her arms around me and tugged me tight until I laid directly on top of her, and then she clamped her legs around my back. Her hips notched upwards, encapsulating the head of my dick so that just the tip was inside, and I wanted to roar with frustration. "Don't you dare leave me. Please don't stop. Please, please, please don't stop. Don't ruin this."

The scent of her swirled around me as my face planted on her neck, fogging my brain. "This isn't right Emma. That was your first time. Why didn't you say—I mean, the windows?"

"I wanted to, but I knew if I told you, then you would have stopped. And come on, really? How many twenty-six-year-old virgins do you know?"

"Fuck me."

"Yes, we've been doing that. I'd like to do it again, please."

I tried to pull away again, but Emma held on tight. She was shockingly strong in her thighs. "Ems, this is not the way it should have been. Fuck, against the wall? I took you against the fucking glass window. I was sliding my dick against your ass. Fuck."

My dick, though, was unperturbed by being where he was, happily notched for just a little bit as she milked the tip. As she did that, I was losing my mind because I could feel the tingling along my spine, and I just wanted to fucking slide back home and take her fast. Hard. And in a slow punishing grind. Yes, the punishing grind. That would make up for her lying to me.

She shook her head. "I'm sorry. Come on, Bridge. Don't be mad."

I was furious. "How am I not supposed to be mad, Emma? You're supposed to talk to me."

"If I'd talked to you and told you, would you have done it?"

"Fuck, no. Or, I would have done it in the bed."

"We're in the bed now."

"Emma, your fucking first time should not have been against a window."

"You didn't enjoy it?" Her voice was soft, unsure

I blinked down at her like she was insane. "Did I enjoy it? Don't be daft."

"Don't be a dick."

At the mention of him, my dick surged forward again, sliding in an inch. And it was a real force of will to pull back. But then, devious minx that she was, she lifted her hips even more, impaling herself on me. And I hissed. I had to push back with a hand between us and placing it on her hip, holding her down. "Do not do that."

"Are you mad at me?"

"I'm *incensed*."

"Fine. Can you finish fucking me anyway?"

My gaze searched hers. "What is wrong with you?"

"Nothing. There's nothing wrong with me. Fine. Get off."

She shoved on my shoulders, and I could tell that I had said something wrong. As her hand shoved on my shoulders, I grabbed her by the wrists and pinned them over her head. "There's nothing wrong with you physically, and you are the most stunning woman I've ever seen in my goddamn life. Clearly, I want you. And I am desperate to finish this. But we have to talk, Ems."

"We've been talking our whole lives. You've been running from me. If you didn't want me, you didn't have to kiss me. You did that. I didn't force you."

I hung my head. "That's not what I'm saying, Emma. I could have been gentler. I could have made this good for you."

"But you wouldn't have done anything. I just wanted you, Bridge. However, you wanted to have me. And now you wrecked it."

I pulled her close to me. "Come on, Ems. Do you know how many times I pictured just dragging you to the floor, shoving up your skirt, and sinking deep? Never mind who the fuck was in the room? Never mind who the fuck is watching?"

"No." She shook her head and averted her gaze.

"Every goddamn day since we kissed since you were fifteen, every time you crossed my mind, my brain just froze up at that image. Me losing control and tearing your clothes off of you and fucking you until you screamed my name and thought of nothing else for the rest of your life. That is what I think when I'm near you. And your first time, it shouldn't have been like that."

"If you would just shut up, I'll go. And then you don't have to have any regret."

"You think I regret this? That's why... Oh fuck. You were so tense. I could have made that easier. I would have gone down on you for an hour, at least. I am dying to taste you. I wouldn't have jumped the gun."

She shoved at me again. "I don't want that. I just wanted you. The real you. Not the one you show everyone else. Not the one that is tempered or in control. You. That's what I wanted."

I frowned down at her. "Ems—"

She shook her head. "No, I wanted you. You're always in control around me and holding yourself together. And for me, against the window was my perfect first time. I didn't know that you'd be so big. That was uncomfortable at first, but then you made it so easy and it felt so good, and I just... I'm sorry, I'm not good enough and not experienced enough yet. But if you could just show me what I'm supposed to do, I can make you come. Or maybe you don't want to? With me?"

I stared at her incredulously. "Are you kidding me? Can you not feel the pulse of me against you?"

She frowned and focused, her gaze hard on mine, and then she blinked in surprise. "Oh yes, the pulse is very, um... loud."

I nodded slowly. "Yeah, all the blood is concentrated right in my dick. I am desperate to have you. I'm just..."

"Can we talk about this another time? Either get off, or let's finish. Please?"

"Ems."

"Bridge."

I sighed then leaned down, kissing the column of her neck. "You are all I've ever wanted. I just didn't expect you to not be with anyone before me."

"*You* are all I've wanted. And at first, Mum did her round of perfect Indian boyfriends, but I just haven't found anyone appealing. At school I dated a little, but they were fumbling and none of them were you. So in the last couple of years since we've reconnected, I thought maybe... But you had Mina. And now you don't have Mina, and here I am naked and you don't want me. So maybe you should just let me up."

I watched her. How could she think I didn't want her? "Keep your hands here."

She blinked up in surprise. "Why?"

I shook my head. Jesus, why was she always so difficult. "Because I'm trying to be gentle this time."

"I don't want you to be gentle."

"I was too harsh out there in the living room. I'm going to be soft with you."

Her gaze snapped to mine. "I don't want soft. I want you or nothing at all. Give me you."

She lifted her hips again, and the tip of my dick was inside and I just... *Fuck. Fuck. Fuck.*

"Emma, I..."

"I want you, Bridge. You. *All* of you."

And then I surged forward. The angle changed everything. And being able to see her eyes go wide and then start to roll into the back of her head, the satisfaction was instant. I still had her wrists over her head, and I started a slow grind and palmed her breast, dropping my head down and contorting myself just enough so I could lick the tip. Her body bowed. And then I notched myself tighter against her with a hand on her shoulder, bringing her down so there was no escape from me. When I released her arms, she looped them around my neck, holding me close, and I buried my face in her neck, grinding, keeping up the pace. When she started to whimper against me and her teeth sank into my shoulder, I shivered. "Fuck, Emma. Oh God. I just... I want you so bad."

Her whisper against my skin was a promise. "I've always been here. Always."

Then I picked up the speed, each thrust a promise. Each grinding movement a fantasy coming true. I simply was a goner. I was at a loss for words. And then I felt it again, the quiver around my dick, her harsh breaths against my skin, our slick bodies sliding against one another. She was calling my name, begging, begging, begging, and breaking apart around me. I sank my hand into her hair, fisting it back, pulling it and tugging it, angling her head so that I could kiss her and then swallow her scream, swallow my name on her tongue as I shattered into a million pieces inside her.

Chapter Sixteen

Emma

I eased out from under Bridge's arm with a side shuffle as quietly as I could.

I wasn't running. I was just creatively making sure that I didn't wake Bridge.

I was sore... everywhere. Hell, I was sore in places I didn't even know I could be sore. And God, my pussy felt every residual stroke from last night, like an echo.

Bridge Edgerton was huge. And every sex fantasy I'd ever had about him came to life last night. Granted, I could never have imagined what it would be like with him. And admittedly, I should have told him that little detail I'd left out. But everything had moved so fast.

We were kissing, and then he was lifting me, and we were against the window, and my body was on fire. Literally on fire. He had doused us both with gasoline and lit a match. I just figured he wouldn't notice.

I thought *I* wouldn't notice, because where the hell do you find a twenty-six-year-old virgin these days?

And now I was achy and would never be able to erase Bridge

from my psyche. I mean how the hell did anyone follow up that act? Who knew Mr. Buttoned-up was actually a porn star.

Then, of course, I hadn't wanted to leave him hanging. Just call me a giver. Also, I didn't want to get marked as bad in bed. And well, I'd wanted him again. If my obsession with him was bad before, no one, and I mean no one was ever going to match it now. He was a standard no one could meet.

And yes, the sex was some *you should probably have stretched first* shit, but the thing that got me, that pierced me straight to my soul, was the way he looked at me. The way his breath would hitch just before he'd kiss my shoulder or the way he would moan into my neck, or the way his hands would tighten just a little in my hair as he angled my head before diving in to kiss along my jaw, my neck, my shoulders. Those little soft, endearing points that showed me that he was fighting for control and that I made him lose it. That was what would forever stamp and imprint on my body and my brain.

Second, of course, was that unrelenting quest for orgasms. Jesus. That man, with his fingers, and oh, that dick. Wow. The thing was, I'd had no expectations of orgasms because everyone I'd ever met said it was just impossible for your first time or until you found a rhythm with someone. And if I was being honest, Bridge was the only person I had ever wanted so badly that I couldn't breathe.

His deft fingers and skill were unmatched. Because now that I knew what the big deal was about kissing and making out and sex, I wanted to do it again.

In the shower, I let the stinging heat flow over my body, and my fingers played on my lips. They tingled and were still swollen from last night. Or was it this morning? I wasn't sure. Because this morning, Bridge had used his fingers. God, it was like he knew exactly where I needed to be touched, and he knew how to deliver, all without taking anything in return. When I reached for his erection, he tucked my hand away and held me close, telling me that I was going to need some recovery time.

I felt cheated. Because I didn't want recovery time. I wanted *him*. But then, I had drifted off to sleep because I was just so tired. And now, I was hiding in the shower because I had no idea what the hell was happening.

I had *shagged* Bridge Edgerton. Or rather, *been shagged* by Bridge Edgerton, and I wasn't sure I was going to walk right for the weeks to come. The problem with shagging Bridge Edgerton when you had been fantasizing about it for half your life was, you had no idea what the hell to do after. I had no delusions. Bridge did not love me even if he wanted me sexually.

Last night may have been one of those circumstances, but this was not some permanent gig. And the sooner I realize that, the sooner I would be on the road to survival. Because at some point in the future, he was going to get tired of me, and I needed to ready myself for that. I would have feelings about that, and I was going to need to mask them.

I was so busy ruminating that I didn't hear the bathroom door open until the shower door opened as well, and I squeaked in surprise. "Jesus Christ. You scared me."

It was then that I got the full effect of a naked Bridge. He stepped into the shower with a smirk on his face. All bronze skin, cut muscle with... Wow. Goddamn, was that a V? He had a very defined V with eight pack abs. His dark hair flopped in his face, and his sexy smile said, 'I am the epitome of sin and bad decisions.' It was like someone had drawn him from my fantasies. And God, I wanted him again.

"You left bed early," he grumbled.

I nodded. "Yeah, you know, I figured we have an early flight. Don't you have work to do?"

"Not 'til eight. And we are flying private, so we don't have to be in a hurry."

I swallowed hard. Admittedly, I wanted to shower and be fully dressed before he was up, but that was not going to happen now. Oh, boy.

He lifted a brow as he reached for the shampoo. "Emma, did you run from me?"

I shook my head. "Nope. I'm not exactly the running type." I lifted my chin, trying to appear brash and brave. It was just bullshit.

He stepped closer again, and there was nowhere for me to run. When he reached for my hips I swallowed hard. "You okay?"

I nodded. "Of course, I'm fine. Totally fine. I am the okayest of okay."

He snorted a laugh, and to watch Bridge Edgerton laugh was a thing of beauty. He had a dimple that peeked out just on the right side. Perfectly straight, even teeth that I'm sure orthodontists had assisted in. A jaw that gave Henry Cavill a run for his money, and those startling silver-gray eyes. He looked like a more handsome caricature of that guy from that one sex movie I'd seen on Netflix. And while the movie itself left much to be desired, that man was... wow. But Bridge was even better looking than that. What was I doing with someone like him? Why had someone like him been my first? Because from there you only went downhill.

"Ems, you look like you're freaking out."

"No, I'm not freaking out. I'm *fine*." My voice was an octave too high, and I was talking too fast.

His gaze ran over me as he pulled me under the stream of the water. "Oh, yeah?"

His hand reached around to my ass and squeezed gently. I moaned as he asked, "Are you sore?"

I swallowed hard. "Not too bad. You know, you obviously, uh, know what you're capable of, so you know, just a little."

His brows furrowed. "Emma, you have to talk to me."

"We're talking right now. We're talking. See?"

He sighed and then dragged me under the full onslaught of shower spray. There were three heads, one directly in front of us that was a softer spray, one above that was rainwater spray, and then one set in an angle.

"Come on."

I swallowed, annoyed with myself. "It's just that I'm feeling embarrassed."

His brows rose. "Why?"

"Well, I mean, you figured out about my virgin status, maybe because I was bad at it."

His brows stayed raised as his mouth opened, and then he did a sputtering impression of Porky Pig. "Are you mad?"

"No." I rethought that. "Maybe a little."

He laughed. "Emma, clearly, I was having a *very* good time."

My inner diva stood up and stretched, arching her back, preening, crazy woman that she was. She apparently had forgotten that our vagina was on fire.

"I just want to make sure you're okay. I wish I'd known it was your first time. I would have been more gentle."

I blinked at him. "You wouldn't have stopped?"

He huffed the chuckle, squeezing my ass again. "I think by the time we kissed, you and I both knew that I *couldn't* stop. Unless, of course, you wanted me to. But as long as you were willing, there was no stopping me. I was tired of fighting it."

"What were you fighting exactly?"

"I made a promise to your brother, and a big part of me has always been trying to honor that. You and I, since we were young, have had these two combustible energies. I was a fool. I should have done this a long time ago."

I smirked and bit my bottom lip. "So yeah, that happened. That was fun."

He leaned in and brushed his lips over mine. "That was more than fun. Are you sure you're okay?"

I nodded. "Yeah, yeah. I'm a little sore, because wow, I did not know that you were working with *that*. But um, yeah, I'm good."

"Good enough to try it again?" he asked in a low rumble.

My head snapped up, and I blinked rapidly. "Oh, you want to?"

"Ems, I'm not yet thirty, heterosexual, and you're fucking fit. So yeah, I want to. Especially after this morning."

"I thought maybe you didn't want me this morning."

He chuckled as he nuzzled my neck. "Ems, when a man wakes up with a morning wood and then fingers you to orgasm, it's safe to say he wants to."

"Right. Yes, of course."

"Also, are you going to explain to me how come you're a virgin at twenty-six?"

I shook my head. "It's not that big of a deal. People are virgins all the time."

"Right. But you, Ems? A wild child?"

I was not having this conversation with him. "Can we talk about this later?"

He watched me. "Sure, we can talk about the wheres and hows later, but we should probably address something first."

Oh, God, what now? "Yeah, sure. Anything. Although, maybe out of the shower?"

He shook his head. "No. I have every intention of fucking you against that wall right there. You see that little bench?"

I nodded. "Yeah?"

"I'm going to have you plant your hands on it in a moment, and then I'm going to take you from behind, okay?"

I blinked slowly. "Wow."

He nodded. "Mm-hmm. But first, just so there are no questions, because you seem to have a lot of questions in your eyes, you and I, we're going to try this. We're not going back to an inconvenient arrangement. We're here. I think we need to stop fighting this. Are you in agreement?"

His thumb was dusting over my hipbones and it was very difficult to think. "Um, mm, hm, mm, mm-hmm."

"Use your words, Ems. I need to hear you say it. That you want me to fuck you in the shower."

I snorted a laugh. "Um, right. Yeah, in the shower. Great."

He gripped my hips firmer. "Say it, Ems."

I lifted my gaze to his, and I could see that he was deadly serious as his teeth grazed his bottom lip. "Bridge, I want you to fuck me in the shower."

"Well done, Ems. Next thing, I fully acknowledge that we are doing this now. While married, we will be shagging often."

What the hell did he mean by often? At some point, I was going to need to walk. And shagging him constantly was not going to let me do that. "Um, I acknowledge that while we are married, we shall be shagging."

He nodded slowly and started to massage the top of my ass with his thumbs, kneading the muscles. The action made my knees feel like jelly, and I could only lean against him, pressing my breasts into his chest. "One more thing."

"Mm-hmm."

"We're just going to go ahead and see where this marriage thing takes us. No definitive end date like before."

My stomach did a flip on that. "Um, Bridge, I don't—"

"Hear me out, Ems. We agreed to do this, and it's unorthodox, so why don't you let me date you or whatever it is you want to do? But give me a chance. A real one. No running. I don't like how it feels when you run away from me."

Oh shit. The one thing I'd always wanted to hear from him forever. And he was saying it now. "You want to have a relationship?"

He nodded slowly. "I do. You don't have to stay married to me forever, but I want a real shot. A real chance is what I'm asking."

Was I going to grasp what I'd wanted wholeheartedly from the time I'd known exactly what love was, or was I going to run like he said?

My inner diva practically punched me in the vagina.

We want sex. With him. All the time. Date him. Marry him and date him, I don't care. But do something with him.

I cleared my throat. "We'll see where it goes. But I still want your help. And I want to be involved with everything you do for Toby. Partners."

He leaned in and kissed me. His lips were a whisper, a soft brush. "Partners. I'm just asking that we try."

"Yes. I want to try. With you."

He slid his hand up my body. Briefly palming my breast and rubbing a thumb over my nipple before sliding it up over my collarbone and cradling my cheek in his enormous palm. "Now, I need you to go over there, plant your hands down on that bench, and I'm going to lick you until you shake and you beg, and then I'm going to fuck you again until I shake and beg. Sound like a plan?"

Oh, boy. All I could manage was a nod as I walked over to the bench seat and turned.

"Bend over, Emma."

I flipped my hair and glanced at him over my shoulder. He was stroking himself. And if that wasn't the hottest thing I had ever seen, I didn't know what was. From the root, one smooth stroke up to the tip and then a slow glide down, the soap that he'd used aiding him up and down over the thick massive length of his erection. What was that? Eight, nine inches? Heavens. No wonder I was sore.

"Legs wider."

I inched my legs apart, and then I felt it, the crisp swat of his hand on my ass. "I said wider, Emma." With a sharp gasp, I complied. And then his hands smoothed over my lower back and my ass as he murmured something that I couldn't quite understand, but it sounded like he was pleased. And then Bridge Edgerton knelt behind me, palmed my ass, and dove in, mouth first.

I might have been a virgin, but I was far from innocent. There were moments when I thought that I would lose my virginity and just toss it aside, give it to someone so that I would not carry it around with me anymore. And I had men who swore that I would change my mind about fucking them if they just went down on me or something along those lines, but *nothing* ever felt like this.

Bridge consumed me. Full-on ravaged. His mouth locked on to my pussy and his tongue dove straight in as he sucked and licked and parted my folds with his thumb and his tongue, and then licked up to that secret dark spot, the same one he'd teased last night and licked thoroughly. There wasn't any part of me he left unexplored.

And he was right about the shaking. And the begging. Especially as his tongue sought my clit and he circled and teased and then sucked. But really the begging started when he slid in two fingers. Oh so gently, all while he sucked on my clit. There was begging. Fine. I screamed. And begged. Pleaded even for him to just hurry up and let me come.

God, I don't know how long I stood there like that, bent over, ass in the air. It could have been minutes. It could have been hours. I was in a space where time stood still and all that existed was Bridge and his tongue and his fingers, and pure bliss as it hummed over my skin.

And just as I was about to teeter off into oblivion, he pulled back. I whimpered a cry. "Bridge, where are you..." I didn't get to finish that because he stood quickly, aligned his dick to my cleft, and pushed.

All I saw were stars, and my body tipped over into fucking oblivion. The explosion in my body was so swift it nearly knocked me out. Gray edged my vision as the stars started to blink in and out, and he pulled all the way back and then slid back home again. "Oh my God. Oh my God."

Behind me, he ground out tense words through what sounded like his clenched teeth. "Fuck, Emma. Fuck. Fuck. Fuck. Why do you feel like this?" And then he held perfectly still. And started to pull out.

I reached behind and grabbed his ass. "Where the hell are you going?"

"Fuck, Emma, I can't. I can't. I'm not using protection right now."

I blinked rapidly. "What?"

"I'm clean. Just for the record." He pulled out. "Stay here. There's something in the drawer over there."

I reached for him. "What? No. No, no."

"Ems, we have to. Come on." His voice was pleading.

"I have clearly never done this with anyone else."

"Which is why we need a condom, okay?"

"But you just said you're clean."

"I am. And I have never not used one before. I wasn't thinking. You feel so damn good that I am going to come inside you, again and again, and fucking again. We need to get you some plan B after."

"No, wait. You're not listening Bridge."

He moved to leave again and I grabbed his ass and held him in place. "Motherfucker, Emma." He was dragging in deep breaths through his nose and his hands clenched on my hips hard. "Do you understand how close I am to coming right now?"

"No. Yes, but I mean I'm on the pill. It's to regulate and to stop the bad cramps and you don't need to know why, but I am on the pill."

His gaze met mine and his lips parted. And then he picked up his pace.

"You're a naughty girl. You could have told me this last night." *Slam.*

Me, screaming.

Him pulling back. "Such a naughty girl. You teased me." *Slam.*

Another scream from me. Honestly, it was more of a sob, really.

"You filthy." Slam. "Naughty." Slam. "Tease."

I chocked on another sob. "Bridge, please. Oh my God, please."

Slam. And then it was happening again. That explosion from deep down in my body, threatening to override everything. Hard reset on my brain, my soul, my body.

And this time, Bridge grabbed my shoulder with one hand, kept the other hand on my hip, and then pushed the pace hard. He smoothed his hand over my hip to my ass and one of his fingers found my pucker. He brushed it gently. "I can see you're teasing me now. You want me to have every part of you, don't you?"

"Yes, oh my God, just..." And then I was gone again. My knees buckled, and then he roared behind me, holding me tight against him. I could feel the kick of him inside me as he filled me deeply. And I knew I had agreed to try with Bridge Edgerton. And before it was all over, he was going to completely destroy me.

* * *

Bridge

I kept my mouth shut about myself and Emma. Because really, it was none of their fucking business.

You're still mad about the Mina thing?

Fuck Mina. This wasn't about Mina. This was about me and Emma. I just didn't want everyone to know. And I was going to respect that for now. I could see where she was coming from. I didn't have the best track record. And telling the lads was impossible because there would be interference.

East and Ben would have something to say. East tended to be like a gossiping teenager. Wanting the dirt, but then daring to have an opinion. Ben normally would shake his head and say, 'What's the most beneficial?' Drew was the more carefree of the four of us. But I deserved this. I deserved her. And there was a part of me that was terrified I'd fuck it up. So I wanted her all to myself at least for now. That way she'd never leave.

That sounds like some stalker shit.

No, it was not stalker shit. I just knew that she was cagey.

Inclined to run away. So, I wasn't going to run her off yet. Anything she wanted, she could have right now.

I sense the pattern. Were you like this with Mina?

No, I was not like this with Mina. She'd seemed so fucking perfect. Whatever I wanted, I could have. A threesome, I could have it. An open arrangement, I could have it. Not that I'd taken her up on her offer. Matter of fact, I'd been gassed. What was the point of having me if she wanted an open relationship?

I wasn't so naive as to think that just because you're married didn't mean you didn't want to fuck other people, but the idea was that you didn't because you made a promise to this other person. A vow. An oath. The more I thought about all the red flags that Mina had given me along the way that I just ignored, the clearer it became that I should have asked more questions a lot sooner.

But when I turned up at Ben's the night before I was supposed to marry Emma, I was feeling nervous that they would see the shift in me. I texted her as I stood on Ben's veranda.

Bridge: *I'm still waiting for my notes.*

Emma: *You can wait all day.*

Bridge: *Are you already here? Are we going to sneak off?*

Emma: *I'm almost there. I came from work.*

Her job was another point of contention. And well, as far as the lads were concerned, she did have a need to continue that ruse. One we could exploit when ready.

I didn't bother ringing the doorbell, and I found Ben and Livy snogging on the couch. I quickly turned around. "Oi, you two knew I was coming. What is wrong with you?"

Ben groaned. "Mate, go back out. Knock. Then give us a minute."

I smirked. "Liv and I both know you'll only need one."

Liv snorted and then rolled off of her husband. "Honestly, Bridge, you could have given me a heads up. I could have gotten behind before you came in."

I laughed. "I can go back out, but then it would be awkward

because you know I'm listening. Ben is going to put on a show because he's proud of his performance. You're going to try not to scream Livy, but we've all heard you scream already. Which was awkward for the rest of us."

Livy just laughed. "Oh my God, must you remind me? I had no idea you were there."

I grinned. "Or, you're going to make me insanely jealous that I didn't sweep in and grab you up myself."

She was already shaking her head as she came over to give me a hug. I gave her a squeeze and over her shoulder, I winked at Ben. "Then it would be my name you're calling. 'Oh Bridge. Oh my God. Right there.' Except it would take me longer than a minute."

I pulled back and Livy swatted my arm. "Bridge. Enough."

"Oh, come on. I love winding him up."

Ben shook his head. "Nope, you can't wind me up today. I'm in a good mood." And then he eyed me closer. "And you seem like you are too."

I shrugged. *Play it cool.*

He continued to analyze me closely. "Even before the devil took over your life, your best mood was really sort of grouchy and scowly. Right now, you don't look grouchy. And you aren't scowling. Oh, actually,"—he leaned forward, assessing me as he slid an arm around his wife's waist—"Oh my God, is that a hint of a smile? Are you sick? Are you dying? Is that what's happening?"

I shook my head. "Fuck off."

Ben chortled. "Can't mate. You wouldn't like me that way. So honestly, what's got you in a good mood?"

"Nothing. I'm just as grumpy as I have always been."

He laughed. "If you say so."

Livy watched me too. She was more perceptive than Ben and East were. "He's right. You look happy about something. Are we finally done with Mina? Did she get all her shit out of the house?"

I furrowed my brow. "Uh, I haven't really looked."

"Bridge, you are letting her run all over you. Just like you've always done."

"I am not. I just haven't really been invested in anything she does. I'm barely there, so I'm not paying attention."

"You've moved Emma in now. I don't know how vindictive Mina is, that can't be a good combination. You're liable to come home to a pile of ashes one day."

I shrugged. "My money is on Emma."

Livy grinned. "Mine too. But Mina is devious and mean, so let's not go exposing Emma to that, shall we?"

I nodded. "You have a point, but Emma can look after herself. She doesn't need me."

Livy's brow lifted. "Uh-huh. Aren't you the same one who forbade her from working for Middleton?"

I frowned. "Yes, I'm still unhappy about that."

"Well, what happened to 'she can look after herself'?" She gave me a cheeky smile.

"That's different. He's dangerous."

"And Mina is not?"

"Mina is devious, yes. Self-indulgent, absolutely. Dangerous? No."

Livy shrugged, went back to the couch, picked up an earring, slid it back in her ear and then scooped her hair back as the curls fell over her shoulders. "If you say so. But I don't buy it. I see danger there. But you would know her best, right?"

What was she getting at?

East and Nyla arrived next. Hugs were given and drinks were poured. Drew turned up finally. He barely greeted us before he poured himself a scotch. I slid my gaze over at East and inclined it toward Drew. Was he just drinking a lot because he liked the scotch? Specifically, his Macallan that Ben always stocked up on. But he'd been off for a bit. More than a bit. Months now. East had said something about him having an affair. Drew denied it, of course. And then he'd sort of admitted to it, but I had no idea what was going on there.

Maybe we just needed to have some lads' time away when we finished with Middleton. Take a holiday. Once Livy and Nyla showed up, things got complicated. We had our focus elsewhere. Maybe it was time to head out to the villa in Greece. It was one of our properties for our special visitors. We could all take a holiday. Recharge. Get back to basics.

East just made a face that said, 'I don't know mate.' And Ben, well, Ben was watching him like a hawk, but I didn't know if he was going to do anything about it yet.

Telly turned up, still without Carmen. Her wife, apparently, had gone to Bristol. And the only reason I knew that was because I had gossiped with East, because the London Lords has to keep tabs on anything new about our little group. I was waiting for Emma to turn up. I kept looking at my phone to see if there was a text from her, but there wasn't.

Finally, the doorbell rang, and I almost sprang up to answer. But in a tragically cool way.

Oh yeah, real cool.

She bounded in with a smile to everyone. "Sorry. Sorry. I got held up at work. I know this is a party in my honor, I suppose." She was all smiles for everyone. But to me, she gave me a head nod and scooted by with barely a touch.

I scowled at her and whispered, "What the fuck?"

"Remember, we're playing it low key."

Yeah, but low key was fucking annoying me.

As my gaze narrowed on her, I had an overwhelming urge to scoop her up, bring her over, and show her how she was supposed to greet her husband properly.

One, you're not her husband. Two, you should keep a low profile. Three, you're supposed to be playing it cool. Isn't that the way you two would always react to each other before? Pretend she didn't exist.

Yes, but things were different now, weren't they?

Yes, different, but the same. You're supposed to be playing it exactly the same.

Goddamn it. I hated this already. I hated it. Memories of her lips on mine, and that breathy little sound when I hit that spot deep inside kept assailing me. Tickling my soul, forcing me to remember. Oh, fuck. I needed to take care of the erection in my trousers or somebody was going to notice.

I turned my gaze away from her and focused on something Telly was saying. She was telling us about how, so far, she hadn't found anything on Middleton either. Or his clients for that matter. Nothing that wasn't already public knowledge.

And then everybody was talking about the merger and some other bullshit about some other thing. And fucking Emma wouldn't look at me.

And like an obsessive fool, I tracked her every movement. Every step she took, I was tracking her.

Goddamn it. I was a goner. Without even trying. Fucking hell.

When the Middleton portion of our meet up was over, Emma and the girls went up to try on something for the wedding, and Drew frowned at me. "Wait, are we doing the two-wedding thing tomorrow?"

I frowned. "Why would we do two weddings?"

"You know, a British one and then a Hindi one."

I frowned at him. "Why would we do a Hindi wedding?"

"You know, to give Ems the cultural thing."

I stared at him incredulously. I was going to kill him. "Why are we friends with him again?" I asked the others.

East just blinked at him.

And Ben, well, Ben scowled.

Drew just frowned and shrugged. "What? What's wrong with you lot?"

Ben and East left it to me. "You recognize that Emma isn't Hindu, right? She's Catholic. Just like Toby was."

Drew's eyes went wide. "But she's Indian. Isn't it cultural?"

Was he that daft?

"Just because she's Indian doesn't mean she's Hindu. Where would you get that?"

"Well, she ordered vegetarian at dinner the other night, right?"

"Maybe she just likes vegetarian stuff. You have also seen her eat a steak."

His brow furrowed as if something in his brain just couldn't compute. "Fucking hell. All this time, how have I not known?"

"Maybe you're not paying close enough attention, for starters."

He went and poured himself another scotch, which was another set of problems that we would deal with later.

"All right, I heard from the old lady that she's very excited to be part of our little shindig tomorrow, so lads, just remember we're being watched the whole time." I shifted my gaze to Drew and waited for him to acknowledge.

"Yeah, yeah. Why is everyone looking at me?"

Ben sat back. "Mate, you've been real keen on the bottle lately. What's happening?"

Drew lifted a brow. "What? You're my father now?"

Ben shrugged. "No. But the way you're hitting the bottle, it says something is wrong. So what's wrong?"

He shook his head. "Nothing. I'm all right as rain. Everything is fine."

Ben watched him. "Look mate, whatever is happening, you can talk to us about it. Or if not, at least keep your shit tight. No fuckups tomorrow."

"I'm not the one who's going to fuck up." He pointed at me. "It's that one. That one is going to fuck up. He's bloody shagging her."

My head snapped around to meet Drew's gaze. "The fuck?"

"I can tell from the looks you've been giving her and the ones she's been sneaking to you. Did you think we wouldn't notice?"

Oh, he was slick. It was a classic diversion. If everyone was looking at me, no one was looking at him. "I'm not shagging her."

Unfortunately, my lie must not have been convincing enough because East piped in. "The fuck? Are you shagging Emma?"

I shook my head and lied through my teeth. "No. I'd be in a much better mood if I was."

It was then that Ben's gaze narrowed on me. "I'm not saying you are, but if you were, you know that would be foolish."

East threw up his hands. "Little Tobes? Are you trying to tell me you would shag little Tobes?"

"First of all, keep your fucking voice down. Second of all, I'm not shagging anybody. Remember, you lot put my dick on lockdown."

East shook his head at me. "You, of all people. You know how important this is. I know you're pissed off about Mina, and I understand you are angry. Which I get, but you would shag little Tobes? Fuck."

"You think I'm in a right strop about Mina, do you?" I leaned back and crossed my arms. "I wonder why I'm on a scruff about her? Maybe if my mates had seen fit to tell me that she was a plant from my father, I wouldn't be in this mess nor be in this drama, right?"

Ben cursed under his breath. "Okay, okay, everyone relax. Bridge, just be careful with Emma, yeah?"

"No, bullshit. Why am I being warned about Emma?"

East pushed to his feet. "Why? You know how emotional she is about this. There is zero negotiation with her about any of this. She walked right into Middleton's office and took a bloody job because we weren't moving fast enough. When it comes to her brother, she cannot see straight. She can't. And you're going to fuck with her?"

"Is that what you think I'm doing? Fucking with her?"

"You haven't been able to keep your dick to yourself since you found out about Mina. Instead of manning up and just saying how twitched you are about the whole situation, you've been fucking your way through London. And that's all well and good with anybody else, but not baby Tobes."

"You recognize she hates it when we call her that, right?"

East looked at Ben for help and threw up his hands. "Are you listening to this?"

I don't know what it was about Ben. But it was like he saw a little too much. "Bridge is the least stupid of all of us. He's not going to do anything to jeopardize any of this, is he?"

I frowned then. "Who gets the stupid award then?"

Ben tipped his thumb toward Drew. "That one."

Drew flipped him the bird. "Fuck you."

But Ben grinned. "Are we not going to talk about Mandy Williams?"

Drew winced. "Ugh, mate, that one? Why are we bringing up old shit?"

"Just so you'll have a perfect understanding of why you've been a knobhead every time, and why no matter how much you try, it's not going to be East or Bridge. Certainly not me."

"How was I supposed to know her father was best mates with the Prime Minister?"

"Pay attention."

Drew sat down with his glass, tugging up his trousers as he went down. "Whatever. I'm not a knob head."

East rolled his eyes. "Yes, you are. You're still our mate, but you are. Also, you didn't know Emma wasn't Hindu and that she was Catholic, so that makes you an extra knob head."

He sighed. "Fine, whatever. If it makes you feel better to say that."

I scowled. "Are we done here?"

East turned his attention to me. "Not if you're shagging Emma."

"Who I shag is none of your fucking business. Also, when did you become the self-appointed protector of Emma?"

"It's supposed to be you. But right now, you're looking at her like she's bloody steak and you haven't eaten in a month. So, you'll forgive me if I don't believe you."

"You think I have shagged Emma? Let me ask you this, would Emma shag me?"

And with that question, all the lads relaxed.

Ben sat back. "That's a good question. Unlikely. I don't know what you did that pissed her off in the past, but she's not exactly your biggest fan."

"Yeah, thanks for the reminder." I hated that they'd caught that.

Ben sat forward. "But you need to clear the air about Mina, mate."

I shook my head. "Bygones." They were bygones, weren't they?

"You say it's over, but how can it be? You're clearly still tweaked about it."

"You know what, we're not having this conversation. I don't want to talk about this."

Ben leaned forward and placed his glass on the table. "Look, we know we fucked up. And we never really had the chance to clear the air."

"Consider it cleared. I'm glad I know. I just... Why didn't anyone trust me enough to tell me before?"

Ben pressed his lips together and slid his gaze to East and Drew. But he didn't say anything because it wasn't his style to toss the two of them under the bus like that.

East ran a hand through his hair. "I knew your Dad's plan to let Mina into your life. It was a shitty judgment call and you weren't supposed to get hurt, but you did. You were unhappy. I made the call. That was my fault."

I turned my attention to Drew when he said, "You know what mate, you wouldn't listen at all. And when someone won't listen, you can't tell them anything. We would have lost you if we'd said anything. So we just kept as close an eye on her as we could, but not really telling you about it, and maybe that was a wrong choice. But we did our best for you at the time."

I thought about that. Would I have listened? Now I could look back and say that I would have if they'd just fucking told me. But maybe that was the appeal and lure of Mina. I couldn't see. I was blinded by her. Unable to see anything beyond her perfection.

I nodded. "It's something to think about."

East gave me a nod. "Yeah mate, think about it. Whenever you want to talk, I'm here."

And I knew they would be. I was just going to have to figure out something to get past it.

Chapter Seventeen

Emma

I was getting married today.

It was the most surreal feeling. I'd woken up in Bridge's bed, which was probably bad luck, but who the hell knew, because this wasn't exactly a real marriage.

Didn't you just tell him that you are going to give it a chance?

I had said that and meant it at the time. I *was* going to give it a chance. But it was safer to hedge my bets. And this marriage was so unconventional already. Not at all the proper order of things. I was agreeing to date, not to be married to him forever.

Fuck. Had I really agreed to this?

I patted the bed next to me and the sheets were cool. I'd heard him moving around the floor, maybe gone to the gym or downstairs to do a lap in the pool. I wasn't sure. I rolled over to my side of the bed and grabbed my phone. In all of this craziness, I hadn't called Mum. And if I was getting married today, I should probably mention it to her. Except, what was I going to say?

Automatically, I dialed speed dial number one, and she answered on the second ring. "Darling, why are you calling now? It's the middle of the night."

Fuck. "Sorry, Mum. Why are you up?"

"Oh, I just got back from this midnight exhibit at this fabulous art gallery here in New York."

I blinked. My mother? I didn't even know she liked art galleries. "By yourself?"

"For your information, I am a grown woman and I can go to art galleries by myself. But I was with some friends and Pinky Auntie."

I frowned. Friends? My mum had friends? Oh sure, through the years she'd made friends with other mums. You know, play group mums and all that sort of thing, making sure that I had people to talk to. I just assumed that those were her friends. And yes, there were people she had dined with every now and again, and she had her best friend Aunt Tildy. But Aunt Tildy lived in Ireland. So who were these *other* friends?

"Who are these people? Do I know them?"

"Sweetheart, I know that it's confusing for you, but I have people in my life other than you now."

"Yeah, I know. I just didn't know you knew that many people in New York, that's all."

I could hear her sigh. "Yes, love. For all you know, I'm even dating."

I coughed and then sat straight up. "What? Who are you dating? I already told you that if you are going to start dating you need to let me do the picking. I don't trust your taste."

She laughed. "Sweetheart, I'm not going to do the Tinder."

"Please, no, Mum. Never Tinder. There are other options. Bumble, Raya, I mean, you are a famous artist after all. You could apply for Raya, that's the one where famous people meet other famous people. Oh my God, what if you dated someone like Brad Pitt?" Famous was a stretch, but she'd had a piece bought by a Kardashian, so that was something.

Mum laughed. "Oh my God, darling. I love that you think that I could pull Brad Pitt."

Mum was beautiful. I wanted to look exactly like her in twenty years' time. Her skin was still smooth and unlined, thank you melanin. Her hair was still dark, though she aided it along with hair color every now and again. Her henna treatments took all bloody day. And she kept in shape. Yoga. Running. She even took a hip-hop dance class once. I wondered if she was still dancing. "Mum, you're a hottie. Agreed. Everybody would think so. I'm just curious about who you are dating."

"I didn't say I *was* dating, I said I *could* be dating."

"Right. Mm-hmm. Look, I for one am all for it, but I just want to be part of the experience."

"Sweetheart, you would not be dating these men. *I* would be."

"Yes, but I want you to make good choices."

"You don't think I'm old enough to make these choices for myself?"

I frowned at that. "No, you are. It's just... It's hard out there. Dating."

"Yes, I know."

Suddenly I was the mum. "Ah, wait, are you using the Indian matchmaker?"

She sighed. "Are you still angry that I made you go to the matchmaker a couple of years ago?"

"Yes, actually. I told you I didn't want to date, and you insisted that Chara Auntie was the best match maker. And the matchmaker insisted that I didn't need such a demanding job and said I gave off alpha-male energy."

She sighed. "Perhaps that was not the matchmaker for you, but love, I don't want you to be alone. I just want you to find someone you love and who loves you in return."

"Mum, about that..."

"Are you seeing someone?"

I could almost hear her perking up. "Ah, what are you doing?"

"Okay fine, if you must know, I just turned off Netflix. I was watching in the background as I finished a snack."

"What are you eating for a snack?"

"Oh my God, the judgment. A brownie sundae. I was starving."

"Why are you starving? It's not dinner time. It's the middle of the night."

Why did I sound like the adult in this conversation? I wasn't wrong though. Wait a minute. "Mum, why did you need to snack in the middle of the night?"

"Jesus Christ, I may have eaten an edible. They had them at the exhibit. They were part of the experience, and I was hungry."

I sat there blinking for a moment. "How many of those did you have, Mum?"

"Oh relax, they cut them up into tiny little pieces. One of my friends I went with cautioned us against eating more than one. She said it's easy to think, 'Oh I'm not high at all,' and then you eat several more and then you're high."

"Well, at least that was smart advice, but Jesus, Mum."

"Oh, please. Like you've never had an edible."

I refrained from answering that because I'd had one. I was so high once because I'd been the moron who had eaten a whole one. The paranoia was real.

"Mum, that's not the point. I have something to tell you."

"What is it, love?

"Okay, keep in mind I don't know how to say this. And it's a long story. But do you remember Bridge?"

"Of course, I remember Bridge. He only spent his secondary years in and out of my house. What kind of question is that?"

"Um, well, you see, we are, um, seeing each other, and we're going to marry tomorrow. Today. Whatever."

There was a long pause. "Jesus Christ, I must be higher than I thought. I thought you said you were getting married today."

"Um, it's a very, very long story, but he needed a wife, and I said I'd help. And then in the course of it we just... Well, we started seeing each other, and I know you're probably worried. And this is not how you wanted it done and you want a traditional wedding for me. I know all that and..."

"Oh, I think it's lovely."

I paused. *Lovely*. "Is that the right word?"

"Yes, it's the right word. I love Bridge. I've always loved Bridge. You know this."

"Well, yes. But as Toby's friend. Not as like dating me for real."

"You know, I've always thought he was a lost soul, but if you're seeing each other, I'm happy. But I'm very concerned that you're getting married because I'm not there."

"Mum, don't worry. This is not a *real* wedding. Ben is going to marry us, and it's very low key."

"I hear you. But what is happening?"

Quickly, I ran Mum down the logistics of everything that had happened and how they had a big deal on the line, but I left out any details about Middleton. And then she was silent again for so long I thought maybe she'd hung up.

"Oh baby, I'm worried."

"There's the right reaction. Worried is a good thing. Worried is the right word."

"No, love. I'm not worried about you marrying Bridge, because obviously he can look after you if need be."

"Mum, I don't need looking after."

"Love, every human being on this planet needs looking after. Let me just be really clear with you. We all need love in our lives. We all need someone who's going to see us to the end. And love for more than just one person. We network. No one dies alone. But I know how you felt about Bridge all these years."

It was my turn to sit there dumbfounded. "What?"

"Sweetheart, I'm your mother. I know what a thing you've had for Bridge Edgerton. He's handsome and stoic, and you were always trying your damn best to make him smile or to make him crack. One of the two. How could I not see?"

"Oh God, did everyone see?"

"Probably everyone who knows you well. Which isn't many people because you don't let that many people close. I'm glad you two are seeing each other. But I don't want the scenario to cloud your judgment. You deserve everything, not just a part of someone."

"Thanks, Mum. And believe me, I'm taking the actual relationship slow."

Uh-huh, yeah, real slow. So the bendy athletic sex, is that slow?

"If you're sure, love. Can I watch? Live stream it."

I smiled. "You know what? I think Telly and East can make that happen."

"What time is it?"

"It's 4:00 p.m. UK time. Are you sure?"

"Look, if I can't be there for my daughter's first fake wedding, what kind of mother am I? Of course, I'll be there. I love you."

"I love you too, Mum."

"Just one question."

"Yeah, Mum?"

"Is this one of those situations where your father would be there?"

I coughed. "My father? Hell no. It's a private ceremony. No unwanted visitors."

She sighed. "Okay. But it might be one of those things that maybe you'd want to tell him."

"Do you know what? If he could somehow magically wind the clock back and appear at anything that was remotely important to me, then he would have the right to be there. But until then, no."

She sighed. "I can see why you feel that way. All right. I love you. I guess I'll see you when you get married."

"Yes, I guess you will."

When I hung up with her, I frowned at the phone. Why did she bring my father up? He was the last person I wanted to think about right now. And he was certainly the last person I would ever allow at my wedding.

* * *

Bridge

I stared at myself in the mirror. I was really fucking doing this. Jesus Christ.

Emma had left an hour ago to go get ready with Nyla and Olivia at East's place. I had arrived at Ben's ten minutes ago. Getting dressed had been quick. And there wasn't much to do because everything had already been taken care of. The bastard actually had a mini ballroom for these kinds of things. He'd gone from a man who hadn't wanted to live in his house to making sure it was as ostentatious as possible. It was unbelievable.

But I was proud of him because there had been a time when he avoided this place like the plague because he'd been burned, by a friend of Mina's, no less. So that made sense.

Someone knocked on the guest room door and I called out, "Come in."

I saw the tousled blond hair first and then the wide grin when he popped in. His shirt was undone as was his tie.

"Ah, there you are. Handsome devil. If I didn't love Olivia, I'd give you a go."

I laughed. "You couldn't have me. We'd fight to be in charge."

Ben coughed a laugh. "Mate, please. Never say that again."

I grinned and winked at him. "So, are you ready?"

Ben nodded. "Just a couple of buttons, and then I'm tying the bow tie and I will be Alexander Skärsgard's more handsome brother. The question is, are *you* ready?"

I shrugged. "I mean, I am a handsome devil. So yeah, not much to do here except stay looking good."

He rolled his eyes this time. "Mate, I know about you and Emma."

I frowned. East was such a little grass. When in doubt deny. "I don't know what you're on about."

He sighed. "Bridge, you think I don't know you? I know you've had a thing for her since we were kids."

I swallowed hard and shoved my hands in my pockets trying not to give anything away.

When denial doesn't work, double down. "I don't know what you're on about."

He crossed his arms and leaned on the door jam. "There was one time when Tobes got stuck on some project at school. He sent you home. I was headed home too, but you refused to come with me. You didn't want to take my father's charity or whatever, so you took a train. He asked you to watch out for Emma. You forget you told me you kissed her."

I blinked. "That was a long time ago." Also I needed to stop sharing shit.

"Was it? Bridge, you think I don't notice you never let yourself have anything good? Even with Mina. You tried to turn a pig's ear into a silk purse because you were getting exactly what you thought you deserved."

"I'm not sure what you're trying to say about Emma. Do I deserve her or don't I?"

"Emma's the best. I love her like a sister. And you absolutely one hundred percent deserve her."

I relaxed marginally. "But there is nothing to worry about there because deserve her or not, she's not mine." But I could make her mine. I just needed time without interference from the lads.

"If you say so. But I can see you. And I know you want her. So, I'm asking, are you going to marry her because you actually want her? There are easier ways, mate."

"That's not a fair question. My hand was forced."

"The shit with Mina was fucked. For my part, I'm sorry. I never wanted to go along with it. I would have just told you."

"I know. Hell, you did tell me, multiple times in wicked fashion, how much you despised her."

"I can't help wonder, if I'd told you the truth, would you have listened?"

I shrugged. "You know, I've been thinking about that a lot

lately, and I'm not sure I would have. Maybe East and Drew were right. I am stubborn."

Ben nodded. "We all can be. I guess what I'm trying to say is if this is real for you, make it real, make her yours. You deserve it. Take the bloody vows seriously."

"Are we going to talk about *your* vows?" I asked.

Ben grinned. "We've had our hands full. Besides, Olivia didn't want to get married until this is all over. And we're already getting pretty close to that now. Besides, you know me. I live for the big, splashy ceremony, yeah?"

I smiled at that. "You deserve nothing less."

"Same goes for you. East is right. Stop looking at her like you want to eat her like steak. And secondly, good. You both could use some happiness. And we're almost there. As soon as we find our angle to press on Middleton, he's done. We can all finally get on with our lives."

"The old man tried to talk me out of it." I blurted it out. The words just tripped off my tongue.

Ben frowned. "What?"

"At the meeting, he implored me not to marry her."

"Is that just to fuck with you?"

I shrugged. "I don't think so, actually. I just find it odd. I'm not sure why. But it's gnawing at me."

My mate shifted on his feet in a move completely uncharacteristic of him. "So since we're here sharing deep darks and all that, and you're about to get married, I'm not saying you need to tell Emma about the situation in Austria today, but you should do it soon."

I blinked at him. My surprise made me stagger back a step. It was rare that I was caught completely off guard. I was so used to watching my back, planning exits, having an alternative. "What?"

Ben sighed and shoved his hands in his pockets. "The scenario in Austria. You've never said anything about it. The way I figure it is, if you wanted everyone to know, you would have said something. I know, it's none of my business. I understand that. I don't even get to have feelings about you not telling me, but I'm Director Prime, remember? I happen to know all the secrets. So, again, if Emma is real to you, then you have to tell her. You don't have to do it today, but soon. Really soon, yeah?"

I still couldn't work my mouth properly. He knew. "How..." I tried again, pushing the air past my constricted throat. "How long have you known?"

He sighed. "My knowledge stems from long before I was named DM. Since graduation from Oxford. There was a letter from her school in your shit when I was helping you move. It fell out. They were talking about the tuition for the next year. I did a little research. I found out about the girl."

I shook my head, blinking. "You've known that all along. But..." I swallowed hard. "East. The research, did he do it?"

Ben shook his head. "No. You know, I do know my way around a little bit."

"Right, yeah. Why didn't you say something?"

"I was waiting for you to tell me. I would never tell. I just wish you'd said something to me, mate."

"It's not what you think."

"It doesn't matter what I think. What matters is that you tell Emma."

I was so flustered that I blurted out, "She knows. Darcy ran away from school for a concert or some bullshit. The school called. Emma was at my house. I had to go and she came with me."

Ben's brows lifted. "Oh. And she's good with you having a daughter?"

I shook my head and I tried not to let the disappointment in his tone bother me. "She's not my daughter. She's my sister."

Ben's brow furrowed. "But on the—"

I interrupted him. "On her birth certificate it says I'm the father, but she showed up on our doorstep when I was not yet eighteen. Mum took care of her. But it was the old man who dropped her off. And then I saw what he'd done by putting me on the birth certificate. That's how Mina knew. She's been trying to use that secret to get me to take her back."

His scowl deepened. "Or what?"

"Or she'll take it to Fredericka. Ruin our chances. But I'm already getting married and the old lady loves Emma, so I'm covered. It's fine."

Ben whistled low. "Fucking hell, Mina. God, I hope that shagging her was at least worth it because the pain that has now followed is bullshit."

"Yeah, I'm not surprised now that I know the difference. Good versus actually good with someone you care about, so I know it wasn't good."

Ben smirked. "So you *are* shagging her?"

Realizing my mistake I shut up. "I said no such thing."

"My lips are sealed. Just tread lightly."

I sighed. "You don't have to tell me. I'm keeping her. A little more could spook her, so I am well aware."

"Anything you need, I'm here. What do you say we go and get you married, huh?"

"Yeah. Is it okay I'm actually excited?"

My best mate grinned. "You're supposed to be excited. Come on, the guests will start arriving soon, so we have to put on a show. Except you'll be putting on the greatest show of all because you actually want to marry your fake fiancée."

"That sounds so bizarre. When will we stop saying bizarre shit like that to each other?"

"Soon, mate, soon. Let's go get you married."

"I'm right behind you."

Chapter Eighteen

Emma

I didn't think I would miss any of the traditional Indian wedding elements. , but I did. There hadn't been days of celebrations.

I never thought of myself as the girl who wanted a very traditional Indian wedding. We were Catholic, so different things to do, but there were still days and days of activities.

I wasn't really a big family person, and with Mum abroad, I suppose I could have asked some of my aunties to come. Most of Mum's family lived in Ireland. And honestly, our whole family situation was one of those things that the family never approved of Mum for. So we'd always been on the outskirts anyway.

When Toby had been alive, it was easier because he had that gluing quality to him. People love being around him. He could make anyone smile. But when he was gone, Mum was in mourning. She couldn't bear to be around people. And then she went to New York. She was deeper in the Indian community there, and she had aunties and friends. When we moved back outside of the obligatory visits and nods and smiles and bringing presents and food, always food, I had no one.

Which was such an odd feeling. Because in New York, I'd been surrounded with family all the time. Aunties were always telling you how you have to study and work hard. And as I got older, aunties started bringing around unmarried eligible bachelors. I was only twenty-five, but they were insisting I get married before I was too old.

You mean like what you're doing right now?

This was different. This was for work. It had a very specific purpose. At least I kept telling myself that. The problem was, I was even more connected to Bridge than I had been before. I cared about him.

You idiot, you love him.

Jesus. I was a mess. A freakin' disaster.

The **Mehndi** artists painting the intricate design up my arm smiled up at me. "Are you okay with this? Do you like it?"

I smiled down at her. "Yes, Tasha Auntie. It's beautiful."

"You know, it's so much better when it's authentic and a real artist is actually doing it. You can really see the distinction."

"Yes, Tasha Auntie, you are an artist, and a good one at that." And she was. Mum's one request had been to send me the best **Mehndi** artist that she could find in London. And I thought I didn't want the fuss and the pomp of the circumstance, but I did. When I looked at my bejeweled hands and fingers with the gorgeous white **Mehndi** over my fingers and up my arms, a stark contrast to my brown skin, I was happy I'd let Mum do this for me.

It took her another thirty-minutes to finish and another hour for me to let it dry and to fit into my sari. I had gone with silver and white. It wasn't traditional-traditional. I had one of my cousins help me try on a few of the wedding saris she and her friends had worn. There were gorgeous reds and greens, but I wanted something that at least would look a little like wedding-white, without actually *being* wedding white. That way I could blend both my cultures.

As the silver skirt swooshed around my feet and the jewels jingled around my ankles, my wrists, and my chest, I took a deep breath. Holy shit, I was actually marrying him.

Remember, it's not real. The sooner you realize that and you accept that, the easier this will be for you when the time to part comes. You are going to try a relationship, but be realistic. This is a business transaction, not a real wedding. Get that inside your head.

For the love of God. I just had to remember that. This was the **Mehndi** and the sari's fault. If things didn't work out, I would be okay. I could go back to my life... before Bridge.

Once I was dressed and I looked like a bride, it was hard for me to pretend I didn't feel like a princess. Hard to pretend this wasn't real for me.

At about ten minutes till show time, there was a knock on my door. I thought it was probably Livy or Nyla coming to tell me it was time to shake a leg, but when I opened it, it was East. I gave him a wide smile, opened the door, then he gasped and took a step back. "My God, Emma, you look fantastic. Completely stunning."

I gave him a soft smile. "Thank you. I figured, even if this wasn't real, I should at least, you know, make the attempt."

He laughed. "Who said it's not real? It's as real as you want it to be. And I promise you, if it wasn't real before, the moment he sees you in this, it's going to be very, very, very real."

"Aww, stop. I feel like a whole other person."

He hesitated. "Okay. Are you sure you didn't want us to have your Mum here?"

"No, this is better. She's got herself settled there and she's old. It didn't make sense for her to come back and then go back again. So it's fine."

He nodded. "Well, I know that this whole thing is weird. And I know that traditionally, it would be your father who walks you down the aisle. But since yours is a twat, I was thinking maybe you'd let me do the honors."

The simple words I hadn't expected sent a wash of tears to my eyes that I had to rapidly blink away or they'd ruin the heavy mascara and the dark liner I was wearing. "What?"

"Yeah, you know, the whole wedding thing... Walk you down the aisle?"

I sniffled and kept blinking in the hopes that this teary madness would stop. I was going to ruin my makeup, and then I would look like a dying raccoon.

"Aw, don't cry, Ems. Had things been different, this would have been Toby's job. And since Ben is officiating, give me something to do, please."

My lip trembled. "I-I don't know what to say."

He grinned and proffered his arm. "Good thing for you, you don't have to say anything. Just take my arm and let's do this. You'll be fine, Ems. We're all here for you."

I took hold of my bouquet and East helped me adjust my veil.

"Like I said, if it's not real now, it will be as soon as he sees you."

All I could manage was a trepidatious smile because if not, I was going to bust a leak. And while I had seen many an Indian bride crying on her way to the altar, I did not want to be that girl. I was strong. I could do this.

As East led me down the hallway on the third floor at Ben and Livy's ridiculous mansion, he stopped at the elevator. "Oh, come on, I'm not chancing you tripping on your sari."

I laughed. "I'm not that clumsy."

"No, you're not, actually. You're stunning and beautiful and elegant, but I want you to make your entrance."

I snorted a laugh. And just like that, East had helped the tears dissipate. By the time the elevator landed on the main floor and we stepped out, I was feeling calmer. Happier. Ready. And as we walked down that long hallway and then made the turn toward what could have been an exceptionally large dining room or a very small ballroom, East stopped. "Are you ready?"

I nodded. I didn't know how it happened, but magically, the doors opened and my breath caught once again. Nyla and Livy and Telly had been exceptionally busy. The room looked like an explosion of white gardenias and roses everywhere. The seats inside were covered with white fabric and tied with silver and white bows. Everything was perfect. It was elegant and majestic, and I couldn't have asked for more. And there were people of course. Not a lot, but enough to make me realize this was actually happening.

I recognized them as I stepped forward. Team Winston Isles also had shown up. There was King Sebastian and his wife, Queen Penny; Ben's cousin Roone and his wife Jessa; Sebastian's cousin, Prince Tristan and his wife, Ariel, who was also Penny's best friend. Everybody was there except prince Lucas and his wife Bryna, as they were on an extended honeymoon. What were they all doing here?

I'd met them off and on through our various adventures over the past year. And I liked everyone enormously, but I hadn't asked them to come. I thought this was just perfunctory. Fredericka was also there with her daughter and her nephew. There were a couple of people I didn't recognize. They looked perhaps a little shabby in a suit. Slightly rumpled.

I turned to East as he said, "Well, just because we said small and unassuming didn't mean we weren't going to go all out. Jesus, most of us thought Bridge was never getting married. This is all for him really."

I grinned up at him. "Thank you."

And as I turned back to look down the aisle, there was Bridge in his dark, perfectly tailored, black Marc Jacobs tuxedo. Dark curly hair pushed mostly off his face, with a stray curl or two trying to flop onto his forehead. He was perfectly clean-shaven, making him look so much younger, which was probably why he wore stubble most of the time to look older and more menacing. He'd been looking at the floor, but then Ben elbowed him. He glanced up, and his eyes went wide.

Ave Maria started to play, and East led me on our first step. I almost wanted to run. But instead of running away, I wanted to run straight into Bridge's arms. How whacked out was that?

Only a little. Look at him, he's beautiful. And for a whole year, he's going to be yours.

I couldn't think about what would happen beyond that year. What I needed to do was grab on to this time with both hands and live it to the fullest. No regrets. East looked down at me. "You're beautiful. Come on, keep moving."

"Thank you again."

"Of course. Now, let's get you married to your miserable fiancé before he comes down here, throws you over his shoulder, and carries you down the aisle himself."

"That is so Bridge."

East chuckled as we started to walk. "Isn't that just?"

* * *

Emma

This was not a drill.

The look on Bridge's face, told me that he 100% meant business. And teasing him wasn't going to work out well for me.

I shoved against him, and he stumbled back. The look on his face was nearly feral and he snarled at me. "Emma, it's time to stop fucking about."

"I'm not fucking about Bridge. I don't want to talk right now."

His brow lifted. I took a step back, and he took a step forward. "You're going to need to be explicit here, Ems. If you don't want to talk, what do you want?"

"I thought I was already really clear. I want you to fuck me."

And damn him, the way his lips twisted into a smirk was more than I could handle. He was all fire and sin and lightning energy. "Ems, do you know what you're asking for?"

"Yes, I do."

"I get the impression you want to run."

I smirked. "Maybe you should get the impression that I want you to chase me."

His brows lifted. And then he gave me a full-blown grin. The smile of Bridge completely unencumbered. One who was having fun. I knew if I was going to play this game, I needed to be ready to run. And I was.

I grinned back at him, but I was already turning to run. I bolted down the hall. When his thick forearm wrapped around my waist and he brought me up against his hard body, I sighed, my legs going melty and heat pooling between my thighs. When he braced me up against the wall, all I could do was pant. "That's not fair. You didn't let me get very far."

"You've already been teasing me too long, Emma."

"I was barely even teasing you."

"Oh yeah?" I could feel the thick length of his erection against my ass and my lower back, and I moaned, dropping my forehead to the wall. "Would you just do it."

He laughed. "Do what?"

"Hurry up and fuck me already, Bridge."

He loosened his arm around my waist, and I started to turn but he stopped me with a firm hand on my hip. His other hand grabbed both of mine and lifted them above my head. I tested the strength of his grip and found out that his body was just as powerful as I had always thought it was. I wasn't getting out of this until he was ready to let me go.

"Tsk, tsk. Stop struggling. I don't want to hurt you. Unless you're telling me to stop. And then we'll stop."

I groaned. "So what, you'll just walk away?"

He leaned in close against my ear. "Yes. I'll walk away from this interaction, but not away from you. I meant what I said. You and I we're, trying to make a go of this marriage however we started it. So if you don't want me now, that's okay, I can wait."

His whispers were harsh against the shell of my ear, and I shivered. He knew I wanted him, but he was willing to walk away if it wasn't what I wanted.

"Yes, Bridge, I'm saying yes."

"Yes to me, or yes to a quick fuck in the hallway?"

He knew, but he was going to make me say it. "Yes to both. I want everything."

"That's my girl."

And then I felt the sharp smack of his hand on my ass.

"Ow!"

"That's for making me beg." But then gently he soothed the gentle hurt. And to my horror, I was wet. So goddam wet.

"Oh God. I think I like it."

"You want me to spank you, Ems? Is that what you're asking?"

My voice wavered. "I don't know. I've never done it before—"

Another smack on the other cheek, and I shuddered. "Fuck, Bridge."

"Open your legs for me, Em."

I did it as I was told.

"Now tilt your ass up nice and pretty for me."

When I complied, he rewarded me with two additional smacks.

I was shivering, rolling my head back and forth on the wall. I knew I was in good hands. Problem was, I couldn't touch him, and I wasn't sure I liked that.

When another smack landed on my ass, I moaned. "Oh... my... God." It was like every smack was a direct line to my clit.

He released my hands then. And the next thing I knew his hands were quickly removing my wedding sari.

There was no patience, no slow seduction. He was going to give me what I wanted, which was rough and fast like our first time. The first time I knew exactly what it was like to be owned by someone. Body and soul. Bridge was the kind of lover you read about in books. Possessive and domineering, but sometimes so gentle it made you ache.

When instructed, I lifted my legs out of the scrap of my lace panties. His hands gently smoothed over my cheeks.

"I didn't think I'd be able to see the red on your skin, but you redden so prettily."

I swallowed hard. "Bridge?"

He hushed me softly, his hands gentle now. "I don't want to hurt you, Ems.

Something about the way his voice broke told me this wasn't about the spanking. This was about something more.

"Then don't."

He leaned forward, kissing the nape of my neck, and I could feel him nodding. "I'll do my best not to."

And as his hand smoothed over my abs, a finger dipped down into my cleft, making me weak. "Oh my God. Bridge. I need—"

His chuckle was pure cockiness. "I know what you need. But I'm going to need something first." And then he was kneeling behind me.

"Bridge? What do—"

What I'd expected was the hard ridge of his erection. Claiming me, possessing me.

What I hadn't expected, was the soft caress of his tongue, firm but insistent. His hands grabbed onto my ass, held me in position, and then he dove in. Lapping at me, holding me open for him. Leaving no fold unexplored. When he started to hum over my clit, that was when the shaking started. I broke apart, screaming his name.

"Oh my God. Bridge. Bridge. Bridge." If I was being honest, I had no idea what I was saying. Nonsensical ranting and raving and begging. I knew there was begging involved. But he was unrelenting. Completely focused on his task.

The second orgasm was almost punishing because I hadn't been allowed any rest, and my knees buckled. But his hands, God, his hands held me right where he wanted, and he didn't stop. It was going to be death by orgasm. Which I felt like I was here for, but in practice... wow. I knew I would be a puddle on the floor in moments. But I didn't fully lose it until his tongue snaked from my center to that tight patch of skin just beyond and then licked over my ass. I gasped so loudly. "Bridge, oh my God."

"Hold tight, I'm still eating."

"Oh God, Bridge, you can't—"

"Never interrupt a man when he's eating, love."

And holy hell, was he eating. He didn't stop. I was completely bare and open to him, and he was making sure that he left no part of me unexplored. Every part of me was his to own, his to claim, his to devour. With the third orgasm, I really lost full control of my legs. I just couldn't stand anymore. I started to slide down to the floor, and he let me until I was on my hands and knees trying to crawl away. But he stopped me. "Where the fuck are you going?" He growled.

"I need a minute.

"We're not done."

And even as I slid down until I was face-planted on the floor with my ass only a little lifted, he still lapped at me, still licking all of me, tongue penetrating someplace I never knew a tongue was supposed to go.

And I was going to lose my mind. *Fuck*.

"You taste so fucking good. All of you. You taste incredible.

"Bridge, I don't think I can."

"Oh you can."

My face was buried on my forearms, and I had no other choice but to enjoy the ride. Because Bridge was going to town. And I had a feeling that he intended for me to be here a long while.

When his fingers joined the party, I automatically lifted my hips, seeking contact.

"Yes, that's it." As his tongue licked my pucker, he slid two fingers inside my slick channel and gently pumped.

More nonsensical words. More moaning. More begging.

But then I hit this almost nirvana moment where the bliss just kept rolling through me.

Behind me, all I heard was his satisfied moan and grunt. I'd never heard him like this. I'd never seen him like this. And all I could do was submit. All I could do was just let it happen. This was like a dance where he led and I followed and enjoyed every goddamn moment.

And holy hell, it was incredible.

When he separated from me. I could feel the cool air on my skin, and I gasped. "Bridge, oh my God. What have you done to me?"

He chuckled then. "What I've done is shown you exactly what I should have done our first time. But I was impatient and a complete twat. I don't think I'll ever forgive myself for that. I shouldn't have done anything other than eat you that day. And I'm probably going to spend the rest of the year making up for that."

"Oh. Well, I wholeheartedly encourage you making up for it. After all how dare you." I meant to be sassy, but honestly, I think I was just mumbling.

"Excellent. Put me in my place." I could hear him removing his clothing, the zipper, the buttons on his tuxedo pants. I could feel him shifting behind me.

His whole big body enveloped mine as he leaned over me. Strong arms bracketed next to mine. I could feel the length of him notched against me, and I gasped. "God, you're so big. Why are you so big?"

"Fuck, why do you know exactly what to say to me?"

He rocked his hips once, twice, and I rocked mine back toward him. And when he slid home easily, he hissed and I moaned. And we stayed like that for several seconds. Both of us too afraid to move, to break that connection.

I could feel his forehead drop to the back of my neck. "Fuck, Emma. That's so good. Why is it so good? It always feels so good with you."

I meant to be sassy. I did. I wasn't trying to be emotional. But what came out was, "It's because you love me."

He stilled, the thick length of him pulsing inside me. I felt so full. I could feel every inch of him. And then he whispered against my neck. "You're right. You're absolutely right."

And then he started to move. In this position, I could feel every inch of him. He was so deep. I felt so full and so tight, like I was going to burst. But he was taking his time. That extra orgasm he seemed to want, he was content to take his time giving it to me. I could feel him all over my skin, his legs on the outside of mine, our toes semi-intertwined as we moved together.

His abs moving along my back. The kisses and nips along my neck and my shoulders. Whispering dirty things to me about how I was so fucking tight. Asking me if I liked it. And all I could do was mutter something along the line of, "Umph."

And then he started to whisper. "This is *mine*. Always mine. Don't you forget it."

I was the idiot who was agreeing with him. "Yes, yours. Only yours."

Because that seemed like the thing you did when you wanted someone to keep going. You would promise them anything. Anyone who argued that idea was lying. Because look, he could have asked for my life right then and I would've given it to him and said 'Gladly here you go. Just please God don't stop.'

I could feel the pressure building. But in my position, I couldn't make him go faster, deeper, anything.

Sensing my frustration, he eased back slightly. "Rise up on your knees, love."

I groaned. "I don't know if I can move."

"Oh, you can move. All you have to do is raise up on your knees but widen them. And then you can still lay flat. Like a butterfly."

Understanding what he meant, recognizing the yoga pose, I did what he said. And oh my God.

That opened me right up. And then he was on his knees right

behind me. Slide, retreat. Slide, retreat. His pace was even but not quickening. And then I pushed up onto my forearms, and he cursed under his breath, grabbing my ass with both hands and giving me a gentle smack. But he picked up the pace. "You're a naughty girl. You want me to lose control?"

All I could mutter was, "I want you to have everything."

And then I felt something at my ass. Finger? Thumb? And he massaged the tiny hole. "Even this?"

I shivered thinking about his tongue there. "Yes. Even that. You can have whatever you want. Just keep making me feel this good."

His thumb pressed against my ass, and he slid it into the first knuckle, and oh my God, I was so full. Too full. I started to shake, and his thumb slid in deeper. Then he began working his thumb and dick in tandem. Slide with his dick, retreat with his thumb, slide with his thumb, retreat with his dick. Faster, faster, and faster until I was pushing back on my forearms, helping him ride me.

And then he looped a hand around my belly, slid down, found my clit with absurd ease, and started rotating and flicking. All while he fucked my ass with his thumb and put that beautiful dick to work. "Oh fuck. Ems."

I could feel it. His cock kicking inside me. He pressed and rotated harder on my clit.

Forget seeing stars, the darkness on the edge of my vision told me this one was going to put me out. I wouldn't be moving for a while.

It was only when I surrendered fully, arching my back, my pussy going so wet, so slick, with Bridge moving over me, that I started to break again. When I started to break apart I slapped my hand on the hardwood floor. "Fuck, Bridge. I'm coming."

"Oh fuck, you're so tight. I can feel it all."

The voice wasn't the deep baritone I'd gotten used to. It was softer. More vulnerable. More in awe? And then I was breaking apart, and all I could hear was him roaring behind me, "Never leave me again. You are mine. Forever. Forever, you understand?"

All I could do was nod feebly and mumble, "Yours." It was like our little pact. Because under no circumstances would anyone ever be able to make love to me like that. Ever. Bridge had given new meaning to ruining me for anyone else. He was mine forever. After something like that, I was never, ever letting him go.

Chapter Nineteen

Bridge

Was it creepy to stare at her? My wife.

Only when you're watching her sleep, and that's extra creepy.

I brushed my fingers on her shoulder. "Ems, wake up love."

Love. Watch yourself, or she'll know.

Once again, I shoved down my feelings about Emma. It was safer that way. She was prone to spooking. If I didn't tell her, she wouldn't run. And then I could just hide my feelings and give her time to fall for me. I know she said she'd always had a thing for me, but that was different than the reality of *being* with me. I knew what I was like. I knew that reality would never match up to whatever fantasy of me she'd built on her head. So my job, besides protecting her and keeping her safe from Middleton, was to make her happy. Maybe she could see that I could actually be more than a means to an end.

Good luck with that.

I had a plan. I was going to sweep her off her feet. And I was going to work at not being an arsehole. And I was going to get her the only thing she'd ever asked me for, vengeance for her brother. The plan was airtight.

What about that arsehole part?

When she only mumbled and nestled further under the covers, I took one end of the duvet and slowly tugged it down. She whimpered and tried to scoot down with it. "No, you don't, love. Up you get. We have somewhere to be."

"Nooo. I don't want to. What kind of monster keeps me up most of the night but then won't let me sleep in? You're awful."

"You know, this is not the first time I've been told that, but it's already ten. If we don't get a move on, we're going to miss the whole day."

She groaned. "It's only ten? Oh God, just let me sleep until twelve."

"No. It's rare I get a day off. You're coming out with me."

She grumbled. "I don't want to come out. You kept me awake until four."

I grinned down at her. "Was that me, or was that you?"

"That was you. I was ready to throw in the towel at two."

I grinned. "Fair enough." After a brief nap, I had woken her up again. But at the time, she hadn't really complained. She was just feeling the exhaustion. "Oh, come on, you like it when I wake you up with my mouth."

"Yes, I do. But ugh, why do I have to get up?"

"Because we have a date planned for today."

With a mumble, she rolled over and cracked open an eye. She looked absolutely stunning. Her hair, a rat's nest of disarray, her brows furrowed, her lashes, thick and full and tangled, and her arms covered in the gorgeous white **Mehndi** design running through her hair.

"This is cruelty. Why are you this mean?"

"I'm not mean. I swear. Now come on, get dressed. Do you need help in the shower?"

She moaned. "Yes, but no. If you actually want to leave here, then no. I know you. You can't keep your hands to yourself."

I gasped and clasped a hand to my chest. "That, is bullshit.

Honestly, I'm insulted. I know how to keep my hands to myself. You just never seem to want me to."

She groaned and grabbed my pillow, and I could see what was going to happen. I could have ducked, but I didn't. I let her hit me, full on the face. And she snorted a laugh. What I didn't see coming was a secondary smaller pillow she had hanging off of the side of the bed. When I got broadsided with that one, I jerked in surprise, grabbed the pillow, and it was on. I added tickles for good measure. She squealed and kicked and grabbed the pillow. Emma was quick on her feet. Dodging, and ducking, and diving, and before I knew it, she was on me, tickling me for all she was worth, and it was torture.

I was ticklish. Extremely ticklish. I'd forgotten because... Who the fuck dared tickle me?

"Oh God. Stop. Stop. Stop. I'm really ticklish."

Emma's hands went still immediately. "Oh, I didn't know you were ticklish."

"Yes, well I am. Don't tickle me."

She lifted a brow. "Wait, you can tickle me, but I can't tickle you?"

I lifted a brow. "Yes, that sounds fair."

She drew her fingertips up over the edge of my ribs. "That sounds fair to you?"

I nodded sagely. "Yes, clearly I'm bigger. And so the bigger person gets to control the tickling."

"Oh, really?"

I could see the mischief on her face, the light dancing in her eyes, and I knew that she was going to torture me. When she clamped her knees a little tighter over my hips, I tried to cross and pulled my arms to stop the impending assault, but it was too late. She was fast and nimble with her fingers. I was roaring with laughter. And then I lifted my hips and easily rolled her off, until she was beneath me. Again. Just the way we'd ended up this morning.

"Now, I feel like I told you I was ticklish, and you utilized that information against me."

"Well, it's a war. That's what happens. Sorry not sorry."

And that's how we spent the next twenty minutes, the endless tickle fight. And somehow it ended with my hand up the T-shirt she'd tossed on in the middle of the night, grasping her breasts, scooping my thumb over her nipple. And it was tit for tat, so to speak, because then her hand went straight into the joggers I'd put on this morning. Once her hand cupped around my dick, there was no thinking, no focusing, no angling for my win at war. She had me. And the next thing I knew, we were shoving my joggers and boxers down, and I was driving into her with the strength and force that made my soul shake.

She gasped and then dug her nails into my shoulders. I thought that was how we were going to finish, but Emma was stronger than she looked because she bucked me and rolled us over so she was on top. She yanked her T-shirt off and gave me the view of my life. My wife, hips astride me, beautiful brown skin, her hands scooping up her body, the stark white of the **Mehndi** in perfect contrast to her skin, sliding into her hair as that silken blackness fell over her shoulders. It wasn't long before my hands gripped on her hips tight, and we were both coming. Her with a loud enough scream to very likely send the servants scrambling. When she dropped onto me, chest panting, she laughed. "That's what you planned all along, wasn't it?"

I grinned. "Some version of that, yes. But I really planned for the shower."

"I knew it. You had nefarious plans all along."

I did.

It took us another thirty minutes before we were both showered and dressed, and I was tugging her along by her hand. Not toward the cars, as she thought, but onto the street. "Well, I know you, so I must feed you."

"Yes, dear husband, you know me so well already. Feed me Seymore, feed me," she laughed.

I laughed with her as I dragged her down toward the café. "Today, we are like a normal couple. We did everything backward, so now we go forward. I'm taking you on a very long date today."

Her grin was resplendent. "You do know the way to my heart, don't you?"

And I did. When we reached the café, they already had our order ready and they sat us in a quiet corner of the courtyard.

"Oh my God, I think I love you."

My heart seized as my whole body stuttered. What did she mean? Did she *love, love* me? Was that just something to say? Was she just that hungry?

But the way Emma gleefully ran to the table with mimosas on it, I realized that she meant that in a facetious way. She was happy and thrilled that I had fed her, and that I had already pre-ordered things and gotten everything ready for her. Excellent. I was glad I didn't ask for clarification.

But watching the gleeful expression on her face made me so happy. If taking care of her and anticipating her needs could make her that happy, I could make her love me easily.

She plopped on her chair with a gleeful bounce. "Oh my God, I can get used to being married if this is what it's like."

I reached out my hand for her. "Come on, let's work off these calories."

"Oh my God, Bridge, I can't possibly shag now. I'm going to need like four hours of solid rest and a nap. Definitely a nap."

I had to laugh. "That's not what I meant. Although, it's a fabulous deal, but I merely meant no wild rides right after we eat."

She snorted a laugh, and I couldn't help but think how adorable she was.

"We're going to Notting Hill. They're doing a little mini festival thing. Music, art, bands, you'll like it."

She lifted a brow. "We're going to Notting Hill?"

I laughed. "Yes, why?"

"I just see you as, you know, a hotel magnate." She used air quote.

"Well, I do like music, you know, the oldies and such."

She wrinkled her nose. "Oh God, you're ancient. I don't know how I shagged you last night. Frankly, you're over the hill."

I rubbed my chin that had already started to sprout stubble. "Haven't you heard? I'm a baby face. You should have seen me on my wedding day, looking all spry and young."

"Oh my God, you catfished me."

"Yes, that I did. Now come on, to Notting Hill we go."

I had forgotten about the simple pleasures of running the Tube. It was congested with people everywhere. The smells, most of them unpleasant, body odor stench, and motor oil, and who knows what else. And then there were women with too much makeup on, their perfumes wafting the air, all kinds of stuff. But somehow, holding up her hand, walking through the throngs of people, idly chatting about bands we'd seen, music we'd heard, concerts we'd been to, and I felt a glimmer of the me I used to be before drowning out my father and crushing out any remnants of his legacy became my sole purpose. It was fun. I felt light around Emma, young and carefree.

With the lads, it was fun. There were concerts and private showings too. Two years ago, for East's birthday, we'd had, what was her name? Christina Aguilera and Charlie XCS do a private performance for everyone at London Lords. It had been a wild party. But there was something about going to see a concert, being with tens of thousands of other people who also enjoyed the music and just wanted to have a good time. It wasn't as convenient, no. But God, this was more fulfilling.

Emma was having the time of her life. I could see it in her face. There were live bands that she was bopping and singing songs along to. The cover band seemed to be her favorite, because she was unabashedly singing along with the 80s and 90s remixes, old boy band songs, and I couldn't help myself. I danced and smiled with her. Was this what it was like to have fun? To be liked? To enjoy? I'd been missing out on this because I had been in such a rush to be this other version of myself.

Well, you don't have to miss out anymore. You have a year. A year to convince her to be yours for real. A year to submit to this feeling in your soul. And you have a lot of time to make up for.

We had been on our feet for five hours, dancing, and laughing, and eating. God, the eating. I eventually had to call the car to come pick us up because there was no way Emma was going to survive the Tube. And while I'd carried her four blocks to get gelato, via piggyback, she was still wincing and moaning about why did the Tube have to be so far away? Once the car rolled up on the road, she climbed in gratefully and I climbed in the backseat with her. Before I knew it, Emma's head was in my lap. Not in a funny way, but in an endearing way. And she started to snore.

As I ran my fingers delicately through her hair and rubbed her cheek with my thumb, I whispered, "I'll do anything, Ems, to make you love me, and I'm going to have fun making that happen."

* * *

Bridge

"I must admit, Mr. Edgerton, I had my doubts."

I glanced up from my desk to find Fredericka. "I didn't realize we had an appointment."

She shook her head. "No. I was in the neighborhood and talked my way in."

I had to grin at that. "You blabbed your way past my assistant?"

"To be fair, I am terrifying and intimidating."

I had to laugh at that. "Go ahead, have a seat, I suppose. I have a meeting in thirty, but I can attempt to move it if this is urgent."

She shook her head and took a seat, nonetheless. "No, it's not urgent. But you and I are going to have a talk."

I swallowed hard. After everything I'd done, had I still failed? Bloody how? I'd gotten married to secure this. There was no way I'd fucked this up.

With her purse tucked next to her on the floor, she folded her arms. "I know that you weren't engaged."

I sputtered. "No, that's not true. You watched me get married."

"Yes, I did. Honestly, I was quite curious to see how far you would go."

"I don't know what you're talking about. You watched me marry Emma."

"Yes, you got married and I must say that the wedding was beautiful. Absolutely stunning. And, Miss Varma, well... You are the lucky one. I suspect you know it."

"What is this about?"

"What it's about is I know you lied."

No. I was not letting this go. Everyone was bloody depending on me. "Now, just a minute—"

She put up a hand, interrupting me. "I knew the woman you were with at the benefit, Anisa Bucker. She's married to Darien Bucker, the tech billionaire. Her husband is a bore and quite an ass, actually, so I don't judge you for having your fun. But when I watched you trying to weasel your way out of it, insisting you were engaged, I was so curious to see how you would pull it off."

I didn't usually sweat. Hell, my friends like to call me ice. I could freeze someone with a glare, but she had me on a dead end, and I had no way out.

I was perfectly still. Calm on the exterior, churning on the inside. It was like an avalanche. What answers could I offer? All said and done, I'd fucked up, and she'd known all along that I was trying to fix it.

When in doubt, go for the truth.

"Fredericka, I'm sorry. This wasn't the route I would have chosen, but I have to own it because we needed this merger. And the thing is, I have completely fallen in love with Emma. We have known each other since we were kids. She's one of my best mate's little sister. She's smart, and driven, and funny, and God, I mean, she's stunning to look at, but it's more than that. She's completely beautiful on the inside. If you need help with anything, she will find a way to get it for you." I didn't even have to take a breath just to continue on. "She's a complete hell cat and a crusader. She will fight for anyone that she thinks is being unfairly treated and she's got a full dragon's roar. One day with our children, she will protect them with not just her body, but her whole essence. Woe be with the fool who messes with her children. Emma is a full warrior, and maybe I didn't start this knowing how I felt about her, but by the time we got married this weekend, I knew for sure."

Fredericka pursed her lips and raised a brow. "Oi, do you think I'm a fool? Of course, I could tell you're in love with her. Hell, I could tell when we had dinner and you introduced us. How slow are you?"

I blinked. "I beg your pardon?"

She slowed down her speech as if I was an imbecile. "How, slow, are, you?"

I blinked again and then my lips twitched. Oh, she was spicy. "I'm not sure how to answer that question."

"Any fool could see you're in love with her. And of course, I could see why. Even my daughter, who had her own sights on you, I brought her along to dinner that night to see what a playboy you were. But then Miss Varma was a force. And so I wanted to see how far you would go and what you would do to gain my business. I hadn't anticipated that you would actually fall in love and reform your ways. I could tell on Saturday by the way you looked at her that you would not be caught in any more cupboards with billion-aire's wives, will you?"

I sat back and folded my fingers. "No, I won't. She's it. In some ways, she's always been it."

She nodded and then reached down, picking up her massive Birken bag. She reached in and pulled out a large manila envelope.

"I took the initiative and had my lawyers draft the initial agreement. I wanted to deliver it myself."

I blinked in surprise. "Excuse me?"

"My company. It'll be in good hands at London Lords. I'm tired, my dear boy. I don't want to spend time harassing my daughter to get married. I want to start looking after my family the way I should have all these years. Hell, I want a vacation."

I coughed a laugh. "Well, okay. Thank you."

"No, thank you. It's been massively entertaining watching you fumble back and forth, trying not to fall in love with that beautiful woman. Where has she been hiding, may I ask?"

I cracked a laugh at that. "Ah, well, here and there."

"Well, she's a good one. I like her. She's spunky."

"Yeah, that she is."

"You look after her, Mr. Edgerton. I trust your lawyers will be in touch with mine? So, until next time." With that, she made a move to stand up.

I stood up as well and reached for her hand to shake it. She used her other to cover mine, and that maternal wash of warmth had me smiling and aching to call my mother. "Thank you again for understanding."

"Next time, pick somewhere more private, would you? I mean for you and Miss Varma. You wouldn't want the press getting a story about the newlyweds who shagged just about anywhere."

I coughed a laugh. "Right. Absolutely. Thank you again."

And with that, Ben, East, Drew, and I had exactly what we needed to take down Middleton.

Chapter Twenty

Bridge

I walked into East's office expecting our normal Tuesday morning catch-up on projects, but I stopped short when I found not only East, Drew, and Ben, but also Livy, Nyla, and Telly. No Emma though. I frowned. "What's up?"

Ben tapped his desk. That two-finger tap he always did when he was worried about something. From his spot on the couch, East gave me a nod and did that eye-squint thing that he did when he was trying to assess someone's mood. And Drew, well, for once I didn't see him with a glass of scotch in his hand. He was drinking water, and his expression was grim. The women were much better. Livy was giving me her usual direct look, which indicated she meant business. Nyla was leaning against the far window with her hands jammed in her pockets and gave me a nod. Telly... Well, Telly was Telly, and as soon as I walked in and closed the door behind me, she pointed at the open seat and told me, "Park it, mate."

"Aren't we missing one?"

Telly shook her head. "Nope. No Ems on this one."

I sighed and crossed my arms, unwilling to sit. "If you have to tell me something, you need to tell her something too."

Oddly, it was East's voice that got to me. "Mate, you need to sit."

My gaze darted in his direction and then back at Ben. They were both wearing that grim expression of people who were in hell, so I sat.

"What the fuck is wrong? What's going on?"

East started to speak, but then stopped and rubbed his hand on the back of his neck, so Telly took over. "Ugh, fine, I'll do it. We've got evidence that Middleton is fixated on Emma."

"I could have told you that. I saw the way he looked at her. He wants her."

Telly shook her head. "No, Bridge. I mean actually fixated. He's stalking her."

My gaze darted to Ben and I lifted my brow. "What the fuck? Where is she right now?"

Ben placed his hand on his desk. "Mate, easy. Right now, she is at work. We've got Alex planted in Middleton's office looking out for her. He's three floors down. And Livy already tagged her purse. If she moves, we'll know. East is already watching her phone, and he's got Bird's Eye on her."

I pushed to my feet. "You've got fucking Bird's Eye on her?"

East held up his hands. "Mate, when you told me she was going to work for Middleton, I didn't think it was even a question."

"*Mate*, if she finds out, she's going to think I did that."

East shrugged. "I'll be happy to take the fall if necessary."

Bird's Eye was East's proprietary spying software. That was really the only thing it could be called. With Bird's Eye, he essentially knew where every single one of us was at any given time. He could tap in and hear what we were saying on our phones, ambient noises, any background conversations. It was slick. And awful. And dangerous. The one lucky caveat though was that he needed physical access to the phone to install it. And he'd had that on dozens of occasions with Emma's phone.

"You fucking promised."

"Yeah, but I knew it was going to get you if something happened to her. So sit your arse down and listen to Telly."

"Turn it the fuck off."

"Mate—"

"Do it." I'd have security follow her, but I needed her to trust me. And she couldn't trust me if I was watching her like this.

"Fine. Done," East pouted.

Telly had turned her portable projector toward the blank wall behind East, and she flipped up a series of images, using her red laser pointer to direct our attention. "That's Middleton right there, across the street from your place on the day of the wedding. And that's him watching Emma's place on one of the days that you all had your little spat and she took off. That is you and Ems in Notting Hill. You notice that bloke there,"—she pointed at various faces as she spoke—"that bloke back there, and that woman right there? They are all with Crime Tech Security. They have a contract with Middleton and his father. He's watching her every movement. There's nothing she does that he doesn't know about."

I cursed under my breath, running my hands through my hair. "Fuck." I needed to think this through. "Fine. We need to vamp up security at my house. She has to have a bodyguard, whether she wants one or not. Only those people that we trust and know can't be messed with."

Ben nodded. "I've already talked to Roone and Ariel. They're sending us a temporary assist from the Winston Isles. The Royal Elite will be here this evening. Two guards on rotation until we get our own people in place."

I nodded. "Thanks mate."

He nodded. "Emma's not just yours; she's ours. She's family. Of course we will protect her."

"And she doesn't know?"

Telly shook her head. "I don't think she does. If she did, she would have told me. And she certainly would have told you, especially now that you're married."

I ran my hands through my hair and started to pace. Normally Ben's office felt expansive and had more than enough room. It was the bloody size of my living room, which was nearly a thousand square feet. But now it felt like I was choking. Like there were too many people in the room and there was not enough oxygen for all of us. "Fuck, fuck, fuck, fuck. I should have anticipated this. I let her go to work for him. I fucked up."

East shook his head. "No, mate. We all did. We all agreed."

"We agreed, but Emma is my responsibility."

The room went silent. Everyone sort of looked away from me except for Livy, who lifted a brow as the corners of her lips tipped up in a slight smile. Fucking hell, I just outed myself as being completely in love with my wife. But that was a problem for another day. The current problem was keeping her ass safe.

"All right, we have to get her out of here."

Ben nodded. "I was going to suggest that. But you just got married, and I didn't exactly think you'd go for that."

I rounded on him. "The safest thing for her is to be far the fuck away from him. So yeah, pack her up. I'll send Ollie and Alex and Liam with her."

Our recruits for the Elite would be an excellent cover as an official work trip of some sort. They'd been training, so they'd be able to protect her for now, and then we'd get more private security. I'd put her in a fortress so tight that Middleton could never get in.

And she'll never get out.

That niggling little voice at the back of my brain tried to talk me out of the safest plan, because that part of me wanted to see her every day. Now that I had her, I couldn't let her go. Could I?

Let her go? You're going to lock her up, far away from you.

"It's the only way. Let's get her a flight plan and get her out of here tomorrow."

East was in agreement, but only somewhat. "I agree we need to get her out of here, but that will make Middleton suspicious. We need to be a little more delicate with it. Don't forget that we've already got Alex in play. If it gets bad, he can help. Let the Royal Elite turn up, and we'll make a move by the end of the week. We need to give her a reason to be gone. I can forge some medical records and make it look like her mum's ill and she's going to New York. Obviously, she won't be going to New York. We'll get some security for Pamma Auntie, just in case, and then we'll quietly move Emma out of London. I personally think the Winston Isles is the best option. The Royal Elite is right there. Obviously, we have protection from Sebastian and Penny. Anyone who turns up and doesn't belong in the Winston Isles, there will be a travel case on them."

They'd already been thinking about this. Why hadn't I been thinking about this?

Because you were distracted by your dick. You were busy falling in love. And they were busy actually trying to protect her.

Fuck. I overlooked something because I'd let emotions get in the way. And I knew better. I absolutely knew better. What the hell was wrong with me? Why did I think that I could be a protector?

Had I protected Darcy appropriately? Sure. She was in a boarding school, but nobody knew anything about her. I'd put her in a tower to protect her from people like Mina who were holding her future at their fingertips.

Putting people in a tower only makes them want to run.

I cleared my throat. "Fine. I'll break the bad news to her. Do we have eyes on her now?"

East checked his laptop. "Yup, she just left the office. She's in a car. Looks like she's headed toward Soho, so she's probably coming here."

I glanced at my watch. We were supposed to have lunch at noon. She'd left early to come and see me.

"Does Middleton have eyes on her now?"

It was Telly's turn to speak. "I tapped into the CCTV. I can't tell which cars are which, but I'm assuming he does. I'm trying to get a hand on it now."

"Fuck. Of course, just when I get something good."

Ben's voice was soft. "We'll figure this out, mate. This is happening to all of us."

Drew sat forward. "Bollocks. Are you lot really trying to feed him that right now? Obviously, he's gone and fallen for her. That's why he's all wound up about how much danger we put her in. Don't you lot realize? We are poison. Everything we touch turns to shit. Ever since we went on this little quest, everything has gone to shit."

We all turned to stare at Drew. "Mate, what the fuck are you on about?"

"We started this. Van Linsted went down, but we ran a bowling ball to the pins of the Elite. We're going after them one by one, and in the process, we've crippled the institution. We're just bulldozing our way toward this without even considering what this would mean to each of our lives. It nearly cost Livy her life, and Nyla, more than once for that matter. And God help us, what more is coming?"

Nyla shrugged that off. "We've handled everything well though. Some things are inevitable and we really don't have a choice but face it head on. We can do this. Together. As always."

Drew shook his head. "Yeah, don't you see though? You lost your father in the process. We are a poison, and you all know that. And now it's happening again, this time to Ems. Baby Tobes is in trouble. And once again, we're going to do what we always do, fuck it up and leave a trail of bodies."

"What would you have us do then, Drew? Just let it go? Pretend that they didn't kill him?" Ben asked.

Drew ran a hand over his face. "Fucking hell, do you hear yourself? Yeah, they had a hand in it. But taking them down won't bring him back."

Livy cleared her throat. "Look, this won't solve anything. There is an urgent matter at hand that needs to be addressed, and you guys need to pull yourselves together and agree to disagree. Whether we like it or not, all of us are in this. We can't avoid that. But for now, I think you four should talk about it. Nyla, Telly, and I will just head downstairs. Maybe meet Ems early and grab a drink. We'll keep her occupied Bridge."

"Nah, don't bother. I'll go down myself."

Drew shook his head. "Of course, way to check out, Bridge. You don't want to hear it, but you need to. We *all* need to hear it. This is a mess of *our* making. We can stop the madness, or we can continue on and get Ems killed. It's up to you."

I glowered at one of my oldest mates. "She's not getting killed. Over my dead body. And we're going to get what we need."

He sighed. "The three of you, I love you like brothers. But you have to realize, sooner or later you are going to get someone else killed. And I pray to God Emma's not fucking next."

* * *

Bridge

As I waited for Emma to come home, I tried to think of another alternative, anything else I could do, another way out of this. But after a fantastic lunch where she'd been happy and talking about our new projects and possible new jobs, she'd been happy, and glowing, and resplendent.

And yes, we had gone to shagtown on my desk, because I was that arsehole. I really was. Instead of just telling her what I knew and what we were going to have to do, I had acted as if everything was fine. Because I'd been looking for a way out where I wouldn't have to walk away from the only woman I'd ever loved.

Security sent a notice on my watch which told me she was home. And it was another ten minutes before the *clip-clop* of her heels hit the marble entryway. The two of us had already made plans for how we were going to completely demolish and fix the house. Get rid of all the Minaisms. All the areas that Mina designated as mine were much too dark and heavy. Emma knew that. The first time she'd seen my office, she'd told me it was all wrong and that everything else in the house was too frilly, too girly, a merry French countryside theme and that was not my style, and it certainly wasn't Emma's.

The first thing Emma had done when she moved in was take off her shoes and put her feet on Mina's antique French country-side coffee table, and then really, really slouched down into the one piece of furniture I actually liked, which was an oversized couch. At six-two-and-a-half, I needed room. I had laughed and asked her what she was doing, and she said, "Pissing Mina off."

I'd known right then that I was going to like having her there. She stopped at the study and peeked in. "Hey, I'm home. Did you want to get a curry, or do you feel like cooking something? Because I do *not* feel like cooking something."

I laughed. "You never feel like cooking something."

"Oh my God, accurate. My poor mother, somewhere she's insulting me because how in the world could she end up with an Indian daughter who does not know how to cook proper Roti? Well, actually, I do know *how* to cook. I just hate the process. Loathe it."

Just hearing the lilt of her voice was enough to make me smile.

Emma talked fast. A mile a minute stream of consciousness. But somehow she was still thoughtful and smart.

"Can you come in for a sec?"

"That's what you said at lunchtime, and then I ended up with my legs splayed on your desk and you ruining my hair."

I grinned. "Well, you look better that way. And I'm not sorry I did it."

"Uh-huh."

My smile fell as I tried to think of a subtle way to break this to her. "Actually, I need you to come here."

Her brows dropped immediately, and gone was the playful teasing in her eyes. "What is it?"

She sat down and crossed her knee, brows furrowed. I slid a manila envelope over to her. "In there is a new passport for you and an itinerary."

She blinked. "I'm sorry, I don't understand. Why do I need a passport? I mean, are we doing the name change thing? I didn't think we were. How the hell did you get my passport?"

I sighed. "No, it's not your real passport. It's not in your name. That's your new name."

She lifted her gaze, confusion etched on her brow as she gave me a shaky smile. "I don't understand. Is this part of the whole secret society thing? Your wives and girlfriends get secret passports?"

I shook my head. "No, just you."

"Okay, why is your voice like that? What the fuck is going on, Bridge?"

"Ems, this is already hard enough."

"What is hard enough? You have to talk to me."

I ran my hand through my hair and pushed up from my seat. "I'm sending you straight to the Winston Isles."

Her eyes went wide. "I'm not going any-fucking-where. What's wrong with you?"

"Middleton, he's been stalking you for weeks."

She sat stock still. "What? What are you talking about?"

"We had a meeting today. Telly showed these photos of Middleton at your mum's house and across the street from Ben's on the day we got married. He even had men following us to Notting Hill."

Emma did a headshake that made her look like she was glitching. "No, um, I don't... Wait, there was a team meeting without me?"

"It happened before we were had lunch. I didn't know about it until I walked in. Because it was so sensitive, they wanted to talk to me first."

"That is some bullshit right there. They talked to you first like I'm the little lady? Fuck that."

"I know, I know. I think they were trying to protect you."

"Well, I don't need that kind of protection. Whose fucking grand idea was that?"

"I don't know. And that's not the point. The point is you have to go."

Her eyes went as round as saucers. "The hell I do. I'm not going anywhere. Look, if you're worried, give me a bodyguard or something. Hmm, preferably someone hot."

I ground my teeth. "Stop it. Stop right now. You're not fucking doing this. Middleton is coming for you. He's been watching you, checking your phone. He is dangerous. You can feel it. You said so yourself. So I'm doing what I need to do. I am protecting you. I don't want to do this. I don't want things to be this way, but I have tried to think of a way I can keep you safe and keep you with me, but I can't find one."

"In all of the thinking that you've done since the secret meeting, you haven't once called to talk to me. Instead, I come home, and what did you do? You gave me an edict. That's bullshit."

"What the fuck am I supposed to do, Emma?"

"You talk to me. This afternoon, you fucked me senseless instead of talking to me and asking me for ideas about how to solve this. And now... Now you give me this?" She tossed the envelope back on the desk. "I don't want this. I'll go stay at Mum's."

"You can't. He knows your mum is in New York. He will send men there. Money is no object to him, and he is obsessed with you. What do you want me to do?"

"I want you to talk to me. Instead, you're giving me edicts and telling me what I will and will not do. Fuck you, Bridge."

I could see it then. I recognized that I should have told her this afternoon and I should have asked her how she wanted to handle it.

But you know she would have chosen wrong. You know it.

I did know it. Which was why I had chosen for her. Something she saw as the ultimate betrayal.

Chapter Twenty-One

Emma

I couldn't breathe. I couldn't think. I just needed to drive. I pushed out of my chair and flew through the house. I just needed to be alone, but I could hear Bridge's steps thundering behind me. He caught me on the stairs and grabbed my arm. I did a quick twist of my wrist to bring my elbow down to my side and he was forced to release me. But instead, he grabbed me at the waist and brought me down on the runner.

"You will listen to me. You have to go."

"Fuck you," I spat back.

He jerked as if I'd hit him. "Ems, be reasonable."

"Reasonable? You're asking *me* to be reasonable?"

"Look, it's not ideal. You and I have just gotten started. But I can't protect you here."

"My God, you don't get it."

His eyes went wide and he shook his head a little bit. "*You* don't get it. Your life is in danger, and you want to argue with me because I didn't tell you sooner? Because I solved the problem?"

"See, that's just it. Right there. The solving of the problem. I'm not a problem to be solved, Bridge. Fuck, I am your *wife*."

He shoved away from me and ran his hands through his hair,

still crowding me on the stairs and not giving me much room to move. "You *are* my wife. Sorry if you don't like it."

"You know that's not what I'm saying. If you have a wife, someone you care about, you share things with them. You talk to them. You communicate with them. You don't give them edicts and expect them to be obeyed."

"I'm sorry you don't like it, but thems the breaks."

"You're out of your mind. And I more than don't like it; I hate it. So I'm not going to do it."

"You're fucking insane. You're getting on that goddamn plane."

"Over my dead body. You will have to pick me up and transport me there yourself, kicking and screaming the whole way."

He glowered down at me, and I hated what I was feeling. The sexual need between us was too vibrant, too hot, too much. I wanted him. Even after what he'd just done to me, I wanted him. Even though he had just broken the promises he made that he would not try to control me, that he would talk to me, that he would love me.

He didn't make you that promise.

It had been in the vows, and even though I knew the vows were bullshit, I believed them. And so now my heart was breaking.

I tried to scoot backward on the stairs, but his fingers hooked on my dress and he tugged me right back down.

"Oh no, you don't. You are not running."

"No, I'm not running. I'm walking away. There's a difference."

"We're going to hash this out. You and I, we're going to talk about this. We are going to fix it."

"There is no fixing this, Bridge."

"Yes, there is."

"No, there's not. Because you made me a promise and you broke it. You could have done anything else, *literally*, anything else. At lunch, you could have said like, 'Hey, we have a problem. You have a stalker.' And I would have been reasonable and said, 'Well, fuck, what are we going to do?' You could have laid out some options in front of me, but oh no, you and your merry band of misfits decided that you need to parcel me off like I'm some precious piece of artwork and lock me in a tower. Fuck off."

I turned around and tried to scoot once more, but he pulled me down and my knee hit the corner of one of the steps and it smarted. "Ow."

Immediately, Bridge's hands were on my leg. "Are you hurt? I'm sorry. I just... You can't run away, Emma."

"Isn't that what you're trying to make me do? Run away?"

"Don't be smart with me. You know I mean you can't run away from me."

"Oh, yeah? Watch me." This time I was quicker, evading his grasp and running up the rest of the stairs to the second floor. I made it just around the corner to the library when his massive arm looped around my waist once more, picking me up off the ground.

"Stop running, Ems. Please. God, I just want to protect you. Do you understand what *I'm* dealing with right now? I just started this thing with you. I mean, really. And now I have to give you up?"

I fought his grip. "You are choosing to give me up."

He growled in my ears. "Stop it, Ems. You'll hurt yourself if you keep this up."

But I couldn't hear him over the heartbreak. I just couldn't. I was throwing elbows, weeping, and kicking my legs, and Bridge just stood there holding me to his body. He lowered his face into my neck as he said, "I'm so sorry. I'm sorry it took so long to realize I had feelings for you. I'm sorry it took me so long to do anything about them. I'm sorry it took so long to recognize I could have you and deem myself worthy of having you. I'm sorry it hurts you that I made a decision without you. At the same time, if it will protect you, I don't give a fuck. So you are going to calm your ass down."

Just when his pleas and his apologies were starting to hit me in the heart, he had to go and say that. I elbowed him in the gut. He *oofed* but wasn't letting me go. I managed to scoot my body down, out from under his grip, and I turned around and faced him. Tears were streaming down my face, and that made him hesitate. "I don't trust you. You made me a promise and you lied. You're sending me away. I don't want to go. I want to stay and fight."

"And that's the problem, Ems. I don't think I can let you."

"So, not only are you sending me away, but you're also telling me that I'm incapable of fighting?"

"This situation? Yes. This fucker Middleton... Your brother died, and he and his family covered it up, and now he's stalking you. You think I'm just going to stand by and let that happen? You think I'm just going to let him hurt you? As much as I care about you, do you think I'm capable of that?"

"I'm not saying you're going to stand by, but let's talk about the options. All I'm asking for is a fucking conversation. I'm reasonable. If you told me it's really not safe and I could see it for myself when you laid out all the reasons, I might have made the same choice. But you didn't give me one."

I shoved his chest because I could see that he had finally gotten it. The reason I was mad was not because I had to leave and I didn't want to leave him, but more because he had taken the choice out of my hands. I swung toward the bedroom, making a left and then a right before I got to the next staircase. And he still followed. "Ems, what are you doing?"

"I'm going to pack a bag."

I could almost feel the relief wash over him. "Oh God, okay. Okay, I'll help."

"No, twatface. I'm not packing a bag to run off to the Winston Isles. I'm packing a bag to go to my mum's."

And just like that, I could feel the heat of rage coming up behind him. The force of it was so strong it nearly blew me over, and I backed up against the wall of the narrow staircase.

"What?"

"You heard me. I'm heading to mum's. I'll make my own choices from there. I don't need your help."

"Yes, you do. You think I'm going to let my wife walk away when I'm trying to keep her safe?"

"You're not going to have a choice. I'm leaving."

"Remember the first night when I caught you in my suite? I will keep you locked in the safe room if I have to."

"And that would be kidnapping. You will break us forever."

He reached for me, but I shoved at his chest. He reached for me again, and I shoved again, but this time, he grabbed both of my hands. "I love you. Do not do this."

I tilted my chin up. "You have a funny way of showing it."

His lips slammed down on mine, and even as I whimpered and fought against his hold, against the way his body just overtook mine, crowding everything out until all I could feel was him and his energy and his anger, and his... fuck, his love. I succumbed. His tongue was hot against mine, and I was weak. He knew it. I knew it. But then he made this whimper at the back of his throat, and against my lips he whispered, "Please don't leave me. I just... I need to keep you safe."

It made me pull him closer and kiss him harder. But then I had to push, because I knew he was going to hurt me much more than anyone else could. I had to leave and think and figure out my own best solutions. If Middleton was stalking me, that was real trouble. So home wasn't a perfect idea, but just for a night, I needed to regroup and make a decision in the morning. By myself, since apparently, all my friends and my ever-loving husband didn't see fit to speak to me.

I pushed his chest, and he released me immediately. "Ems?"

"No, Bridge. You don't get to throw a love bomb at me and make my brain go to mush. I'm in possession of all my faculties, and I'm not staying here. I'm not dumb. I'm not going to do something stupid. But I can't stay another day with you. Not like this."

And then I left him in the hallway and headed to our room to pack my things.

* * *

Bridge

I hadn't slept.

Last night wasn't the first time I'd slept on a floor, but sleep last night was impossible. I'd parked it in in front of our bedroom door, but the moment the clock hit 6:00 a.m., she vacated the room and left, stepping over my body as she went. She didn't even take much, just a weekender bag. I asked her where she was going and she told me she was not telling me.

I told her I just needed to know if she was safe, but she said, "I'll text you and let you know I'm safe, but don't follow me."

As if I had to do that. I had a GPS tracker on the car. She had gone to her mum's house and stayed there exactly thirty minutes. The driver knew better than to leave her. And then she'd come out with another bag and had him take her to the train station. And from there, I had no idea where she went. Fuck. Why did I let her go? Why did I listen? Why did I give her space?

My phone rang and I jumped at it. "Emma?"

"Nope, the next woman in your life. Well, half-woman. I don't know. Young woman. How's that?"

I sighed. "Hi, Darcy."

"Hello, big brother, what's the matter?"

"Nothing is the matter. Are you okay?"

"Yes, I'm okay. I was actually calling you about going to a concert, but you sound awful. What happened? Did you fuck up with Emma?"

"Why is it that you assume *I* fucked up?"

"Oh please, she is literally the coolest person you know. If something went awry, it was your fault, not hers."

"You only think she's cool because she's a lot like you."

"Exactly. The coolest person I know."

I sighed. "I did something she didn't like. And now she just left."

My sister was silent for a moment. "Jesus fucking Christ, Bridge, did you cheat on her? Jesus, how fucked up are you?"

"Language. And the answer is, pretty fucked up, but no, I would never do that. Are you kidding me?"

"Okay, so you didn't cheat. What made her run?"

"I made her a promise, and I broke it. But for her own safety. She took a car but she ditched it, and I don't know where she is."

"Bridge, I'm sorry."

"Yeah, it's shitty. And I'm pretty bollocksed in the head about it."

"Well, I mean, go get her then."

"I guarantee you, she does not want to see me."

"When was the last time you listened to what somebody else wanted?"

I frowned at that. "I listen."

"You sort of listen. But here's the thing, you're my big brother, and I know how intelligent you are. And by virtue of you knowing a lot of things, you tend to make decisions *for* people. People don't always like that. They at least want to be consulted about their own lives."

"You think that's what I do to you?"

"I think that's what you do to everyone. You can't help it. But for some people, especially people like me, people like Emma, the more you do it, the more we fight it. And then we just either die a little on the inside and let you take over, or we cower, or we run. It looks like Emma's running."

I considered that for a moment. "Darcy, I'm not trying to keep you from being you."

"No, and we're not talking about me right now."

"Well, aren't we a little?"

"You know, I was glad you came last time. Talking to Emma

gave me some perspective. I'm a little hard on you to get your attention, but it's not like you're the one who abandoned me."

"No, I'm not. But I can be rigid at times. I get that."

She laughed. "Are you sure rigid is the right word? Obstinate maybe is a better one."

"Fine, obstinate. Slightly."

"Oh my God. Do you know where she is?"

"Well, she went to her mum's, but she's not there anymore. And I don't know where she went after that."

"Think about some places that belong to both of you. Some place that there's a memory you share or something."

I racked my brain. "Oh, actually, I might know where she is. And East has Bird's Eye on her phone, so I should probably just ask him."

"Or there's that. I don't even want to know what Bird's Eye is, and I don't want to know if you have it on me."

"I don't."

"Don't ask for help. Find her on your own. It would mean more."

I ran my hands through my hair. "What concert are you trying to go to?"

"It's just an Ed Sheeran concert. It's in Italy. Please, can I go?"

"Yes, but you have to take my plane. Who's going with you?"

"A couple of girlfriends."

"No boys allowed."

She sighed. "Fine."

"See, it's called the art of negotiation. Just send a note to my assistant to deal with the details. You'll stay at the London Lords hotel there and take the plane. Anything else?"

She chuckled. "See? You're doing it again. But this time it's for my benefit, so I'm happy about it."

"I love you, Darcy."

She was silent for a moment. "You know you don't usually say that, right?"

I frowned. "What?"

"You know, that you love me. You never say it."

My gut twisted. "Of course, I say it."

"No, I say it and you say, 'Me too.' Or I say it and then you give me a kiss on my forehead and hug me tight, or you do awesome things for me. Or you say, "I know, love.' Or you tell me I'm the most important person in your life. Any of those lines, but you never say I love you."

"Fuck. I really am a shitty parent."

"You're not a parent, you're a brother. But I heard you this time, and I like the sound of it, so keep saying it."

"Yes, Darcy, I love you."

"I know. My point wasn't that I don't think that you do. I know you do. It's infuriating sometimes, but you're very, very clear on that."

"Well, at least I'm clear on some things."

"Now go get your woman."

I was dressed in no time. I didn't bother shaving, and my driver was lucky I'd even taken time to brush my teeth. On the way to her parents' flat, I texted the lads and told them I wasn't coming in. And then I asked East if he turned off Bird's Eye like I'd said. His response was immediate. "Yup, as soon as you said it, I had it off."

"Can you put it back on?"

It took a second for him to answer. "No, I can't do it again without access to her phone. Once I shut down that door, that was it."

"Fuck."

"What's wrong, mate? Did something happen to her?"

"Well, she's gone missing. Not because of anything untoward, but because I fucked up. So I need to find her."

"Do you want me to check her cards and stuff?"

"Yes, but no. I need to find her on my own, I think."

"All right, you do that."

I went to the rooftop across from her parents' flat only to find she wasn't there. I ran my hands through my hair as I plopped on one of the seats she'd set up. Where else could she be? How little did I know her that I didn't even figure out where she would go when she was upset? And then it occurred to me that one of the best times I could remember with Emma had been at her mum's house in Essex. Pamma Auntie never really used it because it had been a guilt house from Emma's dad. But that weekend we'd been there, the last time she and Toby and I had all been together, we'd had a grand time. Emma and I had kept the bickering to a minimum, and it had just been fun. We played games and enjoyed ourselves. And I thought I finally knew exactly where to go.

It took another hour to get to Essex. When I dashed out of the car and ran to the house, I could see the lights on in the sitting room. She was there. My heart hammered as I banged on the door, hoping and praying she would open it and I wouldn't have to pull out my lock-picking kit.

But as it turned out, I didn't need it, because Emma yanked open the door.

And I lost it.

"Never do that again. Never leave me again and not tell me where the fuck you're going. You left. You promised me you wouldn't leave, and you *left*."

Her mouth opened to say something, but then she closed it. I grabbed her, slammed my lips over hers, and kissed her hard just so she could feel the fury and frustration that I was feeling. Then I released her. "You do not leave."

"It wasn't at night. It was in the morning. It was already dawn."

"Bullshit semantics, and you know it. You left."

"Well, you controlled me."

"Fuck you, Emma, you left me."

Her face softened. "I'm sorry, Bridge."

Her apology hit me in the chest. "What?"

"Well, on the way here, I sort of realized how worried you probably were, and while I wanted you to worry, I *didn't* want you to worry. So, I'm sorry."

"Look, just come back and we'll figure this out. I screwed up. I fucked up bad. I know I'm domineering and overbearing, and there's no explaining that. But please also know that all the shit in my life made me need to be in control of everything around me, and I know I can't do that with you or with Darcy. Can you just please come home so we can talk about this?"

Her hand went to my chest, right over my heart. "Bridge, I'm sorry that I made you worry. I'm sorry that you were scared."

My hand wrapped over hers. "Okay, then come home. Just—"

She shook her head. "I am sorry, but I'm not coming home."

And just like that, Emma Varma broke my heart, again.

Chapter Twenty-Two

Emma

I had known he would come for me. I expected it. I knew the car he'd given me, or rather that I'd taken, had likely been tracked. I turned off my phone in case that was being tracked too. When I finally turned it on the next morning, I had fifty messages. Twenty-five of those from Bridge. A handful from Liv. East, Ben, Nyla, and Telly as well. Each of them looking for me, worried about me. I just needed space. My friends, my family, each one of them, had tried to handle me like I was a child. Which was just the biggest pile of bullshit I'd ever heard in my life. And then there was Bridge, Mr. Bright Idea, with his plane tickets to no man's land. Ugh. What the fuck was that about?

He cares about you and he's worried.

I wasn't an idiot. I knew Middleton was a problem. I knew he made me uncomfortable. And now I knew he was dangerous. A threat and a force that I should be wary of.

But what bothered me incessantly was why Bridge hadn't just talked to me. The way he just sat there and handed me that envelope and told me I was leaving, like I was a child. Like Darcy sent off to boarding school.

I told myself I was never going to be in that position again, begging someone to love me enough to include me in the decision making. I wasn't that person. And I couldn't accept the fact that Bridge was doing this to me. Him, of all people.

And I had to admit that Bridge's little display, sleeping in front of the door to prevent me from leaving, that had given me a pause. No one had ever tried to stop me. No one had ever insisted that they cared. Except, that was hard to reconcile too. What man would try to take away my voice? Not that I didn't agree that leaving town might be a good idea. I was no fool. I was trying to figure that out right now. How best to do that and what strategy would provide a good outcome for me.

I wasn't really surprised when he showed up on the doorstep for the second day in a row.

"Ems let me explain. Let's talk, please."

I shook my head. "I know what talk means."

The corner of his lips quirked into a smile. "That's not why I am here."

"It might not be why you're here, but we apparently can't seem to help ourselves. So you stay right there."

"Emma, it was fucked up. I was wrong. I shouldn't have tried to send you off. I was worried and scared, and I did what I always do. I tried to fix it and control it. Throughout my life, I've had this belief that when you can control things, you don't have to be the scared kid in the dark, not sure of how you're going to take care of your mother, or your sister, what you're going to do for food, not only today, but into tomorrow and the next. Those are my survival instincts. Right now, everything is telling me to take care of you. Make sure that you survive. I can't just watch you walk into danger. I care too much about you. So we are going to figure something out somehow, because I'm not okay with that outcome."

"I see what you mean, but my point is that you didn't have to control me. All you had to do was *talk* to me. If you'd just done that, we could have figured this out together. But no, you had to charge in like Captain Save-a-Ho. I'm an adult, Bridge. I'm not

Darcy. And while I acknowledge that I don't know everything, I need you to at least respect me for fuck's sake."

"I know. Look, I just I came to talk to you. I'm scared for you. I tried to pretend like I have it together, like I know what the fuck I'm doing, but I don't. I really fucking don't. Knowing that you're in danger, that you could be hurt, that worries me. I can't allow it to happen. So just tell me what to do, what to say, how to be. I just can't have you walk away from me again."

I stepped back to let him in, even though I knew it was a bad idea. I suspected I would wind up on my back or against the wall with my legs wrapped around his hips, moaning his name, because I craved his touch. That was the problem. I had always craved him. But it was more than want, stronger than longing, and my resolve melted.

He shut the door behind himself and leaned against it. "Thank you for letting me in."

"You're not staying. Like I said, I'm sorry I ran. I just need to process what the fuck is happening, and I couldn't do that in your house. After the other day, it started to feel real, you and me."

"It is real for me. A hundred percent."

"I don't know if I can trust that, Bridge. At the first sign of trouble, you reverted back to your old ways, and that tells me this isn't real. That feels like I'm just a thing, a chess piece to be shuffled back and forth across the board. But you forget that the queen is the most powerful piece on the board and she has a nasty bite. You would do well to remember that."

"Ems, can you please give me a chance? We'll just talk. Let me stay here with you. I have to make sure you're okay. I have to make sure *we're* okay. Look, I'll sleep in one of the guest rooms if that would make you feel better. Any of the guest rooms. I won't bother you. I promise."

I couldn't let him think I was still in that state of mind. I was angry, but I wasn't cruel. "I'm okay. We're okay. I'm just trying to get past this anger about the fact that you guys blindsided me. But other than that, I'm good. We're good. I wanted to tell you that at lunch, but we were distracted."

"Yeah, because I knew I was doing something that was going to make you angry. I wish you'd told me."

"Well, I wish you'd told me."

"Right. So what would you do differently?"

He pushed away from the door, and I took a step back. "Not that, Bridge. We can't solve all of our problems with sex."

"We're not solving our problems with sex, Ems. Yes, we fight, but that's normal in any relationship. But we need to somehow reach a resolution, right?" The look on his face was that of sincerity and longing. I swallowed hard. I was weaker than I thought I was. I couldn't resist him. I knew exactly where this was going to go.

He took another step toward me. "I always loved this house, you know." He must have sensed the discomfort that I felt because he attempted to change the topic.

"Me too. I hadn't come here in years. Mum kept coming for maybe a few years after Toby died. I just couldn't, but mostly because I wanted to lock up all of the good memories of him inside this place. They will be here forever. But Bridge, I'm not shagging you," I blurted out.

He nodded. "Of course not. I don't deserve that. I need to earn your trust back."

I furrowed my brow. "Okay, then why are you coming toward me like that?"

"Like what?"

"Like you plan to eat me."

Actually, that's not the worst thing that could happen.

No. Damn it. Focus.

His smile was slow at first, and then a devilish grin spread across his face. "Because that's exactly what I plan to do."

The back of my thighs hit the couch, but the smile on his face set off alarm bells in my brain, so I'd backed up with a little too much force. The next thing I knew, my legs were up in the air with my hand on the soft plush material of the couch.

"Well, I see you're amenable."

I couldn't help it, a laugh escaped even though I did not feel like laughing. "Oh my God, Bridge. You knew the couch was there."

"Yes, I did. You're the one adamant to run from me. You need to be coming toward me so that we can fix this."

"I'm not going to have sex with you."

"Okay, maybe not. But I'm sure as hell going to try."

And then I felt his firm hands on the backs of my thighs and applying firm pressure to have me open my legs.

Oh, fuck.

When his large palm pressed over my mound, I shivered. "Oh my God, Bridge."

"Shhh. I'm going to apologize properly. And we are going to fix this."

Oh God, it was what I wanted. I wanted him so much, I could've died in that moment. And then I remembered that manila envelope on his desk as he stared at me, expecting me to just take it and be grateful, and the surge of rage was renewed. With a couple of twists and grunts, I sat upright, and Bridge backed up.

"Ems? What's wrong?"

"You're not going to blind me with orgasms and think that everything's fine. It's not. You were trying to push me away with that 'take this envelope and your IDs in it' bullshit. Like I'm some kind of whore you're packing out. I'm not fucking Mina."

He scowled at me then. "That's enough, Emma. I've never treated you like Mina."

I shoved him. "You did then. Just like her. She pissed you off too, huh? In cahoots with your Dad and all that. Is that what you do with all the garbage? Just put it out?" I shoved at his chest again and he barely moved.

"Emma, stop it. That's not what I said. Don't talk about yourself like that."

I shoved again, and this time he caught my wrists. "Enough, Emma. I can see what you're doing. You want to fight because you don't want to feel it. That pull, the fact that we need each other. I get it. So shove at me all you want. Hit me. Fight me. But I'm not leaving, and I'm not letting you run. One way or another, we're dealing with this."

"Just because you say so, right?" I tried to wrench my wrists free, but he was too strong. And I remembered what I learned in self-defense class and the training that Liv, Telly, and I took with Nyla. I went to raise a knee, but he immediately blocked it with one of his.

"Kitten, if you want to fight, we can fight. But I don't want to hurt you."

"Let me go, Bridge."

"I will, but only if you promise you're going to play nice."

I took a deep breath. "Okay, fine."

The moment, he released my wrist, I went to deliver an elbow, but he smirked and blocked it easily, turning me around and wrapping his arms around me from behind. "Somehow I knew you weren't going to play nice."

His breath was hot against the shell of my ears, and I shivered. "Let me go."

"No. Not until you and I have come to an agreement and try to figure out our shit. You can fight me all you want. I'm not going, and you're not leaving."

"I'm not making love to you."

That was probably a lie because my core was melting. The heat coursing through my veins told me I was weak and I was likely going to cave.

"Why don't you say that with more conviction next time? Because right now, you're rubbing your ass against my cock. Do that one more time and your ass and my dick are going to have a very stern conversation."

That should have scared me. That should have had me stilling. Instead, I turned my head so I could meet his gaze partially, and then I very deliberately rotated my hips into the steely length of his erection.

"Well, now you've gone and done it, haven't you, princess?"

"I'm not scared of you."

"That's good. I'm glad to hear it. Because that will make this a lot more fun."

Chapter Twenty-Three

Bridge

I woke to scratches in on my back and sore muscles. Okay, so that had happened.

Emma and I were, point-blank, volatile. She had this way of pushing my buttons, and I had this way of pushing right back. When we were working, we were really working. We made the best partners.

But when we weren't working... Jesus fucking Christ. Last night, she'd needed to work out a little frustration. I was pretty sure I'd have love bites on my neck and scratches on my back.

Last night was something akin to our first time, raw and a little out of control.

And you weren't exactly gentle last night either.

I knew I must have left my fingertip imprints on her ass and thighs and there was at least one love bite on her ass.

Last night, that was the version of me that she needed. But sometimes she needed someone who could be gentle with her. Someone who would give her not just what she needed, but let her have fun as well.

I could be both. I had to be able to be both.

She stirred against me, and I kissed her shoulder. "Good morning."

She groaned immediately as she tried to roll over. "Oh my God, I think I've got bruises up and down my back."

I winced. "Fuck, I'm sorry."

"Don't be. I think I landed a couple of good hits myself."

I glanced down at my collarbone where she'd bit me. Slightly red and discolored, but not too sore yet. When she saw me looking at it, she started to lick and kiss it. And then just like that, my cock stirred.

She groaned. "Oh my God, I was just kissing it to make it feel better. How can you go again?"

"Well, your ass is cupped up against my dick and I'm remembering you biting me, so yeah, I could go again."

"Okay, fair enough. So could I, but that's not the point."

I chuckled and kissed her shoulder again. "I skived off of work yesterday, so I've got to go in."

"Oh yeah, you should."

I could feel them; her walls were going back up. Safety and protection. "Hey, don't do that. We're not done. Our marriage is as real to me as any other. So no more shutting down. Neither one of us."

"You're the one running away now." She didn't meet my gaze.

"No, I'm not. This is work. I would love for you to come to work with me. There are a million things at London Lords that you could do. Things you could be great at. We have a crisis management department."

"I know. You think I haven't already looked at the jobs? I even considered applying using a fake name hoping nobody would notice."

I frowned at that. "Why would you use a fake name?"

"I don't want any preferential treatment. I want to be hired because I'm good."

"I know you're good. And besides, don't you recognize that

that's how these things happen? How these geezers get richer? Someone hires someone's kid. Gives them a fuck load of money to do not much. Sometimes you get lucky and they're actually decent at what they do but not usually. But if you know someone who is capable of helping you, use it to your advantage. Always."

"Wow. Thanks, Daddy Warbucks."

"Sorry. I guess you don't need that lesson from me."

She sighed. "No. Sorry, it's a personal thing. I know I'm good, but I want other people to be able to acknowledge that."

I nodded. "I get it. So if you are interested, come to the office and we'll discuss this further. How about we do probationary status? You can come in, have a look at the files, and then give some recommendations. We give it to a client. If they like it, then I'll know you're good, and you'll be assured that's why you're getting the job. How's that?"

Our eyes met, and the longing I saw there was the last straw for me. I slammed my lips on hers and my hands slid downward. But Emma stopped me halfway. She grazed her lips over mine but said, "We can't keep doing this."

"Yes, we can, Ems. We need to keep talking. We need to keep communicating. What you said last night about us solving our problems with sex... We just haven't learned to fight fair enough yet. I want to be able to talk to you and to make up with sex. As hot as fighting with sex can be, I don't want to see your skin with bruises unless they're from my handprints on your ass. Anywhere else, I don't want to see. I don't want to be the cause of those."

I could feel her inhale deep, hold it, and then expel the breath. "I'm sorry." Slowly, she turned around in my arms, wincing and groaning as she did. "Last night was a mess. I knew when I saw you on the doorstep what was going to happen. I knew you were mad that I ran, and I was mad that you tried to control me. I knew we were going to end up with me with my knickers down and bent over a flat surface. But I'd let you in anyway because I wanted it to happen. I just feel like we are volatile."

"We *are* volatile. But like I said, we belong together. So, you and I are going to learn to use our words better. And I get it, we can't go home. I fucked up, and I need to earn your trust again. But will you please let me bring security here?"

"Isn't that going to tip off Middleton?"

"We're using team Winston Isles. Royal Elite will come in. They'll cover you at least until we can figure out our next move."

She laughed. "I can see you're trying. You can't help it, but you're trying. And I appreciate that."

It was tough. I wanted to just carry her on my shoulder and put her on the goddamn plane and get her the fuck out of there, but she was right. I couldn't just solve our problems by force of my will alone. Especially not if it was going to alienate her. I needed to work with her, not against her.

"So I'm going to go to work, but security will come. I just ask that you not leave the house, okay? And can you turn your fucking phone back on so we can track you through old-fashioned means?"

"I'm surprised East hasn't already been tracking me."

"No, he hasn't. Well, not now anyway."

She lifted a brow. "What's that supposed to mean?"

"How mad will you be if you found out he had Bird's Eye on you?"

She went still in my arms for a moment, and then she leaned forward to kiss the bruise on my collarbone. "I'm pissed off, but I think that's on him and not on you."

"Yeah. And he was trying to keep you safe. You know East. He's all about safety."

"Right. Okay."

That was all she said, leaving my mind to try and decipher what she meant. "Okay, we are doing this? Okay to security? Okay to East turning on Bird's Eye? I need you to be clear and specific."

She tucked her head and whispered against my skin. "Okay to everything except Bird's Eye."

That tension that had crawled into my heart and wrapped

around it, squeezing it over the last few days, eased at last, but only marginally. It would be a long time until I could breathe easy again, but if she was agreeing that we'd work together and to having security, I could live with that. "All right. You and I are a team."

"Well, we are having conversations about becoming a team, how's that?"

"Fine. Conversations about becoming a team."

When she kissed my bruise again and I tucked her against me, I just prayed to all the Gods in heaven that I would be able to keep her safe, because Emma Varma was everything to me.

* * *

Emma

To say that I was still mad was an understatement. I was ticked the hell off, but these women were my friends and they'd done what they'd done to try and keep me safe. Though it was still bullshit and I was still mad about it, I did need their help. So when Telly picked a neutral location for us to meet at her flat, I'd agreed to meet them with my security in tow.

When I walked in, the girls were already there. The atmosphere was kind of tense, but not in a heavy kind of way. It was like they were trying to assess my reaction, given they'd done me wrong. Casually, I murmured a soft, "Hi."

Telly planted her hands on her hips. "How mad are you? And how long are you going to stay mad? Just so, you know, we all understand."

Despite myself, I wanted to laugh. That was Telly for you. Always there and ready to make you laugh with a joke. She could also make you feel ridiculous. "There's a reason I'm mad and you know it."

"I know. I know. We fucked up. We three queens are eating some crow." She sang and mimicked the tune of that Mark

Wahlberg movie about bank-robbing army guys. 'We three kings are scaling some gold, something, something.' I couldn't remember it. All I remembered from that movie was Mark Wahlberg. I could be forgiven for that.

Liv jumped up from her seat and came over, wrapping her arms around me and squeezing me tight. She was taller than me by an inch, and her curls were up in a messy bun. She had glasses on. "I'm sorry. I would have called and warned you had I known. But we were in a meeting, and it was more along the lines of protecting your safety. So I made a judgment call, which was wrong, mind you. Will you forgive me?"

I nodded my head as I hugged her back. "Yeah, fine. Whatever."

Nyla came over then too and proffered two bottles of wine. "I've got you your favorite. Sweet and soothing wine. None of us will even have a single sip. It's just for you."

"Just wine?"

"No, not just wine. I also got you your favorite almond cake from the bakery. You know, the American one that has like real American cookies? Yup, that one. Am I forgiven?"

I rolled my eyes. "Whatever."

Nyla snuck in to wrap her arms around both of us. Over her shoulder, Livy called, "Telly, you're coming here. Now."

And then I was surrounded by friends squeezing me and pulling me into their protective barrier. "Okay, okay, enough with the touching."

They laughed and finally let me go. I found that I missed their warmth. They were my friends, and they really did only want to take care of me.

Once the wine was poured and the cake rolled out, I ran my hands through my hair and pulled it into a ponytail. "All right, spill it. How bad is it?"

Telly blew out a long breath. "Honestly? Really bad."

"Wow. Take it easy there."

"Hon, I wish I could. I really do. But it's bad. Really, really,

really bad. He's been watching you. The problem is, I don't know for how long. Was it from day one? Does he know you tapped into the system when you shouldn't have? If he does, that means the information we have is useless because he's changed or modified it. But if his following you is a recent thing, we have some leeway. But the problem is, he will search and wonder if you sabotaged him in some way. He'll come looking for answers. We don't want to be around for that."

"Right. Why can't any of this be simple?"

"Well, vengeance is rarely simple. Especially if you want to make someone pay. So, that's where we're at right now ladies. The question is, Ems, what do you want to do?"

I took a long sip and sat back. "I don't want to leave. You guys are my family. I don't want to run and hide. I want to face this head on. I can't pretend I'm not scared. That would be foolhardy. Besides, I'm not good with pretending. But I'd like to be really, really clear about what I'm dealing with first. Ascertain the facts and go from there. Right now, the only fact I know is that Middleton is dangerous, just like his cohorts in Toby's death. I've known it from the moment I knew he was part of Toby's demise, and it was solidified when I took the job at his company. I thought I could handle it. But that was naive. I fully understand that now. What I saw in his eyes at the Price job sent a chill down my spine. Any luck on finding Weston Price's wife by the way?"

Telly shook her head. "I have searched and searched. She hasn't a single credit card, and I haven't caught her on the CCTV anywhere."

"The kid?"

"That's worse, or better, depending on how you guys see it. There was a Jane Doe little girl recently put into foster care who can't remember much on account of being so traumatized. All she is telling anyone was that she wants her momma and Spooky the Bear. If I can get in touch with authorities, show them a picture of the Price girl and find out if it's her, it would make it a lot easier without having to notify Middleton."

"Where was she found?"

Telly winced. "That's the thing, she was found in Barcelona."

My eyes went wide. "Spain?"

Telly nodded. "Yep."

Nyla stepped forward. "Yeah. I've already got Interpol checking because then maybe we can get access a little faster. I did a little back-channeling and discovered she was found on the ferry, all alone in the loo. One of the female passengers found her. So, if we can get a photo, we'll have confirmation and then we can get her father to her safely."

I chewed my bottom lip. "I'm just worried because, what if the dad was in on it?"

Telly cringed. "Goddamn it. What are you saying? We've got some kind of trafficking situation?"

"You mean like the first time?"

Livy shook her head. "Now, I know it's easy to jump to conclusions, but we don't have any proof of that. And other than Toby, we don't know of anyone Middleton has actually harmed. So other than being a creep and potentially dangerous, we have to tread carefully here."

I crossed my arms. "Stop being reasonable."

My phone buzzed, and I picked it up. An unfamiliar number popped up. "Um, let me take this."

I strolled out onto the balcony while the girls poured more wine. "Hello?"

"Emma Varma?"

The voice was a deep baritone. Vaguely familiar but I couldn't place it. "Yeah, this is she."

"This is Lord Edmond Edgerton."

My stomach twisted. "Bridge's father? Are you fucking kidding me?"

"Ah, yes, I was warned that you have a way with words. Ever loquacious."

"What is it you want?"

"I recognize that it may be too late, as you have already married my son, but there's something important you must know. It's urgent."

"I have nothing to say to you."

"I see he's already poisoned your opinion of me. Fair enough. I'm just asking for a meeting at a place of your choosing. Somewhere quiet. I'm actually not trying to cause trouble, I just want to warn you of something. It is important, and it could mean life or death for you and my son."

I didn't want to believe him. But the idea of life and death for Bridge... That worried me. "I don't believe you."

"And I recognize that you don't have a reason to. You're already married. You already won. My influence around my son is over. But he needs your help, and he doesn't even know it."

"I'm afraid I can't do that."

"Miss Varma, this is a matter that is of utmost importance. Let's just say that in our line of work, there are always ways to listen in, and I can't let this information get out. If this became public, it would be too late, and Bridge will pay the price. I am sure of that."

Bridge?

My heart squeezed. What could it be that could harm him? All of my instincts told me I needed to protect him. I had to. I loved him too much. "Where?"

"Wise choice, Miss Varma."

"I'm not sure about that, but just so you know, I have security."

"You won't need them. I will do you no harm."

"Said the wolf to the lamb."

"If you bring security, I won't talk. This is a matter of life and death. I'll text you the details." And then he hung up.

Just what the fuck was he going to tell me? And was this a meeting I was going to take?

Chapter Twenty-Four

Emma

This was a risk. I knew it. But I was willing to take it if it could help Bridge. If it could protect him. The thing was, I knew how he felt about his father. There was no way, under any circumstances, that he would let me go if I told him. That was just another locked-in-the-closet situation waiting to happen.

The only option I had was to go and meet Lord Edgerton and tell Bridge afterward. Because, as I'd learned from life, it was always better to ask for forgiveness, than for permission.

Are you sure about that?

No, I wasn't sure. When he'd texted me with a location, I'd given him a counter suggestion. A place I knew well enough to get in and out of. A place I'd be able to ditch my security if I needed to.

This is a bad idea.

It was. It one hundred percent was a bad call. And Bridge would be furious.

There was a theater on the corner of Charring Cross and Cranbourne Street, The Hippodrome, home to *Magic Mike*. Also home to one of Central London's popular casinos. It would be crawling with people. While it was madness with the throngs of people, the

285

theater itself had a back entrance along a side alley street. And the older Lord Edgerton had agreed to meet me there.

I would need to ditch my security, otherwise Bridge would come charging in and throw me over his shoulder before I got any good information.

He's doing it to protect you. Do you think this is a good idea?

No, I really didn't. But if the truth was going to keep Bridge alive... Jesus, was that even a question? I knew that was dramatic, but they worked in a world of espionage and secrets, lies and assassinations, and poisonings and power brokering. This shit happened all the time. And it was my job to protect him if I could. Just like it was his job to protect me.

You see how he came up with that argument now?

I knew it now. Everything he had done he did because he cared about me. I was having a hard time reconciling this Bridge with the man I'd been chasing for so long. Wrapping my head around it. My reaction to him had been immature. And I really couldn't continue on with that if I wanted to keep him. The fact that I even had an option to keep him was shocking.

Six months ago, I never would have thought that this was real. That this was possible. But maybe it was. I just had to get his father to leave us alone first. The old man had tried to control Bridge with Mina. He needed to see that I wouldn't be intimidated.

There was a girl at Middleton Communications named Natalie, perfectly nice Natalie. She seemed to like me, and even better, seemed to despise Middleton. So when I made drink plans with her to meet at the Hippodrome, she'd jumped at the chance. She kept asking me if I wanted to change our venue, which I knew meant the Hippodrome was a little too wild and crazy for her.

But I insisted. Told her I had a friend in the show and he might want to have a drink with us after. Unfortunately, I was going to cancel on her. And while security was busy trying to locate me, I would be able to meet Bridge's father. It would be easy to slip my detail. I knew that wasn't safe, but I couldn't see an alternative.

Are you sure about that? Because this is the exact kind of shit Bridge was talking about when you agreed to cooperate with him and work things out between the two of you.

This would be fine. It was only going to be a ten-minute conversation. And this was meant to protect him.

At six-thirty, I was out of the house and in the car with the appointed driver, Daniel. Daniel had beautiful brown skin with a shock of curly ringlets that stuck up in every direction. His hair looked so silky and springy, I wanted to ask him what the hell he was doing with his curls. Daniel was the type of fellow who brooked no argument. He was by the book and strictly business. Perfectly polite. Businesslike. But not exactly chatty.

I could tell he was tense about the traffic in Central London. I could feel it in the way he carried himself. It was the least ideal place for security and perfect for exactly what I needed. When he let me out at the Hippodrome, he pointed out my security detail. "You've got Jason over there and Ryan to the right. They'll stay back, but be aware that they're there so that you're not spooked later."

"Thank you, Daniel. I should be done by eight, but I have your number. I'll text you when I'm ready."

He nodded. "Yes, miss. I'll head over to find parking, but I won't be far."

"Thank you."

Then I stepped out and went into the Hippodrome as planned. I had my oversized purse and a plan of action. But even as I walked through the doors, the tension coiled in my neck. Everything in my body told me this was a bad idea, but I'd already committed. Jason and Ryan stuck to me like glue. But then one of the earlier showings of *Magic Mike* let out, and the hallway was flooded with women. Which was my exact opening. I timed it perfectly to slip into the bathroom. Once inside, I quickly hurried to the last stall because I knew at some point the lads would forget decorum and come in looking for me.

In the stall, I quickly changed out of my skirt and put on a pair of leggings and trainers. I then turned my reversible shoulder bag inside out after dumping the contents.

Then came the wig. It wasn't a great wig, but it was just right for my disguise. I tied my hair back into a ponytail and then tossed it on, hoping that at the very least, no one would look too closely. I framed the bangs around my face. When I stepped out of the stall and looked in the mirror, I was a completely different person. My skin would be a dead giveaway, but hopefully the camouflage would work. There was no reason for them to be looking at me. And there was a throng of women outside, so I could easily blend in.

I grabbed a pair of glasses and shoved them on my face, which helped complete the look. And then as calmly as I could, I walked out into the massive rush of people. I got jostled and shoved, but that was fine because I was heading not in the direction that I'd come in, but the other direction where there was another exit. I felt bad because the lads would get an earful from Bridge if something went wrong, but this would take only ten minutes. Maybe they wouldn't even know.

The guilt ate away at me, but I needed answers.

I was at the exit in moments, and there was a limo parked just along the way. One of the doors opened, and a hulking man stepped out. I hesitated, assessing if I had the space and time to run back to the Hippodrome. But then a second man stepped out after him, an older version of the man I loved. His hair was salt and pepper, and his full beard was white. He was bulkier than Bridge was. His eyes were wrong though. His were bright blue, while Bridge's were silver gray. He didn't have Bridge's lashes, and I could see he lacked the cleft chin, but the cheekbones, nose and forehead were all Bridge. Bridge's lips, the set of the eyes, and the cleft chin must have been his mother's genes. "Lord Edgerton, your security is unnecessary."

He gave me a wan smile. "Forgive me if I don't agree. I'm

surprised you don't have security, even though I clearly warned against it."

"You just can't see them."

"My, my, isn't that a feat?"

I tipped my head at him. "You're so busy watching me and the street, but you're not looking up on the rooftops." A totally bullshit lie. But the older man frowned as he glanced up above and then gestured for me to get in the limo. "Oh, after you, I insist."

He rolled his eyes, but climbed in. When I followed, his hulking bodyguard stayed outside, and I said, "I hope he has body armor on."

Edgerton's lips thinned. "Surely my son isn't that paranoid."

"Well, you are. And you suggested that I should be. And by extension, that means your son."

"Touché, Miss Varma."

"All right, I'm here. Stop wasting my time."

"Right, straight to the point. Of course you are. How could you be any different?"

"What do you want? Why did you contact me?"

"It's about you and Bridge. I know I'm already too late. I tried to convince him against it. Obviously, Bennett is Director Prime, so he used his privileges and was able to get your marriage certificate and license through without any problem, but see, there *is* a problem."

"I thought you'd get to the point, but this is just bullshit, isn't it?"

"I promise you, it's not."

I made for the door, and he clamped an arm on my bicep. In the side flap of my purse, I had a Taser. I reached for it and quickly pulled it out. He frowned at me. "Miss Varma, that's not necessary."

"Oh, quite the opposite. It's very necessary. You are touching me without my permission. So kindly take your hands off, and you won't get zapped. I haven't used this thing in a while, so the voltage might be way off."

He released me. "I'm sorry. There's no need for that."

"Uh-huh. You scoot on back and let's make sure you don't have the urge to touch me without my permission again."

He frowned. "You're just like her."

"Who's that now?"

"Your mother. I know her and your father very well."

My stomach pitched. "What the fuck are you on about?"

Lord Edgerton sat back, leaning insolently against the door and spreading his legs out in front of him. "I'm very close with your father. Because I know your family, I'm inclined to watch out for you. My dear, why is it you think I didn't want you to marry my son?"

I shrugged. "Because you're a malignant narcissist who wants to control him?"

His gaze narrowed so quickly I felt a prickle of alarm skipped up my arms. This was a man used to getting his way by any means necessary, and he would not hesitate to end me, physically if he had to.

"Your mouthiness is unbecoming."

"Bridge seems to like it just fine."

You are asking for trouble.

"You really think that your poor attempt at bawdy jokes will deter me? Child, I've seen and done more in my lifetime than you can fathom."

"Says one of the poster children for the Me Too movement. Rich twats with too much money and power. Now tell me, what the fuck am I doing here?

He moved so quickly I had to shuffle back to get away from him. Jesus fuck. He leaned over me ominously. "You will shut your bloody mouth and listen because your life depends on it."

I swallowed hard but did as I was told, all the while searching behind my back for the door handle.

He eased back and smoothed a hand over his hair as if the outburst was out of character.

On the contrary Mr. Cockballs, I see the real you.

"My son, you need to be careful with him. I'm warning you of that against advice."

"Against whose advice?"

"Even I answer to people and the oaths we took. I shouldn't be speaking to you. But I need to warn you because I feel responsible. My son is very dangerous, and staying with him could cost you your life."

I blinked and sat upright. "Bullshit."

"You don't know him like I do. As a child, he put another boy in the hospital and claimed it was an accidental fall. But there was footage that clearly showed Bridge pushed him. He was six at the time. When he was older, he stabbed a teenager then shaved his head... for fun." He sighed. "I'm ashamed to say I thought Eton would straighten him up. That we could educate the monster out of him."

"You're lying."

"I'm not. I bet you he told you the Darcy thing. That I'd made it up. I encourage you to speak to Darcy's mum. She'll tell you that Bridge threatened her. And then during his last term at school, a woman vanished."

The bottom fell out of my stomach. He was lying. I *knew* he was lying. Bridge had told me all about Darcy. None of this was the truth. "What woman?"

"A young student teacher, Melissa Carlisle. Young, beautiful, in her twenties. She was discovered near the Eton boathouse. Stabbed with her head shaved."

A shiver ran up my body. "You're lying. And I'm leaving." I reached for the door, but he stopped me.

"You don't have to believe me. But research it yourself. Look into it. I've got a head start here for you." He tried to hand me a folder.

"I don't want this."

"Take it. You know I'm not lying. Why would I? I have no reason to. I don't care if you like me. I don't need anything from you. I'm just trying to save a life. My son is a murderer." He dropped the folder in my lap.

All I could do was stare at it.

"It's true. Look into it for yourself. Then get yourself as far away from him as you can."

I assessed Lord Edgerton's face, looking for a hint of a lie, any sign of deception, but either he had no tells, or he was telling the truth. Or he was a sociopath. Which was entirely possible. "And if I don't listen to your lies?"

"Another woman could die. I'd rather it wasn't you."

* * *

Bridge

I should have known it was too good to be true. Yes, Emma and I were having problems, but we were working through them to something real. Something that was completely untainted that I could be proud of and be happy about for once in my life. But it was too good to be true, and I knew it the moment I got the call from security.

"Mr. Edgerton, she's done a runner. We have the tracker on her shoes. She's definitely not in the Hippodrome."

If only I could describe this feeling of everything having been fine, perfectly adequate, and then hearing that my wife wasn't where I'd expected her to be. She'd slipped her security, even though she promised me she would do no such thing. And for what? Some clandestine meeting. Luckily, the theater wasn't far.

I arrived less than fifteen minutes from the moment she'd vanished. Of course, it was so like Emma to be badass, so she was smart about it. She'd vanished into a crowd of women. Had she really thought that security wouldn't do everything in their power to keep her safe? That seemed like a miscalculation on her part. I marched to the Hippodrome and found my guys. Jason was most apologetic. "Mr. Edgerton, I'm so sorry. She went to the ladies' loo. We waited but she never came out, so we had to go looking for her only to find—"

I put up a hand. "I'm uninterested in how she got away. I only care about where she is now."

They showed me exactly where she was on the tracker. I took the handheld device from them and followed it out past the back exit into the alley, just in time to see her step out of a limousine. My stomach curled in on itself when I saw the hulking man standing outside of the limousine, and bile rose in my throat.

I knew him well.

That was Anton. The Russian worked for my father.

Please God, please, please, please, do not let her get out of that limousine.

I needed to believe that she had been robbed, kidnapped, transported, into that limo. Anything other than my wife voluntarily being inside with my father. Not the woman who had looked me in the eye and told me that she would love and cherish me for the rest of her days.

Please God, tell me she didn't lie. Tell me she didn't play me. Tell me anything but that.

But then, as I stood in the shadows watching, Emma stepped out of the limousine, her face stricken with disappointment, and following her was my father, looking self-assured, as he always did. He reached for her, and she scooted out of his grasp.

Every instinct told me to go to her and wrap my arms around her. Go and protect her. And then my irrational voice spoke up.

She's with him. They were having a meeting. She slipped security to meet your father. How long has this been going on? How long has she been lying to you? How long has she been his mole?

Unable to wait for her and ask for any explanations, I turned around and went back inside.

I found Daniel right inside the doorway. "Sir?"

She was clearly fine. I had enough anger coursing through my veins to tell them that they no longer had to watch her. But that possession inside me knew I couldn't let her go, because even though Emma Varma had betrayed me, I did love her. Despite how shitty that was going to be for me, I loved her. And she was trying to break me.

Well, only one of us would break. Because as much as I loved her, I also loathed her now. And I was going to make her pay. "Stay on her when she comes back. Pretend nothing's wrong. Don't let her know we know where she went. Trojan protocol."

Daniel's eyes went wide and then he quickly averted his gaze. "Yes, sir. Whatever you need, sir."

And then I went out the way I'd come. All the London Lords cars had diplomatic plates on them, so we could park wherever we damn well pleased without tickets or towing or any of that nonsense, so parking straight outside of the Hippodrome was not a problem.

I climbed back into my car and drove back to the hotel all the while chewing on the bitter betrayal. My wife had betrayed me.

And with the Trojan Protocol, I'd detonated a bomb.

Too severe? Maybe. But she'd made a fool of me, and payback was a bitch.

* * *

This had been a complete waste of time. I didn't believe one word out of that man's mouth.

But at least now I knew full well what Lord Edgerton was capable of. And now I had to explain to Bridge. What was I going to say? 'I know he's your nemesis, but I did it for you.' There was no way Bridge was going to let that one fly. He was going to be well ticked off. And honestly, he had every right to be, because I had expected the outcome and still insisted on doing this.

Why the fuck did I do that? Why did I think that if I did something, the outcome would be different? God, it was the epitome of insanity, doing the same thing over and over again and expecting different results. He had been an ass to Bridge his entire life. And I thought somehow I was special? Damn it.

But this takes the cake. The lies he was spewing.

My mind still couldn't wrap around what he'd said. The pack of lies he tried to sell me. As I exited the limo, he made sure I took the folder, his supposed truth.

Such bullshit. There was no way. It wasn't true.

Are you sure?

It couldn't be true. I knew Bridge.

Even just thinking about it, the bile rose up and threatened to explode.

What did it say about me that I was considering it *might* be true?

Despite what this false evidence said, I knew Edmond Edgerton and men just like him. The pack of lies and manipulations they would use just to control a situation. I had to figure this out. Why would he lie? What would he have to gain? That didn't make sense.

As I headed back to the rear entrance of the Hippodrome, I pulled my phone out of my bag and sent a quick text to Bridge.

Emma: *Can we talk?*

I waited for the three buttons to jump, and they didn't. I frowned. Not that I expected my husband to be at my beck and call, but I knew he was having a meeting with the lads tonight, so why didn't he just respond?

When I walked in the Hippodrome, I went to the restroom and found my guards waiting for me. "I suppose I'm in trouble?"

Both of them stood up as if surprised. "Ma'am," said Jason.

"What? You're just going to pretend you didn't know I was gone?"

Ryan rolled his eyes. "Ma'am, you know you're not supposed to shake your security. If you did, it must be for a good reason. So we knew to wait for you here."

"Don't worry, I will let Bridge know that it was my doing, okay?"

Both of them frowned. "You're telling him?"

I blinked as if it was obvious. "Of course, I'm telling him. The intention was never to not tell him. It was just to buy time to do what I needed to do and then talk to him."

Ryan pursed his lips. "Yes, ma'am."

On the way back to my mother's house, I settled back on the leather seats, inhaling deeply. The car smelled of leather oil and vaguely Bridge's Tom Ford aftershave. I loved the smell. When I had packed a few things to leave Belgravia, I'd taken one of his T-shirts with me straight out of the hamper. One he'd slept in. Not that he usually slept in a T-shirt, but I had been with him and I was stealing the covers. And so it was either completely wrap around me and get the full effects of a furnace or start wearing a T-shirt to bed.

I pulled out my phone and texted him again.

Emma: *Hey, where are you?*

Still no response. No jumping circles. Nothing. I frowned at that and leaned forward. "Hey, Daniel. Do you know where Mr. Edgerton is tonight?"

He shook his head. "No, ma'am."

"Okay, thanks."

I had texted Liv and Nyla just to see if they knew where my husband was. Liv's response was immediate.

Livy: *I think the boys are together.*

Emma: *Yeah, thanks.*

Nyla's response came right after hers.

Nyla: *You must be at your Mum's?*
Emma: *Yeah, but I was thinking about coming home.*
Both of them sent heart emojis. I knew they loved me and Bridge together and their hearts would break for me too. I wouldn't tell them until we were together. I just couldn't. I leaned forward again. "Daniel, I'm so sorry. Do you mind actually going back to Mr. Edgerton's place? I need to get back to Belgravia."

Even if he was annoyed, he would never show it. "Yes, ma'am."

At the next exit, he got off and turned back around, heading back toward London. I couldn't let it go. I needed to see Bridge.

If we could just talk and I could let him know what happened, maybe he would be mad, but he wouldn't hate me. At the front gate, Daniel keyed in his code, and when the gate stuck, he said, "Ma'am, if you don't mind going through the doorway there and just pop in your passcode, I'll see what's wrong with the gate."

"Okay, sure. Thank you again, Daniel. Have a good night."

"You too, ma'am."

My trainers were almost silent on the damp cobblestones. London being London, it had started to drizzle at some point when I was in the limo. But I didn't mind it. I was home. The scent of rain and the feel of cobblestones beneath my feet would forever be marked as a feeling of home to me because this was where I'd started to fall in love with him all over again. I punched my personal ID code into the gate, and the door swung open, allowing me in.

I closed it behind me immediately, and something in the air stilled. Something was off, but what?

I glanced over at the security tower and realized that's what it was; the lights were out. The lights were never out. The lights at the front of the house were on, but they only lit a portion of the yard. What the fuck?

I started walking toward the security gate to see if Daniel had figured out what was wrong with it, but before I could round the stone pathway, a shadow moved behind me. I didn't wait. I didn't ask questions. I did what I'd been taught to do. I screamed and ran like hell. There was another back security gate. Even if it wasn't open or no one was manning it, that one, I could easily scale. I just had to run fast enough.

My heart hammering against my chest and my breathing coming hard, I bolted, holding on to my phone and then deciding to discard my purse. I tossed it behind me, swinging it wildly and hoping it would hit whoever was behind me. I could hear the fast breathing and the heavy footsteps. They were on my tail. Someone was coming for me. Bridge had been right, and I had been wrong. And for the umpteenth time in my life, I hadn't listened to reason, so this was happening. Someone was going to take me from him, and he would have no idea that I had come to talk to him, to make peace, to reconcile. He would never know that I had come on my own to tell him that I loved him too and I wanted to be with him.

The gate was ten steps ahead. Then nine. Eight. Seven. Six. Five. And suddenly, a hand clamped around my waist, heavy and too well-muscled to fight against. I screeched, my legs flailing for purchase because he lifted me too high off the ground to get a good stomp on his instep. The air in my lungs was giving out, but I would not stop. I kept screaming *fire*. I kept screaming *bomb*. I kept screaming all the words that were meant to get people's attention. People outside of this compound in Belgravia. Surely somebody would hear me.

When I managed to finally get a heel into his shin, my attacker grunted, his arm loosening but unfortunately making me pitch forward. I almost fell, but instead, I grappled for the fence and started to scramble. But then his arms lifted me around my middle again and he hauled me backward. This time, I was airborne. Fucking airborne. And then my back hit a solid grassy patch with a thud, and my head started to ring with the ricochet of my brain against my skull. And as I tried to see who my attacker was, my vision grayed. All I could tell was that it was a man. He had a mask on, and I couldn't see much in the dark. Then my vision went black, not because I passed out, but because he'd shoved a black bag over my head. Holy shit.

Someone was taking me.

To be continued in Bridge of Lies...

* * *

Thank you for reading LONDON BRIDGE!

Betrayed by the person who vowed to love me. There is no turning back now. If Emma is playing to win then I'm playing for keeps. There are no participation trophies in this game of love. There can be only one winner. And I never lose.

Read Bridge of Lies *Now!*

You can also read Nathan and Sophie's story right now! Find out what happens when a seductive, jaded playboy with a filthy mouth meets his uptight neighbor and they strike a little ex payback bargain.
One-click MR. DIRTY now!

> "Mr. Dirty is a ***fun and flirty romance*** with *complex characters and a great storyline."* - *Amazon Reviewer*

Can't get enough billionaires? Meet a cocky, billionaire prince that goes undercover in **Cheeky Royal**! He's a prince with a secret to protect. The last distraction he can afford is his gorgeous as sin new neighbor.
His secrets could get them killed, but still, he can't stay away...
Read Cheeky Royal now!

Emma

Turn the page for an excerpt from Cheeky Royal...

UPCOMING BOOKS

Bridge of Lies
Broken Bridge
Gentlemen Rogues

Also from Nana Malone
Cheeky Royal

"You make a really good model. I'm sure dozens of artists have volunteered to paint you before."
He shook his head. "Not that I can recall. Why? Are you offering?"

I grinned. "I usually do nudes." Why did I say that? It wasn't true. Because you're hoping he'll volunteer as tribute.

He shrugged then reached behind his back and pulled his shirt up, tugged it free, and tossed it aside. "How is this for nude?"

Fuck. Me. I stared for a moment, mouth open and looking like an idiot. Then, well, I snapped a picture. Okay fine, I snapped several. "Uh, that's a start."

He ran a hand through his hair and tussled it, so I snapped several of that. These were romance-cover gold. Getting into it, he started posing for me, making silly faces. I got closer to him, snapping more close-ups of his face. That incredible face.

Then suddenly he went deadly serious again, the intensity in his eyes going harder somehow, sharper. Like a razor. "You look nervous. I thought you said you were used to nudes."

I swallowed around the lump in my throat. "Yeah, at school whenever we had a model, they were always nude. I got used to it."

He narrowed his gaze. "Are you sure about that?"
Shit. He could tell. "Yeah, I am. It's just a human form. Male. Female. No big deal."

His lopsided grin flashed, and my stomach flipped. Stupid traitorous body...and damn him for being so damn good looking. I tried to keep the lens centered on his face, but I had to get several of his abs, for you know...research.
But when his hand rubbed over his stomach and then slid to the button on his jeans, I gasped, "What are you doing?"
"Well, you said you were used doing nudes. Will that make you more comfortable as a photographer?"

I swallowed again, unable to answer, wanting to know what he was doing, how far he would go. And how far would I go?

The button popped, and I swallowed the sawdust in my mouth. I snapped a picture of his hands.

Well yeah, and his abs. So sue me. He popped another button, giving me a hint of the forbidden thing I couldn't have. I kept snapping away. We were locked in this odd, intimate game of chicken. I swung the lens up to capture his face. His gaze was slightly hooded. His lips parted...turned on. I stepped back a step to capture all of him. His jeans loose, his feet bare. Sitting on the stool, leaning back slightly and giving me the sex face, because that's what it was—God's honest truth—the sex face. And I was a total goner.

"You're not taking pictures, Len." His voice was barely above a whisper.

"Oh, sorry." I snapped several in succession. Full body shots, face shots, torso shots. There were several torso shots. I wanted to fully capture what was happening.
He unbuttoned another button, taunting me, tantalizing me. Then he reached into his jeans, and my gaze snapped to meet his. I wanted to say something. Intervene in some way...help maybe...ask him what he was doing. But I couldn't. We were locked in a game that I couldn't break free from. Now I wanted more. I wanted to know just how far he would go.

Would he go nude? Or would he stay in this half-undressed state, teasing me, tempting me to do the thing that I shouldn't do?

I snapped more photos, but this time I was close. I was looking down on him with the camera, angling so I could see his perfectly sculpted abs as they flexed. His hand was inside his jeans. From the bulge, I knew he was touching himself. And then I snapped my gaze up to his face.
Sebastian licked his lip, and I captured the moment that tongue met flesh.

Heat flooded my body, and I pressed my thighs together to abate the ache. At that point, I was just snapping photos, completely in the zone, wanting to see what he might do next.

"Len..."
"Sebastian." My voice was so breathy I could barely get it past my lips.
"Do you want to come closer?"
"I--I think maybe I'm close enough?"

His teeth grazed his bottom lip. "Are you sure about that? I have another question for you."

I snapped several more images, ranging from face shots to shoulders, to torso. Yeah, I also went back to the hand-around-his-dick thing because...wow. "Yeah? Go ahead."
"Why didn't you tell me about your boyfriend 'til now?"
Oh shit. "I—I'm not sure. I didn't think it mattered. It sort of feels like we're supposed to be friends." Lies all lies.
He stood, his big body crowding me. "Yeah, friends..."
I swallowed hard. I couldn't bloody think with him so close. His scent assaulted me, sandalwood and something that was pure Sebastian wrapped around me, making me weak. Making me tingle as I inhaled his scent. Heat throbbed between my thighs, even as my knees went weak. "Sebastian, wh—what are you doing?"
"

Proving to you that we're not friends. Will you let me?"
He was asking my permission. I knew what I wanted to say. I understood what was at stake. But then he raised his hand and traced his knuckles over my cheek, and a whimper escaped.

His voice went softer, so low when he spoke, his words were more like a rumble than anything intelligible. "Is that you telling me to stop?"

Seriously, there were supposed to be words. There were. But somehow I couldn't manage them, so like an idiot I shook my head.

His hand slid into my curls as he gently angled my head. When he leaned down, his lips a whisper from mine, he whispered, "This is all I've been thinking about."
Read Cheeky Royal now!

Nana Malone Reading List

Looking for a few Good Books? Look no Further

FREE
Shameless
Before Sin
Cheeky Royal
Protecting the Heiress

Royals
Royals Undercover

Cheeky Royal
Cheeky King

Royals Undone
Royal Bastard
Bastard Prince

Royals United

Hear No Evil

East End
East Bound
Fall of East

To Catch a Thief

Speak No Evil

London Bridge
Bridge of Lies
Broken Bridge

The Donovans Series

Come Home Again (Nate & Delilah)
Love Reality (Ryan & Mia)
Race For Love (Derek & Kisima)
Love in Plain Sight (Dylan and Serafina)
Eye of the Beholder – (Logan & Jezzie)
Love Struck (Zephyr & Malia)

London Billionaires Standalones

Mr. Trouble (Jarred & Kinsley)
Mr. Big (Zach & Emma)
Mr. Dirty(Nathan & Sophie)

The Shameless World

Shameless

Shameless
Shameful
Unashamed

Force

Love Match Series
Game Set Match (Jason & Izzy)
Mismatch (Eli & Jessica)

Don't want to miss a single release? Click here!